The Enemy

John Barnes

First Edition Published in the United Kingdom
in 2022 by aSys Publishing

eBook Edition First Published in the United Kingdom
in 2022 by aSys Publishing

Cover Image: Stock Photo Secrets

Disclaimer

This is a work of fiction. Names, characters, businesses, places, events and incidents are either the products of the author's imagination or used in a fictitious manner. Any resemblance to actual persons, living or dead, or actual events is purely coincidental.

ISBN: 978-1-913438-61-6
aSys Publishing 2022

Prologue

Mount Sinai, Saint Catherine, Egypt

The Bedouin eyewitness said it the way it was. He told it straight. He said that the Russian teenager made a beeline direct to the hidden cave, straight to a point just inside, where an object had lain hidden for decades. Not that he knew what the object was. The police hadn't disclosed it. The eyewitness said that the teenager seemed to be in a trance, as if that provided the necessary explanation. But even so, how could she have known what object would be there? Or even that any object would be there at all? She had never been in Egypt. Never before had she set foot on Mount Sinai. Never before had she been to its summit, nor to the cave in the sun-scorched summit rocks. She had arrived with her parents in the evening of the day before, to St Catherine, the camp of the Bedouin at the foot of the mountain. That much at least the police had worked out for themselves.

The eyewitness said the teenager arrived at the summit in the late afternoon, and he had diverted his flock of goats to steal a closer look. He described her as the most beautiful woman he had ever seen, but he laboured to get the point across. He wanted to go further, as if the matter held some hidden, extra meaning that he was sure would be of assistance. He said, "Her face was that of a goddess, and her body . . . "

The police officer stopped the interview right there. "Okay, okay. No need for descriptions. We have her in custody."

The teenager's name was Anna Kuznetsova and she was arrested for the murder of her parents on her return to the Bedouin camp. The scene of the crime.

The forensics were a perfect match. She had a severe head injury which she could not explain, blood on her T-shirt not all of it hers, and amnesia stretching back two weeks to the flight from Moscow to Sharm el Sheik. The psychiatrist report said that the amnesia was a result of her head injury.

She was found guilty of manslaughter under Section 4 of Egypt's Criminal Code. She was sentenced to sixteen years in jail, but was out in five. And then she made her way to Tel Aviv and then she made her way to Barcelona.

The object was a VHS video tape of the kind sold in the 1990s. It had a white label stuck onto the cover and a time reference scrawled there in black ink. And when the tape was played to that time reference, the protagonist said:

"In the nuclear world the true enemy can't be destroyed. The true enemy is war itself."

Crimson Tide (1995)

Part 1. Before The War

Chapter 1

Virginia, USA

The recruit cleared the stone wall on the top of the ridge, rotated in mid-air and landed in a firing position, his Glock, out in a flash, gripped in drenched hands as if in the teeth of a vice. Rapid yet steady. Unhurried, and in control. Four shots rang out and four bullets slammed into four separate targets, 500 metres distant.

Watching the recruit from the viewing gallery directly opposite Pine Tree Ridge was CIA Deputy Director of Operations Zak Hoffman. Hoffman was a big man. Thick set and muscular. He had a six foot two inch frame. He had sharp, wolf-like facial features, an angular nose and a forehead which sloped backwards to a head of thick, coarse hair which hung and bristled around his big ears.

He watched with the keen, eager attention of someone whose interests are tied up with an approaching decision, and what he saw disturbed him. It was not because the recruit wasn't good enough for the mission. He was bothered because the recruit was *too* good. He was good enough to be considered a real alternative to Lee Ross. Lee Ross and Hoffman went back a long way. They had been through a lot together. Ross was Hoffman's first choice.

The recruit had strength, speed, and control. Above all Hoffman noted his accuracy. His score was displayed to his right on a big neon screen which shot up by four to 35.

Hoffman knew that if he had found the recruit so impressive then so would his boss who was standing to his left. Director Tom Shepperton's hands gripped the wooden rail of the viewing platform, a long black raincoat fending off most of the heavy rain. And if Tom Shepperton found him good, it would be more difficult not to choose him for the mission.

The recruit on Pine Tree Ridge was the top of his group. Elite. The best of the best. His handler had been singing his praises ever since the start of the program. Three months down the line, week eighteen of the program, four weeks from graduation, and the recruit was better still.

Hoffman had decided the time had come to see him in action.

So too had Shepperton. Because Shepperton needed an alternative to Lee Ross.

Lee Ross was Hoffman's rookie, and Shepperton knew that he was not going to change the mind of his Deputy Director of Operations without a fight. Not now that Hoffman had selected him. Hoffman could be as stubborn as a donkey, especially when it came down to deciding on the person to send on a sensitive mission. And considering the nature of the current mission, choosing the right man was crucial to the lives of each and every American. On that point they were agreed.

So why not send Ross? Ross was better than the recruit on Pine Tree Ridge. He had experience, maturity and abilities attested to in the field, not just on a Virginia shooting range.

Both knew how he had breezed through the same training program eight months previously. Just like the recruit, but better. Neither understood why the pilot had decided to change careers and work for the CIA. Neither cared. All they cared about was that someone with his talent stayed the course.

Ross had been 28 years old when he had left the Air Force, the youngest ever to achieve the rank of Lieutenant Colonel. A meteoric rise culminated in him becoming test pilot of the most advanced and expensive aircraft the USAF had ever developed, the Lockheed Martin F-35.

After graduation from the academy they released him into the dirtiest region they had, the Middle East, and told him to clean it up. After six months the stream of body bags filled with well-known terrorists had become a torrent. Success brought notoriety and fame. And even if his dark looks could still allow him to circulate with ease between Algiers, Amman and Addis Ababa, slipping into the Kremlin would be a different kettle of fish.

This mission was different. They were not sending an agent to clean up in some shady, corrupt hellhole. They were about to send someone to do a job which would break every rule of International Relations. They were going to send someone to execute Colonel Alexander Chernyaev, a minister in the government of a partner country. And not just any partner, but Russia, a country capable of destroying their own, their families and their lives.

Colonel Alexander Chernyaev spent most of his life embedded deep within the thick ramparts of the Kremlin. *Smart,* thought Hoffman, *put yourself inside Europe's largest, most secure fortress.* As head of the Russian Defense Committee, Chernyaev needed such security — he was planning: a nuclear strike on the United States of America.

Whichever way Hoffman looked at it, such a mission was risky in the extreme. It was the type of mission which could determine fast promotion, or a long fall followed by years behind bars. There could be nothing left to chance. No slip-up. Nothing to lead the Russians back to Langley.

Lost in thought, Hoffman didn't hear Shepperton's question, the words engulfed by the thunder which accompanied a stroke of lightning. "Excuse me?" he said, turning to face his boss.

Tom Shepperton met the eyes of his "Team Black Ops" head. His face, in contrast to Hoffman's, showed no signs of stress. There was no deep furrowing above his brow. His features were soft and serene, those of someone who sleeps well at night. That was perhaps because people like Hoffman took most of the stress. "You still prefer him, don't you?"

"Who?" answered Hoffman, poker faced. He resigned to deflecting and absorbing a discussion of the best man for the job.

"You know who."

Hoffman nodded slowly. "This guy's good, very good, but … "

"But he doesn't come close to Ross," interrupted Shepperton.

Time to take the bull by the horns. "Sure, Ross has his shortcomings, but they're just because he's so damned good at what he does. At least if we send him we can be sure the job will be done the way we want it. It will be carried out in complete accordance with our needs. With anyone else we may have problems."

Shepperton's face twisted into a deep frown as he turned to Hoffman. "I have absolutely no doubt he will finish the job, Zak, and finish off Chernyaev. But what if he's caught on the way out? No one could expect him to get in to the Kremlin, kill Chernyaev, and get out completely unnoticed. Not even you. There's a good chance he is the best in the world at what he does. He *is* our best. But he's also known. One way or another, he'll be identified"

Hoffman shook his head, aware of the direction of motion. "That won't happen."

Ross was his. He had sourced him, tested him, and recruited him, all in the space of a month. Ross's credentials were perfect for leading a rapid response unit in the Mediterranean, ship-based and drone-equipped.

"There has to be another way, an alternative to Ross," shouted Shepperton as thunder roared again.

The recruit had come back into view, sprinting towards them through the rain and the pine trees. Shepperton's eyes tracked the movements of the recruit.

"You're not seriously considering this rookie, are you?"

"Why not?" said Shepperton.

"Are you kidding me? He's completely untried."

"I count that an advantage. No risk. No linkage. Think about it — if he messes up we'll have deniability. With Ross we won't."

"We're talking about Moscow, Tom, not Harare. There's a chance he won't even make it to the shot. Then what?"

"There's a chance Ross wouldn't make it either."

Hoffman took a deep breath. "Are we at least agreed that Chernyaev needs to be taken down?"

"Agreed," replied Shepperton. "Take another look at the Intel if you still have doubts."

Hoffman reached inside his rain coat. Breaking every rule of the department he headed he had photocopied the latest report.

"You don't need to read it to me, Zak, I memorized it. *Zlatka: Colonel Alexander Chernyaev: Plans for a pre-emptive nuclear strike against an American target operational. Target appears to be Washington D.C. Initial strike to be followed by a full counterforce attack.*"

Hoffman's eyes followed the printout before darting sideways to land on Shepperton. So you believe it?"

"It came from Zlatka, therefore yes, I do."

Zlatka was a CIA sleeper inside Russia. And what a sleeper — platinum blonde, five foot ten with a physique to match. It had been ten years since she had posed on the front of Maxim. Now she was 27 and an escort in the Russian capital. She was in constant demand by the rich and the powerful; by businessmen, politicians and members of the Moscow elite, the *Siloviki*. The previous night, she had slept with Colonel Alexander Chernyaev, and by nine a.m. Eastern time her report was lying on the smooth mahogany of Shepperton's desk.

"Have you had a chance to debrief her? Directly, I mean?" asked Hoffman.

"I got a secure uplink to her on my drive over. What struck me wasn't the details of what he's planning, but that he's in love."

Hoffman felt a pang of disappointment. "With Zlatka?"

"No. Not quite," answered Shepperton, with a smile. He knew Hoffman had feelings for the spy. "He's obsessed by another woman, this time in Barcelona. He's infatuated."

"Lucky for her."

"Not really," continued Shepperton. "You see, there's this girl in Barcelona, Kuznetsova. She's been on our radar for a while. You know it. You've seen intel on her. Well she's also with Alexander's father, our Grand Master himself. Do you understand the issue?"

"Of course I do. But it's a mundane conflict of interests. I'm sure it can be resolved."

"Right. But unless Alexander does a deal with his father, Anna will be unable to escape. Rumour has it that despite being Russian, they caught her in Israel, trafficked her to Spain only to realise she doesn't remember her home or her parents. Not that it matters. But she won't have anything to do with Alexander, despite the fact that he loves her. Or rather, she would have something to do with him if he gets her out of there."

"Just his luck," shrugged Hoffman. "Of course Dmitry would not be happy. We've all seen the photos. He would be losing something big. He wouldn't just let his son take her away from him if . . . "

"That's not all," interrupted Shepperton. "It seems Alexander tells her everything and anything, top secret stuff included. He needs her to confide in, to tell his fears, his doubts. He trusts her completely."

A thought ran through Hoffman's mind. "We could take him out in Barcelona."

The recruit, now close at hand had somersaulted back onto the muddy running track at the bottom of the ridge of pine trees which rose up before them, emptying a third of an AK-47 into a target at 200 meters.

"I can't let that happen," said Shepperton.

"Why the hell not?" said Hoffman.

"Because according to Zlatka, he's staying put in Moscow, until the plan becomes operational."

Hoffman shook his head. "I can't believe this. Are we really looking at a Russian strike? Nuclear Armageddon?"

"The question is not there, my friend. It's can we afford to take a chance? Our station chief in Moscow believes in the rumours. That should tell us something. He believes President Khodorov is the Antichrist. You know it. I wouldn't go that far, but who can say?"

Hoffman thought for a moment. President Khodorov, the Antichrist who unleashes fire on the world. Sure sounded like hell. But the worrying signs were already there. Moscow Chief Of Station, was sure of it. The Russians had doubled up on the rhetoric. They were posturing, ratcheting up tension. Tensions could lead easily to presumptions, to misconceptions, and to accidents. And accidents could lead easily to full blown nuclear war.

The accumulation of problems between Washington and Moscow in itself would not have worried Hoffman, just as previous situations had not worried his predecessors. The things that really affected him were the daily reports from Moscow, from their Chief of Station and from agents like Zlatka: President Khodorov was intent on aggression.

And to have one hawkish son-of-a-bitch in the Russian presidential administration, predisposed towards pre-emptive nuclear strikes and the likes, was bad enough. What was ten times worse was when the country's political leader agreed with him. Russia had lapsed back into a dictatorship, and all the reports from U.S. agents told the same story. The dictator had visions of global grandeur. Khodorov was delusional, but did that make him any less dangerous? Hoffman looked up at Shepperton. "What do we really know of the man?"

"Of Khodorov?"

"Yes. I mean, not the humdrum reading of his resume, but the details surrounding his ascent."

"Ivan Ivanovich Khodorov." The CIA director deliberated for a moment. "For a start his ascent to the Russian Presidency was heralded by a sign in the cosmos which some believe to be proof of his true identity; that is, him being the Antichrist."

"You don't believe it, do you?"

"I do, and I'm dead serious. Zak, look at the astronomical diagrams from the period if you don't believe me. There appeared at that time in the night sky a formation called The Great Cross, a rare alignment of our planets. To some it was an alignment leading to extreme gravitational forces and the end of the world. To others it was a sign that the Antichrist was risen."

"I don't believe it," said Hoffman. "And besides, Khodorov is not our immediate problem."

The conversation had taken a turn towards the absurd, which was as unwelcome as it was disturbing. There was a clear and present threat to the United States and it was his sworn duty to remove it. No matter how worrying it was to see Russia slipping back into the darkness of its past, Colonel Alexander Chernyaev was an immediate problem. He and he alone was behind the pre-emptive strike plans, and it was he who had to be taken down before those plans became operational.

"Chernyaev?", said Shepperton. "Yes. You're right. Every day which goes by brings his plans closer to fruition."

"So do I have a green light for this particular Black Op?"

Shepperton studied him closely, his grey eyes dead serious. "You do, Zak. But think carefully who you send."

"Not Ross?" asked Hoffman.

"Think about it," said Shepperton. "What you've said about Ross is true. He *is* the best. But there's one reason why sending him is impossible, a reason which trumps every positive aspect. Do we understand one another?"

"Chernyaev's father is one of us."

Hoffman understood. Hoffman was a Templar Knight, and had understood the day he heard Colonel Alexander Chernyaev had been promoted to head the Russian Defence Committee of the potential conflict of interests brought about by his rise to the top. What would Hoffman do should he be required to take out the son of his Grand Master?

"Not just one of us," reminded Shepperton. "He is our leader, the Grand Master himself."

Hoffman pondered briefly. "I think you over-estimate Dmitry's reach. Chances are he will never know who will kill his son, especially if we send Ross."

"I don't work on chances and presumptions, Zak, and you know it. Dmitry's a shrewd son-of-a-bitch who would suspect our involvement. And once his suspicions are aroused he would soon figure out that it was Ross. No, we're caught between a rock and a hard place on this one, Zak. Either we act in the interests of the Order, let him be, and hope for the best. Or we act in the interests of the U.S. and take out his son."

Shepperton was right. This time, despite their allegiance to the New Knights Templar, it was necessary to remove an existential threat to the United States of America. This was his home and there was no way he was going to put his whole life in jeopardy out of duty to the Order. But although Hoffman was contemplating killing the son in order to serve his country, there would have been no question of doing it had Alexander Chernyaev been a Templar. Hoffman loved the New Knights Templar, and lived for it. New Knights Templar was a way of life. Doing harm to any one of its members would go against every fibre in his body.

There was a chance they could all walk away from this, but for that the mission would have to be executed to perfection. It would all come down to the kill shot. That and the agent they would send. Hoffman turned and looked at the scoreboard which bleeped three times. The test had come to an end and the numbers showed the recruit had scored 38 out of 40. "I sense you're going to recommend sending the rookie out there on the range?"

Shepperton nodded his eyes following the recruit. "We can't send Ross, despite his credentials, for one simple reason — a reason which trumps everything else."

"Ross is one of us too?"

"Precisely. And if Dmitry suspects the involvement of the Order, he'll kill all three of us."

The Kremlin, Moscow, Russia

Colonel Alexander Chernyaev slumped into the depths of a leather chair in the vast emptiness of a high-ceilinged Kremlin meeting room. The head of the newly formed Russian Defence Committee contemplated documents spread across the smooth surface of the mahogany table.

He was worried. The documents told that the Americans knew of his plan for their destruction. They told that they were preparing a pre-emptive strike of their own: against him. He could have wondered how they had found out, but what good would that serve apart from closing the stable door after the horse had bolted? He was well aware of his shortcomings as a military officer — his addiction to women for one — but he was primarily a patriot. And if the Americans were planning to assassinate him, well, that meant one thing — war, and a nuclear one at that. Attack being the best form of defence.

Chernyaev was in one of the sumptuous State Apartments on the other side of Red Square from the Kremlin, in Kitay Gorad adjoining the buildings housing the Presidential Administration. It was necessary to be cautious but not to hide beneath a bunker inside the Kremlin.

The briefs in front of him changed all that. No more visits to his apartment for the time being. Nor to Zlatka in the mansion he had bought her in a gated community next to Park Parbedy. No more leaving the Kremlin in fact, at least until after the strike.

He sat up and looked again at the reports spread before him, and felt the discomfort on being forced to change plans. There came also a recognition, a realisation that there was something he could not and would not renounce: his weekly visits to Kuznetsova in Barcelona. Only seeing Anna would ease the pain and hurt he was going to experience from losing Zlatka. So the Colonel picked up a phone and dialled a pre-set number.

Lieutenant Colonel Pavel Kazansky, Director of Operations at the Federal Security Bureau, was fast asleep in one of the other apartments on Kitay Gorad. The ringtone identified the caller, and on hearing it the intelligence chief threw off sleep as easily as flinging aside one of the luxury white dressing gowns which adorned the suite.

"My apologies. I know it's late—or early."

"No problem, Sir. What can I do for you?"

"Information."

"What kind of, Sir?"

"To do with my visits to Barcelona and one aspect in particular. If I travel within the next twelve hours, is there any U.S. threat to my safety?"

"Sir. Let me see . . . " The silence of the line was interrupted by the fast clicking of a computer keyboard. After what seemed to Chernyaev as an eternity came the response. "Sir, according to the system there is one potential threat. Lee Ross. Based in Ibiza but active in Barcelona. He could be tasked with your assassination"

Colonel Chernyaev hesitated, and then he said, "Take him out."

Chapter 2

Ibiza, Spain

At 03.00am Ross saw Irina take a call. *Not exceptional,* thought Ross. Each of the four team members received calls at all times of the day and night, him included. Such calls were alerts from Langley or from Israeli Military Intelligence and served to keep the team one step ahead of a high profile operative targeted for elimination by both the U.S. and Israel. An operative of Islamic State, the man not only had the blood of innocents on his hands, but was in the final stages of planning atrocities in certain Western capitals.

Ross had been ordered to work with Mossad, and was going ahead with the mission, even though every bone in his body was against it. Ross liked being one hundred percent in control one hundred percent of the time. With a team of Mossad agents that was impossible. He preferred working in small, hand-picked teams, not those composed of Russian speaking Israelis.

Ross looked at his watch. 06.00. Three hours had gone by since the call.

Irina had checked the room before answering. But she hadn't noticed Ross was awake. His sleeping habits were a mystery to her, despite them having lived together for a week.

Now Ross was sitting on the balcony of the third floor flat at *La Figueretas* watching the beach and the sea beyond. Early morning. Cold, windy, with an approaching storm supposed to hit by afternoon. The sun had just cleared the horizon, and its blood red orb was still visible behind layers of horizontal cloud, bathing his face in a heatless glow.

Ross measured six foot, slim, and athletic. He was former college gymnast. He wore boots, black jeans and a 1942 pattern U.S. Army Air Force "Captain Hilts" jacket. He missed the Air Force. It had been ten months since he had switched to the CIA, a choice dictated by a need to do more against the world's injustices than checklists and test flights.

A doubt troubled him as he looked across the restless sea to the bright horizon — *Could Hoffman have made a mistake by arranging the joint operation with Russian-Israelis, considering the developments in Moscow?*

***

Actually, two things were preying on Ross's mind. First and foremost, the briefs sent to him by Zak Hoffman told that Colonel Alexander Chernyaev had become America's number one threat by far. The man was planning nothing less than the first pre-emptive nuclear strike in history, an attack against the U.S. which would kill most of the American people.

Second, Ross was stressed as always by his obsession, by the need to fight for justice for the downtrodden masses, for those too weak to resist the tyranny of the powerful. He had risen to the echelons of the elite, developing on the way a vision of how the world should work and a burning desire to mould a fairer future for all. The New Knights Templar had been part of that vision, a vehicle for his dreams, a duty and a fascination, a life mission which he would never abandon nor betray. He had lost both parents at the age of five when they had drowned in a storm off the remote Alaskan island where he had been born. The accident had left a void in his life, a vacuum which The New Knights Templar had filled.

Ross had been only seventeen when he had sworn allegiance to its goals. High among them was the search and acquisition of two priceless treasures: the Holy Grail and the Ark of the Covenant. Other Templar Knights had told him at his initiation that those two artefacts were theirs by right.

That better world was 'the Kingdom of Heaven'. It was destined by the ancients to exist when the two artefacts were once again Templar possessions. Only then would humanity ensure the return to Earth of God's son, Jesus.

Following his introduction to the New Knights Templar the goals of the Order became Ross's own, an enduring passion and a preoccupation. And so long as the goals of the Order were aligned with fighting evil in general, reducing international terrorism and diminishing the influence of Al-Qaeda and the Islamic State, his obsession with creating a world safe for the 'Second Coming' complemented his day job.

Ross feigned not having heard the question Irina had just asked him when she joined him on the balcony. After a long silence, she broke it by saying, "Were you on the yacht last night?"

"Yes, I was. Why?"

He had spent the evening analysing intelligence briefs and talking to his controller Zak Hoffman from the lounge of the Panthera, the CIA leased yacht which he commanded. Based in Eivissa, the largest port on the island, the Panthera provided the U.S. intelligence community with eyes, ears, and covert military force in the heart of the Mediterranean. The situation unravelling in Moscow was fast becoming critical, and Ross sensed Hoffman was about to dispatch him to the Kremlin, without an invitation of course.

What gave Chernyaev and Khodorov the right to play God with the lives of millions of innocents? Both men came from his social level, the working class. They should have been able to resist the worst temptations of greed and power. *They should be championing the harmonization of society, not the enslavement of the masses.*

His eyes focussed back on Irina. His earlier doubts concerning the call crystallised into specific questions. Were the three Mossad agents on the payroll of the Russian Federal Security Service, the FSB Federal Security Service or GRU Russian Military Intelligence? What were the chances Colonel Alexander Chernyaev had hijacked them for his own narrow interests? Were they enemies rather than colleagues or friends?

Ross found himself back on the Panthera, that very evening, the second in a row. A live video link from Langley was streaming onto a massive screen above black leather sofas. Ross was sat opposite, on another set of leather sofas, Hoffman filling him in on the latest intelligence. There was now no doubt that the Russian President and his new key military strategist Colonel Alexander Chernyaev had gone completely off the deep end. They were not only nuts, but dangerously so, and the absolute minimum strategy to remedy the situation involved assassinating Colonel Chernyaev. Shepperton had not quite reached the point of ordering a hit on the Russian President himself, but he was close.

Hoffman called Ross back that evening, this time from his mansion in the wooded hills of Virginia, an hour's drive from CIA Headquarters, Langley. There was a three-way video conference in Russian. There was Hoffman, Ross and their Order's Grand Master, Dmitry Chernyaev. It was loud. It was raging. And Ross let it take its course. And then it clicked. The fogginess cleared. Dmitry Chernyaev was not party to his son's dark plans for America.

Chapter 3

The Kremlin, Moscow, Russia

Colossal Colonel Alexander Chernyaev dominated a long conference table in a sumptuous, decorative but ultimately undistinguished example of the Kremlin's Reception Rooms. Opposite him sat the Russian President, Ivan Khodorov. Between them sat the *Siloviki,* Russia's power brokers, the cream of Russia's ruling elite.

President Khodorov drummed his fingers on the conference table, attracting the attention of everyone present. "Gentlemen, we are living in dangerous times. These are dangerous times for Russia, for us, and for our children. America and her allies continue to enclose us, encroaching in on us, weakening our economy and our position in world affairs. In the past they have taken away from us Iraq and Afghanistan. Today they move in against Syria and Iran, removing them from our sphere of influence. And tomorrow -- who knows? So let me ask you: do you want your children brought into a world where Russia has no influence? Would you prefer a world where Russia is relegated to second class status in world affairs?"

A negative comments chorus rose from the table just like an orchestrated cathedral choir.

"We are being cornered, gentlemen. I for one intend to fight."

Khodorov was a tiny man in his late sixties. His wizened features aged him, and his fine brown hair was swept flat across his head. He said, "Colonel Chernyaev, please continue."

The heads of the *Siloviki* swung back to the colossal figure. Like Dmitry, his father, Colonel Alexander Chernyaev, was a mountain of a man with a boxer's face—but his jaw was squarer, his nose broken.

"Gentlemen, what you will be asking yourselves is: why am I here? Why this meeting? To give you the reasons, I present, Rostelecom Vice-President Alexei Nesterov." Alexander indicated his friend seated halfway down one row of the *Siloviki* with an outstretched arm.

Nesterov threw back his chair, and took the floor. He was in his mid-30s, with medium length hair streaked blonde and spiked with product. The refined elegance of his looks was matched by that of his stylish business attire. He gestured to four graphs that appeared on a giant screen which filled the rear wall of the chamber. There were lines and traces from the left to the right, curving up from near horizontal to almost vertical. The quantities they represented increased exponentially, to a particular year that was marked in red on the extreme right hand side of every graph. The year was 2035.

"Gentlemen, the phenomenon you are looking at is developing as we speak. These traces are real." Nesterov paused, letting his first words take effect. "Now take a look at that . . . " A sweeping movement of his hand moved a red pointing device, indicating the exponential portion of the curves rising to vertical above the year 2035.

"This is what scientists have named the Technological Singularity, an event and a time when the world's computers will become self-aware, sometime between now and 2035."

The meeting broke into impromptu discussion. Nesterov snatched a bottle of Perrier from the table in front of him, snapped open the top, and took a long draught.

"Gentlemen," shouted Nesterov, above the hubbub. "The Technological Singularity is fast approaching. And as we approach it, another danger becomes clear: nuclear annihilation."

The heated debate was fast becoming tumultuous. In no mood to let the presentation falter now, Nesterov clapped his hands in rapid succession before continuing. "The processes controlling the launch of ballistic missiles, ours and the Americans, are controlled, as you might have guessed, by electronic systems. Computers, gentlemen. Those computer systems contain bugs as do you, me, our laptops and our smart phones. And as the Technological Singularity approaches, the presence of bugs becomes crucial."

Defense Minister Nikolai Makarov threw back his chair and rose to his feet, unable to contain himself a moment longer. "As far as I am aware, three manual security levels exist expressly for the purpose of preventing such a scenario."

"Thank you, Defense Minister. You are correct. It's true that there are three security levels, each of them necessary for launch of our strategic nuclear missiles, two military and one presidential. And they are as you say, manually controlled. Unfortunately they are linked between each other and to the launch switch itself by electronic systems."

Nesterov walked to his place at the table, finishing the bottle of Perrier in a final long draught. "Gentlemen, there is no way around this problem. Sometime within the next ten years, either our strategic nuclear missiles will launch against the U.S., or their missiles will launch against us. From now on Russia, and indeed the world, is in ever increasing danger of nuclear annihilation."

Colonel Chernyaev got up from the head of the table, thanking Alexei Nesterov, who took his seat. The time had come for him to wrap up the meeting, and his voice thundered, resonating through his immense being and the walls of the ancient building. "Gentlemen, we are being driven into a corner by the Americans. What are we waiting for, a world where Russia is reduced to third-world status?

Do nothing, and our respected colleague has just informed us of the certainty that we will be involved in a nuclear confrontation with the United States.

"I propose an answer. It is an action which I and the President believe is the only hope Russia has of seeing the other side of the Technological Singularity as an intact nation. I will now cede the floor to the President of the Russian Federation who will tell you what that plan entails."

President Khodorov sat motionless at the head of the table, hunched, his elbows wide with his hands clasped together in front of him. It was his characteristic pose, the one he used to give important, earth shattering addresses. "I have concluded that the only fail-safe way for assuring the long-term survival of our nation is a massive pre-emptive nuclear strike on the U.S. in which they will be destroyed. This will take place within the next two weeks. I have entrusted the planning, execution and fine tuning of this operation, to Colonel Alexander Chernyaev. I cede the floor once more to him. Please open the red folders you see on the table in front of you. These are imminent pre-emptive strike plans. With your help, American hegemony will be but a chapter of history, and Russia will rule the world."

Chapter 4

Ibiza, Spain

The Mossad-CIA combination team sat in a line on the terrace of the apartment at *Las Figuretas.* They faced the sea, like a big happy family at the beach. But through the fleeting clouds of an approaching storm, the atmosphere was thick, expectant.

Ross's mobile rang out. The screen indicated the caller — 'Hoffman home'. His mind pictured a mansion, a place he knew and liked. He walked to the other side of the patio, leaving strained ears behind him and looks of feigned indifference.

When he thought he was out of earshot, Ross indicated he could talk. Hoffman said, "Another asset will do the Moscow job. Not you."

"Why?" answered Ross, indignant. He knew he was the best man for the 'Chernyaev job', as did Hoffman and Shepperton. That was something which linked all three of them. That and the knowledge that with every passing second Chernyaev's plans were becoming more concrete, closer to a pre-emptive strike against the United States of America.

Hoffman said, "He is already en route".

Ross countered, "So why are you calling?"

"We need you to find his lover."

"Just give me her name, her location and I will get on it."

"Anna Kuznetsova, location Barcelona, status unknown, but we're working on it."

Anna Kuznetsova. Ross needed a moment. The name, the location, the Russian beauty's involvement with Chernyaev. His initial thoughts? *Anna Kuznetsova? What was she doing mixed up with Alexander Chernyaev?* His one and only meeting with her had been at a social event organised in his honour by his Grand Master, Alexander's father Dmitry Chernyaev. Her involvement with the *Vory v Zakone* was understandable and logical. Dmitry Chernyaev was a Godfather. He was also her 'protector'. So why and how was she involved with Dmitry's son?

"Hold on, Ross," said Hoffman. "I have to take a call."

A minute later Hoffman's voice crackled back down the line. His tone had changed and his words were stressed, hurried. "Ross? You there?"

"What happened?"

"I need you in Barcelona earlier than planned. Tomorrow morning."

"Zak," said Ross aware of the listening crew behind him. "You didn't answer my question. If you're pulling me off this mission I have a right to know why."

"You have a right to know nothing." Hoffman was old school, a forty-six-year-old ex-Navy Seals Commander who would not stand insubordination. And disrespect much less. "I'll fill you in once you are on the Panthera."

Ross bristled at the tone and the words, his response direct, provocative and immediate. "Negative. I need to know now."

The line went quiet. Hoffman was reasoning, deliberating. He might have been old school, but he was a realist. He needed Ross. He badly needed Ross. "Very well, Ross. Colonel Alexander Chernyaev's Gulfstream just touched down in Barcelona."

Ross hung up and swung around, the eyes of Stephen, Irina and Maria meeting his. He looked left to right, then back left. Like a tennis umpire.

Ross said, "I'm afraid I have to leave to Barcelona. Tonight."

To which Stephen pulled an 18 round Glock in a single, fluid movement.

Mistake: Stephen didn't fire immediately. He just held it there, as if executing the move was enough. Ross took out all three.

Chapter 5

Northern Iran

The day dawned crisp, bright and still on a lonely road through the dusty Qazvin plains of northern Iran. The rough road was deserted, save for a black Daihatsu Jeep heading in the direction of Alamut. The vehicle moved at no faster than eighty kilometres per hour, yet despite the fact, its thick, all terrain tires churned the track's thick covering of dust as effectively as a summer tornado.

Despite the day′s early warmth and the lack of rain, the summer had gone, a fact not lost on the vehicle's driver. He loved November almost as much as the winter months. November heralded real autumn weather, good, cold and stormy. And autumn led to winter, the spiritual season, where he could feel stronger than ever the connection between himself and the universe, his land, his people.

Karim Hosseini's jeep left the plains road and rounded a long, corrugated, left curving incline at the start of the mountains. The jeep had power to spare, and Karim felt joy as he dialled in more of it through the vehicle's tough chassis. Soon he knew that he would have to ease off on the speed. The track would become rockier, but he was sure the vehicle could handle it. It was not as rugged as the Toyota

Land Cruisers he was used to driving in the Revolutionary Guards. But he was happy with the old jeep. Old-timers had a charm of their own, especially the Daihatsu Fourtrack. You had to know them to drive them, even more so when the terrain was as challenging as the mountains of Qazvin.

Half an hour had passed since the start of the rocky section, his body thoroughly shaken up. At the top of a downhill section he stopped, pulling the handbrake tight, gripped by excitement. He grabbed the pair of powerful binoculars from the glove box, threw open the door and jumped atop one of the huge granite rocks which protruded from the hillside at the top of the pass.

He wanted to be sure he had got the best possible view of the valley before he allowed himself to look at it. For the first time in four years he had reached a place from which his home could be seen. Though he had lived four years in and around Tehran, the place he was approaching, the farm on which he had spent the first fifteen years of his life, was still his home and always would be.

The view was breath-taking. Overcome with emotion and regret he was struck by an incredible desire to embrace his mother and father. He had been gone a long time. Some of the best years of their lives had come and passed without him—and his best years were passing without them.

They had been getting older, needing him more than ever. And yet he had stayed away. When he was distant, it had been easy to forget the old feelings, the closeness, the love that he had felt as a child. But now that he was close he felt powerless to prevent the old memories of them flooding back.

He remembered how, one day in his very early teens, he rode his father's bicycle to an area of mountains thirty kilometres from their farm. There he spent the day, alone, walking and climbing without a care in the world. Then, as the evening fell, he found himself standing on a rocky outcrop, not dissimilar to the one on which he now stood, struck by an overwhelming desire to be back in his parents' arms.

Though he felt a lump in his stomach, he did not cry. The years of training at the Academy had built a wall around his emotions. They were compartmentalized, pushed deep into his subconscious. When he left the farm he had been but a boy. He was returning a man. And men did not cry.

The steep rocky descent from the pass tested the vehicle's ruggedness even more. It was the first time he had driven in such mountains and his concentration on the narrow rocky track allowed him to forget for a moment what he had felt on the pass.

When he had bought the vehicle two months previously, he had had that very place in mind. The 'back track', as his family called it, was an old mule track through the mountains to the main Tehran road on the plains. As far as he knew it had never been driven in a car; and who better than him to be the first? Someone who knew its soul, its every twist and turn engraved in his mind and in his past. It would take him right under the ancient fortress of Alamut of the Assassins, on the dark side, the north side, which the eyes of the tourist never reach.

He reached the bottom of the descending track where it crossed a river. The ancient bridge was constructed by heavy rock slabs set on massive stone pillars, just wide enough for the jeep's thick tires. From then on the track became smoother. Some sections were paved with rocks, shaped by ancient craftsmen. Others had fallen into disrepair. The road was now running west, towards the sun, half obscured by lowering clouds. The weather was changing fast, noted Karim, just as it often did. But soon he would be home.

As the lake came into view, Karim squinted into the bright distance and caught his breath, transfixed. Across the lake, the clouds were clearing. As he watched, the black cliffs of the rocky peak appeared slowly out of the mist like a ghost appearing in a dream. It was Alamut of the Assassins, the fortress and the mountain — to him they were one and the same. They were revealing themselves to him as they never had before.

He stopped the jeep and stood at its side, captivated by the beauty of Alamut, the ancient refuge of his forefathers. For minutes he remained, as though in a trance, his feet glued to the smooth slabs of the road. He wondered if Alamut had always appeared to him in such a way, or if his years in the city had made him more sensitive to its beauty. At long last, his trance subsided, allowing him to get back into his vehicle and continue down to the lake.

He left the jeep on its barren western shore, confident that it would come to no harm. Crime was non-existent in the mountains due simply to the fact that everyone knew everyone else.

Though the track continued around to the north, to the village of Gilan, his parents' farm lay to the south. The direct route lay along the lake´s rocky southern shore, along a narrow path between the deep water and the series of rock spurs falling direct from Alamut. Skirting the first of the rock spurs he stopped and sat on a rock directly above the clear blue water. He was listening to somebody speaking to him and took minutes to understand that although the words were being spoken at that place, the conversation had happened four years before.

He had needed to visit that place, to relive that moment; his whole life had been determined by the words which were pronounced at that very spot, by the decisions that were taken. Maybe his subconscious knew something that he didn't; that to move on sometimes it is necessary to relive the past. If it had not been for Aida, he would not have gone to Tehran, to join the Revolutionary Guards. He would have stayed on the farm.

"We´ll meet in Tehran at the end of next week," Aida had said at that very spot.

"And what if my father releases me on Tuesday or Wednesday?" Karim had replied. "I doubt he will, but it's possible."

The summer's work was over months before and the farm had never looked in better shape. His father had no real excuse but to let him go to Tehran for the winter. That had been the secret deal between them ever since he could remember. He had said, "When you turn fifteen, I will send you to Tehran, to the house of my brother, but you must promise me you will return."

That day had been four years ago to the day, and Karim had still not returned.

"Then I will try to meet you before," Aida had replied. "Just let me know a day before you get to Tehran. I will be waiting for you."

Then they had kissed, tongue in throat, in the very place where he now sat, above the water and below Alamut; four years ago to the day.

Only Karim and Aida did not meet in Tehran as planned, even though Ali, Karim's father, had kept his word and released his son three days before his fifteenth birthday. Ali wanted Karim to celebrate at his brother's house in Tehran, to be happy, a final gesture of goodwill to the son who had served him and honoured him his whole young life.

Karim waved goodbye to his two younger sisters, Jasmine and Fatima, and to Hassan, his older brother. He kissed Ali and his tearful mother. Leaving them was tough, but staying would have been tougher. He was young and hungry for life, for adventure.

Karim waited till he arrived in Tehran before sending a text to Aida's mobile phone which read: *Darling, I am in Tehran already! I know you are very busy, but I am here. When you are ready to meet me, text me and we will meet.*

Then began the wait. Aida did not return his text that day, and the following day sent him only a short message. It read: *Okay, see you Friday.* On Karim's birthday she sent him her congratulations, but nothing else. No news or apologies for not keeping her word. The weekend passed and still no news. Finally, on Tuesday, Karim, unable to contain his emotions, called her number.

"It´s me, Karim. Where are you?"

"In Tehran," she replied.

"So why don't we meet?"

"I told you Karim, I am busy."

"Too busy even to call me? On my birthday? You sent just a text."

"Look Karim, I will come tomorrow to see you," she said, before adding simply, "See you tomorrow," and hanging up.

Karim couldn't understand her behaviour. What had happened to the plans they had hatched in the long summer months at Alamut? Had the walks by the river, the evenings at the lake, the climb to the top of the mountain all meant nothing to her? He tried as best he could to put her out of his mind for the rest of the day, knowing it was hopeless. She filled his thoughts more effectively than water fills a bucket, and he secretly enjoyed it so, happy with feeling so focused, so much in love.

When the next day dawned Karim had already been up an hour, unable to sleep a moment longer. He prepared tea for his uncle in the cool kitchen of the old house, and served it to him in his upstairs bedroom. He busied himself with preparing the huge rolls of patterned cloth in the front room for the day's business, happy at having work to occupy his mind. Once he had finished, the waiting began in earnest.

He took a bus to the city center and walked through Tehran's historic heart, wondering where Aida was going to choose for their meeting. He bought gifts of perfume for her and her mother in one of the markets he passed through on his way to the river. He sat at an outside café and ordered tea, a good a place as any to kill another hour. Just when the waiter served him his tea, while he was considering how long now he had been waiting for her, his phone rang.

"Aida, where are you?"

"Hi Karim," she answered. "I am in my home, but . . . "

"But what?"

"I can't meet you today, Karim."

It was Karim's turn to cut the line, and he did it instinctively; or rather, rage did it for him. She had pushed him to the edge, and now seemed intent on pushing him over it, into the void. He could not let that happen.

He caught his breath, reacting to the shock. What had happened? Had his sub-conscious cut the line, or had he done it mindfully? It didn't seem to matter. He had done it, and now he would move on. His life was too important to him to waste it waiting.

With the decision came strength and he began to realize how weak he had felt during the past week. He realized how Aida had had a hold on him, had been controlling him. Now the reins of his life were back in his own hands and he wasn't going to give it up.

Four years later, he looked into the shimmering water of the lake. Though the memories lay there still, and with them the certainty that the pain of losing her would never truly leave him, he had moved on. Four years in the Iranian Army, the last two of them in the Revolutionary Guard. It had given him other reasons to live: honour for his country, his religion and family.

Karim stood up straight. The past was the past. How could he be in the midst of such thoughts at such a time in his life? He looked out across the southern side of the lake, his thoughts now only with his parents. Soon he would be with them.

***

The Panthera may not have been the ultimate weapon against international terrorism, the Mafia, global Russian and Chinese hegemony—but she sure came close.

Armament systems lay camouflaged on her deck, prominent among them anti-aircraft missiles. She had a foldaway catapult drone launching and landing runway on her starboard side. And the drones the ship dispatched were built around the legendary GAU-22/A 25mm rotary cannon, with 2000 rounds of cannon ammunition for a two hour mission.

Ross listened to the high-pitched buzz from the twin MEDC jets as they powered the launch towards Barcelona, deep in thought. *When was the last time I had the 5000 horsepower engines revving flat out, steering through such mountainous waves?* He remembered it well, a year to the day since the El-Affendi mission.

El-Affendi had been using his mobile the whole day long. Bad idea. *Don't top Al Qaeda operatives know that modern cell phones are every law enforcer's best friend?* Ross had checked his location, guessed his intentions and received the kill order all within half an hour. Then he crossed the intervening two hundred and forty kilometres of the Mediterranean to the launch zone, executed the mission, and executed El-Affendi.

But now Ross was not thinking of the last mission. A girl occupied his thoughts as the craft approached the midway point of the crossing to Barcelona: a green-eyed Russian beauty named Kira Kamenskaya. Ross wondered how it was possible to assassinate Islamic State operatives with ease, and yet fail to seduce a beautiful Russian. With regret he thought, *I didn't even come close.*

The mission to Moscow was fresh in his mind, not only because of his obsession with Kira, but because it had been only two months ago.

"Seduce her," Hoffman had said when he outlined the mission. "Make her trust you; need you more than anyone alive. Hell, make her love you! And when she does, when she is involved, unable to get out without emotional issues, tell her about you, us and the Templars. Tell her about what we do and how she fits in with it all."

Ross's best friend, Lieutenant Colonel Alexander Bagrov, had set up the meeting. He was a state prosecutor in the General Prosecutor's Office of the Russian Federation, on Balshaya Dmitrovka Street between Pushkin Square and the Russian Parliament. He was a New Templar Knight, but Kira was not. Not yet, at least.

Kira and Alexander Bagrov had been friends since their college days but she had never been approached by the Order. She had remained under their radar. They didn't know her, and if they did, they didn't need her.

That all changed when the Presidential Administration of the Russian Federation short-listed her to become the head of the new

Energy Commission. President Khodorov was creating a second, shadow cabinet to work in parallel with the official governmental cabinet of ministers. And since Khodorov and the *Siloviki* would be able to wield complete authority over the parallel cabinet, it was that cabinet which was going to wield the real power in Russia's future.

Khodorov had noticed Kira during a visit to the Ministry of Education, which wasn't surprising. Kira was not only comparable in beauty to top Russian models, she was tall, curvy, and Slavic, characteristics which mattered, at least to Khodorov.

His admiration grew even stronger when he found out who she was; that she taught at Moscow State University, and that she ran her own energy auditing company. He ordered, right then and there, for her name to be included on the short list of candidates to head the new Presidential Energy Commission .

The CIA soon captured her in communications from the Kremlin, analysts flagging her for further scrutiny. Hoffman found that she enjoyed friendship with Bagrov, and so dispatched Ross from his base in Ibiza to bring her into the fold. Which to Ross seemed naïve, illogical and just plain stupid. Kira was and would remain a patriot, no matter how much money they threw at her.

Ross was filled with excitement and warmth, despite the sea spray and heavy rain soaking through his hair and the outer shell of his clothing. The Panthera was just coming up to the mid-point of the crossing, the wind speed indicator signalling force eight on the Beaufort Scale; a full gale, coming from the south, which meant that the most powerful winds were still ahead.

He dialled in more power, despite the conditions, the twin jet engines whining their defiance. *Lürssen built her to take punishment.* His immediate goal was to be at Barcelona's Zurich Café on Placa Catalynya by 07.30 to get his usual morning caffeine fix while awaiting Hoffman's orders. He also was planning on getting a minimum of three hours' sleep in the apartment rented by the agency at the port.

The thick clouds above blew apart revealing patches of star studded emptiness. *The eye of the storm,* thought Ross. He raised his eyes to the heavens, a full moon meeting his gaze, fleeting behind silver clouds as if inviting him to give chase: a sight which excited and relieved him.

To Ross, clouds and weather were the most visible expression of the true nature of the universe: deterministic. *Cause and effect.* The billiard ball model of the universe. The natural laws of physics determined the formation of clouds, just as they did the lives of men. Watching nature's fury gave him relief from regret. *Since we have no control over matter, nor energy, nor events, nor individuals, what happens was always going to happen. Cause and effect. It made no sense to have fear for the future, nor anguish for the past.*

One last time Ross saw the streaking moon as the storm closed its dark shroud above him. Still he thought of Kira, but now he felt no remorse.

Chapter 6

Barcelona

Inspector Juan Lopez of Cataluña's Autonomous Police, the legendary Mossos d'Esquadra, got up as soon as he awoke. He peered through the gloom with narrow, puffy eyes searching a familiar square white object, hoping it was not about to go off. The alarm clock appeared to him in the dim light. 06.05.

He avoided waking Elena, his wife of more years than he could remember, and crept out of the bedroom.

Downstairs he busied himself with breakfast, wondering why he felt such apprehension. Like a robot he went through the motions, willing his mind to clarity. He prepared a piping hot café latte, baked croissants and squeezed fresh orange juice.

As the traditional Italian coffee pot was heating on the gas flames, Lopez walked over to the window of the lounge, as he did every morning, to take a first look at the weather. The apartment was at Passeig de García Fària, 77, on Barcelona's seafront, and on the 13th floor. The city spread before him to the distant hills. To the right lay the coast, the sea now deserted of ships and hammered by violent weather, its lines of breaking swell stretching towards infinity.

Mesmerised, he stared at the storm, but didn't see it, increasingly aware of the source of his unease. He had had a vision. It concerned his future, and it sent a shiver straight down the length of his spine.

Lopez was Gypsy on his mother's side and had inherited her gift for clairvoyance in all its grandeur. He didn't usually aspire to it, or use it, but sometimes its effects demanded attention. Like right now. He hadn't seen the storm because he had seen an even bigger storm fast approaching, one which would affect the whole world.

The hissing, rasping sound coming from the gas stove transported him back to the normal dimension. The coffee was ready.

***

In a city center hotel, at the very instant of Lopez's vision, a 24-year-old Russian girl bit down hard on the silk scarf tied tightly round her head, trying not to scream.

Screaming was not in her interest. Her mind willed her body against it, against opening her mouth, communicating the pain, though the pain was as real as though someone had just kicked her in her stomach. She knew that such a course of action would bring more pain. Maybe not that day, but eventually, and the pain would continue until the night when another such chance presented itself.

Her eyes filled as she pitted her will against the monster, but not with tears of sadness. They would come later. Her tears were from exertion, from the sustained effort straining her body to its limits.

She had trusted God to protect her. As far back as her memory went in fact, which wasn't that long. Eight years had passed since the nightmare began, but at least she could remember its beginning. Eight years since she had woken at the foot of a cliff in the Negev Desert with a blow to the head and no recollection of a former life. But faith had joined her for the ride, and she clung to it as a baby clings to its mother. Belief that God knew of her and her destiny, that he was out there, clutching the reins of her life, leading her to a better future, steering her towards salvation.

But whatever it was she had signed up for, it was not this. Of that she was sure. This transformed everything. This flicked a switch in her head which allowed her freedom to grasp back a modicum of control from God.

At that very instant she said to God: *It doesn't mean I don't trust you any more; that when you tell me to trust in you, I no longer hear you. There's just a limit to the things my body can endure, and what I am being subjected to, by this monster penetrating me so deeply, with such violence, has pushed me across it.*

The 'monster' had arrived from Moscow less than six hours before, checking into his usual top floor penthouse suite at the Mandarin Oriental. That much she knew. Like she knew his real name: Colonel Alexander Chernyaev, that he was the son of Dmitry Chernyaev, her protector, the man at the head of the organization who had trafficked her from the mountain in Israel.

But did she really know those things, or had she just assumed he had been telling her the truth? *Could he have been lying all along?* Had he been lying when he had told her that he was a minister of the Russian government charged with crafting a new offensive strategy for Russian missile defense? And when he made her believe his plan to destroy the U.S. in a pre-emptive strike, was that true or just lies to impress her? Lies like that were hard to believe. He had even said he needed her, loved her and would do anything for her.

If that was true, he sure had a fucked-up way of showing it!

She had been trafficked to fulfil the occupation of an escort girl in Barcelona. That much was at least true. But not one of her clients had ever subjected her to rape.

Never would she be raped again. *This is where everything changes. My wretched, terrible, tortured existence has led me to this very moment. The forces of the Universe have pushed me to my limit. Not my fault now what happens! Not me who bears responsibility! Afterwards, I will give back to God the reins of my life.*

Anna Kuznetsova was clear that she could not scream, fight, wriggle or wrangle. All she had to do was to wait.

Eventually the monster finished, loosening his fists on her throat. She gasped, her eyes bulging, but she thought, *still I must wait, though my time is coming.*

Colonel Alexander Chernyaev loved Anna for her beauty, and for her body. He would always love her. But he needed sex, and he wanted it to be brutal and violent, sex which knew neither limits nor boundaries. *It doesn't matter how much it hurts her because deep down she wants the same thing.*

But in all of his wisdom, his control, he had forgotten one thing: one of her arms was free and his Beretta M9 was where he had left it, holstered in the camouflage fatigues which lay on the bed. Realizing it was the last thing that went through his head—apart, that is, from the 9mm parabellum bullet.

The shot was deafening, and left a ringing in her ears.

Anna writhed and winced under the Russian Colonel, pushing his rapidly dying body off her own with repulsion. It slouched and slumped to the edge of the bed and then to the floor with a loud thud. Thick red blood escaped from the destroyed head, somewhere between spurts and seepage, pooling onto the timbered floor and filling the room with its acrid, metallic smell.

Anna's arteries were pumping pure adrenaline, not blood, her heart tearing along like a hound on a foxhunt. Her time was short, the clock was ticking, and she was determined to beat it. Her mind raced to a distant court case: *twenty years minimum in a Spanish jail for murder. 'Cos that's the way a court would see it. How could I prove rape? And even if I did, was not my crime still murder?*

Someone would have heard the shot. That person would be dialling reception, or for the police, or for Dmitry Chernyaev. The walls of the Mandarin Orient were thick, but not soundproof. There was time, but not forever. She had two choices: leave within the next two minutes, or face capture, torture and death.

So she put on her clothes and her shoes. She inserted the pistol in her belt, grabbed her handbag and ran out into the corridor.

Empty. She sprinted across to the lift, and slammed the palm of her hand on the down button. The doors opened, and it was empty too. With a shot of relief she took it five floors down, to reception, and walked straight ahead, not daring to look at the receptionist. She walked cool and calm and collected across the lobby to the revolving door. She nodded to the doorman, and exited onto the street. She was free.

Chapter 7

Grenada, Spain

The rays of the high noon Andalusia sun beat straight down on the old man, transforming the furrowed skin of his forehead to a shade of crimson deeper than it had been in the years preceding the nuclear war. Here and there on the top surface of his head, tiny brown hairs had withered and died. In a way they appeared not dissimilar to the stumps of the olive trees that spotted the desolate landscape surrounding him. Two days had passed since the fusion device had exploded 500 meters above the city, turning to rubble and dust what had taken millennia to build.

The diminutive man looked out from the cave entrance across the burnt-out hillside overlooking the blackened city. He strained his blue eyes to see where the Alhambra had stood, thrusting its towers and ramparts skywards for centuries.

Remorse hit deep in his soul as he turned to the young Gypsy woman at his side, noting the fine-boned yet aggressive beauty of her face. A paradox.

She too was looking out to what remained of the Alhambra. For her it would be worse. Grenada had been her city, Sacromonte her district, its caves for centuries the home of her people. "Do you think history will forgive me for what I have done?" he asked at length, fighting a rising tide of emotion.

"I think they will not damn you alone. Men do not live in a vacuum. You acted in the interests of your nation."

"If I am to be honest, I acted more for myself."

"It was your destiny, as being here was mine, and suffering is humanity's. You did not bring together the mass and energy of the Universe, nor create the fundamental forces which determine how our lives unravel. God did. We live in a deterministic world in which each and every one of us bears responsibility, and no one."

Her words went some way to comfort the old man, upon whose troubled face her tender, loving gaze had come to rest. Then she turned her black, Gypsy eyes back out over the desolation. No tears appeared in them however, or rolled down her freckled cheeks. Life had toughened her years ago, and she was weary of it long before any hydrogen bomb had rocked her world. She was tired of living on the edge of a society she loved, unable to integrate into it, to become truly a part of it. She had loved Andalusia as much as her own flamenco culture. But a one-megaton device could not change her, nor destroy the cave that existed still behind her.

Inside the cave a telephone was ringing, its tone oddly familiar. Confused, he turned to the young girl. "I thought you said the blast knocked out the telecommunication systems?"

Seeing a look of surprise written on her face, he knew he was wasting precious time, and ran headlong into the gloomy recesses.

Awakening, he scrambled through the darkness towards the source of the sound. He reached it, grappled with it, and hit the green answer button. "Da?"

"Mr President. I am sorry to awake you at such an early hour but it could not wait."

“What happened?” said President Khodorov, aware that someone of importance was calling, while at the same time trying to dissipate the stress which the vivid dream had generated.

“This is Ambassador Primakov at the Embassy in Madrid. We have a situation.”

Chapter 8

Barcelona

No sooner had Lopez delivered the breakfast tray to Elena, than his mobile began to buzz. As head of The Central Area of Organized Crime, a specialized agency of the government of Catalonia's Autonomous Police, the legendary Mossos d´Esquadra, Europe´s oldest police force, he often received calls from his boss, head of the 'Commissariat General d'Investigació Criminal'. Never, however, had his boss called him so early.

Elena said, "What is it, honey?"

"The Commissar is calling."

It was most likely his father's influence that had propelled him through the ranks at a pace only dreamed about by his peers. Now, just turned forty but with a boyish face that made him seem younger, he was Inspector. It was the only rank in the executive class of the 'Mossos' and he was as keen as ever to emulate his father, the late Commissar Miguel Juan Lopez. He didn't want to do anything to screw it up now.

Elena said, "Why don´t you answer?"

"I thought it must be a mistake."

His wife reached over to the bedside light on her side of the king-size four-poster bed, a symbol of the couple's newfound wealth. "Well it´s not, is it?"

With one final doubt about taking the call crystalizing and dissipating at the same time, Lopez took the call. "Inspector Lopez speaking."

"Juan. You are to report immediately to me at El Complex Central Egara. This is a matter of urgency. When can you be here?"

"In an hour, sir."

"That's too long, Juan. Make it 45 minutes."

"But— "

The line was already dead.

As if some giant catapult had energized his lithe body, Lopez launched himself across the room towards the wardrobe. Elena watched in astonishment as he began swinging open wardrobe doors, grappling with the clothes he found there. In the fifteen years she had known him, she had never seen such behaviour.

"Are you out of your mind?"

"Please honey, not now. I will call you."

He grabbed a few more items, his clothes hanging loosely, and rushed out of the room.

***

On another side of Barcelona, in a mansion on Pearson Avenue, a colossal, black-haired leviathan of a man with a grizzled, fighter's face awoke with a start. The extravagant surroundings of his gilded suite did nothing to protect him from the stark, intrusive noise. As he realized what had woken him, a rising tide of anger swept like a tsunami through his body. *There had better be a very good reason for this . . . or someone will die!*

Dmitry Chernyaev was not a man who took lightly to being woken at 06.30 by a call to his mobile. In fact he was not a man to be woken up at all. Period. And if you did wake him up, you'd better have a very good reason for doing it. Or he would find you. And he would kill you. Men like Dmitry Chernyaev did not act rationally. Nor did he have to, protected, as he was, by powerful forces. So when Commissar Surin, head of the 'Commissariat General d'Investigació Criminal' was finally able to get through to the scowling, threatening exterior of the man himself, he came straight to the point.

"Dmitry, I have some very bad news for you. Your son is dead."

***

It was 7:45 a.m. Lieutenant Colonel Lee Ross sat on the outside terrace of Zurich Café, taking pleasure in his morning fix of pure caffeine. It was a good place to be to people-watch. The well-heeded youth of Barcelona, the trendsetters, the fashion animals all passed by, unable to give him the same attention he gave them. He faced east at his usual table. The wall of the café was at his back, the red orb of the rising sun in his face looking towards the center of Placa Catalunya with its trees and its pigeons and fountains.

Despite the constant checking, Ross was happy. In a place such as Barcelona total relaxation was impossible. In Barcelona there was too much at stake to let down his guard, especially on the day after Colonel Alexander Chernyaev had arrived, unannounced, in the city. He was awaiting orders from above, from Hoffman. Kill orders, he suspected, though he was also expecting them to be hours yet in coming. So he looked at the world going by, especially at the girls.

And they returned his glances, most unable to walk past him without noticing. He was dark with craggy good looks, almost pretty, but manly too, with thick curly hair and blue eyes. There was obviously much sophistication in his attitude, his clothes. He was a little bit too perfect, almost unreal, which attracted their looks more than anything.

You too wouldn't have walked past without giving him a double take. But then you would have fallen unwittingly into his trap. For when you would have done your double take, he would already have done his, and know all about you. He would have seen you approaching, would have taken you in, your face, your walk, your clothes and the way you wear them. You would just have made eye contact with the most successful agent ever fielded in CIA history. And if you were up to no good or had something to conceal, your best bet would be to keep on walking.

Just as Ross was checking out two tall, dark-haired girls, his mobile buzzed, moving in a sporadic, fitful manner across the smooth surface of the steel table. He waited a second before snatching it up, as the second double espresso was served to him by the sprightly waiter.

"Café Zurich, right?" came the unmistakable guttural voice of Zak "the Wolf" Hoffman.

"How did you guess?"

"Listen up, and listen well: Chernyaev is dead."

"Dmitry Chernyaev?"

"No, buddy, but how I wish! It's his son."

"So someone got to him before us. What happened?"

"Shot in the Mandarin Orient less than an hour ago."

"Shot? Shot by whom?"

"We still don´t know, but we're working on it."

Ross's eyes were searching for the waiter. "I will be there in less than ten minutes."

"Not necessary, buddy. As you can imagine, right now the place is swarming with Mossos d´Esquadra. You need to get to the father. We have his phones but no visual."

"I'm on it. Ross out."

Chapter 9

Moscow, Russia

Sirirrat 'Maxi' Kakandee woke with a start to the shrill ringtone of her mobile. Her wrath grew as she became aware of the time.

"Nine o'clock!" *This had better be important.*

"Sirirrat Kakandee speaking."

"Maxi! How fast can you shower and get dressed?"

The caller was her agent, the man who had singlehandedly put her on the map of Moscow's best spiritualists, the ones demanded by the Russian oligarchs who lived on Rublyovo-Uspenskoye Avenue. Since she had arrived in Moscow five years previously, he had tirelessly worked to publicize her, to show the world, and especially those in Moscow just how good she was. Which hadn't been hard; Maxi had a gift for clairvoyance second to none.

"I suppose that depends on who it's for?" she replied, forgetting some of her anger at the prospect of work.

"The Russian President himself!"

"And suppose I told you to . . ."

"Maxi! This time I'm not kidding. I just got off the phone to the President's personal assistant. A car is on its way to pick you up."

"But I . . . but . . ." she stammered.

"Maxi, Get a move on—and put on something spiritual. He's expecting a meeting with a clairvoyant, not a businesswoman."

***

President Khodorov was seated opposite Kakandee in one of the Kremlin State Rooms just off Georgievsky Hall. His tone was low and firm, and yet the way he rushed his words hinted at nervousness. "Let me get straight to the point."

Maxi had picked up his speech pattern and tone, and already knew the reason why he was having difficulty speaking. Her intuitive mind was working overtime, and what it was churning up was extraordinary. "Naturally, Mr President."

"Last night I had a dream."

"That's quite natural. Every one of us has dreams, every night," replied Kakandee, smiling.

"Yes, but the dream I had last night was different from any I have ever had before. Quite apart from the content, which I will tell you about shortly, several other features of the dream make it not only bizarre, but worrying."

Kakandee said, "Go on."

The President rested his elbows on the varnished mahogany of the antique table that separated him from the spiritualist. He stretched out his arms, one hand clasping the other. "In the first place, I remember every single detail of it, which for me is extraordinary. And then, it was so . . . real. As if the event that I saw really happened, or is about to happen. Secondly, and perhaps most bizarrely of all, I had the dream at a particular time, one which I feel may be of relevance."

"When did it take place?" asked Kakandee.

"It took place precisely the instant when, in Barcelona, a high-ranking official in my administration, Colonel Alexander Chernyaev, was murdered."

Chapter 10

Virginia, USA

Zak Hoffman looked towards the wooded hills that surrounded the CIA Headquarters, pangs of fear assailing him. He was worried because he had drawn on his key asset Lee Ross, and because Lee Ross wouldn't stop until he had reached the bottom of the affair. Activating Lee Ross might lead to a precipitation of the matter to levels way above his pay grade. In the case that Ross's actions alerted Senators or Congressmen, and such men found out his allegiances to the New Knight Templar, his days as Deputy Director of CIA Operations would be numbered.

Shepperton will be all over the case in the morning, he reasoned, doing the best he could to cheer himself up. Anything to do with Dmitry Chernyaev demanded his personal attention. Putting Ross onto the case would cover him, provided Ross did not go too far.

Chernyaev's son had been shot. *As if things were not bad enough!* Hoffman got up, advancing slowly through the gloom to his drinks cabinet. He poured a double Bacardi on ice, straight up.

One didn't need a PhD in astrophysics to realize just how Dmitry Chernyaev would see it. An American hit on a man they knew to be behind a new Russian first-strike strategy. *Well there's one easy way to finish the whole affair, a pre-emptive strike against Dmitry before he causes him problems. Use Ross to execute him.*

Ross could make it look like an accident, his speciality. Getting past Chernyaev's army of guards to set it up would be a walk in the park for the ex-USAF test pilot. He could give the order to Ross and be free of the torment.

But there lay the problem. He thought, *I cannot and will not kill my Grand Master.*

Chapter 11

Moscow, Russia

Maxi Kakandee finished listening to Khodorov and drew a long sigh. "Mr President, would you permit me to grasp your hands? In order to gain maximum insight I need physical contact."

It was an unusual request, but one which Khodorov was only too happy to accept. He stretched his hands across the table, grasped her hands and closed his eyes. Silence reigned in the exquisite meeting room, apart from the faint ticking of the gold-plated antique clock sitting on the green marble mantelpiece.

A minute passed. Kakandee released her grasp on the President's hands, settling back into her chair. "Mr President, you are and will always be a great leader of your people. Though your people don't love you, they know they need you. They need a strong leader to take them across difficult times. This is why they chose you for a third term as their President."

She paused, giving weight to the words she was about to pronounce. "Having said that, recently you have taken a grave decision, one which involves the security of your country. Am I right?"

"You are," said the Russian President, shocked. *This woman has truly scary abilities in clairvoyance.*

Maxi Kakandee had cut deep into the realms of her soul, and had clearly seen in the President's future the approach of the End Times. She had seen the End Times as a period of history ruled, not by deterministic cause and effect processes, but by Free Will. She had seen that President Khodorov would be instrumental in bringing down the present world order and ushering in a New World Order. But whether or not that world would be controlled by the forces of good or evil, she could only guess.

She had felt something else during their contact, something that he and she had in common. They both loved the present world, the one ruled as much by Satan as by God. They would both do whatever they could to prolong it. He had the power to do it, and now, by some strange quirk of fate, she had such power too.

She said, "You must reverse your decision, Mr President. You must not strike America by surprise no matter what your advisers tell you. Otherwise, the dream you had of Granada and Armageddon will come true."

***

Putting thoughts of Aida, the past and regret, out of his mind, Karim wondered what would be the reaction of his parents to his surprise visit. Would they scold him for all the years they had lost, or embrace him as a long lost and dear son? He took his first paces towards them, along the top of the smooth rock on which he had come to sit, the lake's small waves lapping below.

Then that he saw it.

Dumbfounded by *déjà vu* and frozen to the spot with awe, Karim beheld a sight which he had dreamed about since childhood. A lone eagle soared above him on the thermals, suddenly closed its wings, and swooped down to the fortress of Alamut.

The words of his elders, of Ali his father and the legends told to him by his mother, came back to him:

He who witnesses the swooping of the Eagle as it returns to Alamut will resurrect the hidden power of the Assassins.

He alone will present the power to the returned Mahdi, the one that he alone will identify. And he will lead the Mahdi, the Islamic world, with the Shi'a at its head, to the final victory against the infidels from the land of Gog and Magog during the Battle of Armageddon.

The eagle landed on the walls of the fortress, hundreds of meters above. He pulled the binoculars to his eyes, twisting its lenses until he focused on the ancient fortress. The eagle was atop the stone ramparts, its wings half outstretched in the classic representation of power.

All doubt about the meaning of the event evaporated in Karim's mind. Allah had chosen him as the one who would lead the fight to redeem the Islamic faith. He had a mission: to lead an insurrection, an insurgency, to spearhead the Assassins' ancient plan. By assassination, he would rid his country of all forces which opposed the one true, legitimate leader of his country, the one that he alone knew to be the Mahdi.

The eagle looked down in his direction, as though to bear more weight, if such was needed, that Karim really was the one Allah had chosen to uncover the Mahdi. It looked away, and then looked back one more time at Karim before, stretching full its huge wings, it launched itself into the powerful up draughts, climbing higher and higher until clouds obscured it from view.

Chapter 12

The black and yellow Barcelona taxi cab cut through the heavy traffic. Lee Ross had promised the driver a hefty tip if he could reach Pearson Avenue in ten minutes and the driver was not going to let an opportunity like that escape him. Times were tough. The crisis was biting ever deeper into the pockets of Spanish citizens.

"Been long in Barcelona?" asked the taxi-driver.

"A week."

"Wow! A week in Barcelona. You like it right?"

"Look, Friend! I pay, you drive. What part of that don't you understand?"

Eight minutes later the Toyota taxi pulled into Pearson Avenue, otherwise known as millionaire's road.

"I didn't tell you to turn off the meter," said Ross. "We wait here a while. Turn off the engine and the lights."

They were 200 meters from a massive three-story mansion flanked on all sides by towering palms. Ross took out a pair of binoculars from the inside pocket of his jacket. He set about making a detailed recce of the building. The risk of a closer approach outweighed possible benefits. The place would be bristling with cameras and God knows what other electronic gadgets. And then there was the army of ex-Soviet military types who serve as the Russian godfather's personal bodyguards.

As Ross studied the complex, he cast his mind back two days to the last time he had studied the Russian godfather's security credentials. On every recent photograph in the database, Dmitry Chernyaev had been accompanied by no fewer than 3 heavily built AK47 totting soldiers. How he wondered, did the Spanish authorities allow him to get away with it? Chernyaev had obviously cultivated powerful connections.

As Grand Master of the New Knights Templar, powerful connections came with the job. But just how far up the chain of the Russian military behemoth did those connections go? Did they, as some in the agency claimed, go right up to the Russian President himself? And now that his son, Alexander, was dead, had things changed?

Although it was too early to tell, one thing Ross knew full well: the revenge for the killing of his son would be terrible. He knew the reputation of the man. He knew how Chernyaev dealt with his enemies. They ended up dead, killed in ways more horrible than anyone could imagine. Like being languidly fed feet-first into the mouth of an incinerator. And if they didn't die, it meant that they were working for him.

Ross scratched his head. *So what kind of hardened professional had killed his son?*

He checked every detail of the house. He checked and rechecked. The system had served him well over the years, saving his life on many occasions. Check and recheck before making a move. And then check again.

The building was flanked on each side by towering palms. A three-meter high wall of lucid Carrera marble ran around the exterior of the property.

Ross shook his head. *How could such an enemy of the United States live on the same avenue as the Barcelona U.S. Consulate?* Less than 500 meters separated the two buildings. Details which begged an obvious question: *Was there a connection between Chernyaev and a U.S. official working in the consulate?* He shook his head, his intuition working overtime, churning facts and events. It was not just a coincidence, and the shooting of his son was going to put the cat among the pigeons in a way no CIA probe could ever do. The trick was to be in the right place at the right time and see what that cat dragged in.

A movement caught his eye in the shadows. Below one of the palms above the left hand corner of the wall, a uniformed figure was moving along the far side of the wall toward the entrance gate. His fatigues suggested he belonged to the Russian army, yet the black beret he wore signified he was contracted to Chernyaev´s own corps. Another movement attracted him, this time at ground level. The huge steel gate was opening as a black armoured Mercedes came into view in the paved courtyard behind.

As he focussed his powerful binoculars on a group of soldiers escorting a creature which looked as much gorilla as human, a warm vibration in the inner pocket of his jacket indicated he had a call from Langley. He picked up the call without taking his binoculars off the 'gorilla'.

"Are you on location?" asked Hoffman. "Do you have a visual?"

"Affirmative," whispered Ross. "I see Chernyaev." The two meter high hulk fitted Chernyaev's description. If he was not the real McCoy, the man was fielding a convincing decoy. "There´s stress in your voice. What happened?"

"He is on the move. My source tells me he's on the move. Do you copy?"

"I read you loud and clear. I will tail him. Any intel on where he's headed?"

"Negative. We will advise you. Hoffman out."

"Roger that. Ross out."

A sleek ultra-heavy Mercedes swung onto the wide, palm tree-lined avenue, its low profile tires screeching sporadically as the driver dialled maximum power through the chassis.

"Follow it!" bellowed Ross to the off-guard driver, his emotions as heightened as the colour in his face.

Chapter 13

The Mandarin Orient lay above and behind Anna as she made good her escape. She made her way downhill in the direction of the coast, walking as fast as she could, putting distance between it and herself, trying to mingle with the tourists.

That wasn't easy. She was dressed in black leather shorts, high heels and a skimpy blue top which accentuated her physique, turning heads along the street. Just shy of six foot, she was blonde with blue eyes despite being of mixed Slavic and Chinese origins. She had been born in Kazakhstan and always guessed her Chinese ancestors must have been from just over the border, in the west of China, where light-colored eyes are common. But right now the exceptional qualities of her looks were the basis of her immediate problem. How could she disappear into the throngs of tourists when she would have stood out from the crowd in any city in the world?

She realised full well that avoiding the Russian Mafia, the *Vory v Zakone,* and escaping the city was not going to be a walk in the park. She had to get off the streets, and quick.

She couldn't go to the place she called home, the Chinese District or Ravel. The Autonomous Police was out of the question too. She would be arrested on sight. She did not possess an ID card, passport, or driving licence. Her only hope was to find help from a third party, from a tourist.

The towering church of Santa Maria Del Mar loomed up ahead of her and then passed as she clip-clopped through the Old Town in the direction of the port.

At the bottom of the hill she came on the huge façade of the train terminal near the port and considered entering, hopping on a train to France, and hiding in the toilet. If she could get to Paris, to the Russian Embassy, she could claim protection, repatriation.

But she changed her mind, and hurried on instead in the same direction, aware of heavy tiredness.

She was fighting to remain in control, to maintain the calm she had shown in the immediate aftermath of the shooting. But she failed. The euphoria associated with freedom had just worn off, replaced by feelings of bleak despair.

She arrived at the quayside and happened upon a bench which satisfied her needs. It faced the yachts and was half concealed by the trunk of a pine tree whose massive branches, twisted and gnarled reached almost to the ground.

She sat down and watched the clouds as they rolled in from the sea on the gale, overwhelmed by sadness, lonelier than ever. Her freedom was a void which she had neither the will nor the capacity to fill.

She saw two young women, casually dressed and laughing, walking along the edge of the quay. One was tall and slender, her hands moving in constant jests as she was talking, as if her words alone could not carry her meaning. Italian, Anna guessed, though her blonde hair suggested otherwise. The other was shorter, her skin cocoa-coloured, immaculate, her hair dark and abundant. Anna guessed that the second girl was Caribbean.

Then she felt dizziness grasp her, her vision turning bright, the sight transporting her to the past, to a time when her life was normal. She was walking in Almaty with her older sister, feeling again the simple, everyday pleasures, things which desperate men had deprived her of for too long. They were memories of a life before the Negev Desert, soldiers and hardship. Or was this the real life, a tough life, where the world was cold and empty.

***

Anna woke with a start, unable to comprehend what had happened, conscious only of pain, of faces emerging out of fogginess.

She was lying on her back on the bench, looking up through the twisted branches of the pine tree.

"Oh thank God!" blurted the blond girl in English. "Are you all right?"

Anna answered, her English confident and unaccented, "What happened?"

The face of the blonde girl appeared close above, her beautiful blue eyes conveying her concern. "You must have blacked out. Are you okay? Should we call an ambulance?"

Anna shook her head, and choked instead of answering, tears filling her eyes. Taking a new breath she said a few words. "No! Don't do that."

They helped her to her feet and walked her across the wide road which runs along the quayside. They found a café and sat her down at an outside table.

"What would you like to drink?" inquired the blonde girl.

"Cappuccino," said Anna, sobbing.

***

At the end of half an hour and two cappuccinos Anna felt renewed. The two girls were from the States and they had a room in a nearby hotel, the Suizo, a five-minute walk along Via Laietana, inside what used to be the Roman City, now part of the central Gothic District.

"Let's take you there," suggested the blonde American.

If only you could know how much you are doing for me right now . . ., thought Anna. She searched for adequate words to express her gratitude, but found only tears, welling up again as if from a volcano of emotion, choking her, preventing her from saying a thing.

Chapter 14

Inspector Juan Lopez´s black BMW pulled at break-neck speed into its allotted parking space at Egara Central Complex in Sabadell, narrowly avoiding colliding head-on with the perimeter fence. Springing from the car like a tiger, Lopez slammed the door behind him and sprinted up the stairs. The building housed the Autonomous Police's Criminal Investigation Department, and he composed himself as he neared the door of his boss, Commissar Siena.

"Lopez!" shouted his boss with indignation. "What the hell!"

"You told me to report to you in 45 minutes, Sir. So here I am, right on time."

"That I did, Lopez. Take a seat."

Commissar Siena terminated his telephone conversation and turned to his personal assistant. "Could I have a minute in private with Inspector Lopez?"

"Sure," replied his personal assistant. "I'll take a cigarette break."

The Commissar wasted no time in beating around the bush. The assassination of Colonel Alexander Chernyaev on Spanish soil, within the city limits, demanded swift, concrete action, and he was in no mood to let the situation precipitate. Least of all was he in a mood to give his erratic, wayward subordinate free rein to conduct the operation. Too much was at stake, his career for a start. "Inspector Lopez, at approximately ten minutes past six this morning Alexander Chernyaev was shot dead in a room in the Mandarin Oriental."

The look of surprise on the face of Lopez confirmed to Commissar Siena that news of the killing had not yet reached social media. "I want you to take personal control of the investigation. Go immediately to the scene of the crime and report on what you find."

"Yes Sir," replied Lopez, with a strange mixture of pride and relief. "You can rely on me, Sir." He saluted and prepared to leave his boss's presence.

"And Lopez . . . ," added the Commissar, as the inspector approached the door. "Do not discuss this with anyone."

As Lopez shut the door to Siena's office, a black Mercedes screeched to a halt outside the front entrance of the exact same building. Its armoured doors swung open and four big men dressed in Russian Army issue camouflage fatigues swarmed out, followed by a rugged mammoth of a man.

Commissar Siena received Dmitry Chernyaev deep in the basement. The situation room was large and disorderly. Its black leather sofas ran down the entire length of one wall, each furnished with a low table. Other black chairs were arranged between laptop computers, fixed telephones and a jumble of black cables. There was an enormous plasma TV tuned to Al Jazeera.

Dmitry Chernyaev was unable to contain himself a moment longer, swinging his bulk round in the doorway to face Commissar Siena. "My son is dead!. Do you understand what this means . . . to me, to you, to the world?"

"Dmitry," began Siena, choosing his words carefully but with difficulty, conscious that his life might depend on it. "I can assure you . . . "

"I don't want assurances, Siena!", he roared, his body trembling and quivering, "I want the girl! And I want her alive!"

"What girl?" replied the Commissar.

"The killer, you idiot!"

It was Siena's turn to be firm. "Sit down, Dmitry!"

"I don't want to sit down, I . . . "

"SIT DOWN!"

Siena didn't take lightly to being shouted at, even by Chernyaev.

Still fuming, the big Russian launched himself into the depths of the nearest sofa.

Commissar Siena pulled up a chair and faced him. He studied his old associate and friend in silence, choosing his approach. They had been through many a challenge in their association with the New Knights Templar. Never before had he seen the Russian in such a state.

The Russian spoke when he was calm enough to do so normally. Despite the pain, his desire for revenge burning in his soul, he needed the Commissar. He needed the Commissar almost as much as the Commissar needed him. "He was shot by a girl. Murdered. We know who she is, but she escaped."

"So who is she?" asked Siena.

"Anna Kuznetsova. She is Russian and we have her passport, so it's just a matter of time before we have her too." Chernyaev looked hard and long at Siena. "I trust you'll bring her in during the next hour!"

"How come you have her passport?" hazarded the Commissar.

"Look, Siena!!" thundered the Russian. "I ask the questions here. And it's me who calls the shots!"

The Commissar got up, facing him across the table. He folded his arms across his chest. Six foot tall, but his eyes still had to look up to the dark giant in front of him. Only two men in the whole world could talk to him is such tones. But one of them was Chernyaev.

"Do I need to remind you, Siena, of your duty to the Order, of your obligations to me?"

"No, Sir, you don't," countered Siena.

"Then you will find the girl and when you do, you will relinquish her to me. That's an order. And by the way, she better be alive."

Chapter 15

Across the road from the Egara Central Complex, roughly 100 meters from Dmitry Chernyaev's black Mercedes, a taxi was parked. Its driver was happy. He had just been promised more tips if he agreed to wait at the new location and keep his head down. He liked such passengers as the man who was sitting in his back seat and studying the building opposite with a pair of high power binoculars.

Ross kept the powerful lenses trained on Egara Central Complex, certain of his ability to pinpoint the office where the meeting was being held.

"So what's your line of work?"

The attempt at small talk irritated the American. "I told you. I pay and you drive. *Ahora esperas, claro*?"

"Si Señor! Claro! Claro!"

Ross extracted his smartphone from his jacket, selecting a fast dial option from the icons on its screen.

"Hoffman here."

"It's me," said Ross.

"What's the latest?"

"I'm at Sabadell, the headquarters of Mossos d'Esquadra."

Zak Hoffman felt sweat forming on his back despite the comfortable air-conditioned surroundings of his elegant fourth floor Langley office. Ross's answer confirmed that Dmitry Chernyaev was pulling out all the stops in his search for the killer of his son. He was calling in old dues from friends and associates. Commissar Siena, Spain's pre-eminent Templar and head of the Autonomous Police's Criminal Investigation Department had been an obvious first point of call. How long would it be now before he too was contacted? A conflict of interests between him and the U.S government was fast becoming a reality. A nightmare. And the worst thing of all was that if Chernyaev asked him to do his duty to the Order, he was not even sure he could do it. Not knowing what else to say, he just said, "And where exactly is Chernyaev?"

"He went in the front of the building, about twenty minutes ago, but his men are still hanging around the car."

"Okay. When he leaves, just make sure you keep tailing him and in touch. I want to know what Chernyaev does before he does it. Hoffman out."

Chapter 16

In the closed circles that characterize Langley's social scene, Zak Hoffman was known as the Wolf. The nickname had stuck as much for his conduct as for his appearance.

Despite his outward presentation, the calibre of his female companions never ceased to amaze those in his social circle. He had a charm and an appeal which preceded him and he would, despite his lone-wolf reputation, be seldom seen without an alluring woman hanging on his well-tailored arm.

Such characteristics had been instrumental in him acquiring a certain reputation in the small world of the U.S. military top brass. That and his military record. A former member of both Delta and Rangers. Winner of two Purple Hearts as well as the only post-Vietnam Medal of Honour, awarded him for his courage during Operation Desert Storm. Nobody possessed security credentials as did Zak 'The Wolf' Hoffman. What the top brass didn't know didn't concern them, or so they thought. Hoffman was a member the New Knights Templar though only Shepperton and Lee Ross knew that little fact.

Hoffman cut the call with Ross, his protégé, ill at ease. Somewhere between anxiety and discomfort. Apart from confirming that Dmitry

Chernyaev was out for blood, which he could well have guessed, the call had taken him to the memory of his father, and to the situation surrounding the last conversation they ever had.

The late Senator Douglas Hoffman had not taken kindly to his son's decision to take a year out to study in Paris. To him the acquisition of languages was a waste of time; time that would have been better spent obtaining a PhD, or becoming a White House intern. Worse still, at the time of the call, Zak had just moved to London, a decision way beyond the Senator's understanding.

The younger Hoffman's career decisions had already crystallized. He had met Oxford student Javier Siena in Rome and had become enthralled by the idea of joining his father's Order. The time finally seemed right to tie the knot between him and the New Knights Templar. "Father," he began, opening that last telephone conversation. "I have something to tell you."

There was a long pause, and the junior Hoffman knew he had his father's full attention.

"I have decided to make the initiation in London, that is, to finally join the Order. Everything is finalized."

A long pause ensued. "Are you absolutely certain, Son?"

"Yes, Father, I am. This is what I want. I see that the best way I can serve myself, my family, and my country is through the Order."

For the Senator the news came as a shock. For a year now his son had refused to even think about joining the Order, despite the constant pressure he put him under. Now for some inexplicable reason he had decided to join of his own free will. He was at a complete loss for words, unable to convey his satisfaction at what he had just heard. "Where and when will the ceremony take place?"

"The location is as yet, secret, Father. You know how it is. I will be escorted by Javier Siena whom I believe you know."

"I do. A good fellow, quite like his father."

"I have to go, Father."

"Yes, Son. I love you."

"I love you too, Father."

In the years that followed, those kind, ultimate words afforded him some relief from the regret which assailed him. Senator Hoffman died two days after the call.

Back at his nineteenth century mansion in the wooded hills of Virginia, Zak Hoffman made a beeline for his bar. He pulled down a half empty bottle of Johnny Walker, poured a large one, and downed it in a single draught. He refilled, and walked, bottle in hand across the sumptuous lounge to the vast window overlooking the garden.

The stresses of that day were accumulating fast, a tightness forming between the eyes with such force that he felt as if his head would split in two. He took a long swig as an incoming call came through on his mobile. "Hoffman here."

"It's me," said Ross.

"You found the girl!"

"I'm afraid she's disappeared. Even the Mossos d'Esquadra can't find her, which says a lot for her ability wouldn't you say?"

"This was not the phone call I had been expecting."

"Don't worry, Sir. I'll have a lead before the evening."

"How can you be so sure?"

"Just trust me."

"All I want to know is that she is safe, free, and not in the hands of the Mossos, nor the Russian Mafia in Spain. And we need to know who she is working for, to debrief her."

"How can you be sure she *is* working for a third party?" countered Ross. Something didn't gel. The Russian girl didn't fit the profile of a sleeper assassin. More that of an innocent bystander. Somebody's collateral damage.

"If she was that close to Alexander for that amount of time, believe me, she killed him for a reason. We have a duty to protect her, whoever she did it for. Find out who it is."

"We will find out, Sir."

"Very well."

Later that evening, Hoffman reached for the control console to the right of the patio windows, dimming the light, allowing his eyes to accustom to the moonlight which flooded the woods opposite. He poured another whisky with steadier hands. The real relaxation he craved was of quite a different nature. He cast bloodshot eyes around him not knowing what he hoped to find, if not the priceless antiques, the walnut dining table, and the impressionist paintings that hung on the oak panelled walls. Where were the women he had lusted for but not loved? Where was the life he had strived but not achieved? Why had happiness eluded him despite the opulence that surrounded him?

Later he awoke in the middle of the night. He pulled gently away from the slumbering form next to him, succeeding not to wake her. He threw on a dressing gown, and went to the bathroom, his body raked by thirst. He let the tap run before placing a cupped hand in its flow, stooping to drink, and then doused the cool water in his face.

"Zak, your phone! Turn it off next time, okay?"

Hoffman jumped across the room to his pile of clothes. *Who the hell knows this number? Apart from …*

He exited the bedroom, answering only when he reached the top of the vast, curving staircase, his voice raucous and agitated, as was his state of mind.

"I presume you were expecting my call, Zak."

"Who is this?"

"Nice try, Hoffman! Don't bother pretending you don't know who this is, or about what it concerns. I know how much time you spend pursuing me. You have a day to give me the girl."

"And what if I don't give her to you? What if she is not mine to give?"

"Then I would have to remind you of your duty to me and the Order. I would advise you to recall the day of your initiation, of the pain I inflicted on your back, and to try to imagine what such pain multiplied by ten feels like. That's the first thing I would do. And if survival is an instinct you possess, the matter need go no further. You took a vow. Don't make me hold you to it."

"And if I still refused?"

"Then reminders would turn to threats, and threats would turn to action, your job, your family, your life. Well, you're an intelligent guy. I'm sure you can work it out."

The line went dead.

Hoffman made no attempt to prolong the conversation, or to call back. It would be useless and besides, it would send a message. It would say: "I am worried." He was worried, extremely worried, but advertising the fact would not advance his interests. He needed to show strength in the face of adversity.

He descended the sweeping staircase into the dining room, for long minutes looking out through the window to the forest that bordered the vast open spaces of his garden. He stared as if caught in the belief that looking alone would provide an answer to his problems. Nothing. Not even the tiniest spark of an idea. So he returned to bed, snuggling up tight behind his female companion, searching relief in her arms.

Chapter 17

The cold air of the Barcelona night enveloped Chernyaev in its steely shroud. He was seated on the veranda of his mansion, pondering the most difficult day of his life. The pain of losing his son was incredible, but it was not the only thing on his mind. Other worries were crowding in on him, one of them in particular demanding his immediate attention: a document which lay in a safe in the depths of his basement, a document in his safe-keeping.

The ancient manuscript was elegant, and it was simple. If the things it beheld were true, then the End Times had begun, times which would lead to the Second Coming of Christ, to a showdown between good and evil. He remembered word for word what the document said.

The End Times would be heralded by the Great Tribulations, a period of time set in motion by the murder of he who would rain fire on the West.

The parchment document conveyed to him on the day of his inauguration as head of the world's oldest surviving military order had not been intact. It had been split after its discovery by the Order in 1947, torn into two symmetrical halves. Already by that date, it had been submitted to numerous tests of its validity. All had been conclusive. There was no doubt at all who wrote it: Ezekiel, the prophet, in 587 BCE.

It had been determined by his predecessor, Bernard De Montbard, that the two halves of the parchment were to remain physically separate until the End Times began, a time which, with the murder of his son, was upon them. De Montbard ordered one half to remain in the custody of the Order's executive, the Priory of Sion. The other half was to be kept under lock and key by the Order's military wing, the New Knights Templar. With the death of De Montbard, that executive power was now him, Chernyaev, while the military wing, the Knights themselves, were head-quartered in London, at Temple Church.

Popular belief maintained that the Military Order of the Knights Templar was effectively extinguished on Friday 13 October 1307 on the orders of the Pope. Coming to power in 1305, Pope Clement V had become indebted to the Knights Templar for safeguarding Christian pilgrims on their journey through the "Outremer," that part of the Holy Land between the coast of the Mediterranean and Jerusalem. Pope Clement was uninfluenced by greed or vanity. He wished merely to create a viable, resilient fighting force to continue to protect pilgrims in the Holy Land.

To this end, he had invited the Grand Masters of the two most powerful military orders of the day, the Knights Templar and the Knights Hospitaller to his residence at the papal court in Poitiers, France, to discuss merging the two orders into a single fighting force. While waiting for the Hospitaller Grand Master Fulk de Villaret to arrive, Pope Clement V and the Templar Grand Master, Jacques de Molay discussed the criminal charges brought against the Knights Templar two years previously. They decided the best course of action was to involve King Philip IV of France. A worse move for the Knights Templar could hardly have been imagined.

King Philip had also become deeply indebted to the Knights Templar, as had most European monarchs, and seized swiftly upon the rumours of criminal charges as a vehicle for wiping out his debt. Proving the truth behind the rumours that the Knights Templar were heretics that used secret rites involving homosexual acts (a rumour given credence by the Templar logo of two knights riding a single horse) would free him of his debt. Better still, as the most powerful king in Christendom, he secretly planned to expropriate the Templar's entire wealth. On 13th October 1307, a Friday, his plan wheeled into action.

At precisely 4am that morning King Philip's order for the arrest of Templar Knights under charges of heresy, idolatry, spitting on the cross and devil worship was executed across the realms under the overarching authority of the Pope. Pope Clement V, elected by the Perugia Conclave after an eleven month interregnum, was bound by a previous agreement with the French King to rule in the interests of both men. If such interests involved the suppressing of the Knights Templar then so be it. They had, since the loss to the Saracen Army of their last stronghold in the Holy-land at Acre in 1291, ceased to be useful.

In the following days, 15,000 Templar Knights were taken into custody across France, and tortured into false confessions of their crimes. On November 22, 1307, Pope Clement V's Papal bull *Pastoralis Praeeminentiae* was issued expanding the persecution, ordering all European kings to arrest Templar Knights within their jurisdictions.

Although most would later retract their confessions, proclaiming that they had been extracted under duress, the fate of those Templars unlucky enough to have been already arrested was sealed. Most were burned to slow deaths on top of bonfires in open fields across Europe. On one day alone, May 12th 1310, 54 Templar Knights, howling their innocence before God, were burned on a field at Saint-Antoine just outside Paris.

In 1312, following the Council of Vienna's decision to disband the order, Pope Clement issued the Papal bull *Vox in Excelso*, authorising the complete dissolution of the order. Contrary to much popular opinion, Clement did not proclaim the members of the Order guilty of the crimes levied against them, merely deciding that the time had come to do away with a largely discredited and increasingly irrelevant fighting force.

The Knights Templar Grand Master of the period, Jacques De Molay, was burnt to death at 6pm on March 18, 1314. As proof of the wrong done to the Knights Templar and of the power of God, he proclaimed that within a year both architects of the suppression, Phillipe Le Bel (the French King), and Pope Clement V, would be dead. With a year of De Molay's execution, the prophesy came true.

Despite the best efforts of Pope Clement and the most powerful secular forces of the time, the suppression of the Knights Templar was incomplete. As with any plan necessitating action, an element of surprise is fundamental. In the case of the French King's plan to arrest all of the Knights Templar, such an element was, to some degree, lacking.

King Philip Le Bel, the Fair King, had by necessity issued the order to arrest the Templars on September 9th 1307, a full month before the date, October 13th set for its execution. Due to an informant, a leak of information from the center of political and military power had, by October 12th, reached the commanders of the Templar fleet of eighteen ships anchored at La Rochelle. At midnight on October 13th, a matter of hours before the less well informed members of the Order were arrested, they set sail.

Well out of harm's way, on the great swell lines thrown up from a mid-Atlantic storm which stretched north to south across the Bay of Biscay, the fleet split into two sections.

La Falcon, the flagship of the fleet, under the command of Roger de Flor, led one part of the Templar fleet towards the north-west on strengthening winds. De Flor was a veteran sailor and had mastered his profession transporting pilgrims, mercenaries, coin and no doubt more besides between Marseilles and the Templar fortress at Acre in modern day Syria.

A hardy forty-year-old with a square jaw and weather-beaten face, De Flor guided the nine ships under his command 1,000 miles towards the north. After passing up the Atlantic coast of Ireland, the ships turned east on heavy seas. After twelve days at sea, they passed south of the islands of Islay and Jura into the calmer waters of the deep Scottish fjords. There, in remote Loch Craignish, the 24 Templar Knights aboard were finally safe. Pope Clement V had already excommunicated the Scottish King, Robert the Bruce, so Scotland was no longer subject to his authority.

The Templar Knights set up camp on the flat, expansive eastern side of the fjord, near the present day village of Kilmartin, eventually founding an abbey from where they began to mend their shattered lives.

The second part of the Templar fleet sailed south west across the Bay of Biscay to the second realm out of reach of forces loyal to the Vatican, Portugal. At the helm of the lead ship was Captain Gerard De Villiers. He safely guided the nine ships under his control into the haven afforded by the great Tagus River.

The fleet did not stop at Lisbon, however, but continued along the River Tagus towards a place they knew would afford them even greater security. Almourol Castle, standing on an island of the Tagus River had been constructed in 1171 by a Master of the Knights Templar Order, Gualdim Pais.

To De Villiers, not only did Almourol Castle provide a secure resting place, somewhere to remain to ride out the political storm and a haven to safely berth the nine vessels of the southern Templar fleet. It was also the closest port of call to his final destination: a well-fortified castle a mere half day's ride on horseback to the north. It would be there, at Tomar Castle, that the sacred military order of the Knights Templar would be head-quartered in the future.

The Order of Knights Templar thus survived, preserved intact in its two geographically distinct locations, Scotland and Portugal. Only the highest echelons of the Order, those holding positions in the executive, understood that the groups of Templar Knights they controlled were incomplete halves of a united whole.

Together, and since the morning of the original schism, the Order of the Knights Templar survived at Tomar Castle. It was there, on December 24th 1307, the day when the sun started its return from its most southern position in the midday sky, that a new Grand Master was hastily chosen. The Order had remained without a Grand Master for ten weeks, marking a division of their heritage into two periods which served to remind future leaders of the Order of the suffering and sacrifices of its previous members. The Order which emerged from the ashes of the Knights Templar was named the New Knights Templar.

The original knights and their descendants waited through the centuries in the humble lodgings of their protectors in Portugal and Scotland. Members of the Order waited too in monasteries and abbeys across Christendom and the Middle East which had remained sympathetic to their plight and believed in their cause.

They waited for news of the relics they had been tasked with protecting, the Ark of the Covenant and the Holy Grail, artefacts whose rediscovery would mark and seal their resurgence. They communicated between themselves in their far-flung hiding places using secret codes passed from hand to hand and mouth to mouth.

Any news of the emergence of the Ark was meticulously studied and verified. Above all, news of the reappearance of the priceless relics was studied at Tomar Castle in the twentieth century, the century leading up to the year in which Templar mythology stated the Ark of the Covenant and the Holy Grail would reappear in the realm of men.

The Order had remained confident through the centuries that the hiding place of the Ark and the Holy Grail was not far from Jerusalem, as were the indications of how to find them. They had concentrated their intelligence gathering systems in and around the holy city.

In the winter of 1946, the first rumours of a significant discovery began circulating in those tight Templar circles, news that the Bedouin had found something extraordinary in the mountains on the shores of the Dead Sea.

Templar Knights rushed from their hiding places to the area of the discovery, becoming the first educated people to analyse what the Bedouin had found. The documents were written in Aramaic on parchment or papyrus. They had little problem in finding out what those documents said. For centuries their whole raison d'être had been the deciphering of information from ancient sources.

They read the scrolls in great detail, systematically photographing passages that pertained to the Ark of the Covenant, the Holy Grail or to the End Times, the much heralded period leading up to the Battle of Armageddon. Time was short. News of the discovery had already been leaked, and soon, they knew, they would be required to hand them over to the Israeli state for custody.

Then they found the key passages they were looking for.

One Old Testament scroll in particular had attracted their attention. It was different from the vast majority which had been written by the Essenes, a Jewish sect and kept for centuries as a kind of library. It was older, written in Ancient Hebrew, and made of papyrus with a silky touch. After paying the Bedouin healthily, the New Knights Templar whisked it away into the desert for further scrutiny.

The first detailed analysis was undertaken at St Catherine's Monastery, in Sinai, an old Templar refuge. It indicated with absolute certainty that the script on the silky papyrus had been written by the hand of Ezekiel, the prophet exiled to Babylonia after the destruction of Jerusalem and the Solomon Temple in 587 BCE.

The silky papyrus scroll contained the lost information that the Templar had been searching for through the centuries; information on where the Ark of the Covenant was hidden, who could lead them to it, when the End Times would begin and who would usher them in. They realised the danger of the information, and split the document into two halves, separating the whole. Only when the End Times began would they permit the two halves to be brought back together.

***

Dmitry Chernyaev stood up in the lonely expanse of chairs and tables on the patio of his mansion and stretched his arms wide above him.

The time he had been waiting for was fast approaching. As Grand Master of The New Knights Templar's executive branch, he was the custodian of half of that very same scroll, that original silky parchment. And though he knew word for word what it said, that night, the night of his longest and most terrible day, he become overwhelmed by a desire to see it.

He went inside, stepped into a glass lift and took it to a place where the temperature remained constant, three levels down, to the basement.

With careful hands he extracted it from the safe. It was difficult to believe it had been written 2,666 years previously, and yet, the tests had been conclusive. It had indeed been written by Ezekiel in 587BCE, year of the destruction of the First Temple. It had lain preserved in the desert surrounding the Dead Sea ever since. He laid it out on the wooden table which took up one side of his basement, so that he could study it. Written in Ancient Hebrew, it read:

The End Times will be unleashed:

When 966,666 days have passed since the destruction of the Temple.

When he who would consume the West by fire is assassinated in Spain.

The uncovering of the Mardi, the Angel and the Antichrist will occur as the Ark of the Covenant reappears in the realm of men.

The reappearance of the Ark will end the era of history ruled by Determinism and herald the era subject to Free Will.

Three people will be necessary for the establishment of the Kingdom of God, LR Lee, AK Anna and KK Kira.

Chernyaev skimmed his fingers along the bottom of the delicate papyrus, caressing the unevenness of the edge, caught in deep thought. The differences between the other margins of the relic were obvious. The sides of the papyrus scroll were brown in colour, the same as its surface. The bottom was rich yellow. It had been torn, not cut, at a recent date.

Chernyaev knew the legend, that the original scroll fragment had been ripped in half shortly after coming into the Order's possession, days after its discovery by the Bedouin, in 1947, in a cave on the Dead Sea. He knew that the fragment in his hands had been conferred to the Priory of Sion, the executive of the New Knights Templar, that is, to him. He knew the bottom half had been retained by the New Knights Templar themselves, their warrior soldiers, the military side of their operations. *That,* thought Chernyaev, *meant only one thing. The other half was being kept at Temple Church, London.*

Dmitry Chernyaev shook his head in disbelief. The power of God was truly great. Was it not written in the document in his hands the truth that God existed? Had God not determined exactly everything that had occurred in the intervening 2,666 years? How could anyone argue that God did not exist after Ezekiel his prophet wrote that following 966,666 days of seclusion, information concerning the Ark's hiding place would reappear after the death of his very own son?

But 966,666 days had not yet passed since its occlusion. Neither had such information reappeared. All that Ezekiel had predicted was that the End Times would begin once "He who would attack the West is assassinated in Spain."

With the assassination of his own son, a man who had indeed planned the destruction of the West, Dmitry Chernyaev guessed that the End Times had indeed begun. That made perfect sense. The event which had just befallen him preceded by two days the ending of the period of occlusion of the Ark of the Covenant, a date he had worked out many times.

As Templar Grand Master, Chernyaev alone was privileged with knowing the exact date of the Ark's occlusion. He alone, therefore, was able to calculate when it would come out of occlusion, as he had done on many occasions.

Every time, the date he had worked out was the same. 966,666 days would pass in two days' time, December 21. In two days, he would be able, no, *be required,* to begin the search for the Ark. On that day the period of seclusion of the Ark of the Covenant would end, and he would find himself in London, in Temple Church, to receive the other half of the papyrus scroll.

Chernyaev smiled. *In two days, the information on where the Ark lay will no longer be divided between the two arms of the Order. The information will be finally complete, and it will be mine.*

Chapter 18

The Euromed from Renfe, Spain's national railway company, was not the cheapest way to get to Alicante. That would have been the twelve hour coach from the Alsa transport company. It was not even the cheapest train. But it was the fastest.

Anna bought the ticket in the late morning in the cavernous interior of Barcelona Sants train terminal. The purchase used almost all of the money the two American girls had given her, and she felt a lump in her throat as she thought of them. She had had no choice but to leave them, having promised herself right at the start that she would not bring them into danger. They had already done so much. They had saved her life.

She made her way towards her train, along the end of the platforms. She felt uneasy, without knowing why. It wasn't to do with the day before. She had avenged the rape on the spot, compartmentalizing the pain and the emotions and moving on. No. Something else had put her on edge, something from her subconscious.

Someone in the ticket office had recognized her. *My photo has been released by the police!*

She had to get out of sight fast, and so she skirted the side of the platform keeping to the walls. She found her train, her carriage and her numbered seat, a window, and sat down. She wished she had used the time with the girls more effectively, to change her appearance, to cut, dye and perm her hair. There was a copy of El Pais discarded on the seat opposite, so she snapped it up and disappeared from view, willing time to fly through ten minutes thirty seconds to the 11.36 departure.

By eight minutes to go her heart was racing along like a thoroughbred. *If only I can get out of this godforsaken city, to a deserted beach, to Alicante!*

Six minutes. A guy dressed in a heavy leather jacket entered the carriage, distinct from the tourists and businessmen forcing themselves and their luggage aboard. He was catching the attention of females both in the carriage, and outside, on the platform. He came straight to where she was sitting, taking a seat opposite without even looking at the seat numbers or checking his ticket. "Hola!"

American, she guessed. "Hola!" she replied, forcing a smile.

Four minutes. Her galloping heart missed a beat. *Mossos d'Esquadra.* They began moving through the carriage, checking IDs. The newspaper was not going to help.

She glanced at the American and found him staring back. *Was I so obvious?* With a sign of his eyes he indicated the table between them. She ducked under, disappearing from view.

Chapter 19

The armoured limousine cut through the Moscow afternoon traffic like a hot knife through butter. Though the driver had driving ability, the ease with which it sped towards its objective, the Kremlin was due mainly to the intermittent siren tones it emitted and the flashing of the blue strobe lights on its roof. Some drivers dodged out of its way while others held their ground, used to the sight of such government cars driven by impetuous, arrogant drivers.

In the front passenger seat sat Dmitry Chernyaev, just arrived on his private jet from Barcelona, still reeling from the news, struggling to believe that Alexander, his son, was dead.

The vehicle reached the end of the wide, three-lane Lenninsky Prospect as the rain increased in intensity. A blue-white flash of lightning touched down close followed by the crash of thunder, loud and powerful. Each had no more effect on Chernyaev than his driver's attempts at conversation.

The sight through the storm of the soaring, red bricked ramparts of the world's most secure seat of power jolted Chernyaev back to thinking about the practicalities of the meeting. He said, "Take me through the Spasskaya Gate."

"Yes Sir," replied the driver. The limousine chauffer had already been advised that he must approach the meeting place through that very gate, the "Saviour Gate" but was in no mind to seem rude. "Any news Sir, about the time of your meeting?"

"No."

The driver took his eyes briefly from the road and glanced at his boss to ascertain his mood now that he again seemed to be paying attention to his words.

"I was told the helicopter had already taken off from Gorky Two," his boss carried on. "The President has another meeting after mine is over, which he will get to by helicopter so we'll need to be quick."

"But the weather! Don't you think that the weather . . . "

"Look, son, just drive!"

Exactly a minute later they were being waved through the huge, imposing gate tower from the cobbles of Red Square by two drenched agents of the Kremlin Regiment.

Chernyaev's driver wasted no time skirting the Kremlin Presidium, immediately to the right of the red brick Spasskaya Tower entrance gate. He had that very morning received telephone instructions from the Presidential Administration. They had been as short as they were clear: *Drive directly through the Spasskaya Gate to Building No. 14, the Kremlin Presidium, to the triangular building immediately behind.* He knew what that meant. The meeting was to be held at the President's Official Residence in the center of Moscow, otherwise known as the Kremlin Senate.

After long seconds, the building came into view between tall pine trees as they finally neared the end of the long façade of the Kremlin Presidium. A large neoclassical gem in the form of an isosceles triangle, the shortest side of which lies adjacent to the Red Square wall of the Kremlin, the building had been originally planned to house the Moscow branch of the Governing Senate of Imperial Russia. Now it was the President's first choice for informal meetings.

Chernyaev's black Mercedes rounded the pine trees on the corner of the Senate building's main wall, and pulled to a stop under the triumphal arch which split its huge yellow façade.

Chernyaev was protected from the rain by the arch, if not from the wind which continued to gust around the classic stone Doric and Ionic order columns which adorned the building's facade. The driver fought to steady the door as he shouted to Chernyaev. "You are requested to enter the building by the Rotunda Hall."

Chernyaev looked over the top of the car and across the rain drenched inner courtyard towards the huge cupola, the Russian Pantheon as it was known. "Why didn't you drop me over there?" said Chernyaev, gesturing towards the other side of the courtyard.

"The Presidential Administration insisted that I drop you here and direct you to your meeting with the President, which will be in Rotunda Hall, beneath the cupola. I protested, but to no avail. It seems the President always meets his most respected guests in this way."

The Russian President had said goodbye to Sirirrat Kakandee, the Thai spiritualist, minutes earlier in the study of his third floor apartment, entirely satisfied. The meeting had gone well. He was now prepared for the meeting with Dmitry Chernyaev. Thanks to Maxi Kakandee, he knew exactly what the big Russian was going to ask him, and knew how he was going to answer.

Khodorov looked out from his third floor office, the one used by Lenin and Stalin before him, down to the courtyard below. He lifted a pair of binoculars to his face watching as the hulking, muscle bound figure fought the winds and driving rain across the Rotunda Courtyard. He smiled broadly. *So the Grand Master is angry!*

Khodorov arrived beneath the giant dome of the cupola and approached Chernyaev, careful that the splendid acoustics of the room did not pick up the sound of his soft footsteps on the smooth marble floor. Chernyaev was standing in admiration of the vast, domed hall, his anger and pain forgotten for an instant.

"Beautiful, is it not?" came the voice of the Russian President close behind him, amplified by the rotunda. Chernyaev swung around, a fluid movement despite his size.

"Mr President. The time for negotiation between my organization and Russian government departments is over. We now must act in the face of American aggression."

"Dmitry Ivanovich . . . "

The Templar Grand Master was in no mood for negotiations. "Mr President, if I may . . . " He had not been fazed by Khodorov's choice of meeting place. Neither was he intimidated by being constrained to walk across the rain soaked yard, nor by the stealthy approach of his host. He was out for blood, American blood. He looked down upon the small, wizened President, seeking steely, steadfast resolve.

"As party to the last meeting of the Presidential Security Commission I take it you are aware of the danger the U.S. represents to Russia. If we do not take America down, the world and our descendants will never forgive us. We have been given an opportunity Mr President, one we can't afford to slip through our fingers. The time has come to act, before it is too late, before America has destroyed our world and its cultures."

Khodorov said, "What exactly are you proposing I do about it?"

"Not what my son wanted. Not a total pre-emptive strike. Not yet at least. That would involve certain retaliation on behalf of the Americans, and without my son at the helm the consequences would be catastrophic not only for Russia, but for the world."

"So what kind of reaction are you contemplating?"

"What I propose is something much more limited. Something my son believed in, despite his plans for the full strike."

The Russian President studied Chernyaev's face closely in the dim light diffusing into Rotunda Hall from the 24 windows situated 27 meters above their heads. "So do you propose a limited strike?"

"Along those lines. The detonation of a mobile device exactly mid-way between the Pentagon and the White House, taking down their political and military power. The area is open, not too well patrolled. Executing it would be child's play. The biggest problem would be getting the bomb into the U.S., something my organization can accomplish."

"Dmitry Vladimirovich," began Khodorov, a look of severity crossing his ageing face. "Following the death of your son I have no longer the intention of launching a nuclear pre-emptive against the United States. Not yet at least. That strategy required your son, a master of nuclear military strategy. Without him, I prefer to wait a more appropriate hour."

"Mr President . . . America's expansion must be stopped. They are in our yard, knocking on our back door, and the inevitability of an accidental nuclear strike against us due to the approaching Technological Singularity is real."

"Dmitry. My decision is final. There will be no pre-emptive attack against America at the present time."

"This is an outrage!" shouted Chernyaev. "This is not the end of the conversation, Mr President!"

"What time is it in Beijing," asked Chernyaev to his driver. He was kicked back and fuming in the reclined black leather seats of the executive car as it sped back out through the Saviour Gate onto the still drenched cobbles of Red Square.

"Beijing is plus five hours, Sir."

Time for plan B. Chernyaev dialled a pre-set number on his smartphone, to a private number in the top secret prison of the headquarters of the Chinese military, in the Western Hills Complex of the Taihang Mountains just west of Beijing. If the Russian President would not willingly give him a nuclear weapon, he would have to be coerced into giving it to him.

The number of Li Bo-Yuan, a Russian — Chinese double agent still held in the military base began to buzz. He might have been incarcerated, but he had a phone, and was still the deadliest asset Chernyaev could call on. And the most persuasive. Desperate times call for desperate measures. And as desperate measures go, the one involving Li Bo-Yuan was as desperate as they come.

Chapter 20

Anna would have been totally invisible if it was not for the almost imperceptible rising and falling of a thick, brown, U.S. Army Air Force leather jacket that had been draped over her.

Officers of the autonomous police, the Mossos d'Esquadra, had arrived seconds after the vanishing act was complete, and left almost as quickly. Ross could have chosen any of a score of approaches to get rid of them, making full use of his gift for dramatics. He could have waved his Spanish government ID identifying him as a military attaché to the American Embassy in Madrid in their faces.

In the end, it turned out to be unnecessary. No sooner had he began to assail them about the legality of their request to see his passport that a voice cracked over the train intercom indicating the doors of the train were on the verge of closing. Looks of resignation passed across the faces of the agents as they realised their time was up.

From inside the leather folds which enveloped her, Anna heard a hiss of escaping air followed by a dull thud.

"It's clear!" whispered the American, his voice deep and confident. A blinking blue eye emerged first, looking straight at Ross, soon followed by the rest of her.

Ross remembered the face. He had seen her seven months previously at a New Knights Templar party thrown in his honour by his Grand Master. For her he would have been just another random guy in an evening of indistinct, alcoholic haze. She would not remember him. Of that he was sure.

He noted her chiselled features; the piercing blue of her eyes, her full lips. Ross thought, *a Russian beauty, with more than a hint of the East.*

"They're gone?" she asked.

"Yes," replied Ross.

Anna sat up on the double seats opposite. "Why did you help me? I never asked you to?"

"Your eyes asked me to," replied Ross. "I was happy to be of service."

"Do you expect me to thank you?"

"Thank me?" Ross observed her with curiosity and interest. He sensed her scent too, strong, intoxicating, and mixed with the sweet smell of her respiration. It was a powerful combination. His look was searching, and Anna returned it. They seemed to be testing each other. "No, I don't."

The Renfe Euromed was streaking through olive groves and citrus plantations well outside the city. Bright rays of sunshine angled into its air-conditioned interior. Anna was staring out of the window, and Ross could tell that she was searching her words. Finally she said, "What did you say your name was?"

Ross lied, "We have not been introduced! My name is Ross. Lee Ross."

"Funny!" said Anna.

"What is?"

"I could have sworn that I have met you."

"Really? Well if our last meeting was anything similar, I am sure I wouldn't have forgotten it. What is your name?"

"Anna."

"Russian?"

"Yes."

"On the run?"

"Obviously. They're always looking for beautiful Russians to kidnap. For escaped escort girls too. Not that I am one. But this is Spain, and there's conflict. Probably they got a tip off that a blonde Russian had escaped from one of the Mafia dens in the city."

She was getting too close to the truth, but the American was charming, and she had no reason to care telling him.

"So you're in the Russian Mafia?" hazarded Ross.

"In the Russian Mafia?" Anna laughed, momentarily switching her view back out of the window. "No. I am not *in* the Russian Mafia. I'm out of it. Today I took a decision; to leave."

"Do you have a passport?"

"Why?"

"Okay. No! Stupid question."

"Yes." She cast her eyes back in his direction, focussing them on his, their aspect gentler now. "Thank you, for helping me back there."

"It was my pleasure."

Anna fell back into the soft luxury of the seat. Two minutes later, she was fast asleep.

Chapter 21

Six hours had passed since Li Bo-Yuan had made good his escape from the Western Hills military complex in the mountains west of Beijing. The operational headquarters of the Chinese military behemoth was thought by the Chinese to be escape proof. And it probably was, to most, but not to Li Bo-Yuan. Because not only was Li Bo-Yuan ex-GRU Spetsnaz, Russia's most skilful Special Forces. Li Bo-Yuan was also a killer with the full privileges of lifetime membership of Chernyaev's *Vory v Zakone.*

The six hours had flown by in a flash, consumed by his body's sheer appetite for life, for killing. He had spent six years in captivity, and six times, after each new victim of his escape, murdered in cold blood, he had uttered under his breath the name of the man he held responsible for everything he did, was doing and would do. The one man he blamed for his years in captivity, for his pain under torture, and for the responsibility of the murders he was now committing: Zak Hoffman.

Six years had passed since the Chinese had captured him in Henan's remote Huo Guo Shan. Huo Guo Shan was the Chinese's secret mountain. He had been snooping information about a military installation buried in its depths, one presumed by the Russian government's military intelligence, the GRU, to be a site of stockpiled nuclear warheads.

It had been six years too since Anita Shu Pin, the Taiwanese-born specialist and his accomplice on the mission had disappeared from her office in Suzhou. Six years since the Chinese had handed him over to the Americans, hoping that the Americans would finish him off and spare them the task.

Six years since Zak Hoffman had tortured him to find out who he worked for, convinced that it was Dmitry Chernyaev.

He never broke. Despite the pain of Hoffman's amateur torture attempts, he had been able to summon the mental and physical strength to resist. Then he had turned the tables on his interrogator. Through the agony he had shouted out to Hoffman, "I know your name, you son-of-a-bitch. Run and hide! Run . . . and hide! When I am released, and I will be released, I will hunt you down. Run and hide! Zak Hoffman!"

Hoffman, not he, was responsible now for everything he did. His unique situation gave free rein to murder, to mutilate. And when he got to Mr Zak Hoffman, he would torture him to death.

Crouching in the shadows of a side street in one of the two Beijing embassy districts, Guo Yang, he looked at the watch stolen from the last guard he had martyred. 02.50. How many more would be killed that night in the name of revenge?

Not that he cared. Why should he? He hadn't been the creator of the deterministic world in which he lived, responsible neither for his actions. Whatever he did was for the good of mankind, ordained by God who had created him and determined his path.

There was movement in his field of view. Focussing his dark, narrow eyes on the spot he saw a People's Liberation Army soldier heading his way with a slow, methodical gait. Still crouching in the undergrowth on the opposite side of the street, he allowed himself one last look at his smartphone, reconfirming the target's location, entry route to the United States Embassy, known location and status of guards.

Seconds later, a dull thud reverberated through the Guo Yang night, unheard by the tall guard, his brain destroyed by the supersonic bullet.

Bo-Yuan sprinted across the smooth asphalt of the Beijing side street to the place in the pine trees where the tall guard had stood. He did not need to dispose of the body, or move it. The power of the bullet had done the job for him, taking him across a low wall. At a point on the perimeter fence offering a clear view of the U.S. Ambassador's residence, he checked his smartphone one last time for the position of the Ambassador's bedroom. He rechecked and then swung the heavy rocket propelled grenade launcher off his shoulder, took careful aim, and fired.

Chapter 22

Anna flinched in her sleep as the train braked heavily, her eyes open in a flash, seeing Ross sat next to her.

Ross smiled. He had not moved a muscle since she had dropped off, primarily out of a fear of waking her. Sleep could be a precious commodity in such situations, and her future was anything but secure. Ross knew that she needed all the sleep she could get, but now that she was awake, he straightened up, saying, "You were out of it."

"How long?"

"Two hours."

"Did your eyes ever leave me?"

"No, not really."

She struggled to sit up straight.

"Don't you have anything better to do?"

"Apart from protecting beautiful Russian women?"

"Yes, apart from that."

"No."

"Do you have a girlfriend?"

"No."

"And why not?"

"Freedom. Why spoil a good thing?"

"What about children? A wife and a family?"

"Don't need it."

"Aren't you afraid of waking up one day and finding yourself old and alone?"

"Better by far than waking up old and alone with an old woman!"

"You're a selfish egoist."

"Me? Egoistic? Oh, please! The most egoistic people on the planet give all their love to one person, bringing children into this cruel world to suffer without asking their opinion first. Just because they don't want to be lonely when they get old. Let's face it; the gift of love is strongest at the start, not the end. Serial polygamy is the way to go. Let me ask you a question; what do most people regret when they get to the end of the road?"

"Not having had enough fun by any chance?"

"That's exactly right! And let's face it, sex is great fun when you know how to practice it, in the right way, the way which avoids hurting people, avoids emotional pain."

"I see," said Anna. "You're God's gift to women!"

The Euromed train pulled into a small, nondescript station somewhere between Valencia and Alicante.

A group of law enforcement officers were standing on the platform as it pulled into the station.

The look on Anna's face told Ross she had seen them.

The doors opened. A group of four agents entered, moving through the carriage. This time their movements were hastened. They were targeting women. Blonde women. One of them noticed Anna and made a beeline. "Your ID miss," he asked, in perfect, unaccented English. *The Russians must be hiring well-educated hit men these days*, thought Ross.

"We're travelling together," said Ross. "Is there a problem?"

"Doesn't the lady have a voice?"

Their education obviously only went so far. "She doesn't speak Spanish or English," he said. "Maybe you speak Russian?"

"Miss, show me your ID."

"On what grounds?" answered Ross.

The agent turned to Ross, annoyed by his second attempt to intervene. "Excuse me?" he said, a mix of frustration and arrogance in his voice. He had done such 'checks' before and wasn't used to there being a 'body guard' present when he had to capture a runaway.

Ross said, "You heard me. Any self-respecting law enforcement officer in the world would know that in order to demand to see a person's ID, the officer is required to state the reason. May I see your warrant card?"

"My what?"

Ross said, "Are you deaf as well as stupid?"

The agent decided enough was enough. Taking no more chances, he drew his pistol, and Ross ended up looking straight down the barrel of a Beretta. "You two will have to come with me!"

"I repeat my question," countered Ross. "Under what grounds do you need to see her passport?"

The display of calm only fuelled the imposter's wrath. "Get off the train!"

"If you insist!"

On the platform, the two were corralled to the entrance of the station. A low yet solid wall of massive yellow sandstone blocks lay between them and a sprawling car park where it looked to Ross as if the town's weekly textile market was just being set up.

The car park was covered by tall cypress trees, interspersed by newly set up stalls displaying all kinds of materials from the finest quality silk to the cheapest denim. Ross estimated the distance between the place where he and Anna had been carolled and the market to be two hundred meters. Half the length of a standard lap in a stadium. The fastest he could cover it was thirty seconds. With a girl in tow he would be lucky to cover it in forty five. Then he saw one of the agents reach for his handcuffs.

With a movement as fluid as water and quick as lightning, Ross pulled his Beretta from inside his jacket. In the first two point seven seconds he disabled three of the four agents. The fourth one he disabled a second later. Leg shots. Messy, but effective. They wouldn't be able to point a gun at anybody for weeks, let alone recapture escaped slaves.

The echoes from the gunshots soon died down, replaced by wails of agony emanating from the fake police officers. Two other police officers appeared from nowhere, on the other end of the platform.

"Run for the market!" Ross shouted to Anna, pushing her in the right general direction before launching himself to the deck, which he hit firing, emptying the rest of the contents of the first magazine. One bullet took out the fifth officer, while his comrade dived for cover onto the rail tracks.

Ross ran after the Russian, catching up with her as bullets ricocheted around them off the solid asphalt of the parking lot. Anna let out an agonizing shriek, falling heavily, her head hitting the hard asphalt of the road with a dull crack. Ross somersaulted over her, landing in a perfect firing position, facing his adversaries. Two more shots rang out across the station followed by distant cries.

The Russian lay there, knocked unconscious by the force of the impact. She had taken a bullet, a flesh wound in her right leg. The entrance and exit holes were clean, but blood was seeping onto the road. No broken bones, no complications. Nothing in Ross's view that a week's rest and care wouldn't put right. He scooped her off the tarmac and continued towards the market at a trot.

At the first stall of the market a black-haired woman peeped out from behind a white Ford Transit. She was dressed in a colourful full-length skirt and black top.

Ross asked "Is this your van?"

"Yes."

"She needs a doctor, fast!"

"Lay her in the back," said the black-haired woman, flinging open the rear double doors. She unrolled a roll of denim over the top of her purchases, and helped the American lay the Russian on top of it before attending to the bleeding leg.

"I can drive you to a hospital."

"Not a good idea," said Ross. "We need a private doctor. No questions."

Ross saw a look of comprehension cross the black haired woman's face. She was used to life on the edge of society. People in any kind of trouble had to be helped. It was her people's tradition. And when the trouble involved the police, the desire to help was even greater. She said, "I know such a doctor. But . . . "

"What?" asked Ross.

"She is far from here."

"How far?" asked Ross.

"Depends how fast you drive. She lives in my home town. You drive. I will direct you from the back, while I take care of the girl, make sure she doesn't die or anything." The black haired woman was already applying a tourniquet made of a piece of denim to stem the bleeding.

"And where exactly is your home town?"

"Granada, Andalusia."

Chapter 23

The woman's name was Amparo Mayo Montoyo and she was the most capable clairvoyant in the whole of Spain, if not the entire world. She had never paid much attention to the gift, nor pursued it. But from an early age she had known that, if she tried, she could see the future of just about everyone. What she saw in most of the people she touched frightened her. She saw their dark sides much more clearly than their good sides for the simple reason that the dark side of most people was dominant.

What she saw when she held the tall Russian girl, however, made her catch her breath. Not only was she different from everyone she had ever held, ruled entirely by her good side, her future could not be read. It was as if for her, the normal cause effect relationships which rule our lives did not apply.

The short messaging service, SMS for short, is a powerful tool for those who need to convey urgent information without ambiguity. Amparo could never understand why some people did not send her a text when, as often happens in Grenada, her phone went outside the zone of signal coverage. Her job as a trader of textiles and jewellery in the gypsy villages which surround Grenada took her often into such zones. So frequently she lost time and money when an important client called her about an earring or piece of clothing for some gypsy sweetheart, and did not send a text.

So when Amparo realized that she urgently needed to meet her friend Dr Marie Teresa Juan, Maria to her friends, she was in no doubt how she was going to set about it. She texted it.

URGENTLY NEED YOUR HELP. ON ROUTE TO GRENADA FROM ALICANTE WITH AN INJURED WOMAN WHOSE SURVIVAL IS CRUCIAL FOR THE SAFETY OF OUR HOMETOWN. ETA 20.20.

As soon as she had sent it a doubt seized her mind. Something was wrong. What, she wondered was the connection between the girl in her arms and her home town? Why was it that she and only she could influence the future of Grenada? Was she herself influencing it by taking her there, putting at risk the security of the city she loved? For the first time in her life she understood that some people's future is not already written. Whatever was true or not about the Russian, Grenada's survival was tied to the survival of the girl lying unconscious in the back of her van.

Maria Juan and Amparo Montoyo had been friends since the second grade of high school. It hadn't always been that way, because before being friends they had been enemies.

They had been born into different communities, into different worlds on two sides of the same city. Maria was from the center. She had grown up in the shadow of "El Moro," the huge statue of the "Arab" on the edge of the Jewish district. Some said the statue of El Moro looked more like a Jew, but to Maria such distinctions made no sense and no difference. Arab or Jew, they were living in a city of immigrants, a city founded millennia before by the Moors from Africa.

Sandwiched between the Alhambra and Plaza Nueva, Maria's district was filled with bars and restaurants, bakeries and tea-shops, catering as much to foreigners as to locals.

Though her father had followed an illustrious career in engineering, it was only when he approached retirement that his most remarkable talent had revealed itself. On one of his then frequent trips to Israel, he had by chance become caught up in an archaeological dig on the edge of Mount Zion. From that moment on, archaeology had been his life.

Maria was Jewish, middle class, but above all Spanish. Her skin color and fine-boned facial structure revealed Middle Eastern roots. Though she lacked the aggressive, gypsy beauty of Amparo, her gentle features and beautiful hazel eyes more than made up for it. She had a fine, perfectly straight nose, high cheek bones tapering to a narrow chin and black wavy hair.

Amparo was everything that Maria was not. She grew up in Albacin, the Moorish district clinging to the slopes of Sacromonte. Its narrow streets and alleyways were filled with tourists, Arabic tea houses and cats. It was a place where Arabic is spoken more than Spanish, where all streets lead steeply, over steps and cobbles, to one place; El Mirador de Sant Nicolas. And if one continued in the direction of the hills, one reached the caves of Sacromonte overlooking the Alhambra, for centuries the home of the gypsies of Grenada.

Amparo started the fight which made her and Maria best friends. An acquaintance had told her that Maria had something going on with the boy that she liked. She sustained the rumour and for days studied Maria for a sign of the truth. After school one afternoon, walking out of the gates, she caught sight of the two of them talking. She dropped her bag, and laid into her, kicking and punching. By the time it was broken up, Maria's glasses lay broken on the road. She hadn't put up a bad fight, but Amparo had the advantage. The ferocity of her attack had been difficult to counter.

Weeks later, Amparo felt sorry for Maria, and ashamed for her action. She had heard that Maria, despite her Jewish roots, had a gypsy blood cousin. She approached her one evening at the school gates, in the same spot that she had made the attack, and apologized.

Following that day, the two become friends, inseparable at school and in their free time. Nobody could say anything bad about Maria, otherwise Amparo and her cousins would find them and deal with them.

Chapter 24

Everyone has a special place, a quiet place, where they go to think, to be at one with the world. An hour after receiving a call from the U.S. embassy in Beijing, China, CIA Deputy Director of Operations Zak Hoffman found himself at his special place.

The rocky bluff in the forest jutted over the Potomac, affording magnificent views up and down the river. He would have missed the hidden path which led to the bluff the day four years ago when he had come across it, had it not been for his three-year-old Springer spaniel, Bobby.

Bobby had been so caught up in his pursuit of ground squirrels that he had not responded to his calls. Hoffman had had a time constraint that night, so when Bobby did not appear, he had little choice but to go in after him, following the frantic barking which led him only deeper into the forest, and eventually to the bluff.

In the years which followed his discovery of the 'Secret Path', he had been back to the bluff a mere handful of times. His job hardly afforded him time for such luxuries. Sometimes, notwithstanding, it had been absolutely necessary; his career on the line, or his life.

The severity of his present predicament made the five previous "situations" pale into insignificance.

In the darkening sky above the rocky bluff where he now stood, silently contemplating the universe, himself, and his place in it, two ravens were soaring in the powerful up draughts of an approaching thunderstorm. *It is said that ravens mate for life*, he thought. *What better place than the strong winds above the bluff to exhibit their 'joie de vivre', their love for each other, for life itself.*

Watching them, Hoffman was struck by a powerful realization. While the ravens were free to escape on their wings through the night from the storm fast approaching, he was trapped. The assassination of the U.S. ambassador in Beijing could mean only one thing. *Li Bo-Yuan was out of jail.*

Chapter 25

To say the operations room at Mossos d'Esquadra headquarters was a hive of activity would have been an understatement of grand proportions. Chaos reigned. Yet despite it, at its very center, directing operations, Javier Siena felt in control, shouting orders in rapid succession to the agents sat behind computer screens and video monitors. The search for Anna Kuznetsova and her unknown helper at the train station had been under way for twenty-five minutes. Nothing had come up.

Siena shouted to an agent on the far side of the open plan office. "Agent Villars! I am still waiting for the CCTV from the station forecourt. What's the problem?"

"It should be available in a matter of minutes, Sir, five at the most."

"I don't like the word 'should' Villars," Siena shouted back. "Use the word 'will'. Come on guys. How difficult can it be? We have access to the most sophisticated intelligence gathering resources in Spanish history. And what about the roadblocks?"

"Nothing yet, Sir," replied a tall officer sat right in front of him. "Either they got out before they were set up, within ten minutes of the shooting, or they are still inside the town, lying low."

"If I had wanted analysis, I would have gone to an analyst!" barked Siena, curtly. "Just give me the raw data!"

"Sir . . . ," shouted another agent on the far side of the room, beneath one of the gigantic windows.

"Agent Mayo! Give me all you got!" yelled Siena, sensing a glimmer of hope.

"Sir, the initial report and analysis from our agents at the hospital is in. All four police imposters were shot by the same gun. Each in the thigh, by a shooter who himself was moving. Only . . . "

"I know, I know," Siena interrupted him. "Only a handful of people in the world are known to be capable of such shooting."

"That's exactly right," replied agent Mayo. "Should I run a list?"

"Run it!"

Running the list was the last thing Siena needed to do. It was the easiest answer to give to the agent in order to free his mind for the search for a solution to a widening crisis. He already knew enough about the shooting to know exactly who was helping the girl: Lieutenant Colonel Lee Ross.

The CIA was involved, which fitted. Anna had been close to Alexander Chernyaev. Everyone in Barcelona knew he had been infatuated with her. It was inevitable that the CIA would go after her. Alexander Chernyaev was Russia's mastermind of military strategy. A man who the Americans knew was a fierce proponent of a pre-emptive strike nuclear strategy. What surprised Siena more than anything was how quickly America had got to her. Had the CIA learnt all the lessons from their recent failures?

Chapter 26

Night had long fallen by the time Hoffman reached his BMW, his pet terrier Bobby jumping up and down happily beside him. His mobile rang as he was climbing into the driver's seat. Just as expected, a Beijing area code appeared on the screen of his vehicle, already attached by Blue-tooth to his mobile device. He settled back into the seat and hit the respond button on the underside of the steering wheel. "Code in."

There followed a brief silence followed by a tone which signified the caller had been verified and that the line was secure.

"Hoffman."

"Sir, this is agent Mills in Beijing. We have news regarding the assassination of the ambassador."

"Go on, Agent Mills," replied Hoffman.

"I am not sure if you remember, but five years ago you interrogated what we believed to be a rogue CIA agent. The action was sanctioned by the Chinese in an attempt to encourage the suspected double agent to come clean about his connections to the Russian military."

"I remember," said Hoffman, sweating, despite the cold. "Go on."

"We have just been informed that he escaped last night from Western Hills, taking down five of their personnel in the process."

"And how does this affect me?" asked Hoffman.

"Well, Sir . . . " came back the agent, "It seems the Chinese believe Li Bo-Yuan to have carried out the assassination of our Ambassador."

"That would seem very likely, Agent Mills," said Hoffman. "Li Bo-Yuan is a psychopath with a pent-up frustration after six years in detention. He hates America and his psyche tells him that by carrying out such actions he is doing God's work. He believes he is some kind of Crusader, a Templar Knight on a mission to free the world of America's tyranny. That is what he told me in his interrogation. In his deranged mind, the New Templars will fight America, the New Saladin. Thank you, Agent Mills."

"Wait, Sir?"

"Agent Mills?"

"There is something I think you should know," said Mills.

"What is it?"

"The Chinese say that the assassin, presumably Li Bo-Yuan, left a note at the place where he fired the rocket propelled grenade round which took out the Ambassador."

Hoffman sighed deeply, fighting the 'I knew it' feeling.

"Get to the point, Mills! What did it say, this note?"

"It said FOR HOFFMAN, signed THE TEMPLAR."

***

"Sir!" exclaimed Agent Villars.

Siena, who had been pacing up and down the aisle separating the two sides of the office, stopped dead, turning to the window. "Agent Villars, this had better be good."

"The CCTV footage from the station should appear on the big screen . . . Now!"

The large screen on the far wall flickered into life, revealing a fish eye view of the station forecourt and car park.

"Fast forward to the time of the shooting, approximately 12.25," ordered Siena.

"Yes Sir," replied the agent.

"Stop there!" shouted Siena. Two figures, a man and a woman, had just entered the field of vision of the digital camera, running away from the camera's location. "That's Lee Ross!" he pronounced. "Run it!"

They watched the grainy footage as two running figures fell to the ground, Ross somersaulting gymnastically across the girl. The move was awe-inspiring, firing at his pursuers before picking up the girl in his arms and continuing to run towards the now deserted textile market visible in the middle distance. They watched as Ross approached a white Transit, receiving help from a dark haired woman who happened to be there.

"Zoom in on the white van," ordered Siena, "Is it possible to get its number plate?"

"It should be. One moment," said the agent. "Yes . . . There it is. 1346 YAC."

"Run the trace!" commanded Siena.

Chapter 27

Lee Ross kept the Ford Transit at a steady 140km per hour, a compromise between speed, the prevention of mechanical problems, and avoiding any complications with the law. Amparo had kept the vehicle in good nick; the engine took the journey in its stride.

They arrived at Gran Via in the center of Grenada, Ross looking for signs to the Alhambra.

"Go straight to the end of Gran Via, to Placa Nueva, and carry straight on," directed Amparo from the back.

"The old Jewish quarter?" said Ross, barely disguising his surprise. Although his only visit to Grenada had been more than two years previously, he remembered that most wealthy gypsies continued to live on Sacromonte, mainly in the many beautiful gardened villas or 'carmens' overlooking the Alhambra. "I had presumed that you lived in a villa on Sacromonte."

"I do, but it's best if we take Anna to Maria directly, and she lives in a carmen below the Alhambra."

The subject of the discussion jogged something in Ross's mind. Now he understood why he had been so ill at ease during the second half of the trip. *The van was traceable.* How could he have overlooked it? They were lucky to have got this far. All it would have taken was for a wide angled digital camera to have been set up outside the station for the police, and anyone who paid them, to know where they were going. There was a chance that there had been no such camera at the station, but taking chances was not how Ross liked to work. He took the next turn off the main street, and stopped the truck.

"What's wrong?" asked Amparo.

"This truck, where is it registered?" asked Ross, his voice laced with anxiety.

"What difference does it make?" answered Amparo, "The girl needs professional help fast. I don't think we should be wasting time discussing to whom the vehicle is registered! For Christ sake Lee, she needs help!"

"It matters because they will be able to trace it."

"It's registered to Maria, but in Alicante, where she has a house, and brothers."

Ross didn't like the sound of it. Not one little bit. But Amparo was dead right; the Russian girl was quite literally dying from loss of blood. Worse than just unconscious, she was in a coma, which complicated everything. If he didn't get her to a doctor in the next hour, they could well lose her altogether. He didn't relish the idea of taking her there, but the idea of explaining to Hoffman the circumstances surrounding her death grabbed him even less. He didn't have a choice.

***

"Sir. I have an address. A Ford Transit registered to one Maria-Theresa Juan, Calle Aragon 37, San Juan de Alicante."

Siena picked up a phone and dialled a number he knew by heart, a mobile number in Moscow, Russia.

Dmitry Chernyaev took the call even though he was in a meeting, leaving the table without explanation, apart from the usual "I have to take this."

"What have you got?" said the Russian.

"We have a location for the girl," said Siena. "Would you like me to send a team?"

"That won't be necessary. Send the name and address by secure line to Li Bo-Yuan. You have his number. Tell him that he is to call me as soon as he lands." Then he hung up.

Slipping his mobile back into its pouch, Dmitry Chernyaev lingered long in the corridor of the Kremlin, trying to focus his mind.

On 21 December, the very next day, he would be able, no, be required to begin the search for the Ark. The thoughts he had had the previous night came back, flooding back. Everything seemed to be fitting together as a gigantic jigsaw puzzle in which the pieces are people and places. Again he was filled with wonder at the thought of God's wisdom, and of the Ancients who could predict so well his own place in the future course of history.

21st December. It would be the first whole day after the end of the Ark's occlusion, 966,666 days previously. The next day would confer on him every right, according to his Order's own rules, to demand the other half of the scroll fragment. The scroll fragment would once again be capable of being read by one person, in a single draft.

No longer would the military arm of the New Knights Templar prevent him from finding the whereabouts of the Ark. All he had to do, according to the rules he had read more times than he cared to remember, was to get to Templar Church before nightfall tomorrow. Those rules said he had to be accompanied by two witnesses who had also to be Order members.

Now that the time had come to choose those two witnesses, he chose without hesitation. He plugged in another number on his mobile that he knew by heart. This time, it was a mobile in Washington DC which began to ring. The mobile belonged to Zak Hoffman.

Chapter 28

The white Ford Transit approached the carmen at 20.30, local time, 20th December. Maria was standing at the entrance, as she had for the preceding half hour, her long black hair blowing in the icy wind which descended from the Sierra Nevada high above.

Ever since she had received the message she had been gripped by an anxiety she had not known for years. Unable to sit down, drink coffee or anything at all, she had gone outside in the hope that the mountain air would bring her some relief. Now she was running ahead of the vehicle as it entered the yard through the wide, stone arched entrance. "Park over there, next to the house!" she shouted to Ross, indicating a space next to her Land Rover. Ross obeyed, swinging the vehicle into a tight circle and reversing into the space at impressive speed.

Amparo threw open the rear doors even before the vehicle came to a halt. The girl's condition had deteriorated. Her skin colour was grey and ashen, sweat appearing in beads on its surface. Deep trauma, deep shock. Despite the tourniquet, she had been unable to prevent the loss of a large quantity of blood, which had spoiled all the textiles which had formed the makeshift bed.

"Grab her legs," Amparo yelled to Maria. "Quick!"

"I'll take her!" said Ross at the vehicles rear door, inserting his arms under the Russian, and lifting her out. "Lead the way."

"This way," said Maria, preceding Ross into the two story stone house. The entrance to the house led straight into a vast space. At its center was a table, a solid piece of hardwood fashioned in the middle of the last century, that seemed dwarfed by the grandeur of the room.

"Lay her on the table," commanded Maria.

As soon as the Russian was laid out, Maria set about saving her. The gunshot wound had not broken any bones. A pillow was found. Amparo gently lifted her head as Ross placed it underneath. Maria checked her vital signs. She set up an intravenous drip to replace the liquid she had lost. Then, Ross's mobile buzzed, so he walked away from the table, leaving the two Spanish women engrossed in their endeavour. It was Hoffman.

"Ross."

"Code in," came Hoffman's rasping voice.

A second after introducing the six-digit code, a bleep indicated the line was safe.

"You are to meet me tomorrow afternoon, 16.00, Temple tube station, London. And come alone."

"But, Sir, with all due respect, the girl . . . " began Ross before being interrupted by the voice of Hoffman, coarse and severe.

"That's an order!"

Ross was about to say something, but then stopped. The line was already dead.

***

On the other side of Eurasia, Li Bo-Yuan was strapping himself into a gigantic business class seat, staring straight ahead with cold, emotionless eyes. The ten hour flight to Madrid would give him all the time he needed to analyse the intelligence information he had received before passport control at Beijing airport from the hand of a GRU Russian military attaché.

"Your in-flight entertainment program, Sir," had said the officer, smiling. "I already gave it a brief once over. You'll need to make hard choices. Maria is a gypsy, always has been, always will be."

"Your best shot?" asked Li Bo-Yuan.

"The phone records look promising. They'll lead you straight to her. Good luck Sir!"

Chapter 29

December 21st 07:30 a.m.

Temple Church, London

Temple Church lies hidden, tucked away in a gated community of law firms and mansions a stone's throw from the River Thames. The Templar Knights built it towards the end of the 12th century, at the time when they were the height of their influence and power. Originally circular in shape, it had over the centuries been enlarged to include a large nave, well lit and tall.

At 07.30 a.m, inside his office in the depths of the church's ancient crypt, the leader of the military branch of the New Knights Templar, the Reverend Bernard-Jones, was engaged in a careful operation, extracting a fragment of an ancient parchment document from within the safe where it had been kept for decades. It was one half of the fragment of the Dead Sea Scrolls which had been kept by the Military New Knights Templar, after being carefully passed from location to location since its discovery in 1947. It indicated the place the message it bore would be released, London, that very day, 21 December, the day when it would be united with the other half, the half kept by the head of the Executive branch. Dmitry Chernyaev.

***

Temple Church, London, 12:55 p.m.

Ross had an unbroken view across the deserted square which encircled Temple Church, from the corner of the alley which led to The Strand right across to the tall stone column which bore the Knight Templar logo. He liked to arrive at such meetings ahead of time. It gave him time to check the surroundings, time to think of a backup plan in case things went sideways, to check, double check and check again. That was his system, and time and again, such checks had proved the difference between life and death.

Five minutes had passed since he arrived, and Ross caught himself wondering why Hoffman had changed the location of their meeting so many times. First Temple Tube Station, then a pub called the Knights Templar, midway along Chancery Lane, and finally, Temple Church itself. It showed a high degree of insecurity, or a troubled mind, or both.

Then there was yesterday's phone call when he had just arrived at the "Carmen." Hoffman had gone U-turn about the girl. Why was she no longer a priority? Was the meeting in London so important to leave behind the girl who had just executed the agency's number one target? He was under no illusions that it depended on their allegiance to New Knights Templar, something confirmed by the location of the present meeting, at a place both men knew to be a hotbed of activity for the military arm of their order.

A man entered Ross's field of vision wearing a fashionably cut black leather jacket, blue denim jeans, walking with a wolf-like gait, no doubt trying to appear inconspicuous. It was Hoffman.

They exchanged glances and signs as soon as they saw each other, meaning, *meet you in five minutes once we have both determined that the coast is clear.*

They met beneath the tall plane trees of the little square which surrounded Temple Church, at the base of the column on whose summit stood the Templar logo, a statue of two men riding a single horse. The trees were alive with a gusting strong wind which had remained after the passing of recent rain.

Ross said, "Weren't we supposed to debrief the girl? What happened?"

"I didn't have a choice," replied Hoffman.

"So this is about orders?"

"Of course it is. And you know it."

They walked, circling slowly underneath the plane trees. Hoffman said, "I'm sorry about the girl. How is she?"

"She's in a coma. The shot brought her down by hitting one leg while she was running at full tilt. She fell, driving her head onto the tarmac with one almighty hit. She just needs rest and is assured of it in the place where I left her. She is being taken care of by two angels, a Gypsy and her Jewish friend, both Spanish women, young, honest and kind. She will be fine."

"Good work," said Hoffman. "When this meeting is over you can return to debrief her."

"Naturally," replied Ross quietly, his eyes fixed on those of his boss. "Tell me about the meeting. We came here under directions from the Order right?"

"Obviously," said Hoffman. "I was summoned last night . . . "

"The Grand Master is here?" said Ross, his heart almost missing a beat. He realised for the first time of a connection that he should have made before leaving Spain. This time he was not acting.

"Yes. Why?"

The initial pang of anger morphed into fear. It bit down deep inside his stomach, as he realised with certainty that something was dreadfully wrong. No longer was he in control. He had left the girl unprotected. "Dmitry Chernyaev is here in London?" Ross could not believe what he was hearing. "Why didn't you tell me that we were going to meet the Grand Master?"

"Steady, son, keep your voice down," replied Hoffman. "Firstly of all, I couldn't tell you. We are meeting the Grand Master. There are rules, protocol . . . "

"Protocol!" interrupted Ross, fuming now. "Sir, with all due respect, there is protocol in my duty to the U.S. government too. Do you understand what you have done? You have compromised the operation!"

"You mean the girl?"

"You're damn right, I mean the girl."

"I thought you said she was safe."

"Safe is a relative term, is it not? I said she was safe because until about twenty seconds ago I believed her to be safe. That was before I knew that Dmitry Chernyaev brought us here. Knowing that information, I would say that she is decidedly unsafe, because I know the man, and what he is capable of, as do you. Let me guess. He specifically told you to bring me with you."

"Yes, he did."

Silence reigned as the facts sunk in. The Grand Master didn't do anything without considering every possible consequence, covering possible angle.

Hoffman said, "Look Son, if we have been played, so be it. But need I remind you that we belong to the New Knights Templar, a sovereign military order and do not have a choice when summoned? If the girl's safety has been compromised, you only have yourself to blame."

With that, Hoffman looked at his watch, reached for Ross's black leather jacket collar, turning up the collars, and saying, "It's time! We have a meeting to keep with our Grand Master."

The interior of the church was filled with the rays of the sun on the year's shortest day, flooding in through the tall arches of the stained glass windows, bathing the chancel with its golden luminescence. Candles burned on metal stands beneath the towering stone columns leading to the sanctuary on the right, their fumes filling the church with their pungent odour, providing fragrant heat to the vast, stone clad space.

To the left of the entrance, where the two Americans had come to stand, lay the most ancient part of the structure, a circular space whose thick stone walls enclosed the effigies of twelve Templar Grand Masters. At its very center stood a dark-haired man, a concrete bunker in a suit, his face scowling, speaking already without welcome or courtesy. "You refused to give me the girl. I understand. I would have done the same if I had been you. She was party to sensitive information, and carried out her mission to perfection."

"It's not what you think," began Hoffman, approaching his Grand Master. Ross was fuming at his side following the Russian's every move with two narrow slits for eyes, a Doberman waiting to pounce.

As a member of the Order, Ross had, in the past, done 'cleaning' jobs for the Russian. But this was different. This concerned Anna Kuznetsova, and in affairs to do with her, he was first and foremost a CIA operative. Debriefing her had been part of his job and his duty. It was up to him how he chose to serve the Order to which he had already given so much, and his Grand Master had crossed a sacred line, interfering in something he should not have interfered with. To him, Anna Kuznetsova had become one of theirs, and had the right to expect protection when she needed it.

"What the hell is that supposed to mean?" snarled the Russian.

"She does not work for us," countered Hoffman, calmly.

"Is that your idea of a joke, you ignorant piece of shit? We're here talking about the woman who killed my son, and you make jokes?"

"With all due respect, Grand Master," replied Hoffman, "your son was planning the destruction of my country."

"He was," said Chernyaev, more steadily. "Then he was planning something with good reason, for the good of the world. Humanity is tired of America's tyranny, its imperialistic ambitions and international police operations disguised as spreading democracy for the good of mankind."

"And what the hell is that supposed to mean?" growled Hoffman, using Chernyaev's words for effect. He may have been caught off guard by the overt aggression of the Russian, but he was a CIA Officer and a patriot, and he did not take kindly to criticism of his country.

"You will help me carry out his will," said the Russian.

"And what was his will?"

"It's a small affair. You will take out the Pentagon and White House with a small nuclear device."

"The hell I will!" flared Hoffman.

"Since when was any of this negotiable?"

"You forget I am American and I love my country. There are certain things that I can't do, even when ordered to by you, my Grand Master."

"I expected as much," said Chernyaev. "Which is the reason I secured myself some extra negotiating power, extra leverage, before coming to this meeting."

"I presume you can only be talking about a certain Chinaman?" said Hoffman, aware of the connection.

"Your intellect serves you well," said Chernyaev, smiling. "I am. And I hope you like the sound of your own screams, Mr Hoffman, because you have just reserved a meeting with Mr Li Bo-Yuan, who has been waiting patiently for six years to thank you personally for your treatment of him during your last meeting."

"Then I hope he is more skilful than you in getting what he wants," replied Hoffman, with an air of finality. "This meeting is over."

"This meeting is over when I say it's over," thundered Chernyaev, the words echoing off the walls of the nave like ricocheting pistol shots. "You may or may not believe me when I say that your meeting with Mr Li is already reserved, unfortunately for you, in your not-so-distant future. Your thought processes are, after all, out of my control. What is in my control is how prolonged the torture will be when he finally catches up with you, if you continue to refuse. Have you already forgotten that Li Bo-Yuan is *Vory v Zakone*? Let's just say that what you do for me today will reflect favourably on how Mr Li treats you."

The words *Vory v Zakone* hit Hoffman like a bolt of lightning. He felt the blood drain out of his head as fear sank in, his face turning white as a sheet, the connotations of the term *Vory v Zakone* conjuring up terrible images in the conduits of his mind. Silence reigned in the huge Temple as Hoffman sought options, soon feeling another thought taking root in his consciousness. For years he had absorbed the order's teachings that at the beginning of the End Times, America would be taken down for the good of humanity. Was it not possible that he too could be instrumental in that process, allowing for the long awaited and illusive turn around in his personal fortunes?

The color in Hoffman's face began to return, as a realization took hold that he could be a part of history, not just another statistic for Li Bo-Yuan and *Vory v Zakone*. He took a conscious step back from the brink, aware that he was now being asked by his Grand Master to fulfil his order's *raison d'être*. He was being given a chance to use the Templar *modus operandi* to usher in the new era of human history. There was still time to reconsider his position, his demeanour changing from one second to the next.

Chernyaev was aware of the change in Hoffman's immediate attitude, saying, "Are you ready, Mr Hoffman, to use the Order's *modus operandi* to rid the world of America's tyranny?"

"I am ready to do my duty, Grand Master," replied Hoffman.

"And are you ready to help the Order to detonate a nuclear device in Washington D.C.?"

"I am," replied Hoffman.

He turned to face Ross, who, like a good soldier who knew his place, had remained silent throughout the whole exchange. "Lieutenant Colonel Lee Ross. We meet again."

"Indeed we do," replied Ross. Hoffman's sudden capitulation to the Russian's demands had left him stunned. He had not been as indoctrinated about the order's ultimate goals as had Hoffman. Although Ross knew about the myths surrounding the order's involvement in the End Times, he was at a loss to understanding Hoffman's behaviour, attributing it instead to a fear for his life from Li Bo-Yan and Chernyaev's *Vory v Zakone.*

Chernyaev said, "Gentlemen. We are on the edge of the End Times, the end of the period of human history ruled by determinism. The beginning of the new era of human history, the Age of Aquarius, will occur when an artefact so powerful that it laid waste whole armies, will come out of occlusion. The Kingdom of God on Earth will begin when the Ark of the Covenant once again finds itself in the realm of men.

"It has remained hidden since the Fall of Jerusalem, in 587 BCE, when the Israelites were exiled to the land of Babylon. At the time of the destruction, a priest, Ezekiel, wrote in a document that 966,666 days would come to pass before the Ark's return to the realm of men. The document itself lay untouched until 1947 in the dry interior of a cave at Qumran, on the shores of the Dead Sea.

"The order to which you both belong was tasked at its creation, in 1115, to protect the hiding place of the Ark, a place which according to Ezekiel would be revealed to them at a later date. Gentlemen, today, that day has arrived. The document which Ezekiel wrote, 2,666 years ago to the day, this day, 21 December, in which he discloses information regarding the return of the Ark, information on the medium, the person who will lead us to it, is present in this church."

Chernyaev reached into the inside pocket of his black raincoat and extracted an envelope. From inside the envelope, he extracted a piece of what looked like parchment, old and jaded.

"This is a fragment of the papyrus document which Ezekiel wrote," continued Chernyaev. "As you can see, the bottom of the document indicates that it has been torn, at a relatively recent date. The original document was split into two at the time of its discovery, in 1947, in the mountains overlooking the Dead Sea.

"One half, the one you see, was conferred by the New Knights Templar to the Order's executive branch, the Priory of Sion, and eventually to me, its Grand Master. Written in Hebrew, it indicates that, 966,666 days after its creation by Ezekiel, the 21 December of this very year, this very day, we will be able, no, let me correct that, *be required,* to begin the search for the Ark.

"The other half was retained by the order's military arm, the New Knights Templar, to be reunited with this half only on, or after, this very day. Only on this day, will the information contained in the united document have meaning. It is the definitive proof that we live in times ruled by determinism. God planned the events leading to the Ark's discovery, as he did all events in the present period of human history. However today marks the beginning of the End Times, the day on which the information regarding the identities of the people who will usher in the New Age will be released, those who will lead the world to the hiding place of the Ark."

Hoffman and Ross stood thunderstruck by the speech. After Chernyaev's words faded into silence in the stillness of the luminous church, Hoffman found his voice. "You mean the other half of the document in your hands is in the possession of the military arm of the New Knights Templar, and will be reunited with it today?"

"I mean exactly that," replied Chernyaev.

"But that's impossible, because the members of the military branch of our Order are all in the Holy Land, where they have remained for centuries, hidden in various monastic orders which dot the region with their sacred structures."

"There you are misguided, my friend," said Chernyaev, relishing the moment. "One Knight, the leader of our Order's military arm, is closer than you think, guarding the other half of this manuscript." He looked at his watch. "In a matter of minutes the missing parchment fragment will be delivered to me in person by the Master of this Temple, the Reverend Bernard-Jones, leader of the military branch of New Knights Templar."

A door at the far end of the chancel creaked open, a tall man coming forth dressed in the black and red robes befitting a Templar Knight, the Red Cross emblazoned prominently on the white of his tunic.

As he approached, the three men standing on the threshold of the great circular church could see that he was bearing an envelope on which appeared a wax seal, red in colour. The tall man stopped short, and saluted the three men in the typical and traditional Templar manor. "Gentlemen, members of the Order, this way please."

The Templar Knight led them through the chancel and into a tiny square room beyond the sanctuary. At the room's center was an antique yet simple, wooden table, surrounded by four wooden chairs upon which the knight invited his guests to sit down. "Before we start, gentle knights, a formality; in order to entrust you with the document inside this sealed envelope, a seal which I alone and in your presence must break, I need to verify your identities."

He took out a leather-covered book from a drawer hidden beneath the surface of the table. "The instructions I received, along with the envelope, approximately one month ago from a trusted friend and fellow Knight, were quite clear. It's written that I must open this envelope only in the presence of three members of the order, one who must be our Order's Grand Master. The Grand Master, I see before me."

The tall, military knight looked directly at Dmitry Chernyaev, nodded, and then turned to face Hoffman and Ross. "Please, gentle knights, identify yourselves."

The two Americans presented the tall knight their passports, which the tall knight checked against the names of the order's two thousand members appearing alphabetically in the book in his hands.

The whole process was finished in a matter of minutes. Finally, the tall knight looked at the men and smiled. "Today is a historical day for the world. With the release of this document, we as a race are entering the fabled End Times. They are times of great change, great challenge and great meaning for humanity, for the world. America's tyranny will come to an end as the world enters a period of Free Will. The world has become a sad place.

"The power of Satan is approaching its zenith. He has penetrated us all, poisoning us with his evil desires. The world is full of those who pursue power, influence, material wealth and carnal pleasure. The masses do not work, and yet want the well-being that work alone can provide. They steal, rape, murder and use each other more than any time in history.

"The world must change. Today, that change will be set in motion by the release of information contained within this envelope. The document inside contains the name of the person who knows the present location of the Ark, the medium who will lead the world towards the Kingdom of Heaven. It also contains the names of people who will help her in her quest to find it."

Holding his breath, the military Knight broke the seal, extracted the papyrus with complete deliberation and care, and handed it to the Grand Master. Dmitry Chernyaev laid it out flat atop the great wooden table in front of him, directly under the piece that was already in his possession, noting with satisfaction the exact fit of the tear line. Apart from his position as head of the New Knights Templar and *Vory v Zakone*, he was a scholar trained in ancient Hebrew. He read the text, the simultaneous translation, in clear, yet faltering English. It was but two lines in length:

Anna Kuznetsova from the land of Gog and Magog will usher in the New World by opening the trail to the Ark. She alone in the human realm knows its location.

A Grand Master, Lee Ross and Kira Kamenskaya are links on the trail, instrumental in its discovery.

No sooner had the Grand Master terminated the translation than a feeling of elation coursed through Chernyaev's body, as Hoffman and Ross stood in open-mouthed surprise. Anna Kuznetsova was the medium!

Anna Kuznetsova was the medium, the fabled one with the power to locate the Ark. What no one present knew was that she had been close to finding it eight years previously when amnesia had struck her down, lost and lonely in the Negev desert.

"Anna Kuznetsova?" repeated Hoffman, stunned. "She is the medium? She is the one, mythical being one who knows the location of the Ark, hard-wired into her head?"

"Apparently she is," said the Grand Master. "The document in front of us confirms it."

Hoffman could hardly believe his lucky stars. A feeling of elation surged through his body, just like it had coursed through the body of The Grand Master moments earlier.

The tall knight got up, clearing his throat. "Esteemed Grand Master, gentle Knights, I must request leave. My work is done and my time short, so if you wouldn't mind, I will show you back into the chancel. Feel free to stay there as long as is necessary. I am sure you have much to discuss, discussions that I will not be party to. Our church is now closed, so you will be at peace until tomorrow morning."

The three men passed back into the chancel. The tall knight saluted in typical Templar fashion, and departed.

Of the three men now standing, only Ross felt anxious.

Hoffman turned to face Chernyaev, saying, "Do you know where she is?"

"My dear Hoffman!" said Chernyaev, grinning broadly. "Your skill at playing games is considerably less profound than your ability to secure vital assets. I know very well you and Ross got to her before we did."

"So?" said Ross, offended by the big Russian's condescending tone. "What is your point?"

The Russian broke into a spontaneous laugh. He was going to enjoy Hoffman's discomfort at all costs. Then his face changed, from mire to wrath. "Your country killed my son! But the girl who pulled the trigger is in my custody, not yours. I will find the Ark, and Russia, not the United States will control its power. Despite that, I will hold you both to your previous words concerning the destruction of Washington. This meeting is over."

Chapter 30

Muxamel Airport, outside Alicante, Spain, gelled perfectly with the needs of the *Vory v Zakone*. A coarse runway, covered for most of its length in old black asphalt, minimal security arrangements and a fence which runs around the dry, dusty perimeter, excellent and sturdy in places, but inexistent in others. There was no airport lighting.

Luckily for Dmitry Chernyaev, the details of Muxamel Airport were well known to the chief pilot of his Gulfstream private jet, a pilot used to the semi-illegal requests often forced on him by his boss. So when he was told about a delicate mission to fly a package from Spain to Israel, he did not hesitate in choosing Muxamel. Such missions were why Captain Bill Brown got into Business Aviation in the first place. After twenty-two years flying F-14's and F-15's he had switched to fly Airbuses for Delta, only to find the boredom of long, transatlantic flights almost intolerable. Flying Gulfstreams for people like Dmitry Chernyaev was as close to perfection as it came for the fat, ageing American.

He was sat on the flight deck at Moscow Vnukovo, his co-pilot running through the final pre-taxi checks, feeling the excitement reaching a peak. "Fuel; checked adequate, weather en route; checked clear, slight headwind, weather at destination; checked slight wind 023, flight plan; filed."

"Call the tower to request taxi," commanded Captain Brown.

When Li Bo-Yuan approached the top of the small, rocky road which led from the dry river bed to Muxamel airport's perimeter, the jerking and bouncing of the black Ford Transit reached a maximum, its wheels climbing over the uneven surface thanks more than anything to the skill of the driver.

The vehicle reached the top of the road hewn roughly out of the bare hillside, just as the wide, flat escarpment on which the airport had been built came into full view before them. Amid a cloud of dust, the vehicle came to a halt, its tires screeching intermittently on the limestone.

No lights illuminated the overcast night or the three strands of barbed wire which constituted the perimeter fence. Li cut a hole in it, and then he got back into the truck, swung it around so that it faced back the way it had come, its nose pointed back down the slope towards the dry ravine from which he had just driven. He selected the handbrake, climbed into the back, and threw open the rear doors.

Of the two passengers lying in the back of the vehicle, only one was conscious and she lay there uncomfortably. Amparo Montoyo's hands were tied behind her back, her feet bound together at the knees, and her mouth gagged by some pieces of her own textiles which had been wound around her dark, pretty head.

Li Bo-Yuan had been at a loss to know what to do with her, hoping for at least some kind of indication from Chernyaev during the two and a half hours fast driving it had taken to get from Grenada. He now guessed that such mundane matters were the last thing on his master's mind. Not that it really mattered, since he knew exactly how to get rid of her, feeling sure his choice would appeal to his boss.

As for Maria Juan, the other woman who had helped the killer of his son to escape, Chernyaev had other, more elaborate plans. Those plans could wait. Her time would come soon enough.

To the sound of the mumbled cries of Montoya, he dragged the unconscious Russian woman towards the door by her legs, throwing her dead weight onto his muscular shoulder before heading for the perimeter fence.

Li Bo-Yuan heard the plane's jet engines long before he saw it descending through the thick low cloud, a high pitched rasping hum audible over the noise of the strong breeze which rustled the low palm trees which dotted the landscape. December clouds were often that thick, and they often descended in the lowering temperatures to two hundred meters, as they did right then, obscuring the Gulfstream's landing lights till the last thirty seconds.

It came in low over the escarpment's northern extremity, touching down in the first fifty meters of the runway despite the lack of runway lighting. It ended its landing run, and turned round to head back up the runway. Li Bo-Yuan, seated back in the passenger seat of the Ford Transit, reached for the handbrake, disengaged it, but kept it pulled, taking one last look at the Gypsy girl still tied up in the rear. Then he released it and jumped, not waiting to watch its last journey into the rocky ravine, nor the explosion, nor the fire which followed.

"Get on," shouted the co-pilot from the open cockpit as the Gulfstream approached the end of the runway. "We have no time to be fooling around."

Li Bo-Yuan was in no mood to argue with such sound advice. He grabbed the folding steps of the still moving aircraft, the unconscious figure of Anna Kuznetsova hanging limply from his shoulder.

Climbing steeply through the low clouds less than a minute later, the Gulfstream banked towards the east, destination Jerusalem.

Chapter 31

Two Months Later

"Do you remember that they used to call our father Doctor of the 'Gitanos?'

The group of brothers and sisters, her siblings looked at her, searching for an indication as to her meaning. That's what little Christina was best at, thought Maria Juan, the eldest of the seven, and what she admired most in her younger sister. To her, the reason behind her words was clear. Christina had always been like that, at least ever since she could remember. In fact, her first memory corresponded to her sister. They had been playing at the cemetery gates, with the poor Gypsy children who lived down the road. She remembered they were approached by an adult. The Jewish adult made them cry and the game ended. Before that, was the void, the dark years secluded by her subconscious, the years that her sharp intellect knew she remembered, unable to penetrate its secrets. Those were her lost years.

"How could I forget?" said Javier, raising his voice as if to drive home a point. Although off duty, he was still dressed in the uniform of the Guardia Civil. "How could we forget? He was called the Gypsy Doctor."

Maria would always come to Christina's rescue, unable to bear seeing her out of sorts, especially when she knew Christina had acted for a good cause. This time, however she wondered if she could.

The atmosphere was tense. It had only been two hours since the terrible news had reached them, from Moscow, and things needed to be said. For that, everyone present was thankful to Christina. It was the chance to get things off their chest, the chance that everyone needed.

"It doesn't matter what they say," exclaimed David, the second brother, who sat at one of the room's large windows, towards the south. "He was still our father." He was a well-built six footer, a muscular figure worthy of a model for a Greek statue of antiquity. Outside the sun had risen to its highest point for the day, yet still the yellow disc only barely cleared the ancient olive tree which grew just outside the open door.

"What do you mean by that?" chipped in Jose, the second to youngest of the four brothers. His nerves had been on edge ever since hearing the news, and he seemed ready to seize any opportunity to let off some of the pent up anger and frustration that was silently consuming him. The quiet one of the group, his mother had been his world since as long as he could remember. What was he going to do now that she too was gone?

"What do you think I mean by that, Jose? He was Jewish, our mother was Jewish. We are Jewish! And despite everything, he worked to help the 'Hungaros'."

Despite his harsh, critical words against his father, David missed him just as much as his younger brother. Two weeks had passed since the police discovered his mutilated body on a snow covered slope below the cliffs of the Sierra Nevada. As to the cause of the mutilations, they could only guess.

Was the economic crisis gripping the country, precipitating it to unknown depths, reawakening the sleeping ogre, the spectre of neo-Nazism that had swept Europe following the previous economic crisis, the 1930s? And who better than to be the first victim of the rising tide of discontent, than the head of the oldest surviving Jewish family in Spain?

Among the siblings only Maria was sure of the killer's identity. She had decided to keep what had happened that terrible night secret. Of course her brothers in the police knew all about the strange and violent death of her best friend, Amparo, whose body had been found at the foot of a ravine at Muxamel Airport, Alicante. She had been burnt to a cinder, along with Maria's Ford Transit. The case remained unsolved.

Christina couldn't stand the atmosphere in Javier's living room a moment longer. Was it only her who felt to such a point the pain of the loss of their parents? Was it only she who felt the fear of being alone in this world? She was close to them all, but who now could fill the void that she felt in her heart? She got up and left the room, followed by Maria. They walked out to the veranda, where a warm breeze was blowing in the olives trees.

"Maria!" began Christina, sitting down in an old wicker chair next to her sister. "You were always the wise one, our leader. What now that our parents are gone? What will become of us?"

"Oh don't worry, Little One!" said Maria. "We will overcome it. Everyone dies, don't they?"

"Yes, they do. But not everyone's father is thrown off the highest cliff in Spain! Not everyone loses their second parent two weeks later in some bizarre accident in Moscow!"

The door to the wooden chalet was flung open as David too emerged from the living room to participate in the 'second meeting'. With Maria and David both now outside, everyone knew that the second meeting was where things would be decided. The living room meeting had just been relegated to observer status in the corridors of power of Grenada's Harari family.

David was dark, in looks as in character; a dark horse. He had coarse raven black hair cut short as was necessary for an officer in

Spain's Guardia Civil. He pulled up another wicker chair to the table where his two sisters were sat, below one of the ancient olives which pre-dated by decades the stone walls of the villa.

"Still no leads?" asked Maria.

"About Mum or Dad?" answered David as Javier too emerged from the stone chalet.

"Both."

"Still nothing about our mother. The Moscow Police are not speaking to us and when I called the Spanish Embassy twenty minutes ago they told me they should have more information in an hour."

"And what about Dad?"

"The investigation is continuing, he said. You know I'm not authorized to . . . "

"Nice try, David! But it's me, Maria, you're talking to! Don't start to try to keep something from me!" She had power over her brother, as she did over each one of her siblings. The oldest by two years, and now with their parents dead, she was head of the family. Everyone accepted it, even David. He secretly felt grateful to her for assuming the role. It would give him more time for the investigation itself, which he knew, would be lengthy. He looked up to her more now than ever. The look on his face communicated all this, and on seeing it, Maria relaxed. "What do you know?"

"We're treating it as anti-Semitic. But it's strange."

"What is?" asked Maria.

"There hasn't been an anti-Semitic attack of this type in Spain since before the civil war. We could be wrong."

"What makes you believe it's anti-Semitic?"

"The way he was killed suggests a religious- racist element."

"You mean the way he was thrown off the top of a cliff?"

"Precisely," said David matter-of-factly. "There was no evidence of a motif other than that. When heretics were being hunted by the Inquisition, it was common practice for people suspected of heresy to be thrown off cliffs."

"But nobody is hunting them anymore."

"In the Middle Ages, cliff top trials were commonplace. But we are living in the 21st century. However, lest we forget, our forefathers were one of the groups most persecuted by the Inquisition. Most had to leave. Our own forefathers stayed, but our case is unique. In general, Jews had to leave, convert, or die. Is it not too far-fetched therefore to imagine that some modern day nationalist group might want to execute a Jew in a way with historical relevance?"

"What other signs were there at the scene of the crime?"

"No sign of robbery. His wallet was actually still on his person, including his cell phone."

"Could we go back to the scene of the crime?" asked Maria, just as the door once again was flung open, with even more force.

It was Marco, the youngest brother, his eyes irritated, testimony to more out flowing of emotion. "I'm making coffee," he said. "Anyone want some?"

There were various signs of approval to his offer from the outside meeting, and he disappeared as quickly as he had arrived.

David said, "You suggested going back to the scene. I was just thinking the same. I am sure the scene was not completely checked."

"Could we go this afternoon?" asked Maria. "How about now?"

"It's a good idea," said David. "All of us can go, whoever wants to. The more eyes the better. The area of the cliffs is extensive."

The door flung open, revealing Marco bearing a tray full of steaming espresso and café latte.

***

The long grind up the barren mountainside had separated the siblings into two well-spaced groups. David led the first group followed closely by Maria and Javier. Their superior speed up to that point was due not only to their physique and general fitness, but also to their motivation. Ambition drove David and Javier as strongly as their desire to find and punish the killer of their father. As for Maria an overwhelming sense of duty sufficed by itself to propel her at least as fast as her brothers up the steepening and worsening slope.

Maria made the most of every breath-catching pause that David took, scrutinizing the way ahead not only for the best route, but also for any signs, anything out of the ordinary. There was nothing. The slope ahead went on as it had begun, covered with stones and talus which had fallen over the millennia from the cliffs above. Above them started the first snowfields and the place where their father's frozen body had been found.

"Do you think they will make it?" asked Javier half an hour later when he caught up to his two siblings high up on the snow slope. He indicated the following group with a nod.

"No," said David, looking at the procession of tiny, slow moving dots far below. "They will turn back. Look! The weather is changing."

Indeed it was. The wind had increased, tugging at their nylon anoraks with force. Across the snow slopes, lowering clouds were blowing in over the top of the Sierra.

"It'll be snowing soon. We'd better get a move on," said Maria, scrambling below and around David before he had a chance to stop her. Not that he wanted to. Despite his well-honed body, he was tired from breaking trail through the deep snow. Maria was fitter than both her brothers, her lifetime hobby of pole dancing now coming into its own. She wasn't going to let any snowstorm come between her and the trail of her father's killer.

"Watch out! The rocks are coated with clear ice!" shouted Javier from below. He had slipped while trying to gain height faster by taking a direct route up the rocks to the left, only narrowly avoiding a fall. "Stick to the snow," he shouted again, this time the words drowned out by the sound of the wind. He was a climber however, with real climbing boots and mountain climbing experience gained during his military career when he was based in the Pyrenees. He continued up the rocks.

Javier's mind was freer now than it had been in months. It was clear. He reached the top of the rocky spur in no time, sweating profusely from the effort despite the falling temperature. He had beaten his siblings to the top of the snow slope due to the riskier, yet faster route.

"That was the craziest thing I ever saw!" shouted Maria, as she traversed into Javier's earshot across the top of the terrifyingly slope.

"How old are you, Javier?" asked David as he too arrived at the place where the snow met the rocky spur.

"Thirty-eight," answered his brother.

"Carry on like that and you won't make forty!"

The top of the spur seemed as good a place as any to take stock of the situation. The snow plastered rock soared above and to the left until it disappeared into the swirling cloud. With their backs to the rock, three hundred meters above safety, they huddled on its leeward side. The temperature had dropped further. They looked each other in the eye, each aware of the thoughts each was thinking. What was going on? The temperature was well below freezing and snow was falling thickly.

Were they dreaming? Had they missed something, or had the Sierra Nevada suddenly become Siberia?

Javier said, "I'm not sure I can carry on much further," the words blown back down his throat. "I feel bad!"

"What's wrong?" shouted back Maria, her words barely reaching him.

"It doesn't look good."

David and Maria exchanged glances. Javier was behaving strangely. They had noticed it first in the patrol car on the approach, and then again on the snow slope leading to the rocky spur.

"What do you mean?" shouted Maria. "After what you just did the rest of the way will be a walk in the park. The body was found at the top of the next snow slope. Just up there!"

She indicated the general direction into the swirling snow clouds which filled the sky around them. The force of the gale was tremendous, and she wondered if she had ever experienced such a storm.

"It doesn't look good," repeated Javier. He was right. It didn't look good. And what was stranger was that David and Maria were oblivious to the fact. All they could think about was to continue to the final destination of their poor father. But what possible evidence could they hope to find there now, in such a storm?

"Come on, guys, let's go back!" he said. "There's nothing we can do up here now, not today."

"You go back," shouted Maria. "We'll go on!"

"Why?" he shouted at their backs as they began the long upward traverse across the last snow slope, their bodies hunched and close as they fought against the hurricane. "This is crazy!"

***

Half an hour went by and Maria was alone. David too, had turned back. What is going on? Why are my strongest brothers acting so strangely? Why have they both turned back?

Her questions were answered only by the wind.

She thought of her childhood, of her youth, of her little sisters and brothers. They had looked up to her all their lives. She was the perfectionist, the success orientated pragmatist, the role model, a difficult role to play. The continual fighting, the striving for success, the living up to an ideal which she neither understood, nor cared for. She could never see the point in it. All she knew was that she had to keep going toward some unknown goal, an aim that was always out of reach. Just like right now, except that right now, things were different. She could feel it. She knew the goal lay just above her, just out of sight. If only the hurricane, the stinging spindrift which stung her face, the condition of the ice under her feet would allow her to continue just a little more, then she could win.

She reached a huge ice covered rock which protruded from the middle of the steep snowfield, and rested, flattened low to escape at least some of the wind's fury. She thought of the Gods of the ancient myths of Greece and Rome which her father had read her when she was a child. Could it be that her past had destined her to be there, so the same Gods to which referred Homer in the Odyssey were able to punish her for some of her sins?

As she lay there in deep reflection a change came over her. The gusts, though violent, talked to her, soothing her fraught emotions and relaxing her. She looked ahead, aware of a presence that she could not identify. What she knew, she could feel. She knew what her senses were telling her, screaming in her interior that the power of the storm was approaching its zenith. They told her she had to go back, right then and there, to her brothers who would be waiting, frozen by the blizzard and by fear for her safety. They had told her that to go on was suicidal. Why then was she excited and energized? Why was her soul ever more motivated to reach the final resting place of the soul of her father? What primordial entity was drawing her to her death just as the singing sirens drew on Odysseus? Then she saw it.

A huge stone cross appeared out of the blizzard, at the precise location of the death of her father. Maria stared at it for a moment, dumbfounded, unable to comprehend what her eyes were telling her. Was she dreaming? She blinked repeatedly, squinting through the swirling snow, then looked again, expecting it to be gone. It was still there.

***

One week later

"How will you find him . . . , or they . . . ? The killers I mean?"

"Father will help me," said Maria.

"Have you lost your mind?" said David. "Our father is dead."

"To me he is not dead, David, his soul is alive and talking."

"Talking? How is he talking to you? Maria! You sound crazier every minute. What happened to you up there on the Sierra?"

"Ever heard of spirits, David? His soul hasn't left our realm, and is communicating with mine, talking to me, leading me to his killers. Do you understand?"

"No!" said David.

"I'm not asking you to believe me," said Maria. "Just come with me. Come to Jerusalem."

"Give me one good reason."

"I'll give you two. Your sister feels very scared and needs you and you are my closest brother. David, I have always looked up to you. Since as long as I can remember, you never let me down. Well now, I need you more than ever. I'm frightened. I feel like I am on the edge of a cliff. That something is pulling me over, into the abyss. Evil is everywhere. The Neo-Nazis or whatever it is. I can feel their eyes wherever I go. It is tracking me, just like it tracked Dad, just like it tracked Mum."

"You think it was Neo-Nazis who killed them both?" asked David. It was something the Guardia Civil had already considered and rejected. At the present time they were still approaching the case as an accident, or suicide.

"David, I don't just think it, I know it."

"What exactly did you see up there?"

Maria seemed reluctant to talk.

"Come on, Maria! What is it?"

"You wouldn't believe me anyway," said Maria.

"Try me!"

"A granite cross! David! Whoever killed Father erected a stone cross where his body lay!"

A shiver came from nowhere and ran down his spine. It was something about what his sister had told him, the look in her eyes, the way she told him. The Celtic Cross was a well-known Neo-Nazi motif, believed by some to represent the supernatural power of communication between the real and the spiritual realms, and far, far beyond.

Chapter 32

Nine weeks had passed since the meeting at Temple Church, and the euphoria Dmitry Chernyaev had felt on hearing that Anna Kuznetsova was the medium had well and truly disappeared. He had taken revenge of a sort against one of those involved in harbouring his son's assassin. That, at least, had been gratifying. But the actions he had authorized Li Bo-Yuan to take in Spain had been nothing more than the normal actions taken against anyone who crossed him. They lacked the spiritual.

He was seated opposite Anna Kuznetsova's motionless body as it lay in the warmth of the sun on a terrace of an elegant villa in East Jerusalem overlooking the ancient stone walls of the castle of the City of David. A long procession of doctors had passed her by. They all had left after telling similar stories. Anna could wake at any time from the deep coma which still gripped her. Or she might not.

"She had severe concussion, but will wake soon," said one. "It's a question of when, not if," said another.

Yet still she did not wake.

Chernyaev walked across the room to her bedside and held her hand. He had hoped the direct sunlight on her skin could trigger a reaction. He lifted the hand, which had fallen to hang beside her, and placed it on her stomach, admiring her beauty. He discerned her perfectly straight nose, the chiselled chin and blue eastern eyes. *Russian, very Russian, but with essence of the Orient.*

"What secrets do you hold in that pretty head of yours?"

Suddenly, he became aware that he was shaking, and not for the first time. Though he wanted to feel close to such beauty, he could not. All he really felt was wrath. He was angry that Ezekiel had promised him so much and given so little. He had promised him the world, the end of America's tyranny, the end of Satan's rule over men, the beginning of the new era, the Kingdom of God on Earth. And what had he, the Grand Master of the Christian Sovereign Military Order of New Knights Templar got? A sleeping beauty!

He looked at her one more time. If the deterministic world of which Ezekiel had written was ruling his actions, he only had to do what his heart had been telling him since the death of his son. And for the first time in many weeks he felt hope.

Whatever I do now will also have been ascertained in the writings of Ezekiel. A great army from the land of Gog and Magog would descend from the north to the Holy Land to begin the battle of Armageddon.

Then, staring at Anna, something hit him. That army was from Russia! *How could I have waited nine weeks to understand what was glaring at me? I don't need Li Bo-Yuan to bring pressure to bear on Khodorov. I can use my own prosecuting attorney, Alexander Bagrov.*

Reaching for his jacket, he slipped out his smart-phone, and left the presence of the sleeping beauty.

Chapter 33

Keeping her silver Toyota Aurius at one hundred and forty kilometres per hour, Maria covered the better part of the Iberian Peninsula in a matter of hours. Spain may have been in the midst of a deep recession, teetering on the edge of bankruptcy, but who knew for sure? Was not the economic crisis only in people's heads? A virtual crisis manufactured in Brussels to squeeze every last Euro out of the poor? Whatever was true or not true, Maria at that moment felt happy that her country had invested in smooth, fast highways.

Only when she was passing Toledo, forty minutes from Madrid, her destination, did she slow down, her attention caught by the red of the sky above the towering fortifications of the medieval hilltop town. The sun had set, but its illumination remained, shining on a bank of high clouds over the plains to the North West, turning them deep purple.

Tomorrow will be wet, thought Maria. When she was young, her summer holidays had always been spent on the Spanish plains, and such a sky always preceded bad weather. It didn't matter. She didn't plan to stay in Madrid for more than one night. She remembered her brother David's words as she climbed into her car. *Just take everything and get back here!*

If only it would be that easy! Their father, in the years of his retirement, had become an archaeologist of fame, caught up in many a scrape in foreign lands in his search for lost artefacts. Those searches always ended in success, and eventually his ability to pinpoint the location of lost artefacts reached the attention of the media.

Then the University of Madrid invited him to give lectures. They gave him his own room on campus to accommodate the huge volumes of field notes which his searches had generated. The room and his death had been kept a closely guarded secret, so Maria had reason to hope that his collection and documentation had remained untouched by the University.

The 'Ciudad Universitaria Di Madrid' was completely deserted by the time she reached it. Finding it had taken longer than she had expected despite the GPS device which flickered away on the dashboard in front of her. She turned it off. Technological innovations always drove her to frustration.

She parked on the wide, tree lined avenue which ran straight through the massive red bricked campus buildings, dividing them in two. It was her first time in Madrid. She had the address, the door code and the keys. Good to go.

Chapter 34

The dream was wrong. The screams filled his mind for long seconds before becoming transformed into something else. Something about them was wrong. Their tone was different. An invisible force was moving the speaker towards their source. Suddenly it struck him that his own muscles had been activated by a familiar tone, dragging his half sleeping body across his bed to the phone. Croaking deeper than a toad, Lieutenant Colonel Alexander Bagrov of the Russian Federation Prosecution Service spoke into the receiver.

"Da!"

"It's me, your Grand Master," said Chernyaev. "I have a job for you. Come tonight to Rock-n-Roll."

"But I . . . ," began Alexander, realizing he was speaking to no one. The line was dead.

***

Chernyaev's unmarked BMW seven series pulled up outside the entrance to the club. It was ten o'clock. Two hefty bodyguards descended first, looking the street up and down before allowing their boss to descend. He entered the restaurant to find Alexander sat at his usual table in the far end of the main hall, opposite the bar, the dance floor, and a cohort of dancing girls. The Grand Master sat down opposite the most successful prosecuting attorney in Russia's history.

***

Maria descended the smooth marble steps from the building's second floor for the last time, her arms full with two boxes of documents which looked like they were about to fall at any time. She managed to hold on to them, locating the car keys in her pocket and pressing a button to unlock the car door. The car's lights blinked on and off in the wet, Madrid night. She fumbled with the rear door before it opened, throwing the last two boxes towards the rear seat. As she let go of them, one caught on the seatbelt causing it to flip in flight, spilling its contents onto the floor of the car. Maria cursed as she saw it happen.

The box that had flipped open contained the most important documents of all, the contents of her father's desk, the documents her father had been working on at the time of his death.

As she stooped down to pick them up, one of them, a sealed black file, grabbed her attention. So she took it in her hands.

She climbed into the driver's seat, straightened up, broke the seal, and untied it. As she opened it, something very strange happened. As if the contents of the file had been on a spring they jumped out at her, and fell onto the floor of the car.

Maria could not be sure if something bizarre had just happened, or that it was simply her tiredness and short nerves which were playing tricks on her senses. As she took the papers off the floor she saw on the white paper of the black file's cover page a title scrawled by the hand of her father. She read it and her heart jumped for the second time:

Possible Resting Places of the Ark of the Covenant.

Had Father been looking for the Lost Ark, the source of God's power on Earth, the place where God dwelled?

Her first thought was to call David, so she reached for her smartphone. Then something else unexpected happened, and she changed her mind. She felt a wave of fear, which seized her tight.

Though she did not know it, her Middle Eastern blood understood it as a presentiment. But from where and from what? What could it be about? There were four hours of fast driving ahead of her to Alicante, and she decided then and there to make it five, to take it easy on the road. No risks.

***

David was waiting for her when she arrived, sitting on the stone patio of his second house, a villa, outside Alicante, his robust figure silhouetted against the backdrop of the sea which shone in the near distance. The sun had risen just an hour before, and as usual David was enjoying coffee, one of his morning pleasures, taken after a cold shower. Maria went through the gate of his garden from the road where she had parked, the black file in her hand.

They embraced with a tight hug, and then pushed each other apart, as if two opposite magnets had been forced together. Her forced smile did nothing to convince her brother that she was happy.

"What's wrong?" he asked, seating her down on one of the terrace chairs. "What happened?"

"I don't know exactly," she answered, tears in her eyes. "Ever since I found this file, I have felt panic-stricken. I feel afraid." She handed him the black file.

David felt a sensation of anxiety overcome him. It was as if he had just been delivered a condemnation of death, as if the black file in his hands was proof that in a short time he would meet some dreaded end. He looked at his sister, shaking.

"Don't worry," she said. "It happened to me too. Just like that. It will leave you soon, for you as it did for me."

"What is it," asked David, surmounting the initial shock.

"It's what Dad was working on when he was killed." She got up and helped herself to coffee from the pot on the solid wooden terrace table. "Open it!"

Leafing through the first pages of the file, David said, "You're saying his death was connected to his search for the Ark of the Covenant?"

"I don't know," she answered. Her eyes were on the sea now, not on him, trying to evaluate everything. "But we will find out, won't we?" She turned back to him. "If Father was close to finding the Ark, maybe some spiritual force affected the characteristics of his life, just like it affected me on the Sierra. Already this file, his search, this spiritual premonition or whatever the hell it is, has changed my life."

"What do you mean?"

"Because I drove differently because of it, safer, less risk, less speed. I felt it was a boding from the Ark. It was good. I always drive too fast. Maybe the Ark is protecting me for something that needs to happen. Maybe it is willing us, through the spiritual domain, to reveal its last hiding place. Dad was on its trail, and he was killed by someone unconnected to his search."

"So now the Ark is protecting us in order that we finish the job, to bring it back into the land of men? Is that what you are saying?"

"Yes, something like that."

"Okay, I got it," replied David. There was a pause. Then he said, "Maria, there's something you should know."

"What?"

"I have found something concerning the deaths of our parents. It too is very strange, maybe even stranger than that which we have just experienced."

"What have you found?" asked Maria. She really doubted if her heart was capable of enduring more surprises.

"We have an address for the owner of the car we were tracing, a car we believe was owned by the person who threw Dad off the cliff."

"I don't understand," said Maria. "How did you find it?"

"Sister, you are a doctor, I am a policeman. It's my job to find out such things. Let's just say mobile phone calls, signals, records, video cameras and a combination of all of them led us to him."

"Okay. And where is the address?" asked Maria.

"A name and an address in Jerusalem," said David. "But that's not all! There is something else, something even stranger . . . "

"What?" asked Maria.

"The name and address that the Moscow police gave us for the hit and run driver which knocked down Mum in Moscow is exactly the same!"

Chapter 35

While the people of his country laboured, suffered and died, he tightened the ligature of his power around them. While they became poorer, he became more affluent. President Khodorov of Russia did all this while he promised freedom and prosperity for all.

Knowing exactly what she was doing, Kira Kamenskaya didn't care that she was frustrating the plans of the President of the Russian Federation. It was essential. Khodorov's disappointments were a positive thing. Years of wedlock had taught her all she needed to know about the ways of men. *Deny them what they want most and they will never stop coming.* Provided you already feature one indispensable asset; looks. Luckily for her, she did possess them. She had eyes greener than the ocean is deep, thick full lips, and curves in abundance.

Khodorov was right on the limits of what he could withstand.

Then Kira hit him with an ultimatum.

"You know how righteous I am. You know how upright, guiltless and innocent I am."

It wasn't a question, but Khodorov smiled back at her with an answer in the affirmative.

"Then you should know that I will never be yours unless you come clean. Completely."

"What do you mean by 'come clean'".

"Tell me all your secrets. I want to know every bad thing you've ever done in your life. When I know them all, I promise to be yours. I love you, and I don't want you to keep such things inside you. That's the deal."

Khodorov had grown to trust her. She had never given him the slightest notion that she was anything less than genuine. He had done all the background checks. She was clean.

He invited her to his secret Spanish retreat, more enamoured than ever. The four-hour flight alone had been memorable, direct from Moscow Vnukovo Airport to his Spanish villa's private airfield on the cliffs above Cartagena.

They ended the evening drinking champagne on the breezy, cliff-top terrace overlooking the sea.

He wanted her. Lusted for her, and there was a double bed made up with fresh white linen in the huge bedroom just behind them. Now was the time to make her his, so he began to tell her what she needed to know. "By the time I was elected, I had completed the creation of a political system which controlled every aspect of the lives of Russia's citizens."

"Tell me more. I need to know every little secret, and the big ones too, the unbeknown details of your years in power, all of them. Only then will I be yours."

A waiter in a white tuxedo appeared on the terrace, bringing more Champagne.

Khodorov told her everything. He told her about his life, his mistakes and the women he had loved. After an hour and a half, and completely trashed, it was done. He had kept his side of the bargain. He stood up and took her hand, or tried to.

"But we still have champagne," protested Kira, remaining seated.

And so they toasted each other again, and then again. And then he asked, "Why do you love me?"

Kira cast her eyes back out to sea, aware of his desire. As yet he was unsure of her motives. That was good. Her duty, to herself and humanity was to keep him uncertain, thwarted. She would deny him for a little bit longer her body and spirit, and gain more information about his previous life. What could she, a twenty-seven-year-old see in a man more than twice her age? "I told you I love you, is it not enough? If you wanted my soul as well you should have brought along a priest, not a waiter."

"I just want to know!"

"All right," she said, suddenly drawing close to him. "Let's make one slight amendment to our deal."

"Name it!"

"After I believe you have told me everything, nothing more, nothing less, I will not only give myself to you, body and spirit; I will also tell you why I love you."

"Deal!" said Khodorov, believing her through the fogginess of his mind. For the first time he felt certain they would be together by the early hours, a time fast approaching.

"Deal!" said Kira. "Will you just tell me everything, or should I ask specifics questions?"

Khoderov gathered himself for one final push. "You can also ask me questions about things you may have heard."

Kira said, "Let's talk about the period just before your nomination as presidential candidate."

"You're talking about the bomb attacks that swept me to power; the allegation that the attacks were planned at the top levels of the Russian State, that's to say, by me?"

"Exactly."

"It's true. I did plan them. The people who died during those attacks were martyred for the good of Russia itself. Russia was in danger of being split. The separatists were out of control. With the ageing and ailing Ex-President in power, Russia was a hair's breadth away from total disintegration. Russia needed a strong leader, but only a campaign of bomb attacks could bring the population together to a degree which would allow for my election."

When he had finished telling her about his long list of sins, Kira studied him. She had accomplished her life mission. She had found the Antichrist!

The Antichrist is someone who promises his people everything, yet denies them the thing they need most of all; salvation.

The words of her mother sounded in her ears as did the words of the clairvoyant she had met when she was sixteen. She had done her chart, and from her birthday, 18th December, had calculated the reason for her reincarnation. "Your mission on Earth is to find the Antichrist. That is the reason you came back to this life, to suffer."

Now, eleven years later, she dared to believe it. She faced him, looked at him, and now that she knew who he was, did not know if she should detest or admire him. Was her soul so opaque, so turbid to hide to which side she belonged? Did she fit to the good, to God, or to the evil and to Satan? Most frightening of all; she felt powerless to decide.

Chapter 36

"Grand Master, I am ready for any service to achieve your goal, that of our Order, the end of America's hypocritical tyranny over the world, the spread of their low moral values, the dilution of the planet's diversity."

"Good speech," said Dmitry Chernyaev, seated at the prosecuting attorney's favourite table at Rock-n-Roll club, on Moscow's Chisty Prudy Boulevard.

Chernyaev made a slow sweep with his eyes of the vicinity prior to telling the reason for the meeting. "Very well, Alex, I require a small nuclear device, not too heavy, mobile, and capable of being armed by a layman. It must be untraceable."

"And you believe that I will be capable of assisting you in your quest?" said Bagrov, shaking his head in disbelief. "Need I remind you that I'm a State Prosecutor, not a nuclear physicist."

"Precisely, Alexander. And as State Prosecutor you are unique in our Order. You have the power to blackmail anybody you choose, the commander of Russia's Strategic Nuclear Command included. Use his past against him. Or plant something in his office after you raid it. I can't believe I have to spell it out to you!"

"Okay," said Bagrov. "But I will need resources, money, Swiss bank accounts, and weapons."

"You will have them."

"And where do you plan to detonate this nuclear weapon?"

"That, my friend, is not your concern."

***

The sun had long since set behind the hills of Crevaillent, west of Alicante. The stone terrace of the villa had grown chilly in the evening air and Maria and David had been joined by the other members of the Harari family, just arrived from Grenada. The siblings had gathered just like several days earlier when they had heard news of their mother's death in Moscow. Now an emergency of a different kind was upon them.

Maria and David were no longer worried about a shady group of Neo-Nazis, but about being tracked by spiritual forces centred on the quest of their father to find the Ark of the Covenant. They could feel the Ark manifesting itself through them, willing them to find it before the entities controlled by the side of evil, the forces that had killed their parents.

Its discovery had become their calling. The cold feeling of dread had passed, leaving a feeling of goodwill, of wellbeing. The power emanating from the Ark was good, it was protecting them, affecting them as it had their father before them. Its uncovering had become their duty.

"Well, that's an incredible story," said Christina. "I hope you don't expect us to believe it!"

"Believe it?" answered David. "Everything we have just told you is true."

"Everything?" said Javier. "How can you expect us to believe that the car coming down from the Sierra two hours after the assassination of our father, and that which ran down our mother in Moscow can be traced to the same person? Do you have any idea how crazy the two of you sound?"

David pushed his chair away from the terrace table, pacing up and down the patio, between the table and the wall overlooking the sea. His siblings were used to such behaviour. Ever since he had been a kid, whenever he needed to form a complex idea, to express it in words, he made time for it in the same way.

He came back to the table, but did not sit. Instead he leant against it, his arms folded.

"Until this morning, I would have had to agree with you Javier. But the point is, it's now the evening of the same day, and things have happened. Things have occurred that have convinced me that our family, the oldest surviving Jewish family in Spain, has been chosen by God to reveal the location of the Ark of the Covenant. This morning, I saw documents in our father's possession, that prove of a trail that has until now been kept hidden. He found such documents in Ethiopia a week before he was killed on the orders of one Dmitry Chernyaev."

A collective wail arose from the table.

"You know the identity of the killer?" shouted Marco.

"Why didn't you tell us before?" bellowed Christina.

"Because I didn't know," said David, turning to Maria.

Maria was standing, tears welling up in the corner of her eyes. She had to do it, she thought. David was right. They would forgive her. She too had lost her father. With more strength than she thought she possessed, she turned to meet the aggression of her siblings.

"I brought in the killer of our father through my friendship with Amparo Montoyo."

A look of incomprehension passed over the faces of her siblings as Maria began the long process of explanation. At the end of it they absolved her of all guilt, hugging her each in turn.

"It was not your fault," said Christina. "Just cruel destiny. That destiny, as the destiny of all of us, was written by God. He directed our father to find the Ark and now its discovery is up to us. It was not in his destiny, but it could be in ours! If God so desires."

It was David's turn again to speak.

"God has put us, as a family back on the trail of the Ark, the source of his power on Earth, his power over men, his own dwelling place in the realm of men. It has remained hidden for 2,666 years, and I believe our family have been charged with uncovering its hiding place. The coincidence of the cars involved in the murders of both our parents, their owners traced to a single person living in Jerusalem, is proof that God himself is acting through the cause and effect relationships that rule our world. He predetermined such a coincidence when he had created the Universe. We have no choice but to carry on the work of our father, to bring to light the Ark, so that the Kingdom of God can begin on Earth."

***

The inscription above the passageway through the rocks remained out of sight. It didn't have much consequence, thought the explorer. He already knew what was written there. He had seen it many times before, and every time it struck him in the way it was striking him now. This time however, it seemed more real than ever. He wanted to go back, and read it for himself, but the others stopped him.

"What are you doing?" they said. "You know what is written there, so why do you need to go back?"

They were right. But this time seemed different to the myriad of others. Never had it been so real. Making the decision to go back was always the prelude to the end. Yet this time was different...

For the first time he saw the relationship between his two companions. Though he still could not see their faces, he knew what they were. They were twins. They were pushing him forward along the ancient pathway that had been carved into the mountain by people long dead.

Ahead the tunnel was brighter due to a faint light filtering along it from a chamber chiselled out of the right hand wall of the passageway.

As the three explorers stepped into it, they saw four naked women walking in a circle around a gigantic, ornate box on whose lid appeared two eagles, their wings outstretched. He recognized all four of the women. There was Kira with her large green eyes and thick, perfect lips. The other three were his girlfriends, Oxana, Natasha and Olesya. As he watched them they began to chant, a song without melody, a rising crescendo of words which were only too familiar.

"Don't forget your life mission! Don't forget your life mission! Don't forget your life mission!"

The chanting increased in intensity, transforming itself to a noise less human. It was a ringtone, loud and clear as a bell. On hearing it, his subconscious catapulted him into action, a slingshot into the darkness. He ended up at the source, barely awake, and hit the green answer button.

"I've been calling for two minutes. Where were you?"

"Sleeping," replied Alexander Bagrov, the identity of the caller crystallising in his mind. "What can I do for you?"

"You forgot which day it is?"

He felt a sharp pang, a mixture of regret and fear. Luckily he had done what he needed to and, unluckily enough for his Grand Master, it was bad news that he had to report. "Galochkin is clean. I will not be able to put any pressure on him to agree to help you acquire a portable nuclear device. I am sorry, but there it is."

"Sorry?" shouted Chernyaev. "Sorry?! I think you mean, *Sorry, but by tomorrow I will find an alternative!* Do I make myself understood?"

"You do, Sir!"

"Good," replied Chernyaev roughly. "Then tomorrow I will expect you to report that you have an alternative."

"You will not be disappointed," began Bagrov, hearing the line go dead.

He was not worried by such threats. His friendship with Alexei Nesterov would provide the answer. If anybody held information on high ranking members of the government, a Rostelecom Vice-President did.

Before finding sleep, in his suite on Tverskaya, he lay awake a good hour, seeking to remember every detail of the dream he knew only too well. Never had it progressed beyond the passage way. Never had he seen so distinctly the people who accompanied him. Nor the girls.

He had seen Kira and his girlfriends. The others stayed out of sight, but he knew them to be twins. He even could remember the chant of the women who surrounded the grand ornate chest. "Remember your mission in life!"

My mission? The only mission he knew was the one the Gypsy clairvoyant had told him of on his sixteenth birthday, 16 December. She told him everyone comes back to Earth to complete their mission, to suffer.

"In your previous life you were a witch in Spain in the year 1600. What is your mission this time around? There is a link between the spiritual and physical realm. Your mission is to find it."

Chapter 37

Maria's flight from Madrid to Tel Aviv touched down at Lod Airport, ten minutes ahead of schedule. The aching in her head, first noticeable on the flight from Alicante to Madrid, had become a full-blown headache. Flights always had that effect on her, and the remedy was always the same: a double whisky on ice.

She had relaxed enough to feel excitement for the approaching adventure. Smiling, she remembered the words pronounced by Javier's at Alicante airport as he had thrust an envelope into her hands: "Open it on the plane."

"What is it?" she had asked.

"As I said, it's all you need to know, the address, the name, everything. Have a safe trip!"

***

Israel surprised her from the start. For a start it was much colder than she had expected. *If this was the temperature at sea level what will it be like up in Jerusalem?* She tried to locate the bus stop, dodging in and out of the terminal building in search of a sign.

"What are you doing?" asked a well-dressed young man who had appeared in front of her, barring her way. "Why are you are heading back into the terminal?"

"And so what if I am?" she answered. "Is that a crime?"

"Lady, this is Israel, not the United States." He waved his security agent ID in her face.

"I was looking for the bus stop."

The agent gestured a direction, and then walked off, shaking his head.

"Nice!" uttered Maria, under her breath. "Welcome to Israel."

***

Maria sat in the second row of seats, to the right of the aisle, her seat of choice on all buses. She could keep an eye on the curves of the road, and on the driver.

She was not the only one wide awake on the bus that afternoon, though most of the forty odd passengers were soon lulled to sleep by the steady, rhythmic motion of the vehicle as it climbed the freeway which twisted up towards Jerusalem. Sat in row three, to the left of the aisle, a man had been whistling intermittently the whole two hours.

As the bus pulled into the bus depot, she finally turned to look at him. *What was it about Israel?* It had been the third time she had heard someone whistling since she had landed. Something was not right. Someone was trying to get her attention, letting her know that they were onto her, that she was not alone. With the realisation that she was being tracked, she felt a shiver run down her spine.

***

In the center of Jerusalem Yuval Rozenkranz opened his eyes with a start, his body numbed by hard drugs, sex and alcohol, *not necessarily in that order*. Questions crammed in: *What had just happened and how did it affect me?* He looked around the deserted bedroom. He was now wide awake, wondering why he felt cold, worried.

***

Back at the bus station, Maria caught herself thinking of words from her childhood, forgotten till that very moment, spoken by the old gypsy woman who lived near the cemetery when she had been nine years old.

"One day," the old gypsy had said, "you will meet someone very close to you. Be careful little one. He will change your life, and with it all humanity."

***

They were born the day their mother died. Their father had lost the means to support her, convinced that everything would turn out for the best.

It didn't.

The morning of the accident found him in his usual place, dazed and confused in a drink infused stupor on the sofa in the living room. That sofa had been a gift from the Mayer family next door, an unwanted present or a mistake. Either way, to Ron Rozenkranz it didn't matter, as it had been years since he had bought something for the apartment. Years too since he had bought a single red rose like the ones his wife had got used to when they first met, the ones so loved, so needed.

Due to his condition that morning Ron Rozenkranz hadn't heard her leave the apartment. It was the Sabbath, and the city was sleeping.

Maria Rozenkranz planned to take a bus to the center of the city to a café where she had arranged to meet a Frenchman she had met two months before. Her life had become intolerable, and she had asked the Frenchman for his help to leave her husband before the twins were born.

The way the Frenchman looked at her made her feel young again. He gave her the courage to make the toughest yet happiest decision of her life, the courage to start anew.

But as she walked down the familiar road to the city center, that terrible morning, she felt completely alone. She looked at the others in the street, at people smiling and laughing. She wondered, *Why am I thinking, you are not living? Life is suffering. Life is pain. Mine is the real life, not yours.*

***

The pane of glass had been lying on its edge all night, pushed aside the previous day in its tarpaulin wrapping by the workers on the scaffolding. It had been a Friday afternoon, and the rapid descent of the sun towards the western horizon had all but taken them by surprise. A panic had set in. The start of the Sabbath was upon them at last. In the confusion, no one had noticed that the glass had been pushed to the edge of the scaffolding.

Later, during the night, a stiff wind sprung up, cold and dry. It soon gained in strength, and by three in the morning had turned into a gale. For hours it played with the tarpaulin, as if possessed by the dark side, twisting it back and forth till its job was almost done. The final gust of wind to hit the tarpaulin moved the pane of glass the final millimetre, to the place where it came to rest, in equilibrium, above the street.

As the first rays of the sun's new day hit the scaffolding hours later, the street below was deserted. It was after all the Sabbath.

A young woman heavy with child, was making her way towards it far below. From the puffy look in her eyes, she had been crying. As she walked under the scaffolding a current of air so minute that it could only have been caused by the heat from the day's new sun, lifted the tarpaulin. At the same instant, something in Maria's head, a premonition, made her look up. Too late! It sliced through her with frightening ease.

The first to arrive on the scene was a lady who had just rounded the corner of the street when she heard the dreadful sound. She screamed for help and a group soon gathered, followed by a police car and later an ambulance. Somebody must have called them, or so she thought. The dead woman was taken to Jerusalem's main hospital where her twins were delivered.

***

Yuval had chosen to walk back to his house. It was not far and the heat of the day had given way to a cool and breezy evening.

He walked through the deserted streets just as the light was fading. At the corner of his own street, he stopped dead. A woman was standing on his doorstep. He shouted across at her before she even knew he was there. "You better clear off from my door, lady, if you know what is good for you!"

He insulted her from a distance, "I said get off my porch, bitch! What part of that don't you understand?"

Maria stood her ground, as Yuval rushed towards her. When he was really close, she reacted, putting up her arms to stop him dead in his tracks. "Stop, I just want to talk."

Yuval stopped dead, shocked. Never had a woman been without fear in the face of such tactics.

"Talk?" said Yuval, standing awkwardly. "Do I know you?"

"No," she answered. "But I know you. At least something about you. I know your name for example. Dr. Yuval Rozenkranz."

"Who are you?"

Yuval was a master of disguise, turning on the charm as soon as he became aware of Maria's looks. Her nose was too straight and her eyes were too large, but she was beautiful all the same. *When I have her completely, will she too succumb to my critique of her defects? Will I be overcome by my usual desire to destroy them? Her nose, for example; is it perfect? If yes, I could spare it. If not, I would destroy it, and with it her. Then there were her eyes. If they are perfect, I could spare them, if not, would have to destroy them.* Such thoughts always drove him on after sex. They drove him to kill and to mutilate. Every face, even the faces of super models, had defects. They were defects which he would set about destroying after destroying the life of the possessor of the defect. The perfect face existed only in his mind.

"I want to know what you were doing in Spain earlier this year, and in Moscow a week later."

"I've never been to Russia in my life, and as for Spain, I gave a lecture once at The University of Barcelona, but that was two years ago."

He opened the door to his house. "We can talk in my office. I like to work from home whenever I can. The university has too many distractions."

He showed her through an immense hall into a room which looked more like the control center of a nuclear power plant than an office. He indicated a comfortable chair. "Coffee?"

"I'd love some."

"How do you take it?"

"Black, no sugar," she said, sitting down. The apartment was large, modern and in a state of some confusion, books littering just about every surface. "Look, last month, both my parents were murdered in strange circumstances."

"I am very sorry," lied Yuval, succeeding in suppressing a smile as he busied himself with the coffee. *How could anyone be murdered in normal circumstances?* "What happened exactly, and how does it concern me?"

Life is amazing, he thought. *A beautiful woman brings news of murders in foreign countries into my home, and such murders bring her.* He eyed her legs, using his peripheral vision. Her thighs were strong, naked beneath the short black leather skirt.

"The Spanish police traced telephone calls from near the scene of the crime to an individual who bought a Sim card and a mobile phone in Alicante, Spain, a day before the murder of my father. That individual was you."

"Sorry, Miss?"

"Maria Juan."

"Maria. I am really sorry about your loss. But I did not kill your father."

Yuval's pronounced the words with such feeling and compassion that she believed he was telling the truth.

"And you have no idea of who could have set you up?"

"None at all."

"And the Moscow murder?" asked Maria.

"What exactly happened in Moscow?"

"My mother was run down by a hit and run driver. The Moscow police traced the car to you."

"I don't understand. If I am the suspect of two murders, why have the authorities in Spain and Moscow not contacted Interpol? Why have I not been arrested?"

"Two of my brothers are police officers. They are controlling the investigation from Spain. Moscow agreed to keep Interpol out of it until the Spanish police finish investigating. Of course, you will be arrested as soon as Interpol is brought into it."

"I understand," proclaimed Yuval. "Then I hope you will not decide to bring them into it. I have not left Israel in more than a year. The university has kept me very busy recently."

"What exactly is it that you do for the University?" asked Maria.

"Sorry?" said Yuval, handing Maria a cup of freshly brewed coffee. "This way please!"

Yuval indicated his elegant lounge. "We will enjoy coffee on the terrace."

"You said you once gave a lecture in Barcelona?" said Maria.

"Oh yes," said Yuval. "I am what you might call an authority on medieval military orders. The subject of that particular lecture was the Knights Templar, an order believed by many to be extinct."

Maria caught her breath. She had read files on them from her father's boxes. The Knights Templar had known, during the period of their existence, between 1099 and 1312, the location of a treasure consisting of silver, gold and documents pertaining to reveal the location of the Ark of the Covenant.

The Ark was rumoured to contain the broken tablets, the Ten Commandments lost for the past 2600 years. The last known whereabouts of the ancient wooden chest was the First Temple, the Temple of Solomon, built by the Jews on Temple Mount, Jerusalem. The Jews had escaped from slavery in Egypt, led by Moses across the Red Sea and into Sinai. Moses had spent forty days and nights on biblical Mount Sinai before receiving the stone tablets on which were written the Ten Commandments.

Moses had ordered a box, a wooden chest of specific dimensions to hold the stone tablets. The chest came to be known as the Ark of the Covenant. Wherever the Jews travelled thereafter, the Ark travelled with them, housed every night of their wanderings towards the Promised Land in a tent called the Tabernacle. The Ark, as well as holding the stone tablets, was the dwelling place of the one God. When the Jews arrived in Jerusalem King Solomon built a temple to permanently house the Ark. Solomon's Temple. When Jerusalem and the Temple were destroyed in 587BCE, the Jews were exiled to Babylon, and the Ark was lost.

"Who were the Knights Templar exactly?" asked Maria, savouring the strong coffee.

"When the crusaders took Jerusalem for Christianity in 1099," began Yuval, sitting opposite her at the wooden table on the terrace, "the order of the Knights Templar was created. Their role was to protect the secrets of Solomon's Temple on Mount Zion, among them the location of the Ark of the Covenant."

"But I thought their role was to protect the pilgrims travelling to the Holy Land from Europe."

"That was a cover, a common misinterpretation spread on purpose to lead to their acceptance by the masses. You see, the Knights Templar was the most powerful organization of their time. The base of their power was an understanding that their goals were most noble. Protecting the poor and the weak gave them legitimacy."

"So what became of the secret treasure that they were really protecting?"

"It was never found. One of the Dead Sea scrolls gave us much information, a copper scroll found in cave number three at Qumran. But there was not enough material to locate the Ark."

"A part of the information is missing?"

"Yes," said Yuval. "There are myths and legends saying that the treasure indicated by the copper scroll was the Ark of the Covenant itself. There are also legends that the Templar Knights had found the other part of the copper scroll and taken it to a place of safe keeping far from Jerusalem."

"Where exactly?" asked Maria.

"The legends were passed down from generation to generation in closed circles behind the walls of Holy Land monasteries such as Saint Catherine in Sinai. They tell of a group of Templar Knights who travelled non-stop from Jerusalem to Ethiopia, pursued by a Muslim army. They hid the copper fragment, complete with its secret, in a place whose location has been lost."

Yuval stopped suddenly, his train of thought broken by a realization. For the first time since the *Great Cross* had appeared in the heavens indicating that the Antichrist had risen, he found himself alone with a beautiful woman and did not feel desire to possess her, to rape and kill her. Just as he believed that nothing stranger could happen that morning, he saw the Spanish woman reach for a black leather file extracting an object from inside.

"No! It can't be! This . . . can't be!"

"It is!" said Maria, triumphantly. "It's the lost copper scroll."

Yuval was visibly shaking as Maria passed the copper relic he thought he would never see, let alone hold. "Where did you get it?"

"It was in my father's possessions when I picked them up from his room at Madrid University. He too was a Templar scholar, an archaeologist like you."

"What I mean is where did he come into its possession?"

"In Ethiopia. He was there two weeks before he was killed, on his own, following the trails that had become his obsession."

"Of course," said Yuval. "Ethiopia was where the Templar Knights took it. Do you have any idea where exactly in Ethiopia?"

"I was hoping you could help me with that part," said Maria, reaching into the black leather file. "Most of my father's documents are written in Hebrew. Maybe some of them shed light on that fact. Take a look."

Yuval took the documents. Then he picked up the copper fragment that he had laid carefully on the table. "Amazing! These documents say that there are two copper fragments. And when read together they indicate exactly the location of the Ark!"

Maria was almost too excited to speak. "But the other piece, the other copper fragment? Do you know where it is?"

"Unfortunately it's in Jerusalem City Museum."

Maria felt a pang of disappointment.

"But I have a copy!" announced Yuval triumphantly. He sprang up and crossed the terrace into his office, to a wall filled with shelved files. Selecting one, he soon found what he was looking for.

"Here it is."

Taking out the paper copy of the copper scroll, he folded it carefully so that its edges coincided with those of the written text. He placed it on the wooden table next to the copper scroll.

"Exactly the same font and the exact same size!" said Maria.

"And when you put then next to each other... the words on the right of one combine with the words on the left of the other to produce..."

"Coordinates?" asked Maria, afraid to believe what she was experiencing.

"Precisely."

Yuval hurriedly plugged them into a map application on his smartphone, and ran it.

"A mountain!" he said. "Mount Hashem el-Tarif. It's one of the supposed locations of the biblical Mount Sinai. It wouldn't be the first time this mountain had been investigated as the location of the Ark. The mountain is elegant, symmetrical."

"Where is it?" asked Maria.

"In Sinai, Egypt," replied Yuval. "It's near the border with Israel."

"We can be there in a matter of hours."

"Wait a minute," said Yuval. "Who said anything about going there?"

"What? You mean that we are the first individuals to find the location of the Ark of the Covenant, and you do not want to go there straight away?"

"Of course I want to, but not yet. There are things about that mountain that you should know. It covers an extensive area, and we do not know the exact position. What's more, Mount Hashem el-Tarif is a military zone, under tight control by the Egyptian military."

"Maybe they know the artefact is there. Maybe they want to control it until its location is brought to their attention."

"Maybe," said Yuval. "How do you suggest we find the exact spot?"

"As to that," she answered, "the answer is elegantly straightforward." She reached inside the leather case and slipped out another copper scroll fragment. "This is the second copper scroll that my father found in Ethiopia." She ran her finger along the first words of the inscription before continuing speaking, "This, I am told is ancient Hebrew for *directions*."

At a complete loss for words, Yuval literally snatched the second scroll from Maria's hands. "So there were *three* copper scrolls?"

"I expect it is some sort of insurance policy. Anyone possessing only one or two of the three scrolls would never be able to find the Ark. Perhaps those Templar Knights, who hid these two deep down in Ethiopia, were pushed for time, deciding that their hiding place would be good enough for two of the scrolls. Maybe they planned to re-hide them separately at a later date. Maybe shortly after hiding them they died, killed by the Muslim army who encircled them. But whichever is true, the location of the two scrolls was lost to the Templar and to humanity until my father found them last month.

"How fast can you be ready?"

"Excuse me?" answered Maria, unsure of what was going on.

"How fast can you be ready to leave?"

"You mean to go to Egypt, to the mountain?"

"Yes, yes!" said Yuval, agitated.

"I just arrived," said Maria. "All my possessions are in that tiny blue bag over there."

"Even better," said Yuval, eyeing his watch. "That makes things easier." He found a large backpack and threw in a pair of binoculars, ropes, climbing equipment and various other items. He didn't know what to expect but as sure as hell was going to be prepared for anything. "If we leave in half an hour we can make it by nightfall. That mountain is only five hours away, the way I drive that is."

***

Just as night was falling across the desert sky they passed into Egypt. The drive through the Negev had taken them four hours, not five. From the Taba crossing, on the Red Sea, it was but a short drive to the base of the mountain. By the time they reached it the desert sky had become full of stars.

"Will we start in the morning?" asked Maria as Yuval's Land Cruiser pulled into a parking spot below the mountain's eastern slopes.

"Of course, unless you fancy breaking your leg in the dark."

"Where will we sleep?"

"In the tent."

Already she had taken a liking to Yuval. He was handsome, with blue eyes, an athletic physique and long black hair. She thought him to be the roughly same age as herself, and had become aware that the similar climates of Grenada and Jerusalem had given them similar skin colour. He had a gentle, charismatic way about him which was sure to give an array of female admirers back in Jerusalem.

Half an hour later they slid into their sleeping bags, gazing up at the burst of starlight which filled the sky. A fire burned beside where they lay, stretched out on the tent fabric, extra insulation against the hard rocky floor that was theirs for the night.

Chapter 38

President Khodorov of Russia watched as his life passed in front of him, aware that he had become the first Russian President killed by media. The very same media he had spent years bringing under his total control. In the vision appeared a woman, blonde and sexy. She was talking to Kira.

He awoke with a start and looked around. His black Labrador that had until that moment been sleeping in front of the bedroom's open fire, now yawned and stretched, happy that his master had awoken.

Khodorov found the king-size four poster bed was soaked wet with sweat. He sat up in the silence of the room, relief hitting him like a wave as he remembered the dream. He wrote it down just in case he forgot it by the morning.

Kira had gone to the media, selling him and his secrets to the highest bidder. But was it just that, a dream, a figment of his imagination? Or was it real, some kind of presentiment? He knew there was only one way to find out.

***

"Thank you for coming," said the President when he met Sirirrat Kakandee early next morning. They were seated, once again in one of the Kremlin State Rooms.

"It's always a pleasure, Mr President. What can I do for you?"

"I have had another dream," said the President. "And I want to know if there is any special meaning."

"Describe the dream, Mr President."

***

After listening to him, the Thai spiritualist again asked to take his hands, something that the President was only too willing to do. Finally, she released them and sat back in her chair.

"Mr President. The woman you confided in is not a risk, and never will be. Her heart is true."

The President breathed a sigh of relief. He did not know what he would have done had the spiritualist told him Kira was not his true friend.

"Others in your new Presidential Administration are not, however, so loyal. An individual who controls information and communications has created a system which allows automated recordings of your conversations, even when they take place abroad. A file has been created which poses a threat. Fortunately for you, the existence of this file is as yet unknown to anyone except he who made it. It was recorded in your villa, in Spain. It is a conversation between you and Kira Kamenskaya. It remains on automatically saved disk."

The President was tense, restless, already thinking of contingent plans to intercept the hard disk, to delete it. He knew exactly what the file contained, the confessions he had made to Kira at his Spanish villa.

"There is, however, a small potential leak of this file to the media, which is the reason for your dream. It will happen, unless you intercept it."

"What? Where? I mean who is the leak?"

"I am as yet unable to give you his exact identity, but . . . "

"But what?" said Khodorov, on the edge of his seat, his tolerance for the situation unravelling before him.

"Before I tell you, there are some things I ought to tell you about your chart and the signs affecting your future."

"Go on," urged the President, a cold sweat soaking the fine cotton of his white shirt.

"Just before you came to power, a very unusual distribution of the major planets called the Great Cross came to pass. It was a sign that you would be a great leader of your people, of all men."

"And how does this affect me now?"

"At a fixed number of days from this Great Cross planet distribution, the exact period that as yet I cannot ascertain, you will receive a messenger from Israel. This person will give you the information you require."

"What information?" asked Khodorov.

"The identity of who will leak the information to the media. At present, this file going public will be your only risk to your ongoing presidency."

Chapter 39

They thought the first of the 'directions', was going to be difficult to interpret. They were just too vague:

In the middle of the amphitheatre follow a dry valley which rises from a white cave

"But where is the amphitheatre?" asked Maria to Yuval climbing ahead of her up the dusty slope through the dry, semi-desert bushes.

"That's just the problem," shouted Yuval. "What do they mean by amphitheatre? There's nothing of that description on the mountain. Probably we will be here weeks looking for something that vague. We'll have to survey the whole goddamned area!"

"But the mountain is controlled by the Egyptian military. How will we be able to penetrate it?" asked Maria, out of breath.

"We'll just have to cross that bridge when we come to it, won't we?"

They arrived at the top of a ridge, the landscape on its other side laid out before them.

"That's the mountain!" exclaimed Yuval, indicating with an outstretched arm a flat-topped mountain on the far side of a wide valley.

"That's the mountain?" said Maria, dismayed. "But it's miles away!"

"Who said this would be easy?"

Without waiting for an answer, Yuval started down the goat path which led down from the stony ridge towards the valley.

"That's it!" shouted Maria.

"What?" replied Yuval, putting the brakes on his fast descent to look back.

"Look at the shape of the valley," she said. "The ridges on three sides, one of which we are descending. It's the amphitheatre!"

"Well I'll be damned. You're right! It's the amphitheatre."

Yuval sat down on a rock beside the path, taking out his binoculars for a closer look at the panorama.

"And look!" shouted Maria. "There are ravines running up from its base to the ridges which surround it."

"And they lead to the flat topped mountain itself," added Yuval. "I can see the perimeter fence of the military zone. Maybe the Egyptian military only controls the top of the mountain."

"Let's hope you're right," said Maria. "Can you see any caves in the ravines?"

"No," said Yuval. "Guess we're going to have to search every ravine from its base."

They made their way across to the base of the amphitheatre. At the base of the biggest ravine which led straight towards the summit was a huge cave chiselled by nature's hand out of the white limestone. It was at the point where the ravine disappeared into the depths of the mountain; a sink-hole.

"Look," shouted Maria as the two of them gazed into the abyss. "An inscription!"

Indeed there was. An inscription had been carved into the limestone on the inner top lip of the sink-hole.

"How could someone have carved those words?"

"I can only imagine," said Yuval, "that they must have been suspended on a rope, a rope which was then pushed inwards laterally from a long pole."

"But why go to such lengths to write words in such a place?"

"The Ancients had no way to keep things secret. No codes, no passwords to protect secret files, or hiding places."

"What does it say?" she asked.

"It's too far to read, but if I could just... Where's the flashlight?"

Maria located flash light the backpack, took it out and shined it on the ancient Hebrew inscription.

Through binoculars Yuval read aloud in ancient Hebrew, pausing at every word to write it down in the flip open notebook. The inscription was short and to the point.

What you are searching for lies within

"Couldn't the Ancients be more vague!" exclaimed Maria. "Do you think the Ark is here, and not at the end of the trail?"

"I think this is one of the oldest tricks in the book, a good old-fashioned decoy! If you know anything about geology, you would know that from the size of this sink-hole, the caverns to which it leads would take a lifetime to explore. Any ancient person wishing to explore the caverns down there would have had to make do with oil torches and the like, not to mention the danger of being lowered down there on ropes. Pass me the torch."

The powerful beam of light penetrated downwards. The sink-hole had a bottom, roughly fifty meters below. To one side it led down deeper still, an area of darkness out of the range of their torches.

"Yep, it would take years to explore this cave system, even with modern equipment. The thing is, until you explore it, you would not know if it was a decoy. Smart."

"What's the next sign?" enquired Maria, rolling back along the smooth, water washed rock which formed the edge of the cave.

Yuval took out the notebook from the side pocket of the backpack. He knew the ancient Hebrew words already by heart, but wanted to read again the translation in English which sounded like poetry:

The Enemy

At the top of the ravine

A gnarled and ancient pine

Guards a secret older than time

"Guess that means we have some more climbing to do," he said to her, smiling. He looked at her face, unaware now of its imperfections. He took pleasure from seeing her, happy to be with her, a woman he liked for what she was and not for what he wanted her to be.

The ravine was steep, vertical in places, necessitating a series of wide detours to the left and right up smooth limestone slabs which called for total concentration. They tied into the rope, moving one at a time, protecting each other against a fall.

Yuval took the lead as a flock of mountain goats appeared above him, distracting him in the middle of the difficulties. He was protected from a long fall by the camming devices called "Friends" in rock climbing jargon, placed in the slab's many cracks, the rope falling vertically below him to Maria. He reached the safety of a 'belay' securing himself to an old pine tree which grew out of a wide fissure, at a loss to understand how goats could get themselves into such places. They looked down at him with what he perceived to be their own feelings of incredulity.

Yuval brought Maria up, taking in the rope as she moved delicately up the white slabs to the place he had belayed. He surveyed the surroundings. He noticed that the main ravine, over to the left of the sturdy old pine to which he had belayed, disappeared, merging into the mountains upper slopes. The limestone slabs continued above them, but towards the top of the ravine, a breach in their encirclement of this side of the mountain could be seen. A narrow fissure, a fault line, led up diagonally left towards it.

"Look there," cried Maria. She had appeared twenty meters below him, her face red as much from the exertion and concentration of the climb as from the ferocious desert sun which beat down on her. "Can you see it?"

She was pointing to the top of the ravine, to a place that was now obscured to Yuval. He had not been as laid back as she on the ascent of the steep, difficult slab. He had been leading, concentrating on the technical difficulties, unable to admire the scenery.

"What is it?" he yelled.

"In the fissure line above the vertical ravine; a thick pine, old and gnarled."

"Do you really believe," he shouted back, "that after two and a half thousand years, such a tree will be still standing?"

"What?"

She came within earshot.

"Do you really believe it will still be alive?" asked Yuval. "The old pine tree, I mean.'

"Yes, I do," she said. "There is a place in Italy called 'The Garden of the Gods,' in Basilicata. It contains an ancient forest comprising trees which are three thousand years old. The whole place is absolutely amazing. You feel you are back in ancient Rome. The most amazing of all, the forest of pines is on top of a mountain."

"Okay, you sold me," said Yuval. "It's your turn to lead, do you know where you are going."

"Easy. Just follow the fissure line diagonally to the top of the ravine!"

"Safe!" shouted Maria, once she had reached the gnarled old pine she had seen on her approach to Yuval across the slab below. She had initially been reluctant to use the pine itself to secure herself, but in the end just threw a rope sling around it and tied herself off.

"Take in slack!" bellowed Yuval from below, as he untied himself from his own belay. The rope between them became taut as Yuval began to climb, using good handholds on the edge of the fissure itself. The climbing was easily as hard as on the slab lower down. The holds were bigger but the climbing was steeper, more strenuous, calling for strength as well as good footwork.

"Good lead," he uttered, as he approached her.

"Thanks!" replied Maria, beaming.

Yuval took a look around. "So this is the gnarled old pine tree," he said. "No kidding! It sure does look the real thing. It looks at least several thousand years old. The desert has a way of preserving life like no other environment in the world. Trees live slow and long. That's a fact."

"So what's next on the trail?" queried Maria.

Yuval took his notebook from the side pocket of the back pack and flipped it open.

***

At the top of the ravine, a gnarled and ancient pine, guards a secret older than time

***

"That part we know already," said Maria. Isn't there anything else?"

"There is," said Yuval.

***

Inside the tree, inside the fissure, move the rock, a hole will appear

***

"Inside the tree, inside the fissure?" said Maria.

"It does not make any sense."

"Yes it does. Look there!"

Yuval followed her finger to the other side of the pine's massive trunk. The fissure was indeed wider there than anywhere along its length. They had followed it already for forty meters, and after the place where they had come to, after the tree to whose side they were belayed, the fissure returned to the same narrow size, continuing to the top of the ravine.

"Between the roots," cried Maria. "Look!"

It was then that he saw what she was making all the fuss about. A rock which looked out of place was wedged tight into the fissure.

"Impossible!" exclaimed Yuval. "That rock is olivine, and could not have originated in these mountains."

"There is no way that this place could be the hiding place of the ark," said Maria.

"Let's get it out and see!"

Getting the piece of olivine out from the place it had been wedged was a labour of love. The roots of the ancient pine had grown across and over it through the centuries. With each stroke of the knife its release from the pine's tight grip came closer.

With the last piece of root stripped off its gleaming surface of green crystal, the loosening process began in earnest. Yuval still employed the knife, which he dug in around the crystal's perimeter. He prized it this way and that till finally it began to move.

"It's almost free!"

"There!" shouted Maria, as her hands rushed in to grasp it.

Both explorers looked at the space behind. Millennia had passed since human eyes had looked at that place, and yet what they saw gleaned as bright as the day on which it was placed there. The object shone bright yellow. It was gold.

"Buried treasure!" yelled Maria.

"Yes, but not the Ark."

He took a handkerchief made of cloth and very carefully rubbed the surface of the golden object which was itself wedged inside the fissure.

"They certainly picked a safe place to hide it," said Maria.

"Guess they didn't like taking risks."

The cleaning action revealed what appeared to be a solid piece of gold in the shape of a rectangle, the size of a small brick. A gold ingot! Its surface was filled with characters of ancient Hebrew text.

"Another trail?" asked Maria, extracting it with difficulty.

Yuval took out his notebook, writing down the ancient Hebrew letters and translating the words he had seen on the ingot into English.

***

Beneath the words what you are searching for

Lies a passage into darkness

***

The explorers looked at each other.

"Still so vague," lamented Maria.

"Wait," said Yuval. "It does not even make grammatical sense. Beneath the words what you are looking for. .. Are they not the same words as on the inscription under the lip of the cave? Surely there could not be a passageway hidden beneath those words? We shone the torch at those words, and there was nothing below them, only a sheer drop of fifty meters to the floor of the sink-hole."

"That's because we did not *know* there was something there," said Maria. "We did not know to look there."

Yuval said, "And even if there was a passage beneath them, it would have been too simple as a place for the hiding place of the Ark. A sink-hole on the mountain that some scholars believe is the same mountain where Moses received the original tablets. It's too easy to guess, and would already have been found centuries ago."

"Or maybe not. One rarely looks for the things that seem too simple. The cave is not exactly accessible. We had to climb up to it from the base of the ravine, a distance of one hundred meters up difficult terrain. It's worth a look."

"You're right," said Yuval. "We have nothing to lose."

***

Descending the mountain was considerably easier than climbing up. All they had to do was tie their two ropes together, pass it around the gnarled pine, and abseil. They repeated the process two times before the third one brought them right back at the entrance to the sink-hole. Once they had retrieved the doubled ropes they approached the abyss for the second time.

This time they felt a strong current of cool air blowing up, out of the cave, proof of another entrance. They slithered forward on their stomachs to the edge. On the opposite lip of the entrance to the sink-hole, the ancient Hebrew inscription appeared clearer now. The sun had moved towards the west, to drive its rays further towards the depths of the cave. Yuval shone the flash light into the darkness directly below it.

The light disappeared into the darkness. With the flash light resting on the flat, water worn limestone of the sink-hole's entrance, its light hit rock. Directly under the inscription, but way, way back under the overhanging rock below it, the rock thickened.

"Well I'll be damned!" he exclaimed. "Do you see that?"

"I see it," said Maria. "There could be something hidden below it."

If there is a passageway below the inscription, how could they reach it? There had to be another way.

"How far do you think the bottom of the cave is?"

Yuval trained the beam of the flash light onto the solid bottom of the huge cavern.

"Looks to be about forty, maybe fifty meters," replied Maria. "Wait a minute . . . ! You're not thinking about abseiling in, are you?"

"I sure am," retorted Yuval. "With the stretch of the rope, I might just make it."

"And if you don't?" replied Maria, afraid for the safety of her new friend.

"I'll just have to climb my way out on a single rope."

"I guess it's feasible. Okay, let's make a deal. If you get down, I am coming with you. I don't want to remain up here while you are down in that dark hole."

"It would be safer if you stayed up here, but okay. We came this far, no turning back now."

They found that it would not be necessary after all to tie the ropes together; the doubled ropes reached the bottom even before one of them began their descent, which meant the depth of the cavern to be not more than thirty meters. They could get in, and out, without problem.

Yuval was the first to descend. With bated breath, he swung elegantly over the lip into the abyss, pulling himself to a stop five meters down, hanging in space. He wound the inactive end of the rope several times around one of his legs blocking any more rope running through the descending device. With both hands free, he unclipped the flash light from its place on his harness. Without any control about the way he was facing he waited until he could point its beam of light under the rock inscription. What he saw made him wish he could have been with Maria to share the moment. "It's here!"

"What?" came her muffled answer, swallowed by the cave.

"It's here! The passage entrance is here. About ten meters down under the overhang."

"Great! Any indication about how to get to it from the bottom?"

"I'm working on it!"

He could see that the entrance to the tunnel lay at the top of the overhanging wall of the cave. *Not exactly what I had in mind.* He flashed the light down to examine the wall further to the left of the passageway's entrance. On the far left of the cave, a system of cracks led up vertically to the entrance. It would be a hard climb, even in the sunlight.

Luckily, he had plenty of 'Friends,' camming devices inserted into cracks in the rock used to protect free climbers, and was confident in his ability to climb it. From the cave floor to the passage entrance was about 20 meters. *Yes,* he thought. *I can easily climb that. With Maria holding the rope at the bottom, I can use the 'Friends' to climb back up the rope, following the line of cracks.*

As she descended, Maria took a good look at the passageway hidden below the lip of the sink-hole. She too had seen that the only way to get to its entrance was by climbing the cracks with the 'Petzl Shunt' ascender device sliding up the fixed doubled rope. In other words, the lead climber would be climbing the ropes by way of the cracks. If Yuval were to fall, he would merely swing back to the vertical.

"Can you climb it?" asked Maria, on reaching the bottom.

"Sure I can," Yuval replied. "I will use the 'Shunt' and 'Friends.' It will be too wet to free climb. With 'Friends' and the rope already in place, albeit way off the vertical, I should have no problem."

"Just stand close to the bottom," said Yuval. "And keep the rope taut. It will be close to the rock all the way."

"And when I have to climb?" asked Maria.

"Weigh the rucksack with some rocks at the bottom of the rope, and climb the rope on the Shunt, taking the camming devices as you go."

"Got it!"

Yuval made the final preparations to his climbing rack and then pulled the rope over to where the cracks began. The impending wall was overhung about 4 meters, but the rope itself ran to the sink-hole entrance, under an overhang of more like seven meters. He attached the shunt, pulled the rope tight, and gave the end to Maria. "See you at the top!"

The climbing was testing, but Yuval made fast progress up the cracks. By the time he was halfway, he clipped into a friend he had just placed at full stretch above him, and rested, covered in mud.

"Looks like fun," shouted up Maria.

"Don't worry, you will have your turn soon enough."

When he pulled himself over the top of the impending wall Yuval found himself at the entrance to the tunnel, ten meters under the lip of the sink-hole

"Safe," he shouted down minutes later, once he had set up a belay. "Climb when ready!"

"Climbing!"

Having a series of fixed points on the way up meant that her progress was faster than his. All she had to do was retrieve the 'Friends' for further use, and then keep climbing to the next fixed point. Twenty minutes later she was at Yuval's side at the entrance to the passageway.

Again they embraced. It felt as though they had known each other for years. Both felt happy to be there, to be together.

"We made it!" exclaimed Maria.

"We got to the entrance," said Yuval. "That much at least is sure. What happens now is in the hands of the Gods!"

Maria looked at him strangely, aware of a change. Intuition? Or just nerves? She put it out of her mind, and smiled, putting him at ease, hoping he had not been aware of her thoughts.

Yuval took out the flash light, and aimed it down the passageway. It had been cut by human hands, or at the very least, enlarged, its surface pockmarked by iron chisels. It was similar to the ones which can be seen on Roman walls and Etruscan burial necropolis. He had seen them, studied them. He had even discovered some of them. The Etruscans pre-dated the Romans, having a culture roughly contemporaneous with the ancient Greeks, between 800 and 300 BC. That would mark an extreme age limit for the creation of the walls he was now looking at.

"What do you make of it?" asked Maria.

"Ezekiel wrote that the Ark was lost in 587 BCE. These walls could have been made as early as two hundred years before that date, which means they could definitely have been produced at the time when the Ark was presumed to have been lost."

Once they had secured the two ropes, the two walked along the passageway. It was high, not too wide, but they could walk side by side. Even Yuval, who was six feet tall, did not have to stoop. They walked one hundred meters along the passageway to where it entered a large chamber, the walls of which were clad with granite. The blocks had been fitted together with consummate precision. In the center of the chamber was a raised stone platform, of a dark, fine-grained rock, its surface flat and smooth.

At the center of the black stone platform lay a small, rectangular-shaped recess. At the bottom lay a perfectly flat crystal of quartz.

"What is that?" asked Maria, confused.

"This, my dear, is a perfect example of history's first ATM machine. Look at that wall. Do you notice anything?"

"Is it a door?" She had seen that two of the tightly fitted granite blocks at the center of the wall were aligned inwards, as if attached to a mechanism that could swing the blocks open to a second chamber.

"And the rectangle hole in the black slab. Is it the key?" asked Maria.

"Precisely," answered Yuval, sitting on the edge of the slab. "I need a few minutes."

"What for?" asked Maria, confused.

"I need to think. It is a common misconception that the Templar Knights, mankind's first truly international organization, initiated the world's first banking systems. Following their founding and acceptance into the Roman Catholic fold at the Council of Troyes in 1117, their power grew for two centuries. In order to pursue their stated goal of protecting pilgrims travelling to the Holy Land they created a system whereby pilgrims could deposit valuable items, money, jewels, in one of their many centres of power across Europe.

"The travellers were issued documents certifying that they were in credit to the Knights Templar. They were history's first examples of letters of credit. They could withdraw their funds at any one of the Templar establishments in the Holy Land, or on the route to it. Not carrying money or valuables meant that they were less of a target to bandits on their hazardous journey."

"But why tell me this now?" asked Maria.

"The Templars had been given a wing of the Al Aqsa Mosque in Jerusalem by King Baldwin II as their headquarters. The Al Aqsa Mosque is located on Temple Mount, near the site of the Israelites' First Temple, the one that the Jews built to be the dwelling place of their God, Yahweh, inside the Ark of the Covenant."

"And . . . ?"

"So, since the Templars took control of the area of the Temple Mount, the location of the ancient First Temple, the Temple of Solomon, isn't it possible that they found there relics from the time of the Israelites of King Solomon's rule? History has taught us time and again that what seems to be the idea of one country, or people, was actually copied from another. Therefore," he said, getting up from the slab. "I wouldn't mind betting that the Templar knight's ingenuity in banking resulted from such an idea, given to them by the relics they found on Temple Mount."

"Hence, your supposition that what we are looking at is the Israelite's supreme creation; the pinnacle of their expertise; a machine created to safeguard their most sacred object," said Maria.

"Precisely," confirmed Yuval. "What we have here is a machine which controls the mechanism which opens the huge granite door in the wall in front of us."

"Do you really think it will still work after 2,600 years?" asked Maria.

"No reason why not," answered Yuval. "The temperature down here remains constant all through the seasons, and . . . "

"What?" asked Maria.

Yuval looked up, finding exactly what he expected. The ceiling although made of the same granite stones as the walls of the rest of the chamber, was different in one important way. Its stones did not fit together in the same way. Wide spaces ran linearly along it, from one wall to another.

"The humidity of the chamber is as low as the desert above," he said. "I wouldn't mind betting that those cracks were for ventilation. The Ancients were magnificent engineers. They knew that humidity would corrode the mechanism. Since they went to such lengths to build the place to hold their most sacred treasure, it wouldn't be like them to forget something as basic as ventilation. Do you remember how wet and slimy was the climb?"

"Yes," said Maria, with repulsion. "It was heinous!"

"And yet, do you feel how dry this chamber is?"

"Yes."

They looked at the center of the slab, at the small rectangular hole with the white, crystalline bottom.

"Are you thinking what I am thinking?" asked Yuval.

"The gold ingot! Do you have it?"

He took it out of his jacket pocket where he had placed it hours earlier, unrolling it from his cotton handkerchief. "Gold was the most valuable element known to the Ancients, due not only to its colour. It was valuable because of its inertness and resistance to corrosion. It was also the heaviest. Any mechanism depending on weight for security would be easier to calibrate if the weight of the keystone was maximum. Gold was the perfect choice. The rectangular hole limits the number of objects which any unwitting robber could try as a keystone, thereby limiting misuse of the mechanism."

"Make sure it's absolutely clean and dry," said Maria, reaching to rub her fingers along its surface.

"Moment of truth," said Yuval, carefully lifting the ingot above the rectangular hole.

"A perfect fit!"

He let the ingots full weight come to bear on the white crystal lying beneath.

A low rumbling noise became audible as he released it from his steady fingers.

"The wall!" exclaimed Maria.

The blocks in the center of the wall were moving backwards, swinging into the space that lay behind. They watched in open-mouthed astonishment as another chamber became accessible for the first time in millennia.

The rock doors finished their long slow journey into the second chamber with a low, deep thud. Keeping the flash light pointed down at the ground, the two approached the opening.

Yuval aimed the flash light into the darkness. The chamber was huge. At first they could see only blackness. Then a glint caught their eye. Something had reflected the light back at them. Something gold. Training the beam on the position of the flash of light the outline of a large, strangely familiar object appeared out of the darkness.

The explorers caught their breath in the eerie hush of the darkness which enveloped them.

"The Ark!" whispered Maria, as if frightened that someone would hear her.

"Yes. We found it!"

"We did!" said Maria.

For a moment they stood, spellbound, then walked over to the place where it lay.

The floor, as well as the ceiling, was clad in granite blocks, smooth and perfectly flat. The concentrated beam of the flash light explored the tight fitting granite blocks of the walls too in its ghostly light. The blocks of the ceiling were again interspersed by wide cracks. Those of the floor fitted as tightly together as any Etruscan or Greek wall.

The room was square, twenty meters by twenty meters, with the Ark at its center sitting on a square slab of smooth dark green crystalline rock.

The explorers were stunned by the magnificence of its twin Cherubim, their wings outstretched and touching. Their crystal eyes were aggressive, flashing in the flickering torchlight.

While they stood on the edge of the olivine slab on which rested the Ark, their attention was attracted to something closer to their eyes. The Ark, in all its splendour, was not the only object resting on the surface of the smooth, polished slab. A white marble plaque lay there also, an inscription in ancient Hebrew carved into its surface. As Yuval begun to decipher the characters, Maria caught herself looking at her companion, a strange feeling taking hold.

"What is it?" she said, noticing a change in Yuval. He suddenly looked serious.

"The inscription . . . " he began. "Impossible!"

"What?" asked Maria. "Yuval! What does it say?"

"Whichever ancient people built this shrine, this beautiful, amazing place; knew that we, you and me, and no-one else, were destined to find it."

"Say that again!"

"It says, 'Welcome to the twins, Yuval and Maria'."

Chapter 40

In the deep depths of her bed, and in the even deeper depths of her dream, something major had just changed in the world of Sirirrat Kakandee. Her sub-consciousness knew it instantly. That meant that the rest of her body would find out about it soon enough.

She woke, and said out loud, "What the hell just happened?" When she wasn't talking to herself, she was talking to the two others who shared her dacha with her. Her Border Collie and Siamese cat were much more loyal than people, especially men, who she had given up on years earlier.

"What the hell just happened?" she said again, this time louder, as if willing her mind to clarity. The dog pricked up its ears, surprised.

She had become aware of the Universe, aware of the change.

No longer did time flow like a river from the past to the future. No longer were events determined by the past and the present, propagating their effects.

The world, she realised, had passed into a new age, a new era. The fabled transition to the Age of Aquarius had just taken place, a period of time which would be ruled, not by Determinism, but by the warm, forceless world of Free Will.

Her first thought was of the predictions she had just made, and one in particular. She remembered it clearly. It was the reason her home was now a dacha on Rubalovskoe Shosse, and not some cockroach-infested hole in Perova, Moscow's most criminal area. She needed to call the President of Russia, and fast.

She got through after half an hour.

"Is this a secure line?" she said, as soon as she was connected. Her quick mind had learned much in the weeks following their first meeting. Like the President's fixation with security.

"Safe enough, Sirirrat. What is it?"

"Mr President, you remember the conversation we had last week about the threat from the file? About your dream?"

"How could I forget?"

"And you remember I told you that the information was safe? Except that is, for one person who might reveal it to the world at a future date. I told you that at a certain number of days from The Great Cross planetary distribution, which heralded your rise to power, the identity of the person who could reveal it to the world would be made known to you by a messenger."

"I remember," said the President. "You said this person and this file did not pose a threat. He would come into its possession or at least the knowledge of its existence, after the messenger would inform me of his identity. I would therefore be able to eliminate or imprison him before he made public the recording. There was no risk."

"That's entirely correct," continued the Thai spiritualist. "I told you that whoever he was, he was not a threat."

"Well?"

"Well," began Kakandee, "It's hard for me to say, but.. but.."

"Just say it!"

"This is no longer the case, Mr President."

"How is that?" fumed Khodorov.

"This morning I became aware of a change in the Universe. I know how crazy that sounds, but we do not live in the same era of Earth history as we did yesterday."

"What?" asked the President. "Could you repeat that?"

"Look, Sir; there are certain things throughout history as changes of epoch, era. Yesterday we were living in one, today a different one. I don't know what caused the change. All I do know is that in the present epoch, the predictions I made last week are not valid. I can still predict the future, but in the present epoch, the new era, my predictions will be different from the ones I made before. If you like, we can meet later today, and I will try to understand the future concerning that file."

"Yes," replied the President. "I will get my secretary to call you later this morning concerning the time."

***

Twenty minutes after his early morning meeting with Alexander Bagrov had terminated, Alexei Nesterov arrived at his Rostelecom office in Arbat Street. He looked impeccable. The handsome thirty-six-year-old paid more attention to his looks than most teenaged girls did.

His blue suit was tailored in Paris, his white shirt in London. The scent of Bvulgari aftershave mingled evocatively with the pungent perfume of the gel which fixed his short, thick hair into waves and spikes. He parked his Maserati in the hulking, subterranean car park, taking the lift which communicated directly with his office.

Sitting down in his huge leather upholstered chair sent an electronic signal to Ekaterina his slim personal assistant who was soon walking through the door to his 'empire'. Sometimes he wondered if she actually was the Russian GRU military intelligence agent she and others joked her to be, cunningly sent to keep tabs on him. Rumours suggested so. As head of the recently created eGovernment, eDemocracy and eMedicine internet portals his office was not only bugged, but had video surveillance too.

"Good morning, Sir," she said as she stepped into the room. Her presence was a ray of sunlight capable of lightening the darkest of mornings.

"Good morning, Kate," replied Nesterov. "Any feedback from yesterday's meeting at the Kremlin?"

"It's a bit early," she smiled. "Let's see . . . it started yesterday at 5 p.m., and finished at God only knows what hour!"

"Thank you, Kate."

"And what's all this about the new surveillance system you just set up?" asked Kate.

"Why don't you tell me?" said Nesterov, shocked. "I don't know anything!"

"Well, your email is going crazy. Keeps sending fresh email updates about some automated warning. You should look into it. Might I suggest . . . "

"Thank you Kate, that will be all," said Nesterov, faking a smile. "Go on a Starbucks run for me; a large cappuccino!"

Once the heavy wooden door had closed behind his attractive personal assistant, Nesterov loaded his email client onto his screen.

It was a program he had developed all on his lonesome, its aim to run in the data-center side of the Cloud Internet, a system capable of penetrating any known firewall on any platform anywhere in the world. It had fail-safe and foolproof anti-tracking. It allowed snooping on any politician, domestically, or internationally. All it needed was for the target to access the internet. It worked by introducing a tiny virus into the target system which then busied itself on searching, listening and watching for any signs of illegal activity using a variety of speech and visual cues in the target building. It was not legal, but, having developed it himself, he was more than confident it could never be detected.

Before the weekend, he had typed a target list into the computer on which the system ran. That had been on his computer, and the list had included President Khodorov. It was meant to be the ultimate test of his system. He had attended many meetings in the Kremlin in which the President had participated. He was confident the parameters which he had used to flag voice and video extracts for recording would not be tripped by the President. The President was after all a noble man who valued honesty and integrity in himself and others. If the system was tripped by him, or people inside the confines of one of his many residences, it would indicate a bug in the system.

"What? That can't be right!"

But there it was. The system had recorded a file, and what's more had made an automated summary of it, a summary that he was now reading, on the edge of his chair a mixture of excitement and anxiety written on his face.

It was a computer generated brief. He read it. Then he downloaded the audio file to a flash drive, and put it in his pocket.

He must have lost track of time, because just then the door flung open, revealing Ekaterina, an extra hot cappuccino in her hand.

"You like cappuccino right?" It was more of a statement than a question. Nesterov had already stood up, behind his desk, a brown leather briefcase in his hand.

"Let me guess," replied Ekaterina; "A date with a beautiful girl?"

"You know, Kate, that's why I love you. You never doubt me when I tell you I have eyes for you alone!"

"Who is she?"

"He! I'll fill you in later."

Chapter 41

The Ark of the Covenant left the twins awestruck. Finding out that the Ancients had known that they alone would defile its secrets belonged to the realm of sheer fantasy. They looked at each other in the ghostly light of the flickering torch which shone around them, bouncing and reflecting off their faces.

Maria said, "How is it possible? How could they have known?" The situation was farcical. It was just sheer nonsense.

"Because they had a connection to God!" answered Yuval. "Through the creator of the Universe, everything becomes possible."

His voice died away, consumed by the chamber, silence returning to the dark chamber as each of the explorers contemplated the new reality of their situation, coming to terms with what they had just learned.

"This means they had the power to predict the entire course of history," said Maria.

"Determinism ruled the world throughout their age. They tapped into the fabric of the Universe, able to detect every future event, even the identity of those who would find their most sacred object."

"So much for the radical explanation," said Maria. "But are we really twins? How is that possible?"

He turned to look at her, his face appearing devilish in the faint light, sending shivers down her spine.

"I knew who you were from the moment I saw you standing outside my home."

"No!"

"Yes! We are twins, Maria, born of the same mother who died the same day."

Maria blurted, "No, no, no, no! I have Spanish parents, and they were both killed last month."

"No, Maria. Our mother died the day of our birth. Our father was unable to care for both of us so you were passed to a Jewish organization for adoption."

"How do you know all these things?" she inquired, fighting the emotion that was rising like a volcano inside her.

"Dad told me everything when I was old enough to understand."

"No! My father is dead, and your father, whoever he is, has never . . ."

"Accept it, Maria," urged Yuval. "We are siblings. I knew it the moment I saw you. Don't you feel it too?"

The truth was she did feel it. She said, "So why didn't you tell me when we met?"

"I needed to get to know you first, as a friend," said Yuval.

"Why?" said Maria, feeling drained of all positive emotion, replaced by only pain and loneliness.

"Look, Maria," said Yuval. "It doesn't really matter much what we believe or don't believe about our relationship to each other. What does matter is that we just discovered the greatest treasure in history, and the people who hid it knew that we would be the ones to find it."

Maria looked at him. He was right. Feeling a glimmer of hope inside her depression, she managed a smile. "You're right! Yes, you're right." She wiped away her tears with her hand. "So what next?"

"What next?" asked Yuval. "We open the chest of course!"

"Won't we incur the wrath of God?"

"Another common misconception," replied Yuval. "He or she who opens the Ark will not be killed within a year, as some legends hold."

"How can you be sure?"

"You'll just have to trust me!" said Yuval smiling. "Are you ready?"

"Another moment of truth!" said Maria, feeling back in control. "Let's do it!"

Inch by nerve-racking inch the twins prized the solid piece of carved granite off the top of the wooden chest the jewel-encrusted twin eagles providing the perfect handle. Yuval grabbed it. He braced himself. He didn't want to drop it.

It slid completely off the chest.

"Hold it," he shouted moving under its weight. "Hold it!"

He was now supporting it entirely. He let it down until it rested with its one edge on the dark green slab. He let it rest against the wooden side of the Ark itself.

Recovering quickly from the exertion, Yuval flashed the light, looking over the lip of the chest into the darkness.

The interior of the chest was mostly empty space. But not empty completely. Two groups of tablets were stacked up on each of the two sides of the chest's wooden bottom. They were white, rectangular pieces of marble, about 20cm by 10 cm and 2cm thick.

"The tablets!" exclaimed Maria, reaching in to the chest to pick out one for closer inspection. "Two stacks of them!"

Yuval reached in and extracted one of the two stacks. There were five tablets, made of white marble, complete with inscriptions.

"There are five in each stack," said Maria, grabbing the other stack.

"And one more!" exclaimed Yuval. He reached to a lone tablet right in the center of the chest, its position equidistant between the two stacks.

"Eleven tablets in total."

Both explorers examined the tablets in their hands.

Twisting hers into the light, Maria read her name inscribed in English on the smooth surface. On the other side, a date, plus what looked like a code.

"Look at this!" she exclaimed. "If this is a date, and it certainly looks like it, then it's for tomorrow!"

Yuval flashed the torch onto the marble tablet as Maria passed it to him.

"What do you think it means?" she asked, examining another of the five tablets.

Yuval studied the tablet which Maria had passed him. It bore her name. "These are space-time coordinates."

"They're what?"

"This," indicated Yuval, laying a finger on the upper set of numbers inscribed into one side of the tablet, "is an exact moment in time. This," he said, indicating the lower inscription, "is a grid reference. It's an exact location in space." Finally he said, "And this is your name in Hebrew. It is inscribed on each tablet in your stack."

Maria said, "I don't get it. Why is my name written an all these tablets, both in Roman letters, and Hebrew?"

"What it means, Maria," said Yuval, turning one of the tablets to read the other side, "is that whoever hid the Ark are instructing you to five specific locations, five specific places in space-time, the first of which is tomorrow."

"Me or us?" asked Maria, confused. "They knew that we would find the Ark together, didn't they?"

"The tablets in the stack that you picked up all have your name inscribed on them, see?"

Maria saw her name. It was written on one side of each of the five tablets she had picked up.

Yuval said, "The ones in the other stack are inscribed with my name. Look. Presumably they are the instructions pertaining to me."

He handed back the wallet-sized tablet back to Maria, saying, "This one is yours."

Both explorers gathered the five tablets in their respective stacks and laid them out on the edge of the black slab where the Ark had been placed.

"What are the dates written on your tablets?" she asked, after verifying that all five of her tablets really were inscribed with her name.

"The earliest is tomorrow evening," said Yuval, "at ... 35 degrees 45 minutes North, 15 degrees 32 minutes East. It's got to be Moscow."

"So you don't have much time," said Maria, smiling, then added; "I don't understand. What exactly are we supposed to be doing? The people who hid the ark want us to run them some errands?"

"You have not been working in archaeology as long as me, Maria."

"Actually, I am a doctor!"

"What we have here are the battle orders of Armageddon!"

"In English!"

"From now on, Sister, we are enemies. The coordinates on your tablets are for the battles of Armageddon!"

"How do you know?" asked Maria, bewildered.

"It's written here, on the eleventh tablet!"

Yuval held up the eleventh tablet, the one that had lain equidistant between the two stacks on the floor of the Ark. "It's written on the eleventh tablet that the ten tablets contain our instructions, the battle orders of Armageddon, and that the Universe has passed from a period ruled by Determinism to one ruled by Free Will."

Maria slowly came to terms with what she had been told.

"If what you told me were true, that these coordinates really are the locations of the battles of Armageddon, then you could win this battle right here and now."

"What do you mean?"

"You are a man, and a strong one. I've noticed. If you really wanted to win this battle, you could just kill me."

"There is such a thing as honour. You are my sister. The battle orders will take place as pre-decided, predetermined by God and planned by our Jewish ancestors, the ones who buried this treasure."

"Then you don't have much time," said Maria, checking her watch. "It's 2:10. In twenty-four hours you have to be in Moscow."

"There's an airport in Eilat," said Yuval. "I'll get a flight."

"And what about a Russian visa?" countered Maria.

"As luck would have it, I went to Moscow last month on a business visa, multiple entry and still open."

"Lucky you!" said Maria.

"What about your first space-time coordinates," asked Yuval, a concerned look in his eye.

"I don't know yet," replied Maria "I'll check it when we get out of this place."

A new apprehension was growing inside her. From the little she had seen, discussed, and heard from Yuval they were about to be involved not only in a fight, but one on different sides. How exactly was the battle to begin? And when?

Yuval's attitude towards her didn't seem to have changed. Had he not just said he would honour her forever as a sister? Did that indicate only that there would be a period of grace, and not more, before the battles would begin?

"Let's get out of here," said Yuval.

The explorers struggled with the lid of the Ark for a good minute before it was back in place. Each packed their tablets safely into their backpacks. By mutual agreement, Yuval took the eleventh tablet, promising to deliver it to the Israel National Museum in order to prove the existence of the Ark. They decided that the location of the Ark should be kept secret, known only to them. A safer place for the dwelling place of God would be difficult to imagine.

When they reached the previous chamber, they approached the golden keystone with trepidation. Maria beat Yuval to the mark, and grasped the protruding few centimetres of the gold bar tightly in her fingers, lifting it carefully free of the white crystal. With a low rumbling the granite blocks swung back into place, sealing the Ark once again in its hiding place.

"Another 2,600 years?" asked Yuval, smiling.

"God only knows!"

Approaching the end of the chiselled passage through the rock, at the top of the wall which Yuval had scaled, they were once again able to see without the use of the torch. Maria put it away inside her backpack, taking her eyes off Yuval, and the place where he had come to stand. When she looked back at him, she gasped. He was running, already halfway to the doubled ropes hanging down across the entrance.

"No!" she screamed, watching him jump to the ropes and swing out, ten meters over the abyss. "Don't leave me here!"

"Why not," echoed down his cold answer.

"What about your honour, to me your sister?" said Maria.

"I lied!"

He began pulling up towards the bright sunlight that was streaming vertically into the entrance to the sink-hole.

"Don't do it! Yuval! Yuval! Don't do this."

Already he was half way to the top of the rope, climbing the double ropes with remarkable ease.

"Yuval! Please! Look, I still have the gold keystone!"

It was her last hope of drawing him back. He twisted around on the rope, a look of disappointment on his face. Then he was gone.

Maria had watched him go. It was for the best. He had called the first shot of the battle, and a dirty one at that. He had double crossed her, and so the gloves were now most definitely off.

Maria didn't panic. There had to be another way out. She was absolutely certain. She had 100 hours left of light from the LED head torch she carried in her back pack. Most of all, she was certain her life was not going to end in that cave.

She had the gold keystone. Therefore she had access back to the Ark's chamber. She could gain access to the chamber where, according to Yuval, the cracks in the roof communicated with the desert outside. She was Maria, the one chosen to fight against evil in the lead up to

Armageddon. The Ancients knew all along that she was going to be double crossed by Yuval. They had access to the fabric of the Universe! But did they know that she would survive the first battle?

A thought crossed her mind as she flicked on the flashlight.

The eleventh tablet revealed that as soon as the Ark was discovered, the world would pass into a new era, one where Free Will, not Determinism, would reign. Did that mean that her destiny, predetermined till that point, was now in doubt? If the Ancients knew I would be here, in this cavern, then they also knew I would be present in the other locations inscribed on their tablets! Logically, I will survive till the fifth location. Till Armageddon!

She made her way back to the keystone chamber. She had to find a way out, and quick. If the battle for Armageddon had just begun then many would be depending on her to make sure it turned out right. Yuval was on the side of evil, which meant that she represented good. Only she would be capable of stopping him.

She did a detailed examination of the keystone chamber, learning its every aspect. The exit had to be in the Ark's chamber, but that was no excuse to be negligent. She carefully introduced the keystone, gleaming and magnificent, into the black crystal slab. As its weight came to bear on the white quartz crystal of the mechanism, the familiar sound of rumbling met her ears. Again the massive blocks swung open. She passed through into the chamber of the Ark.

Despite her earlier doubts about the end of the era of determinism, she felt sure that the Ancients had predicted Yuval's betrayal. Predicting an event 2,600 years in the future was proof of their remarkable power. Even if they could not predict what would happen as the world passed into the new era, common sense would have told them of what would have happened next.

"They knew I would come back!" she muttered out loud, feeling a connection to the Ancients. It had been absent on her previous visit to the chamber of the Ark. She turned off the light and closed her eyes allowing darkness to penetrate her mind. *What is the key to finding the exit? Where should I begin in my search?*

For five minutes she stood there, listening, feeling, and contemplating the absolute silence of the mountain. Peace was total. She felt connected to the Earth, to the past, to the Ancients. She needed to give the connection time and energy, to flow from the past to the present.

Her thoughts passed from the darkness of her mother's womb, to her first conscious memory at the caves of Sacromonte. She thought of her mother, her father, the ones who had adopted her. She thought of her siblings, of Amparo. Finally she thought of Yuval, Jerusalem and the Ark.

Then solution came to her. *The key was under the Ark!*

Maria opened her eyes and switched on her powerful LED headlight. Once again the chamber filled with strange, coloured light, her gaze falling on the massive chest.

Moving the lid alone had taken five minutes, even with the help of Yuval. How was she supposed to move the whole Ark now that she was alone? She closed her eyes once more. She willed the Ancients to speak to her across the centuries. They knew I would be alone!

Approaching the center of the chamber, she stepped up onto the smooth green slab of olivine. Yuval had been able to lift the lid alone, but she had seen how he had struggled. In the end, she had helped him lift it back. She estimated the lid alone had weighed seventy kilograms.

She caressed its smooth surface, its golden jewel encrusted eagles. The whole Ark must weigh at least two hundred kilograms.

She put her shoulder to it, giving it a hefty shove. It moved an inch. The olivine slab! The Ancients knew it would move easily on such a surface, factoring in the fact I would be alone on my second visit!

She repeated the action. Another inch. Then once again. Another inch. A few more pushes and she looked down to the place where it had been. A narrow hole led through the dark slab, down into the white rock below.

"I'm supposed to be able to fit down that?" she uttered. "Just how thin did they expect me to be?"

For better or for worse, she positioned herself over the top of the passageway. Removing her back pack and placing it beside her on the black slab, she lowered herself into the hole. When she had inserted herself to her breast, she felt the first step, then the second. With extreme contortions she managed to retrieve the back pack, and with it held above her head, felt with her outstretched foot for the fourth step, and then the fifth.

Eventually the tunnel opened up. At last, she was able to turn round, putting her back pack back on her back. Had the Ancients thrown in yet another control? If she had been any bigger, she would have died in the Chamber of the Ark. *The Ancients even knew my size!*

Twelve hours later, she emerged. She had followed the passageway all night, without a break. After taking false offshoots, she eventually saw a faint light diffusing into the cave system. It led her in the right direction.

She reached the surface at a tiny cave high up on the cliff above the base of the ravine. She took out the binoculars and surveyed the ravine below, the sink-hole and the desert in its vast splendour. No trace of Yuval, only the rocks and dry bushes of the desert. She focussed on the car park. It was empty. Yuval was gone.

She took the tablets out and laid them one next to the other on the rocks at the cave entrance. Which was the earliest? Tomorrow evening. No, this evening! She looked at her watch. Her Breitling displayed 9:50 local time. And the coordinates; 35 degrees 24 minutes South, 8 degrees 5 minutes East. Somewhere in the Western Mediterranean for sure, but the Western Mediterranean was an hour behind. It's 08.50 she thought. *In less than six hours I have to be on the other side of the Mediterranean!*

Chapter 42

At precisely 2:50 local time, Yuval stepped down from the plane at Domodedova Airport, Moscow. He was quietly happy with the way things had gone since he had abandoned his twin sister. He had run to his car, elated by his good fortune. Things had fallen neatly into place. Firstly, she had turned up at his home, just as his father had predicted. They had found the Ark, and he had dealt with her in a way which he admired himself for doing; heartlessly. He couldn't see her future, couldn't know if she would get out alive. It didn't matter. She did not matter. The battle for Armageddon would be fought without quarter.

***

The journey to Eilat took Yuval two hours, most of that time waiting to get across the border. He had spent it wisely, booking a place on connecting flights to Moscow; making the first flight with forty minutes to spare.

He hired a car in the arrivals lounge at Moscow after having checked and double checked the time coordinates during the flight. He had two hours. He had checked and double checked the location.

The space coordinates corresponded with the residence of the President of Russia.

***

At the village of Usovo, his GPS indicated his destination was closing fast, less than five kilometres distant. He stopped to study the final approach in detail. Pulling up to the guard box at the entrance to the presidential Palace, he lowered the window. He was not used to the cold air which blasted him, or to the aggressiveness of the guard.

"I am the messenger!" said Yuval.

"What?" replied the guard, thinking he must have misunderstood.

"I am the messenger!" repeated Yuval exactly as the first time. *What's this guy's problem?*

"Sorry, friend, you must be mistaken. No messengers are on the list of today's visitors."

"No. You don't understand. I am the messenger. Get a message through to your boss, saying exactly these words." Yuval paused for effect. "The messenger has arrived with information."

"But.." began the guard, unsure of what to do.

"Do it now, or you will lose your job!"

***

Maria made it to the car park in less than an hour.

She heard the rumbling of a truck on the road, reaching it just as it passed. She screamed out, waving her arms wildly. It didn't stop.

Another vehicle came into view, travelling in the right direction, towards Eilat. This time she was not going to accept no for an answer. As the Jeep approached, she positioned herself directly in front.

"Stop!"

"What's the problem, lady?" inquired the friendly driver.

"You have just *got* to help me."

"But of course," answered the driver, who was American. "What happened to your hands? Has there been an accident?"

Maria looked down at her hands. They were covered in cuts from the punishment she had put them through on the climb. "It's a long story," she replied, "and complicated. I will fill you in on the way. Could you drive me to Eilat, and fast? It's an emergency."

"No problem. Jump in."

***

An hour later, Maria was airborne, en-route to Lod International, Israel's main hub airport. She used the flight time to good effect, verifying the space-time coordinates of the first tablet. The Ancients had determined her rendezvous with the future in four hours, 2:00 local time, in Eivissa Port, Ibiza.

The second flight was direct to Ibiza, scheduled to land at 2:30 local time. Thanks to Yuval, she was going to miss it. But what did it matter? *Would whoever she was supposed to meet be late too? Would they wait? Did they even know she was coming?*

The Airbus prepared for take-off. She ran her hands over the inscriptions on the first of the series of five tablets in her possession, deep in thought. On one side was inscribed her name in Hebrew. On the other the longitude and latitude of Eivissa, and the time coordinate, later that very day.

She tried to relax on the flight, failing miserably, thinking back to the last twenty four hours, analysing every little aspect. Something was bothering her. She gave up on sleep, and took out the other four tablets instead laying them out on the two empty seats next to her.

"My God!" she exclaimed, so softly that nobody else could hear. Something was wrong. Four hours from the first rendezvous, the second one would take place. "Wait a minute, this can't be right!" She was still talking out loud. "5:00 local time. But where is it?" 35 degrees 45min North, 15 degrees 32 minutes East. "Moscow!" *That means 3:00 Spanish time. If the plane landed on time, it will only give me half an hour to prepare for the second rendezvous.* "If prepare is the right word. I don't even know what I am supposed to be preparing for!"

With the complexities of the space-time coordinates whirling around her head, she flipped the second tablet twice in her hands. She saw something she had missed, a difference from the first tablet. Below the space-time coordinate appeared two extra inscriptions written, like them all, in ancient Hebrew. As she could not read Hebrew, she was none the wiser.

***

Maria fell into a deep sleep. Even the heavy landing failed to bring it to an end. A friendly hostess noticed her when all the other passengers had disembarked from the plane.

"Miss, Miss!" she said, shaking her as lightly as she could.

"What?" said Maria, coming round. "Where am I?"

"Welcome to Ibiza, Miss," whispered the hostess. "We just landed."

***

"Please go faster," implored Maria for the umpteenth time. "I should have been there half an hour ago."

"Lady, I am already at eighty," replied the driver. "That's the speed limit on this road."

"Then go one hundred, I'll pay you double!"

"Will you pay the fine as well?" hazarded the driver.

"If we get stopped, yes."

The taxi pulled into the marina at Eivissa Port exactly fifteen minutes later, and screeched to a halt.

Chapter 43

The Blue Marlin serves pricey cocktails to an international clientele in the Marina of Eivissa Port. Lieutenant Colonel Lee Ross was seated at his usual table downing the last dregs of a Martini and ordering another.

The meeting with Hoffman and the Grand Master changed everything. It had shaken up his world. The Grand Master's words inside the Temple Church still rang in his ears, reverberating deep in his soul.

"Anna Kuznetsova from the land of Gog and Magog will usher in the New World by opening the trail to the Ark since she alone in the human realm knows of its location."

"A Grand Master, Lee Ross and Kira Kamenskaya are links on the trail."

The words may have been pronounced by Chernyaev, but they had been written by Ezekiel. That much had been verified by numerous international scholars. They were written by the prophet in or around the time that Jerusalem and the First Temple had been sacked and the Israelites driven into exile in Babylon.

Hoffman had demanded a piece of the papyrus before he and Ross had parted company with Chernyaev. The Grand Master had agreed to the demand, ripping off a corner of the ancient document then and there which was then subjected to rigorous tests.

Chernyaev did not have a choice. His only motive and concern was the destruction of America's power, the Pentagon and White House. His son had believed in it, and now so did he. America was destroying the world. It was destroying its diversity, its culture. As for Russia, it was still weak, too poor to maintain military parity with the United States. The only way forward was to launch a pre-emptive strike.

CIA sources in the Kremlin had told Ross of the meeting between the Russian President and the Grand Master just after the news of his son's assassination hit the Moscow streets. Chernyaev was out not only for revenge for the killing of his son. He had adopted his son's cause, something he believed in, now more than ever.

He was not only Knights Templar Grand Master; he was a patriot. A world where America did not have a free hand to do as it pleased would be a better world. The world needed multiple cultures; it needed Islam, Buddhism and Judaism as much as it needed security. America had to be taken down, and now that his son was dead, he had assumed the role.

Chernyaev did not have a choice. He needed Hoffman to carry out his plan. If the Russian President was not going to give him a nuclear weapon to detonate in Washington D.C., then he would need alternatives. Plan B was to use Hoffman. Plan C was to use the power of the Ark of the Covenant, something he had believed he was going to secure in Temple Church. With the location of the Ark still a secret, at least until Anna Kuznetsova woke up from her coma, and led him to the hiding place of the Ark, he had no choice but to concentrate all his resources on Plan B.

With Hoffman on board, something guaranteed by his fear of Mr Li, the Grand Master was sure that a way for the nuclear device's entry onto American territory could be found. The resources and the influence of the CIA deputy director were enormous. Chernyaev's main problem was securing a nuclear weapon. Getting it into Washington would be easy.

***

Ross now knew all about Chernyaev's plan. He knew of his role. He had considered the possibility that Chernyaev would try to use blackmail against the Russian President to achieve it. With the President of Russia on board, the release of a device capable of taking out the Pentagon and White House would be a walk in the park. That would be the simplest course to take. The Grand Master would be actively pursuing it.

Ross considered the possibility that Chernyaev would try to use State Prosecutor Alexander Bagrov, a member of the Order, to achieve such an aim. It was possible that Bagrov could pressure a general or two in Russia's Strategic Nuclear Forces Command to release a small nuclear device for the Grand Master's use. But he would need an approach. He would need incriminating information about a General at the very least.

While mulling the events of the previous few days, creating hypotheses, analysing, Ross saw a taxi approach the gate to the marina, about a hundred meters distant.

He watched as a woman got out. She made her way straight towards the marina gate. As he watched her he became aware that she looked strangely familiar.

At fifty meters, he recognized her. Ross never forgot a face. She too had recognized him. He remembered her name when she was only ten meters from him. "Maria!" He threw back his chair as he stood up to greet her. "In all the cocktail joints of the world!"

He noticed her anxiety, which wasn't difficult. The colour of her face indicated she had been in a rush to get there. He showed her a chair. "Is everything alight?"

She sat down, trying to compose herself, wondering where to start. "Lee, right?"

"Yes!" replied Ross. "You have a good memory." Then frowning, added, "How did you know I would be here?"

"I knew someone I had to meet would be here."

"Sorry? Someone you had to meet?"

"Don't worry, Lee, I know how it sounds, and I haven't just gone completely crazy. I have to explain some things to you, but I think I do not have much time."

She took the tablets from her handbag and laid them on the table.

"What I am about to tell you will sound absolutely nuts, but just listen and try to understand. I think some people's lives depend on it."

"All right, I will try."

"I found these tablets less than eighteen hours ago in the Middle East."

"No way!" said Ross picking one up and beginning to study it. "Really?"

"Please, Lee, just listen. Do not interrupt."

"Yes, Ma'am!"

"If you look, on each tablet is a name, my name, on one side, and on the other a reference which is actually a space-time coordinate."

"I see it."

"This is the first space-time coordinate." She held up one of the tablets, indicating the coordinates with her slim fingers. "It's a reference for Blue Marlin, today at 2:00. That is why I came here. I knew I would meet someone, or something, that must be important to a forthcoming situation that is now developing in the world. What I did not know is who or what it would be."

"I kind of understand," said Ross, coming up to speed.

Maria had picked up another tablet. "This space-time coordinate," she said, indicating the inscription on the smooth marble tablet, "is for a location inside the city limits of Moscow. As you can see, it is for 5:00 local time. That means 3:00 Spanish time." She looked at her watch. "Now it's 2:56."

"I understand," said Ross. He took the tablet from Maria, astonished to see her name inscribed in Roman letters. He flipped it over. On its other side appeared Hebrew inscriptions.

"I do not know what those mean," said Maria, pulling her chair nearer, smelling expensive aftershave.

"Only one way to find out," said Ross, getting up. He extracted his smartphone, leading Maria towards the Panthera berthed opposite the club. While he walked he drew the first set of characters onto the screen, selected a program which could read all known languages and pressed enter.

The name Alexander Bagrov flashed onto the screen.

"Alexander!" exclaimed Ross, unable to hide his surprise. He tried to remember if he had read any intelligence briefs recently about his friend.

"You know him?" asked Maria, shocked.

"Yeah, I know him!" confirmed Ross, selecting a number saved in recent contacts. "Any idea about what he can expect at that space-time coordinate?"

As the number started ringing Ross typed the coordinates inscribed on the tablet into another of the phone's apps. Seconds later the exact address flicked onto his screen.

"Rock-n-Roll Club!" said Ross. "One of Alexander's favourite haunts. And he's not picking up. Who else knows about this rendezvous?"

He didn't like it. He didn't like it one little bit. 'Sasha' was the best friend he had ever had. If he was in some kind of trouble Ross was capable of anything to help him.

"No answer!" he shouted. "God damn it!" If his friend was in the club, it was quite possible that he would not hear his phone ringing. Loud music would make sure of it. He picked up the tablet once more, tracing the second set of ancient Hebrew characters onto the screen.

"Who else knows about this rendezvous?"

"Not sure," answered Maria. "Possibly someone called Yuval, from Jerusalem."

"Alexei Nesterov!" said Ross, as the phonetic translation of the second set of characters flashed up.

"Do you know him?" asked Maria following Ross as he stepped onto the deck of the Panthera. She felt an attraction to the strong, well-groomed American, happy to have him aboard. Quite apart from his aftershave and clothes, he oozed confidence. He had a low voice and dark looks.

"Not personally," replied Ross. "Alexander spoke highly of him though. He's an executive with Rostelecom with close connections to the Russian Minister of Communications. I know they are close, close enough to be friends." He looked at his watch: 3:05.

His phone buzzed, and he answered, hearing the sound of loud music coming through his earpiece.

"Sasha! Can you hear me?" he yelled.

"Wait a second!" shouted back Bagrov, "I'll go outside."

"That's better," came Bagrov's voice once he was outside of the club. "Lee?"

"Listen, Sasha, I think you are in danger, at risk from something not clearly defined."

"In danger?" replied Bagrov, laughing. "This is Moscow Bro! Everyone is in danger!"

"Just shut up and listen," said Ross, "you don't understand! I have in my hands specific information that you are meeting with Nesterov. It's been compromised! Get out of there!"

"My meeting with Nesterov?" said Bagrov, shocked and not without instant admiration for the CIA and their quick work. He knew they were good, but Jesus! "How did you know?"

"Never mind how, just get out. Whatever you were to discuss with Nesterov, the meeting is not a secret any more. Sections of the Russian government know about it for sure. If you were meeting to exchange information of any kind, pull out!"

Bagrov thought for a second. His friend was a little too well informed, ringing all kinds of alarm bells. How could the CIA have known that he and Nesterov were to exchange information? He was listening to the sound of Ross's repeated warnings to get out of there just as Nesterov emerged from the club. Bagrov put the phone once more to his ear, this time he most definitely understood.

"Sasha!" repeated Ross. "Get out of there!"

It was already too late. Even if Bagrov had been aware of the imminent arrival of the police minutes before, he and Nesterov would have been hard pushed to avoid them.

The police had secured the entire district, setting up road blocks on all the streets. Just as Ross was shouting his warnings a man standing with the troops identified Bagrov and Nesterov. The man was tall and dark, and of unmistakable Middle Eastern appearance. He nodded to the troops who advanced, manhandling Bagrov and Nesterov to the floor, handcuffing them, and throwing them roughly into the back of an armoured van. The connection was cut. Yuval had won the first battle.

***

"What happened?" asked Maria, seeing the look on Ross's face as she followed him around the deck of the Panthera.

"I'm not sure," replied Ross, redialling. "Russian voices shouting something before the line went dead. He has been arrested."

"You heard some Russian voices?" said Maria, smiling. "He is in Moscow!"

"Yeah, but these voices were voices that mean only one thing: big trouble. We have to go to Moscow immediately." He looked at his watch before searching through his mobile's phone book for the number of his travel agent.

"We? Why do *we* have to go to Moscow?" said Maria surprised, and not a little worried.

"You and I are on a mission."

He understood her reluctance to get involved in a trip to Moscow. All that she had heard about Moscow had not exactly endeared it to her, including the present phone conversation.

"Oh come on!" said Ross. He was smiling for the first time since they had met. It definitely made a big difference. "We have the power of the Ancients on our side don't we? We'll be fine."

"But I don't have a visa?" she protested.

"Leave the travel arrangements to me!"

***

The flight to Moscow left an hour later. Ross was able to arrange for a visa on arrival for Maria using some influential contacts he had inside the Federal Migration Service in Moscow. Three hours into the four hour forty minute flight, she woke from the deep slumber that had overtaken her.

She was exhausted, tired as much from explaining every little detail of her little trip to the Middle East in the departure lounge of Ibiza Airport as from lack of sleep. Her head had come to rest heavily on the shoulder of Ross. Coming round, she found her close proximity to his sweet-smelling skin. It was at the same time embarrassing and pleasant. "Oops!" she exclaimed, pulling her head back from his. "Sorry!"

"Don't be," replied Ross. "I'm not!"

"I was out of it."

"When was the last time you slept?"

"Can't even remember," she said, straightening up. "A couple of hours here, a couple there. You know how it is."

"Only too well."

"I feel apprehensive," she said.

"About what?"

"About the arrival."

"Don't be! You're with me. Plus, the power of the Ark is on our side."

"Maybe. Maybe not."

"Right!"

"Do you think he will be all right?" said Maria.

"Who, Alexander?"

"Yes."

"It all depends on why exactly he has been arrested. First of all, I am sure he has not committed any crime."

"How can you be so sure?"

"Because he's my friend, and I know him better than any man alive."

"So why was he arrested?" asked Maria.

"That's precisely the point. There has to be a reason. The other thing to bear in mind is that Lieutenant Colonel Bagrov has become one of the most prominent State Prosecutors in Russia. If they arrested him, it has to be for a very good reason. And when you read good, you know that for Bagrov it's bad, very bad."

"Why?" asked Maria.

"Because in Russia, when you find yourself before a judge, it doesn't matter if you committed a crime or not. The State will find you guilty, if it's in the State's interest."

"But what about evidence?" said Maria.

"Don't make me laugh! In Russia, courts don't need evidence. The judge decides in view of what he is required to decide for the good of those in power, himself included. In ninety-nine out of a hundred cases, that means the defendant goes down for whatever he or she has been accused of. Period."

"What do you think he will be accused of?" asked Maria.

"I'm really not sure," said Ross. "But it would have to be something big. As a State Prosecutor, Alexander Bagrov enjoys unofficial immunity from prosecution. I just hope it has nothing to do with the Ivanov case."

"I heard that name before," said Maria. "Wasn't he the guy who died in jail in Moscow?"

"That's right," replied Ross. "Sergei Ivanov died after almost a year in pre-trial detention. The state accused him of tax fraud but the case never went to trial."

"Because he was dead!" said Maria.

"Yes," said Ross. "Convenient, don't you think."

"If he was guilty, yes," said the Spanish woman. "And what was your friend's relation to this case?"

"His prosecutor!"

A voice came over the intercom system, informing the passengers that the plane had begun its descent to Moscow Domodedovo Airport.

"Are you ready for this?" asked Ross, regarding his pretty companion, a twinkle in his eye.

"No. But let's do it anyway."

Chapter 44

Half asleep, half-awake, Kira Kamenskaya reached over her husband, hoping the shrill tone of her alarm clock hadn't woken him. That was likely. He was perfectly capable of sleeping through it. Her hands explored the bedside table in the gloom, searching the familiar square object. She failed to find it. Then she became aware that the tone had changed. It wasn't the alarm clock that was ringing, it was her cell phone.

She fumbled with various charger leads on her bedside table before locating it. *Who the hell calls at 5:30?* She saw the caller ID. Lee Ross! She threw a thick white dressing gown around her naked body and made her way to the living room. Then she answered.

"Yes, Kira, I know what time it is, but listen up! Alexander Bagrov has been arrested. I am at the prison where he is being held."

"Let me take a wild guess," replied Kira, squinting through the morning gloom which filled the room. "You would like me to help you to get him out of jail?"

"Precisely!" said Ross. "You are connected. Hell, Khodorov even has a crush on you. There must be something you can do."

"Give me a minute. I'll see what I can do. You'll be on this number, right?"

"That's right."

"And where will you be staying?"

"At the Metropol," said Ross. "And I am not alone."

"Not alone?" asked Kira. "You're with a beautiful woman by any chance?"

"Meet us for lunch and I'll introduce you." said Ross. "Rock-n-Roll has a business lunch menu. We can discuss everything then."

"Deal," said Kira. "12.30 sharp?"

"Deal."

***

Kira arrived at 12.35, saying "You look terrible. What happened?"

"Leave me alone!" retorted Ross.

"And you must be . . . ?"

"Marie Teresa. You can call me Maria."

"Kira Kamenskaya, pleased to meet you."

A waiter approached. They ordered three business lunches.

"How is Sasha?"

"Bad," replied Ross. "We didn't manage to see him."

"So what's he charged with?"

"Accessory to the murder of Sergei Ivanov."

Kira looked shocked. "How can they charge him with that? He was acting under orders from above. Everyone knows that."

"Of course they do," said Ross. "The real reason for the arrest was of course different."

"So what was it?" asked Kira.

"I don't know. I was hoping you could at least find that out."

"How could I?" Her green eyes were intense in the beams of sunlight which streamed into the restaurant.

"Oh, come on!" said Ross. "You meet regularly with the President. You give weekly briefs to his advisers. You head the Presidential Energy Commission for Christ's sake!"

"Listen," said Kira, dead serious. "What I am about to tell you would cost me everything. And I mean everything. My job, my friendships, my family, my life." She cast her eyes around the restaurant. "From what I have heard, Nesterov was about to pass Bagrov a file which contained compromising information for the President."

"What kind of information?" asked Ross.

"That I don't know. Honestly."

"And was the file retrieved?"

"Apparently yes," replied Kira, looking at Ross and Maria in turn.

A silence ensued for a few seconds broken by the sound of Kira's mobile.

"Sorry, I have to take this," she said, excusing herself from the table.

Ross and Maria exchanged looks.

"What are you thinking," asked Maria.

"That she is very brave, talking to us," replied Ross. "Or . . . "

"Or what?" asked Maria.

"Or that we are being played."

"I thought she was your friend," said Maria, confused. "Don't you trust her?"

"I don't trust anybody. I only met her on one occasion, so I can barely call her a friend."

"What about Alexander?" said Maria. "Will she help us get him out?"

"She is too close to the President. Too young, too ambitious."

"What do you mean?"

"She won't help us because it would jeopardize her career. If she tries to help us in any way at all, it will be too obvious. Her actions would be noticed, analysed. She would never be able to work with the President again."

Kira could be seen re-entering the restaurant, her curves accentuated by the black, close fitting business outfit that she wore.

"She is amazing looking," whispered Maria just before Kira came within earshot.

"The President has good taste."

"Sorry, guys, I have to leave. Something came up," said Kira, her curves towering over the low table. "Give my regards to Alexander if you manage to see him."

"I don't understand," said Maria, as they both watched Kira getting into her white Toyota Camry which she had parked opposite.

"Don't understand what?"

"Why would Alexander have wanted to get the file? What could he gain by going toe-to-toe with the President of the Russian Federation? What could he hope to gain from that?"

Ross looked gently at the Spaniard across the business lunches that had just been served.

"Because Alexander was acting in the interests of a higher power."

"Who?" asked Maria.

"Someone named Dmitry Chernyaev."

***

The expensive and unnecessarily exaggerated combination of state of the art technology and luxury of Dmitry Chernyaev's office did nothing to calm the Grand Master's nerves that early Moscow evening. He sat with his back to his desk looking out over Teatralnaya Ploshad towards the Bolshoi Theatre at the other end of the wide, traffic-filled square. The late September sun, a red orb dipping westwards, hung low in the cloudless sky. It threw its dying light across the Russian capital, painting the white city deep crimson.

The scene's beauty was not lost on the New Templar Grand Master as he stared out. His naturally red face was turned redder by the extraordinary evening luminescence. It did something to revive him. It animated him, bringing a modicum of happiness, which the situation with Anna Kuznetsova had left hopelessly lacking.

And though 'blue sky thinking' moments like those had never ceased to bring him the answers to his problems, that particular evening it afforded him absolutely nothing. He was still consumed by anger from his son's death. He was still blinded by a belief in the necessity for taking America down.

The world was a living thing, a being. And that being was in the process of being wronged and corrupted. It was being destroyed by a power interested only in its own selfish goals. America was riding roughshod across whole cultures, communities and countries in the name of nothing more than 'democracy', an idea unattainable due to its very nature and definition.

In the absence of the Russian President providing his organization with the device, his trump card, Anna Kuznetsova, the medium, would have to be played. She was after all, part of God's plan, written by the hand of Ezekiel in a document 2,666 years old, the year when the Ark was lost. He thought back to the second fragment, the piece conferred to his safe keeping from the Knight of the Temple, that night at the Temple Church. Just as he had done already hundreds of times since his receipt of it days before. He already knew it word for word.

***

Anna Kuznetsova from the land of Gog and Magog will usher in the New World by opening the trail to the Ark. She alone in the human realm knows of its location.

A Grand Master, Lee Ross and Kira Kamenskaya are links on the trail, instrumental in its discovery.

***

It was unambiguous. Anna Kuznetsova was the medium. Only she knew the Ark's hiding place, hard-wired into her memory by the higher power that had created her. Through her, he could find the Ark. Through her he could control its power. But she was in a coma.

Irina, his new personal assistant knocked once before striding into his office, clutching a file in her slim, perfectly manicured hands. He liked her confidence almost as much as he liked her looks. Her eyes were dark as was the wavy hair which flowed down over her wide yet womanly shoulders.

"Sir," she said approaching. "The President has accepted your request for a meeting this evening at 21.00 at his Gorky residence." She passed him a fax printout from the President's personal assistant confirming the meeting.

The Grand Master, after casting an eye over the document, rested his eyes back on Irina.

"Alexander Bagrov is still not answering his phone," she said.

The information was worrying. Dmitry Chernyaev had given Bagrov, the highest Russian government official in the New Knights Templar the deadline of that day to secure a mobile nuclear device from Russia's Strategic Nuclear Command. By the time of the meeting, the device was supposed to have been already in the air, outside Russian airspace, en route to Iran. That was his plan A. And that was now in jeopardy.

"Then keep trying!" said Chernyaev. "And hold all non-essential calls."

Anna Kuznetsova. He found it difficult to think of her without feeling a mixture of emotions. Rage. Deception. Respect. She had killed his only son, his only heir. If anybody else in the world would have done it, they would have been long dead.

With Anna, it was different. When he looked at her, he did not see the woman who had killed his son. He saw a woman. She had been used by the Americans and left out in the cold; a scapegoat. He did not blame her for his son's death. Americans were responsible, as they were for most of the world's problems. He could not escape feeling deceived, however. Deceived by her coma, and tricked by fate.

The Ark lay hidden and only he had the key. A key which refused to wake up.

He had had to return to Moscow, so left her under the careful eyes of a doctor and two bodyguards. She was safe. And she was close to where he believed the Ark was located. In Jerusalem.

His train of thought was broken by a knock on his door.

"A man and a woman are here to see you," said Irina. "They are not on your schedule."

"Then tell them to make an appointment."

"It's Lee Ross!" said Irina. "And he's not alone."

"Then show them in."

Chapter 45

Dmitry Chernyaev picked up his mobile and hit a fast dial number.

"Zak, how's your back?"

"Still painful from the beating you gave me, though your sympathy is touching," said Hoffman. "What do you want?"

"Then I'll come straight to the point. I have just been graced with a visit from your protégé, Lee Ross. Did you know that he is in Moscow?"

"I did not," replied Hoffman. "But don't read too much into that. His movements in the course of protecting the free world from the worst excesses of people like the Russian President can take him anywhere. Even to the Kremlin."

"Well, yes, quite," said Chernyaev. "As I was saying, I will get straight to the point."

"Please do."

"During our little meeting, it became apparent that I have something that the President of Russia is keen to possess."

"What is it, and how does it concern me?"

"Anna Kuznetsova," said the Russian.

"And you want to trade her? You want to trade Anna Kuznetsova? After everything you said at Temple Church, you just want to give her up?"

"You're right, I do."

"But she's the Medium? The key to God's power on Earth, whose power you need to complete your son's objective. She's the chosen one, the only one who can lead humanity back to the Ark of the Covenant. She is the most valuable thing the Order has ever possessed. Why on Earth would you want to just give all that away?"

"Because right now the Russian President can give directly the power to bring America down. And give it to me right now. I am not a patient man, Hoffman. My son's death will be avenged without delay. Anna Kuznetsova is still in coma. Maybe she will ever wake up. Now I have the opportunity to get exactly what I need, which is why I need you."

"And how do you need me exactly?"

"I have a job, one I believe only you can accomplish. It's a job which we have already discussed and which you already agreed to. In return for your service to the Order, I will grant you something you will not be able to refuse"

"I . . . ," began Hoffman.

"You will come to Moscow immediately," said Chernyaev.

"But I . . . "

"That's an order."

Chapter 46

Psychologically, Karim Hosseini was as unprepared for the reception meted out to him on his arrival in Moscow as a fish for life out of water. He was a country boy at heart. But his contacts in Tehran had at least made sure that he would look the part. So when he stepped off the Iranian military Tupolev Tu-154 he wore his dark tailored suit with confidence, the three day old stubble on his chin adding a mature look which belied his twenty five years.

After beholding the Eagle at Alamut and recognizing that he was the chosen one who would lead his people to greatness, he had renounced visiting his parents at the farm.

He had, since that day, embraced the expedition of the assassin which would lead him to his destiny. He had embraced the assassination of the enemies of Hassan Khan, his leader, the death of America, friendship with Hassan Khan, and the return of the Mardi, the Twelfth Imam, from occlusion. Those were just some of the duties of the Prophet, the duties of the one chosen by the Eagle of Alamut, the protagonist of the legends told to him by his mother around the campfires of his childhood.

The ageing jet was met on the tarmac by a reception normally reserved for a visiting head of state. It had not been a mistake.

The Russian authorities had received their orders from the highest authority, the President of Russia himself.

The 'accommodation' of the wishes of the Iranian President had been easy for the Russian President to accept. He was not immune to the forces of *realpolitik* which continued to define the world of international relations. Far from being an idealist, the Russian President still viewed the world through the lens of 'Realism' a world which, in the absence of any over-arching world authority, was subject to the primordial qualities of the leaders of its sovereign states, to selfishness, to greed and to vanity. The world of Global Politics was a self-help system, a fight for state survival, for dominance in a 'dog eat dog' environment. And his country at least, was not going to lose out.

The decision to provide a small nuclear device to the Iranians had therefore been an easy one for the Russian President to take. The Iranian President had given his assurances that it would not be used directly against the USA. Russia could hardly afford a nuclear confrontation with the States if it was to survive. Khodorov had been assured that the device would be used for what the Iranian President had described as 'a strategic target in Asia'. In return, the Iranian President had provided him with the only thing which mattered to him; money and power.

Karim stopped dead at the top of the aircraft's steel steps surveying the scene with dismay. A red carpet that had been rolled out from the bottom of the aircraft's steps all the way to the black limousines. It may have been meant to convey some kind of message; to Karim it symbolized the spread of ideas which could only be termed 'Western'.

He cared less for these 'formalities' of the American imposed system as much as America itself, and the ideas of 'liberal democracy' that in the years since his entry to the Revolutionary Guards he had learned to hate.

"Is our red carpet not to your liking?" joked the leader of the meeting party as he advanced to meet the envoy, offering a hand.

The Iranian shook it firmly, his smile broad and unforced revealing a dazzling set of perfect teeth which shone in the bright sunlight.

"It is not!"

"Defense Minister Oleg Ivanov. Welcome to Russia!"

"Karim Hosseini. Iranian carpets are superior in every way to the red carpets imposed by the Americans."

"Well said," said the Russian, releasing his hand from the firm grip of the Iranian. "We Russians welcome any initiative to end American hegemony in International Society. Let's start by adopting Iranian carpets in all future contacts." He turned and presented the other Russians to the Iranian, before suggesting lunch. "If it is to your liking of course."

"How could I refuse such a generous proposal?" replied Karim.

He understood that the forces of 'Globalization' were shaping the world. But for him there was only resentment. He resented the way the West preached and embraced the spread of democracy, of liberal capitalism. To him their neo-liberalism signified nothing but a neo-imperialist rant whose hypocrisy never ceased to amaze him. Was it only he who could see it and them for what they were? The Americans and their European stooges were in the process of re-colonizing the world in a way which employed capitalism as a buzz-word for world dominance.

The U.S. promised the world salvation through economic liberalism and the embrace of capitalization, but denied its most needy subjects any progress at all. It was a globalist challenge to the world's poorest people. The rich and powerful against the rest, the 'haves against the have nots'. A challenge he was determined to face.

The Russian Defense Minister gestured to the door of the nearest limousine opened by one of the three bodyguards. His craggy face appeared to have taken the rigours of war and Russia's physical and social environment in its stride.

Karim was whisked with the presidential meeting party at high speed along the wide purposely traffic cleared Leninsky Prospect towards the restaurant where a table for ten had been booked on the top floor of the Ritz Carlton.

***

The world has come to a bad state of affairs thought Dmitri Chernyaev. People steal, people rape, people do not work. Everything he saw in society was turning bad, the world was living in the End Times, with signs of the Great Tribulations everywhere to be seen. And no one personified the evil gripping 'civilized' society as much as the man who was sitting opposite him. Khodorov.

Khodorov had done more than any one man to destroy the aspirations of tens of millions of his countrymen; hopes of a better life, a modern civilized country at peace with itself and its neighbours.

Khodorov had single-handedly consolidated the power vertical in Russia, and in doing so, had turned back the clock to the depths of its cold, Soviet past. He had dashed the fragile, but strengthening pillars of a democracy which his predecessors had fought to build; throwing them like boats in a storm against some dark rocky shore. He looked at the man. He looked into his frozen eyes, devoid of humanity, and knew that things for Russia were going very badly indeed.

"Good evening Gentlemen, Miss Kamenskaya," said the Russian President, turning his head to the left and the right. He eye-balled each and every one present in the Georgievsky Hall in the Kremlin Grand Palace. "Some of you are new to the Kremlin, some of you not." He looked to his right. "This is Kira Kamenskaya. She is head of the Presidential Committee for Energy, a position she holds in parallel with that as Deputy Chairwoman for Industry and Energy." His head swung ninety degrees to the left. "This is Yuval Rozenkranz."

The President imagined what would be the reaction of the group if he had told them the truth. *This is Yuval Rozenkranz, messenger from Satan.*

Managing to keep a straight face, he said, "Yuval is Deputy Chairman of The Commission for Social Development."

Finally, he turned his attention to the remaining members of the meeting. "This is Dmitri Chernyaev, President of Russia Oil and Zak Hoffman, an American observer." He was hunched, his head held low, hands laid flat on the table in front of him. "This meeting has been convened at the request of comrade Chernyaev," he continued. "I will now give the floor to Mr Chernyaev to explain why we are all here. Mr Chernyaev."

"Gentlemen, Kira Kamenskaya, I have called this meeting to request the release from detention of Alexander Bagrov and Alexei Nesterov."

"And why should they be released?" asked Khodorov.

"Quite simply because they are innocent of the crime of which they have been accused."

"Innocent?" replied Khodorov, raising his voice a tone. "Sergei Ivanov died in jail. If that is not the fault of his prosecutor, I don't know what is!"

"He was following orders from above," replied Chernyaev, maintaining his cool.

"That does not exempt him from responsibility."

"Mr President," began the Grand Master. "As you and everyone at this table are aware, the unfortunate death of Sergei Ivanov is not the real reason for the arrest of Bagrov and Nesterov. That is a pretext. The real reason for their arrest is because of their acquisition of a file containing material potentially damaging to this administration. "The Grand Master turned to look directly at the Khodorov. "Am I right, Mr President?"

"Continue with your speech Comrade," said the President, rubbing his nose to allay an itch.

"I'm taking that as a tacit 'yes'," said Chernyaev. "Then we can begin the negotiation in earnest."

"What exactly do you want Dmitry Ivanovich?" said Khodorov, using the Grand Master's middle name to show respect.

"The immediate release of Alexander Bagrov and Alexei Nesterov from custody," said Chernyaev.

"And what are you willing to give in return for this "accommodation"?" asked the President.

"The location of a religious relic said to be the source of God's power on Earth!"

His words were met with loud chuckles from both the Russian President and the man seated on his left, Yuval Rozenkranz. "Perhaps you are going to tell us next that the Ark of the Covenant has not yet been defiled, that if I am quick, I will be the first to penetrate its secrets, to be the receiver of its untold power?"

"You know of its discovery?" said Chernyaev, unable to disguise a profound look of deception spreading across his chubby face.

The President turned to Yuval.

"Gentlemen, Ms Kamenskaya," began Yuval. "The Ark of the Covenant has been discovered. As one of the two fortunate explorers to have been graced with its discovery, I am also one of the two people on this planet who are eligible to be in possession of its power."

"Eligible to be in possession of its power?" asked Chernyaev.

"That's right," continued Yuval. "The Ark, when we found it, contained an eleventh tablet that gave the conditions for the possession of its power. That tablet is currently in the possession of the President of Russia."

"What are those conditions?" chipped in Hoffman, listening with a mixture of awe and confusion.

Kira put her hand on the arm of the Russian President in order to stop him speaking. "I am afraid we are unable to tell you," she said, "for reasons I am sure you all will be able to guess. As my comrade said, this relic is the source of God's power on Earth."

"It seems, Dmitry, that you are all out of negotiating power at this meeting," said Khodorov gathering the papers spread across the table. "This meeting is over."

"Maybe not," said Chernyaev, taking out a leather file from the black briefcase at the base of his chair. "I may have something up my sleeve, a document written by the hand of Ezekiel himself two thousand six hundred years ago." With consummate care, he extracted the two fragments of papyrus. "This document proclaims that three people, two of which are present in this room, will be instrumental in bringing about The End Times, the passing of the world into the New Era, one ruled by God, or by Satan."

A hush set in, broken by Yuval. "Please, may I see that," he said, stretching out a bony hand across the table.

"You will be able to handle it to your heart's content if you release Alexander Bagrov and Alexei Nesterov," answered Hoffman.

"How can we know that the document is real?" asked Kira.

"I have here the results of its authentication by experts from the British and Israeli museums," said Chernyaev, extracting other documents from the leather case, this time with considerably less care. "These are the original printouts of said results, stamped officially and bearing the names and telephone numbers of the experts themselves. If you would like confirmation, please, be my guest. I am sure they will remember carrying out the verification, so you will have no trouble to make your query understood. It's not every day that they do tests on original Ezekiel written documents!"

"Can we at least be permitted to read them," said Yuval, "to know their content?"

"We have prepared photocopies of the fragments," answered Hoffman, getting up and distributing one copy to each of the three members of the presidential side of the negotiating table. "Below each you will find translations of the ancient Hebrew script into English and Russian."

It was Yuval who spoke first, triumphantly. "This information is obsolete! We know where the Ark is. We've been there, seen it, touched it!"

"And Anna Kuznetsova?" asked Chernyaev. "Do you know who she is?"

All eyes fell on Yuval, whose expression told a thousand words. Perhaps his lack of cool was due in part to surprise. When he had read the name of Anna Kuznetsova that very morning, engraved on the face of the eleventh tablet, he had not in the least expected to be confronted with it in the charged atmosphere of a Kremlin meeting. Apparently unable to control his tongue either, he confirmed what those around him had perceived seconds later in words. "Of course I know who she is. Everyone does!"

"I don't!" pronounced Kira, coldly. "Please, fill me in!"

"Her name features on many Old Testament documents. They say she will appear at the time of the Second Coming of Jesus Christ, analogous to the appearance of the redeemer of the Islamic faith, the Mahdi." Then, turning to Chernyaev, asked: "Why did you mention her name?"

"Because I thought I could use her as a bargaining chip."

Dumbfounded by the Grand Master's response, Yuval's first thought was that he must have misunderstood. "How can you do that?"

"Well . . . " said the Grand Master, enjoying keeping the three people opposite waiting, "because I have her."

Kira said, "What do you mean by that?"

"I have her," repeated Chernyaev. "I control her. I own her. I think that means I have her."

"Leaving servitude out of it for the moment, may we enquire about how you 'got' her, as you so elegantly put it!"

"She killed my son," said Chernyaev. "That makes her mine!"

It was the Russian President's turn to ask a question.

"Saying that we believe you, which of course is at this stage only hypothetical, and saying that we verified her identity, you are prepared to give her up to us for the release of Bagrov and Nesterov?"

"No," replied Chernyaev. "For Bagrov and Nesterov, I would give you only the papyrus fragments. For Kuznetsova I would give up only for something a little trickier to arrange, but nevertheless within your power."

"Which is?" asked Khodorov.

"Two nuclear devices," said the Grand Master. "One now and one held in reserve, primed, operational and ready for immediate deployment."

"Are you out of your mind?" asked Khodorov.

"No, I am not," replied Chernyaev. "As I am sure by now you are aware. The devices must be small and mobile, 10 kilotons yield each, set up on a timer; plus one extra thing."

"As if that was not already enough!"

"Transportation to Iran."

***

Silence fell on the exquisite decoration of the Kremlin meeting room as the sound of Hoffman and Chernyaev's footsteps receded. Khodorov, Yuval and Kira were caught up in deepening thought processes.

Kira broke the spell. "It's too good to be true, so therefore it probably is not. It's a trick. If they know who Anna is, why would they consider giving her up for anything less than complete control of the world? After all, that is what whoever controls her would obtain."

"Not everyone has access to people like Yuval," said the President. "If it was not for Yuval, we too would not know who she is, or what power she possesses."

"You are missing the point," replied Kira.

"Which is?"

"That they *do* know who she is. The source of the information about her is immaterial for this discussion. The discussion should be about do we or do we not make this deal."

"We of course make it," said Yuval. "What are two nuclear devices to us? Even if Chernyaev detonates them somewhere, we will have Anna. With Anna we have the world. The possession of her will bring divine protection in whatever we do, destroying America by a pre-emptive nuclear attack included. That is still what you want is it not?"

"It is," said Khodorov. "So we need Kuznetsova. The release of two nuclear weapons to Chernyaev is a small price to pay for global supremacy."

"And what about transportation to Iran?" asked Kira.

"As luck has it, that detail is taken care of. An Iranian transport plane is on standby at Vnukovo Airport."

"What is an Iranian transport plane doing here in Moscow?" asked Kira, dumbfounded. "Why was I not informed?"

"I arranged for a nuclear device to be supplied to the Iranians to jump start their nuclear arsenal. Peace in the region will be ensured to a higher degree if the two opposing Middle Eastern blocks, the Iranians on the one side and the Jewish state on the other, both become nuclear armed. That way, the Jewish state's capability of stirring up trouble will be forever curtailed."

Yuval, knowing that Kira had been kept in the dark about the President's plans to sell a nuclear weapon to the Iranians, filled her in on the details. "Karim, a presidential envoy of Iran, arrived this morning aboard an Iranian military transport plane at Vnukovo Airport. The President of Iran sent him to take receipt of a nuclear device that will help our interests, and that of the Iranians, and indeed promote world peace by restoring the military balance in the Middle East."

"So we make a deal," said Kira. "We give Chernyaev and Hoffman two portable nuclear devices, of ten kilotons each, in exchange for Anna Kuznetsova."

"Yes," replied Yuval and Khodorov roughly in unison.

"One more thing," said Yuval. "The Spanish woman and the American, the ones who arrived in Moscow to seek Alexander

Bagrov's release, will be required to deliver the nuclear weapons to Chernyaev's associates in Iran. Otherwise the deal will not be allowed to take place."

"Why?" asked Khodorov. "If we have Anna, who cares who receives the weapons?"

"Mr President. You do not know as much about the End Times as I. I can tell you that if you follow my advice exactly, and to the word, your own survival, and that of Russia in the End Times is assured. Karim is potentially a weak link in the chain of events leading up to the catastrophic global events which will consume the world in the End Times. We need to control him as much as possible. Part of that control is dependent on control of the nuclear weapons that will be transported with him to the Iranian capital. That is why we need the two westerners on the flight of the Iranian Transport plane back to Tehran."

"Your explanation is both credible and accepted," said the Russian President. "However, I believe that this Iranian is incurably anti-American. How will he, the presidential envoy of Iran, accept the presence of two western infidels let alone two extra nuclear weapons on the flight?"

"That, Mr President, is the next point we will need to settle between ourselves in the twenty minutes we have remaining before the resumption of our meeting."

Chapter 47

"Comrade Chernyaev, Mr Hoffman," began President Khodorov once the visitors had been brought back into the meeting room. "We will make you the following offer, which will be our final offer to you. For the receipt of Anna Kuznetsova we offer you two fission devices of ten kilotons each, primed functional and ready for immediate deployment. One of the two devices will be transported tomorrow to Iran, where it will be delivered to your representative organization. The other device will be kept here in Moscow until you are ready for its deployment."

"Perfect," said Dmitry Chernyaev, unable to conceal his pleasure.

"This deal, however, comes with one condition," said Yuval.

"Which is?"

"The devices will be delivered to your organization by three people who we alone will appoint."

The Grand Master and Hoffman exchanged glances.

"That won't be a problem," said Chernyaev. "Who did you have in mind?"

"They will be delivered by one Iranian, one American and one Spanish citizen. Their names are Karim Hosseini, Lee Ross and Maria Juan."

Chernyaev and Hoffman exchanged more glances, followed by hurried whispered discussions.

"While we understand the reasons for your pursuit of control," said Chernyaev, "we are suspicious of your motives to use what we see as two of 'ours' for the delivery of the devices."

Yuval stretched his arms forward on the conference table. "We approach this distinctly sensitive operation with a high degree of security. We know already the identities of Ross and Maria Juan. They are 'yours' as you put it, yet individuals in which we place a high degree of trust. We would feel confident about them, and only them, administrating the handover of the nuclear device to your organization. As for Karim Hosseini, his allegiance to our cause is unquestionable."

There followed further hushed discussions by Chernyaev and Hoffman.

"Will the nuclear device be ready for transportation tomorrow?" asked Chernyaev.

"It will be loaded along with the nuclear device destined for the Iranians aboard the Iranian military transport under the supervision of the three aforementioned individuals tomorrow morning at 11am," replied Yuval. "From its arrival in Tehran, the subsequent destination of your device will be under your control, the control of your two agents. You can do with it what you like. The other device, destined for the Iranians, will be under the control of Karim Hosseini."

"And this Karim Hosseini will be aware of and in agreement to these conditions, to the presence of an extra nuclear device on the flight. It seems to me he is not aware of this development."

"I can assure you, Comrade Chernyaev, that Karim Hosseini will be fully aware and in agreement with these arrangements," said Yuval.

"Then we accept these conditions," said the Grand Master. "We expect our nuclear device to be delivered and loaded under the supervision of our agents, Lee Ross and Maria Juan, tomorrow morning at Vnukovo Airport at 11pm."

"Then this meeting is terminated," said Khodorov. "Gentlemen, Miss Kamenskaya, thank you."

Chapter 48

Following lunch at the Ritz Carlton Karim was taken on a whistle stop tour of Moscow's most famous monuments. The tour finished in Kitay Gorod at the seat of the Presidential Administration of the Russian Federation.

After a phone call, one of the bodyguards turned to him with a serious face. "President Khodorov has informed us that he will be unable to meet you this evening. He expresses his apologies. He will meet you tomorrow at 9am."

"Then take me to a bar," retorted Karim, one eye twitching fiercely. He was not stressed, but the day had tired him out. He had intensely disliked the museum tour, but had nevertheless accepted it as necessary ill. "I want to see how Russians party."

"It is not recommended," said the taller and older of the two bodyguards who appeared to wield authority. "We have orders to guarantee your safety. If we take you to a club, we would not be able to achieve that."

"Your orders don't concern me," replied Karim. "And I am sure your boss would not wish that my trip to Moscow did not fulfil my expectations. So I repeat. Take me to the nearest club!"

"Yes Sir," replied the bodyguard. "Driver, take us to Propaganda," he said his rough features breaking into a wry smile.

"Propaganda?" asked Karim.

"Propaganda!" repeated the bodyguard. "It's the nearest club! But be warned: until midnight it will be dead."

The black BMW limousine pulled up outside the club minutes later, the bodyguard and his partner preparing to get out.

"No," said Karim, firmly. "I go in alone."

"But we . . . " began the bodyguard, before being cut by Karim, who seemed to be stamping his authority.

"No buts! I will go in alone."

***

The bodyguard had been right. Nobody was dancing. The club was populated with dining couples and groups, a sea of tables sprawled across the dance floor. Karim stepped down a flight of steps to a bar on the lower level followed by two girls. Both were blonde. Both were laughing and speaking in fast Russian. They beat him to the bar tender and ordered margaritas.

Karim moved to the bar and ordered a cocktail. He didn't need a girl. Who needed a girl? And yet, as he approached the bar, he nevertheless realised he needed a girl like the one sat on the end of the bar.

Since losing Aida he had become a loner. He had not socialised with girls. Nevertheless part of him longed for someone to share his life, to talk to, to cuddle up to at night. He was also sure that if ever the possibility of romance presented itself, it would not be him who would make the first move.

At the most basic level, all beautiful girls knew that all guys would want to be with them. He wanted a beautiful girl who wanted him as much, and him alone, a girl that would not only make the first move, but do it because she was compelled to do it, lacking choice. He wanted a situation in which he would possess something which no other guy possessed. Only then would he feel a connection to a girl. Only then could he consider a relationship.

The girl on the end of the bar was sat on a high chair her long legs accentuating her black mini skirt. She had dark hair and big lips. He must have made some kind of impression because she kept her eyes on him. Eventually she walked straight up to him, her curvy body accentuated by her attire. Karim noticed her beautiful green eyes.

"Nice car," she said, gesturing towards the window.

"You saw me arrive?" replied Karim, thinking, *Russian chicks sure don't miss much.*

"I did," said the girl, her expensive perfume wafting in his face on the club's currents of air conditioned air. That coupled with her looks was already creating an impression. "It was difficult to miss. Look around you! Do you see anyone wearing tailored Armani suits?"

"What's your point?"

He liked the way she talked to him. So many people talk at you, not with you. Not her! His left eye was still twitching as he gazed into her eyes. *This girl would never be mine: too beautiful, too perfect.*

"You're different," said the girl. "Not just because your car is better than theirs. It was the way you walked over to the bar. You have a certain confidence about you which some might confuse with arrogance, but which, if I may, is a quality which your life itself has imposed on you. But, as for your question, no, it's just an observation. Can I ask you something? Are you always so cold to beautiful strangers who come to talk to you?"

"You are presuming that beautiful strangers talk to me."

"Okay. You're in no mood to talk." She walked away.

"What! Are you psychic?" asked Karim to her back.

She swung around. "It's obvious. You probably have a lot on your mind. Not everyone comes to Moscow to acquire and transport a nuclear weapon! Have a nice time in Moscow, Mr Karim."

It was not so much the fact that she knew who he was which surprised him as he watched her curves receding into the smoke filled club. He had not expected to come to the Russian capital and generate at least mediocre interest among the security agencies. It was more his sense of loss. She had, in thirty seconds, impacted and unbalanced him in ways more profound than any other woman had ever done. Even Aida had not done that.

He felt the aggression towards the West focusing into something for him infinitely more important. For the second time in his life he desired a woman. It was not that he desired any less the fulfilment of his dreams; the redemption of Islam through Mahdiism and action. But his immediate interests had changed.

Something inside him had reawakened. He had seen something. Felt something. It was in his zone of action, attainable. It was the first time he had felt such forces, and understood their power. Those forces had spoken to him in a language he understood. Whoever the girl was, he knew then and there that he was not going to be able to pass up on her. He ordered two Margaritas, finished his drink, and strode in her direction.

He found her at a table in a corner of the club, a recess half obscured by writhing bodies.

"This is for you."

He placed one of the margaritas carefully in front of her. The fact that she did not sit alone did not worry him.

"Do you mind if I join you?" he said in accented English, eyeing the 'couple' opposite.

"Please!" she replied, indicating a sofa. "Thanks for the drink!"

"You're welcome."

"Are you wondering how I know your name?"

"Good guess!"

"Well, Mr Hosseini, how shall I put this?" she looked across the table to the 'couple' as if for inspiration. The 'couple' met her regard with respectful smiles and silence. "Thanks to your visit Moscow's governmental agencies are mobilised. The capital is reared, you might say."

"Why?" asked Karim.

"Of course I can't tell you why, Mr Karim. But take it to be so."

"Then why are you telling me at all?"

"Because I like you, Mr Hosseini. I have read your file. You are not like the regular security threats which punctuate our existence. You stand for common good, for honesty, integrity, the pursuit of the ideals which underpin your Shia ideology."

A waitress dressed in tight fitting jeans and wearing a black T shirt emblazoned with the word Propaganda passed their table collecting glasses. From the collection of empty cocktail glasses in front of them, the three friends had had quite a time already.

"As I was saying," continued the tall, curvy and distinctly stylish Russian. "I liked you from your file. The world needs more people like you if we are to avoid future wars which common sense tells us will be more and more devastating in nature. That's why I know your name."

Karim had enjoyed listening to her, especially when she had said the words 'I like you'. It seemed to him that he had heard those words pass her full red lips at least twice. He realized that he did not, as yet know her name.

"We have not been formally introduced," he said, taking a long draught of his margarita.

"Kira Kamenskaya," said the girl. "And this is Lee Ross and Maria Juan."

"Pleased to meet you," said Karim, surveying the little group of three. His next question was directed across the table to the couple. "What brings you to Russia?"

"Business," replied Ross.

"What kind of your business?"

"Oil business," said Ross. "The technology used in exploration of hydrocarbon deposits. Russia is expanding its area of potential exploitation into the high risk environment off its Arctic coast."

"Yes," chipped in Maria. "Though tomorrow, events lead us to head to warmer shores."

"Might I ask where?" said Karim.

"Iran."

"Iran?" repeated Karim, unsure of context, reasons and a million things between.

"Yes," replied Ross. "During a recent deal we were presented with a religious relic."

"A relic?" said Karim, unsure if he had heard correctly.

"That's right, a relic," continued Ross, understanding the Iranian's disbelief at the pace at which the conversation was diverging. He removed one of Maria's five marble tablets from his jacket. "This relic."

"And what is it exactly?" asked Karim, taking the tablet.

"It's a relic written in ancient Hebrew which contains space-time coordinates indicating where we have to be to receive information concerning the future of our planet."

"Okay, you lost me!" said Karim, handing back the tablet.

"Not to worry," said Ross. "All you need know is that we have to be tomorrow at 16.00 in Tehran in order not to miss it."

"And so lies our problem," chipped in Maria, sitting up. "If we do not get to Tehran tomorrow at 16.00 disaster will engulf our planet."

"No, I got it," said Karim trying his best to get his head around two different things at the same time, his approach to the girl and what the hell the couple were talking about. "Let me guess the gist of it: the two of you don't have tickets and the commercial flights are fully booked."

"That's about the size of it," said Ross, slouching back into the sofa along with Maria.

Karim said, "Well. I suppose I could help you out with that. Tomorrow at 12.00am, an Iranian transport Tu-154 will take off from Vnukovo Airport. I could make sure you are both on it."

"Really?" said Maria, sitting back up her eyes gleaming. "That's fantastic! Thank you so much."

"It's really no trouble," said Karim, eyeing Kira just in time to see her deep green eyes looking into his with admiration. *If helping the infidel brought such pleasure, I might have to rethink my whole attitude, my approach to life itself.*

"Thank you for helping my friends," said Kira, lifting her half emptied glass. "Ladies and gentlemen, I'd like to make a toast to international cooperation!"

Chapter 49

The steel elevator hummed with a high pitched whine, conveying its three occupants downwards at incredible speed. Approaching the bottom, yet still one hundred meters above it, it slowed imperceptibly, depositing its three occupants at their destination without so much as a whisper. The 'metro' which linked the Kremlin to the 'Octagon', Russia's equivalent of the Pentagon, was over a kilometre deep.

"Follow me," said Khodorov, leading his guests into a well heated passageway. Yuval and Kira felt like they had just been transported across time as well as space.

"I had heard rumours of this system's existence," uttered Yuval, trying to keep up with the Russian President as he strode ahead. "But never in my wildest dreams did I think I would ever see it."

"Please," said Khodorov. "Save your expressions of wonder for the flight to the Octagon."

"Flight?" said Kira. "How can we be taking a flight to the Octagon?"

"In the strictest sense of the word, yes," said the President. "As I said, wait for the flight before you express your wonder at Russia's lead in the field of transportation."

True to his word, the "flight" which ushered them from deep beneath the Kremlin to the Octagon, the nerve center of Russia's military defied belief. In less than ten minutes the raw power of the maglev train's engines propelled them to the heart of the polygonal fortress situated on Moscow's western periphery midway between Central Moscow and Vnukovo Airport.

From the train terminal inside the Octagon they were escorted by waiting guards through the structure's cavernous interior. They reached a department whose security was even more restrictive. One guard punched a six digit code into the panel beside the huge glass door on which appeared a yellow sign warning of radiation. The door opened with a hiss.

"This way if you please," said the guard, inviting the group inside. "We are entering a protected area, hardened to nuclear attack, one kilometre below the surface."

He proceeded to lead them to a lab where two well-built soldiers wearing black military fatigues were guarding the only entrance.

After their identities were checked, the group entered the lab's spotlessly clean interior. Two soldiers were standing sentry next to a glass and steel table on which stood a huge machine the likes of which they had never seen.

"Here are the two machines that will secure us our dreams," said the Russian President. "Each device is ten kilotons, operational and on a timer. The timer can be set . . . " He moved up to the table and opened the control panel on the side of the device. "Here."

Kira looked at the device, and then at Khodorov. "But there is only *one* machine in front of us!"

Yuval said, "Things are never as they seem. What we have before us are two devices, one hidden inside the other. Karim is not an expert in nuclear physics, and neither are you. The size of this device is much too big for a ten kiloton device, but he will not realise it. Hoffman, Chernyaev and Ross are aware of my plan and have agreed to it. Their device will be split from the other device once they arrive in Tehran."

"How will Hoffman and Chernyaev be sure that these are actual, functional nuclear weapons?" asked Kira.

"Because when we hand them over to their control in approximately six hours, there will be a nuclear physicist in attendance of Hoffman's choice who will run checks to satisfy both Hoffman and Chernyaev. As far as Karim goes, the President of Iran has agreed that the nuclear device they will acquire will be checked on arrival. As you all know, that little detail will be immaterial, as when the Tu-154 arrives in the Tehran sky, he will experience at first hand the functionality of his weapon!"

Kira said, "Okay. I got it. But let's come back to specifics, just so there are no misunderstandings between us. The nuclear device that Chernyaev will receive tomorrow morning at Vnukovo will be checked first by Chernyaev and Hoffman?"

"That's correct," said Khodorov. "Once Chernyaev and Hoffman have verified its operational functionality it will remain in the holding hanger at the airport under our protection until Karim arrives. That will be several hours later. His arrival will be coordinated by us, but we expect it to be around 10.30am."

"So Karim will be totally unaware of the second weapon?"

"That's right," said the President. "Karim will be unaware of the second weapon, and Ross and Maria will have been told not to discuss it with him during the flight. In that way, Karim will not be able to stop the operation. Ross and Maria will believe that the authorization for the transport of the device from the airport in Tehran to the destiny agency, presumably under control of Chernyaev, will come later."

"So the passengers on the flight will be aware of different realities, and will not discuss them on board," said Kira.

"That's right. When he boards the flight with Ross and Maria, Karim will be unaware of the existence of a second device on board the aircraft. It will have been hidden, within the device that he himself alone will have checked with nothing more than a Geiger counter to verify that it indeed contains fissile material."

"And what about Anna Kuznetsova?" said Kira. "Let's not forget the reason why we are going to all this trouble."

"Our agents concerned with securing her are currently stationed in Jerusalem awaiting our word. In a matter of hours, they will move to take control of her, to take her from Chernyaev. When she is safely under our control, we will relinquish the nuclear device to Hoffman and Chernyaev, who will in turn leave it at our facility in Vnukovo airport for the arrival of Karim, tomorrow morning at 11am."

"10.30am," corrected Kira.

"10.30am. Looks like all systems are go for this operation," said Yuval, brimming with self-admiration at having been able to put together such an ingenious plan. Nothing now would be able to go wrong. All systems were in place. Karim had been briefed, and would begin calling the Kremlin in the morning for information regarding the meeting with the President.

The two nuclear devices would have been primed and readied at Vnukovo, and he would coordinate Karim's arrival once Chernyaev and Hoffman had verified the device and left. Nothing had been left to chance. The hour when Anna Kuznetsova would be under his control was drawing near.

Yuval glanced at his watch. 02.45. He took a step back from the nuclear device, focussing his attention on the Russian President. "What time will Chernyaev, Hoffman and their nuclear physicist arrive at Vnukovo?" he asked.

The Russian President looked at his watch. "In a little under thirty minutes."

"So . . . ?" said Yuval. "Hadn't we better get a move on?"

An expression crossed the Russian President's face whose meaning was not immediately obvious to Kira and Yuval whose eyes had been drawn to it.

"My dear Yuval," he said. "You have been my shadow for days now. Have you not learnt anything about me?"

"I got it," said Yuval. "You want to say you're never late, and Vnukovo may be fourteen kilometres distant, but we will get there by the Maglev train."

"Precisely," said the President. "Guards!"

He looked towards the door. The two heavily set and heavily dressed guards who had been standing to attention the whole time came immediately up, and saluted.

"Sir!"

"Transport this device immediately to the Maglev. A carriage has been specially prepared in the middle of the train."

"Yes Sir!"

The two guards called for backup to arrange transportation, finally reporting back to the President.

"The device will be loaded within fifteen minutes," said one. "You are invited to wait in the executive lounge until the operation is complete."

"Perfectly acceptable," replied the President.

A beautiful and exceptionally tall Asian woman arrived at the door, dressed in a black.

"Hi. I'm Vicky and I am your hostess for the remainder of your visit to the Octagon. Would the Russian President and his two respected guests be so kind as to follow me?"

The three followed the agent, exiting the holding room just as it became a hive of activity connected to the transport of the nuclear device. The Asian escorted them to a lounge halfway back to the Maglev.

"Would Champagne be acceptable?"

"Perfectly acceptable," replied Khodorov.

The tall Asian disappeared for a minute, returning with a silver tray and a bottle of Bollinger Champagne. She poured three glasses, her smile gracing the event with gaiety and happiness.

Khodorov and Kira knew the future of the world was in their hands. Yuval was the chosen one, the one whose action, through Anna, would complete their Grand Strategy for control over the planet and its transformation into the Kingdom of Satan.

Chapter 50

The twilight of a Jerusalem morning filtered through the half open window throwing dim illumination across the room. Sounds of light traffic penetrated from the street below, softened by the hum of life support systems running on automatic. The Israeli nurse had passed shortly before three o'clock in the morning, and then returned to the staff room, promptly falling back into deep sleep.

Hours later she awoke to violent shaking.

"What?" she screamed, gripped by fear, and by the rough, strong hands of one of the two Russian bodyguards.

"Where is the girl?"

"What?"

"The Russian patient, Idiot!"

Through the fuzziness of the journey between deep sleep and wakening, the meaning of what had happened began to dawn. "Where is she?"

"That's what you're supposed to know, not me!"

"Let me go, so that I can find her!"

"You better! Otherwise we're both dead!"

***

For the third time in her life Anna found herself putting time and distance between herself and her pursuers. Two hours had passed since she had jumped from the second floor window onto the smooth paving of the street, by a miracle escaping serious injury. She had rolled on landing, gashing only her hands, knees and forehead.

Then she hobbled along the streets, fast as her injuries would allow.

She managed to evade the police and the agents, though she saw them many times, in their cars and on their motorcycles, close at times, searching every street. The shawl given to her by an elderly market stall owner had helped. She had wrapped it around her head and disappeared from view.

She had to find somewhere quiet, far away, somewhere to be alone, to think, to pour out her emotions. She began to run, faces on the street turning towards her in surprise. *To hell with it. If I am caught so be it.*

After ten minutes running the neighbourhood changed and she slowed to a walk, panting heavily. She could smell sweet herbs. The countryside was close.

A group of women came into view up ahead walking in the same direction, chatting noisily. She knew they had noticed her because every now and then one would turn around to check that she was still following. Their presence comforted her.

The dry landscape opened up ahead devoid of houses. There were sheep above the road and a shepherd and his dog were trekking up through yellow fields. Though he too had noticed her, she felt safe, happy. She was walking toward barren hills in the distance whose outlines had been painted yellow by the heat of the sun.

The women in front took a side road which curved down and back towards the outskirts of Jerusalem, cheerfully shouting goodbye, waving their hands as if they had known her all their lives. She waved back, feeling emptiness return.

The road was now slanting diagonally up a hillside. At the point where it was crossed by a dry ravine she took a track which led horizontally towards a grove of pine trees which clung to the ridge. Finally she was completely alone, and far from humanity. She sat down among the pines and poured out her heart.

She cried for hours. When she finally stopped she looked up and noticed for the first time that a Jeep had been parked on the far side of the pine grove. It was pointing uphill, on a track which ran straight up the ridge from the pines. The top of the track was out of view, but it seemed to lead to in the direction of the main road. The bones of a plan materialized in her mind.

***

News of Anna's escape hit Chernyaev while he was waiting at Vnukovo Airport. Hoffman and his nuclear physicist had just left Moscow having confirmed that the weapon was indeed real and functional. He directed his response from where he heard the news, the hangar next to the huge Tupolov transport aircraft. The effect of the news was like a cannon ball from the blue.

"You are all dead!" he screamed into his satellite phone at the bodyguard in Jerusalem. "Dead!" *The imbeciles! Heads would roll and roll, and already had started rolling. Of that reality he was about to make certain.*

A black Mercedes swung around the corner of the hanger, at high speed, its tires squealing. As it came to a halt in front of the Tupolov its doors flew open. He recognised immediately the man who alighted from its driver's side onto the tarmac of the apron.

"I want a word with you," said Yuval, approaching.

"Good," replied Chernyaev approaching him also. "I want a word with you too."

"I suppose you have heard the news, the disappearance of Anna Kuznetsova," said Yuval.

"I have."

"Then I suppose you are wondering how it will affect our deal?"

"Our deal?" said Chernyaev.

"Yes, our deal."

"Can we still talk about a deal?"

"Well, your loss of the girl is a serious development."

"And?"

"Nevertheless," said Yuval, "It does not have to signify the end."

"I don't follow."

"Please," said Yuval, indicating the Mercedes. "Let's continue the discussion in surroundings more conducive to reaching agreement."

***

"Champagne?" said Yuval, pressing a button on the sleek hardwood dashboard. "I like to drink it when I am stressed."

"Who's celebrating?"

"Your loss of the girl is unfortunate. However, it does not mean that the deal is off."

"How is that?" asked Chernyaev, casting a long, suspecting glance at the Israeli.

"I am confident in your ability to find the girl, as I am on your desire to honour your agreement with us. Is my faith mistaken?"

"Absolutely not," replied Chernyaev. "The girl will be found. A team is already on its way to Israel tasked with finding her. In a matter of hours she will be in our hands, and then in your hands."

The Israeli's face broke into a broad smile as he took the bottle of Champagne, tearing off its seal and loosening the cork.

"Then a toast to the success of the endeavour!"

"The endeavour?" said Chernyaev, taking a glass of Champagne. "What exactly do you mean?"

"Our endeavour! Your endeavour to find the girl, and mine to deliver the nuclear device to your agents in Tehran."

"So everything is still on for the delivery?" asked Chernyaev. The bizarreness of the Israeli knew no bounds.

"All systems are go!" said Yuval. "Your agents Maria and Ross will arrive to board the flight at 11.00am, once Karim has done his inspection to verify the weapon is real and functional." He crouched down toward the dash, straining for a view of the device awaiting inspection by the Iranian before its loading into the hold of the Tu-154. He glanced at his watch, and started the Mercedes' powerful 2.8 litre engine. "Karim should be arriving. Shall we?"

"Go!" replied Chernyaev.

***

The morning dawned calm in the Presidential Palace in Tehran. The previous night's festivities surrounding the festival of Eid had turned considerably more radical following the President's receipt of a call from Karim. The nuclear device was real, functional and ready for transportation. A hive of activity in the Iranian intelligence services had verified the conversation between Karim and the Russian President.

"Ladies and gentlemen," began Hassan Khan, President of Iran. He was a dark man in his late forties with thick greying hair, medium height and designer stubble. "Tonight we celebrate not only Abraham, our great Prophet's faith in God. We celebrate Karim whose "Expedition of the Assassin" beholds the Mahdi's imminent release from occlusion. Karim will soon deliver the *coup de grace* in the battle to usher in the End Times, a nuclear explosion on American soil. The Great Tribulations will begin, and will be under our exclusive control. Please raise your glasses to Karim Hosseini, the assassin, whose actions provide for the return of the redeemer of Islam, the Mahdi."

Chapter 51

To Anna's considerable relief, the Jeep was unlocked. She knew the technique for starting it began by pulling out all the wires which led to the ignition, so she ducked in under the steering column and got to work. Subconscious intuition, drawn from endless childhood summers and tough cousins in cars, trucks and the shadier sides of North Moscow drove her to connect several of the wires in specific fashion. It worked. The huge diesel engine rasped to life, all 2.5 litres of it, sending a cloud of black smoke straight up into the sky, and a crescendo cacophony across the hills.

Caution to the wind. Anna floored the accelerator, revving the huge chunk of metal to the limit. The rocky track which lay in front was steep and boulder ridden. It was going to need hard driving, and engine power on tap. So she selected first gear, released the clutch, spun the tires on smooth, polished boulders, and fought to remain in control, gripping the steering wheel with white fists, her teeth clenched. Half way up the incline, the engine died. The vehicle shuddered to a stop. She pulled the handbrake.

As the swirling dust whipped up from the spinning tires began to clear, a movement caught her eye — two men running fast across the hillside. She was out of time and out of luck. But not yet. She still had time. There was still time to restart the engine, to hit again maximum revs, and gun the vehicle upwards.

The Jeep's tires spun even more wildly than before, all the way up the track, over boulders, old tree roots and holes. This time she kept it going, topping out seconds later onto the road on the ridge, which, to her immense relief, was made up of asphalt, not rocks. Smoother and less steep, it ran into the continuation of the main road by which she had left Jerusalem. She careered out onto the big road, narrowly missing a truck. She was cruising along in a Wrangler Jeep on an Israeli highway the wind blowing in her long blonde hair.

Sixty kilometres further along the highway Anna felt safe enough to ease off slightly the pressure on the accelerator. She had put on the pair of sunglasses she had found in the glove compartment, helping her to relax, feeling safer, hidden.

A four way intersection came up. She took a road without knowing why, destination unknown, towards solitude and the desert. The midday sun beat down through the open top, and she felt truly happy. She was driving south on a wide open Israeli highway, pulled once again to an ancient relic like metal to a magnet. She was attracted to a relic written about since antiquity, and a location known only by her, a cave on the summit ridge of a mountain in Sinai.

***

The Tu-154 took off at 11.30am into the dull Moscow sky, fast and with a good rate of climb despite the weight of the two nuclear weapons in its payload. Aboard the flight, Karim settled back into his wide business class seat, the sweet happiness of success surging through his body. Securing the nuclear device destined to usher in the new era of Mahdiism was not meant to be so easy.

Mission success was more or less assured, permitting his mind to race to other matters, to the woman who had unsettled him on his first night in the Russian capital. To Kira ran his mind, to her body, her height and size, and to the extraordinary light and colour in her eyes. He thought of the beauty of her face, and of the way she had kissed him on the tarmac of the airport. He missed her.

Probably he would never talk to her, nor touch her, nor set eyes on her again. For a while now he had known where his final mission would lead him. He felt for the assassin's dagger at his side, touching it for relief from torment, a modicum of reassurance that what he was doing was right. It was there, its long blade real and solid, his faithful friend through the long months of his 'Expedition of the Assassin' through Iran.

Since he had seen the eagle land at Alamut, he had left many such daggers under the pillows of his future targeted assassinations. They were a warning, a threat, a calling card for execution. And he always followed up, without fail and without exception, within a day and a night, removing them definitively from the President's opposition, and from the face of the planet. And at the place of each killing he left a written statement, his motives, goals and ideology, spreading his fame far and wide across the Islamic Republic. Eventually it reached, as he knew it would, the ears of the Iranian President himself.

Soon everyone in Iran knew of him. Karim Hosseini of the 'Expedition of the Assassin' A Prophet and a household name. One recognised even by the Iranian President. The Assassin from Alamut who would clear the way for the return of the Mahdi, the redeemer of Islam.

The huge plane banked towards the south, and levelled out at an altitude well less than normal.

Karim noticed. The Tu-154 cruised at 30,000 ft. *So why is it skimming clouds at 15,000ft?* The seat-belt lights flickered and then went out, so he looked across at the other two passengers, seated in the three seats opposite. "Time to celebrate!" he said, reaching for his carryon luggage. The flight had no cabin crew. The one crew member scheduled to be aboard had telephoned in early that morning complaining of stomach pains, headache and nausea. But the flight had to go ahead. It was a question of security. Iran's security.

Ross and Maria broke off the conversation they were having in Spanish, and turned to Karim.

"Let me guess, Karim," said Maria. "Champagne?"

Part 2. The War

Chapter 52

The blast was triggered by satellite, the origin of the signal traced by the Americans to the Kremlin, Moscow. It occurred at 13.55.35 local, Iranian time, just as the Tu-154 was making its final approach to land at Tehran International. It tore the Iranian Air Force plane apart in milliseconds, vaporizing in an instant its metal, glass, rubber and human occupants. The nuclear fireball expanded in every direction encountering the ground within the first second, two hundred meters below. By the second instant the ball of flame had deflected off the ground, speeding towards the stratosphere, a beautiful, yet haunting spectacle as below, on the ground, ninety percent of the population of Tehran had risen to a temperature of 3000 degrees Celsius. Then came the blast, a colossal eighty kiloton battering ram which obliterated everything left standing.

President Hassan Khan of Iran saw the flash well before the thunderous noise from the detonation reached his ears. He and the members of the Iranian Presidential Guard recited silent prayers for the poor souls in the former city receding behind them as they streaked west on deserted highway 66. They rationalized that what had just happened was fulfilment of the ancient prophecy, that the first battle of the End Times would involve armies from the north, from the land of Gog and Magog, from Russia and America.

President Khan knew that such ideas rang hollow. *I did not trigger the bomb*, he reasoned. *But its presence in Tehran skies was indeed due to me. And to Karim Hosseini.* He had been aware of the possibility of treachery from the way Khodorov had spoken during their negotiations, and had therefore arranged to be already outside the city by the time the Tu-154 approached. But he still cursed the Russian President for betraying his trust, for destroying his city and his people. He prayed for Karim, for his commitment and dedication to him and the Mahdist cause.

Despite what had happened, despite the evil that had been unleashed that day, he could not deny that his unique, long term goal had just reached fruition. The Great Tribulations were upon them, set in motion by the nuclear explosion, the reality behind the biblical tales of fire raining down from the west. Those events would lead to the return from occlusion of the Mahdi, the return of power to the Shi'ites, to the Second Coming.

The red disk of the sun was just slipping over the mountains on the western horizon when the presidential convoy drew up to the entrance of the military complex of Fordow. The four Toyota Land Cruisers slipped into a protected tunnel leading into the mountain, to the place where the Iranian response to the attack would be planned and executed.

The corner of the Iranian desert chosen by Hoffman as the landing zone resembled more the 'empty quarter' immortalized by Ibn Haffani in his 1920s book than the real Empty Quarter of Rub al Khali itself.

Incessant winds whistled across a burning Martian landscape, blasting coarse brown sand into mountainous dunes which stretch from horizon to infinity.

But now a noise filled the air, different from the murmur of the desert wind or the hiss of shifting sands. It was a whining of jet engines, growing in intensity, coming from the north, from a large passenger jet flying at mid altitude. It was a Tu-154, its pilot deliberately diverted, guided off route and off flight level by someone in a comfortable, air conditioned office in Langley. Someone called Zak Hoffman.

The noise from the aircraft's triple jets changed from a whine to a drone as it passed directly over the Empty Quarter, streaking south, towards its destination, Tehran. It receded, softened into a low hum by the familiar sounds of the desert before fading altogether, the aircraft now a speck in the distance.

Then a flapping noise filled the air like the wings of desert vultures. Two parachutists were close, and turned their huge chutes into the wind, having already chosen their landing points.

They landed heavily into the dunes blasting sheets of soft white sand into the air, their chutes hitting down, collapsing, half down, half catching again in the wind, dragging them bodily along. Finally they managed to hit their release clips.

"Are you okay?" shouted Ross.

Maria couldn't reply. Not yet. She needed a second or two, her body still cold from the sixty second free-fall. Finally she took a deep breath and shouted, "Where is Karim?"

"I fear he didn't make it," shouted back Ross, from the other side of the dune.

"Are you sure? Did you see him hit the ground?"

"No, but neither did I see any chute. Guess that's Okay. He died saving the world."

They circled the landing dune making a careful 360 degree sweep with their naked eyes. They sat down on the hot sand of its summit, surveying the desert. No sign of Karim.

"So?" said Maria.

"So what?" answered Ross, surveying the desert dunes.

"Do you think the bomb was real?"

"We both know the bomb was real." He looked up at his companion. "The question is, will they detonate it."

"And the message from Hoffman, what did it say?"

Ross took out his satellite phone from the inner pocket of the jacket, tapping and pressing, until he found the message received during the flight. "Here. Take a look for yourself."

He handed her his phone.

"Mission compromised. Bomb on remote trigger. To be detonated on arrival at destination. Tehran at 13.55.35. Three parachutes stowed under seats 23 AB and C. Bail out in ten minutes from now. Aircraft will be kept at 15,000 feet for the duration of the flight. Your land zone predetermined. Rub Al Khali. Dust off at 13.45 local. Good luck! Hoffman."

Ross glanced at his watch. "That gives us ten minutes to enjoy the view."

Chapter 53

Secret military installation, Fordow, Iran.
Ten hours after the explosion.

The Iranian President was about to be transported deep into Jordan aboard a helicopter which stood on a camouflaged heliport sandwiched between the nuclear proof concrete bunkers and the rugged mountains. It was a Sikorsky UH-60 Black Hawk, one of two recently purchased from the Peoples Republic of China, and armed to the teeth with the latest weapons and counter measures.

The night's clouds were thick, and overcast, pitch black and radiation filled. The military controllers who had planned the flight were taking no chances. It had been ten hours since the destruction of Tehran and another attack was believed to be imminent.

The Americans could be trusted only to do what was in their interests, as could the Israelis, who understood better than anyone the implications of the beginning of the End Times. They knew the Iranians would retaliate, that Israel would be the first in the firing line, and that not all of Iran's military power was located near Tehran. To them, Iran was more dangerous than ever, its military installations, its enrichment complexes, its missile silos protected for years with Russian S300 surface to air missiles. The complex at Fordow was more protected than any.

Three Revolutionary Guard soldiers ran out from nowhere onto the heliport, towards the Black Hawk, barely visible in the gloom of the night under camouflage netting. The helicopter pilots were going through pre-flight checks for immediate take off.

Extraordinary situations legitimized extraordinary actions. In the wake of the nuclear attack, Iran's immediate Arab neighbours had expressed unconditional solidarity, promising 'every possible means' to aid in restoration and recovery from the treacherous Russian attack. So far Iran had remained silent, requesting only overflight permission from the Iraqis and Jordanians. As yet, no-one in the international community even knew if the Iranian President had survived.

***

In the depths of the uranium enrichment and bomb making facility, hundreds of meters below, the doors of lift number eight closed with a hiss. The capsule accelerated upwards for a full thirty seconds before reaching terminal velocity, arriving at the surface minutes later.

"President Khan, your transport is ready," announced one of the soldiers of the Presidential Guard as President Khan stepped out of the glass doors of the lift. "Please follow me."

Straining his dark eyes to accustom to the blackness, the President of Iran nodded his assent. A whine of the aircraft's twin General Electric T700 turboshaft engines became audible as the aircraft's characteristic silhouette loomed out of the murky night. The noise grew to a wailing crescendo as the first of the powerful gusts from the aircraft's four-blade main rotors buffeted the President and his soldier escorts.

"Your essential kit is already aboard, as are your instructions. Good luck Sir!"

***

By the time they approached their first point of contact, the sprawling air base close to the border with Iraq, the noise of the twin helicopter engines had pummelled its way into every fibre of their bodies. Despite the tough, military specification headphones which each wore, Lee Ross and Maria Juan were unsure if their ears were resonating with acoustic energy or whether the humming had penetrated permanently into the neurons of their head.

"In one minute we will be on the deck!" shouted the crew member, a United States Marine whose wrists were thicker than most men's biceps. He and Ross had met before, twice in Israel and once in Egypt, meetings that had ended in a bar, drinking cheap bottled beer. Better times, and better places, but infinitely more boring.

Ross ran through rough calculations in his head. "Taylor!"

"What?" shouted back the U.S. Marine.

"We're still in Iranian territory, right?"

"Hell, you sure don't miss much, do you, Ross?"

"Not much!"

"NATO forces from Turkey secured this base six hours after the attack. An intense onslaught with cruise missiles softened them up real good." The big Marine smiled, before adding, "The Pentagon decided that an operational U.S. base in Iran is our priority following the attack."

"Why?"

"Seems your hunch was right after all, Sir. According to the Pentagon, Iran possesses a home grown nuclear capability, and Fordow is where it's located."

"So what are you not telling me?"

"Look around you! This billion dollar operation, should tell you all you need to know. We're close enough here to take on the base at Fordow directly. If we do not neutralise the threat within the next hours, they could actually bring about the Third World War."

"The nuking of Tehran already did that!"

"That's debatable!" shouted the Marine. "The nuking of Tehran probably wouldn't start anything at all by itself. Many actually think that the situation will not precipitate. Paradoxically, the nuking of Tehran may lead to lasting security."

"That's definitely not the way I see it!"

The Marine looked down from of the aircraft's open door as the aircraft banked in low and tight over the landing area. He was checking the landing zone as the aircraft came up onto final approach. "I know what you mean!" he shouted, "Either way, taking out Fordow within the next twelve hours is what we're going to do. Otherwise the little thing that happened yesterday over Tehran will destabilise the whole Middle East."

"And with it the world!"

"You got it. Hold on tight, we're coming in fast." The Marine looked at Maria who looked like she was about to throw up in her seat next to him. "Ma'am, hold on tight."

Maria nodded her acknowledgement. Then the Marine looked back at Ross, an enquiring look on his rugged face.

"By the way, Ross, what's this mission about?"

"You sure you don't know?"

"I sure don't! Must be pretty big though!"

"Whys that?"

"Hoffman's breaking everybody's balls with getting you there on time."

"And so he should. I'll tell you about it over a beer sometime soon!"

The pilot posed the helicopter gunship softly on the runway. Not bad, thought Ross, considering the speed of the approach. A modified F-16 Fighting Falcon, purposefully flown out for the mission, appeared out of the dingy Iranian night, its engines still hot.

***

If Hoffman had any doubts about the truth behind the authenticity of the tablets revealed to him in the Temple Church, they had been allayed by the events in Moscow and Tehran. There was now no doubt. The End Times were upon them. He understood what Yuval and the Russian President had in mind, for themselves and the planet. They wanted their Kingdom of Satan to rule over the world's peoples.

Global nuclear war was not their intention. They didn't need it, their dreams already being realised. The world had never been dirtier. Satan had already spread his power far and wide. The nuclear holocaust meted out to Tehran was nothing more than an expression of Yuval's opportunism, bringing hell straight to millions without affecting the final objective, of 'living with Satan'.

Chapter 54

Few times in Dmitry Chernyaev's life had he been quite so angry. He was seated in the back of his armoured limousine, en route to the Kremlin. The telephone conversation he had just had with Yuval, coupled with his clear recollections of their last meeting, had left him in little doubt; Yuval had deliberately detonated the bomb. What he was determined to find out was how much President Khodorov knew. "Take me through the Saviour Gate!" he snapped to his driver.

"Yes Sir!"

As the heavy car approached the imposing red bricked Saviour Tower, two security personnel dressed in thick black leather jackets gestured for it to stop.

Chernyaev lowered the passenger window. "What's the problem?" he fumed. "Don't you know who I am?"

"Yes, Sir, I do," replied the guard. "But the President has cancelled your meeting."

Chernyaev was about to get out of the vehicle when he heard his driver shouting behind him.

"Wait, Sir!"

His driver knew that you can't just treat the guys guarding the Kremlin walls like you can some ex-military 'face control' in a

Moscow nightclub on Saturday night. Besides, he had seen someone arriving breathless at the gate from inside, striding purposefully and directly towards them. Maybe there had been a change, and President Khodorov would be able to meet Chernyaev after all.

Despite the rushing of blood and the pumping of adrenaline into his veins, Chernyaev chose to wait. Maybe there was still hope.

The impeccably dressed, clean-shaven newcomer turned to approach the car, and drew a Beretta M9 pistol. He pointed it through the half opened window, and emptied the entire contents of its magazine into the body of Dmitry Chernyaev.

***

A strange feeling flowed through Maria's body as she stepped down from the helicopter gunship. She was mentally and physically drained from the hour long flight and her ears were buzzing and ringing and humming. Her body was telling her to puke, but her mind was gripped by the excitement of the continued roller-coaster ride which had begun when she had first set eyes on Anna.

Uniformed, powerful arms buffeted her like a rag doll as she stepped onto the tarmac. Swinging round she sought Ross who had become her rock. He was the only one she could depend on in the new world of espionage, terrorism and conflict that fate had landed her in.

"I'm right here!" said Ross, his voice calming as he descended the chopper's steel steps behind her. He had noticed her apprehension on the approach, and knew what she was going through. He remembered full well the rigours of his own training seven years previously. She was holding up pretty well. What had taken him months, she was achieving in days. Then there was the nuclear explosion, the incineration of millions of people. She had experienced it first hand, in front of her, across the desert and had not been totally uninvolved in its cause.

They passed from the windy airport runway into the air-conditioned luxury of a Toyota SUV. It transported them across the airfield at breakneck speed, the space-time coordinates of the fourth tablet were fast approaching. If she and Ross were going to be on time at the meeting, they had four hours. Four hours to get to an obscure mountain in Israel. Mount Megiddo.

They now knew the locations of the last three 'skirmishes' of the Battle of Armageddon, as she had now learned to call them. They had deciphered the tablets, and calculated the coordinates. Yuval had won the third skirmish, detonating the nuclear weapon over Tehran. The fourth skirmish was upon them. They knew its location, and now, since touchdown in the helicopter, had a clear idea of the access route.

The vehicle came to an abrupt halt, its tires screeching. A U.S. Air Force pilot pulled open the vehicle's sliding door, got in, and pulled it closed behind him with a loud bang.

"Sorry!" he apologized, pulling up a bulging, tattooed forearm to salute Ross and Maria who sat in the wide, leather upholstered space opposite. "My name is Flight Lieutenant Paul Bremmer and I have been instructed to fly you to your destination."

Ross said, "Lucky you."

"Joking aside, your flight suits are behind you. Please put them on."

The American agent and his Spanish partner spun around, reaching for the flight suits that were lying folded on the rear two seats of the vehicle.

"I should give you a pre-flight brief, but time is limited. We'll do it once we are airborne."

Chapter 55

"The director is on line one," said Hoffman's Personal Assistant.

Zak Hoffman had been expecting Tom Shepperton's call ever since he heard the news of the attack. The White House was taking emergency action. It was 09.30 Washington time, two hours after Tehran had been reduced to rubble.

"Line One," replied Hoffman.

Hoffman arrived at the conference table of Langley's biggest conference rooms, taking a seat while eyeing the top brass of the CIA seated around it.

Director Shepperton cleared his throat. "Gentlemen, all section heads are present so let's begin. As you know, a little over two hours ago an eighty kiloton nuke exploded over Tehran, causing the near instant deaths of an estimated one million people. The bomb was aboard a flight from Moscow, as was one of our agents. Lee Ross."

Shepperton stopped, looking straight at Hoffman.

Hoffman took the hint and the cue to speak saying, "It was an act of Russian aggression."

Hoffman was aware of how it might seem to have happened, but it was no secret that Ross was on the flight. They all had had a chance to read the briefing documents. Probably they hadn't had time. Probably the documents were sitting right there, on the table in front of them.

"Then how do you explain that Ross was on the flight?" asked Shepperton.

"He was on a sensitive mission, Sir."

"But of course!" said Shepperton. "And then can you categorically say that he had no part in this act?"

"Categorically," said Hoffman.

"And what of the present location of our asset and his status?"

"Continuing the mission, Sir. Status alive."

"Current nature of the mission?" asked Shepperton.

"The mission concerns the elimination of the risk to Israel posed by Iran's nuclear arsenal, which we believe to be intact and operational."

"Very well."

The director looked around the rest of those seated.

"Gentlemen, the President is waiting for an intelligence update. What is our proposed reaction to the current situation?"

A clean-shaven man in his early sixties with long, grey hair cleared his throat. "Sir, the response of our forces is to go to Defcon 2."

There was a pause.

A well dressed, burly man, this one in his mid-thirties went next. "Russia is still our principal threat. We know for a fact that they triggered the detonation of the nuclear weapon."

"How do we know it?" asked Shepperton.

"We intercepted the signal which triggered the bomb. It was relayed by a Russian military satellite above the Arabian Sea. Our sources indicate the signal originated in the Kremlin, Sir."

"Does Russia have aggressive intent?"

The burly man said, "Yes Sir, they do. Our analysts indicate Russia is planning a pre-emptive strike against the U.S."

"How do we know it?"

"From their behaviour, Sir, and their willingness to carry out the attack against Tehran. And . . . " he stopped suddenly.

"And what?" asked Shepperton.

The burly man was the head of CIA analytics, a thirty-five-year-old named Mike O'Connor. He was not sure of the necessity of telling all of the CIA's top brass the chilling Intel coming out of Moscow.

"For God's sake spit it out!" shouted Shepperton, as silent moments passed, losing his temper in a rare outburst.

The burly man said, "Sir, we have information indicating the change in Moscow's attitude is due to a new advisor to the Russian President."

Discussion engulfed the table.

"Agent O'Connor!" said Shepperton, "Please continue with your report!"

"The advisor in question is an Israeli by the name of Dr. Yuval Rozenkranz. It seems he . . . "

Again the agent stumbled verbally, unable, or merely unwilling, to continue.

Director Shepperton said, "Agent O' Connor. I will give you one last chance. You will continue with everything else you know about this Yuval Rozenkranz, or I will personally terminate your career out of gross insubordination. Do I make myself clear?"

Nodding his agreement, agent O'Connor continued, unperturbed by the threat, saying, "Incredible as it may sound, the new advisor, Yuval Rozenkranz, believes he is the False Prophet postulated to come to the realm of men at the beginning of the End Times. He arrived in Moscow on a flight from Eilat, though we do not know of his movements before that."

Further waves of hushed discussion rounded the table, but agent O'Connor was not finished.

"What is more, a much more dangerous development occurred when we found out . . . "

In a flash the director was on his feet, rounding the table to finish towering above agent O'Connor.

"You are fired! Leave this office at once!"

"Please, Director!" came cries of protest from the others in the room, most of whom had also got to their feet. "Give him one last chance!"

Calmer heads prevailed as everyone retook their seats, including Shepperton. "I will accept your request," he said sitting, "if agent O'Connor finishes his report without further hesitation."

All eyes fell back onto agent O' Connor. Calming frayed nerves, he looked around the table.

"It seems the threat from Russia is all the more severe, because the Russian President believes he is no other than the Antichrist!"

***

The meeting was over, and no sooner had Hoffman regained his office, when his mobile rang out, startling him. He was even more startled when he saw that the display indicated withheld identity of the caller. Frowning, the Deputy Director of Operations took the call. A heavily accented voice, powerful and straight talking came through the receiver, a voice from the past, but one whose identity was deeply grained in his psyche. "Hoffman?"

"Yes!"

"Key in code."

Holding the device carefully, Hoffman keyed in a six figure code to confirm his identity. It was not strictly necessary, the New Templar's Headquarters in Paris had for years now been using voice recognition software to ID caller identity. The six letter code was therefore, strictly speaking obsolete. Nevertheless, old ways die hard, even in the secretive world of the Templar. He was one of the four New Knights Templar sénéchaux, the principle guardians of the order's secrets.

"There has been a development. We need you to come to Paris immediately."

Hoffman listened to the line go dead, knowing very well that it would. And carefully, and thoughtfully he replaced the mobile back into the inside pocket of his dark blue tailored suit. He called his secretary, and told her to book the next available flight to Paris.

Chapter 56

Six hours into the flight, Hoffman sat back into his business class seat. He liked Air France, always choosing them for his flights across the Atlantic for Templar meetings, meetings which for him had fortunately become less and less frequent. Since its dissolution by Pope Clement in 1314, the Order had gone underground to some extent. With its organizational headquarters in France destroyed by Philip 'Le Bel' it lived on in Portugal and Scotland, countries whose leaders in many ways were not afraid of the consequences of defying the Pope's order, the papal bull as it was known. Of the two countries, it was Portugal which provided real continuity to the order however. Portugal's Tomar Castle set on a rocky bluff above a breath-taking panorama provided the order a real seat of power, one befitting the Order's proud past. Paris, however, even in the years following the Inquisition, continued to be the location of the order's secretive meetings, a tradition which had continued to the present.

A pretty, young and dark haired flight attendant appeared before Hoffman, entering his blurry vision, a half filled bottle of Champagne in one hand and a silver tray in the other.

"More Champagne Sir?" she asked, smiling broadly and dazzlingly.

"Why not?" replied Hoffman, placing his glass waveringly onto the silver tray.

"We will be preparing the cabin for landing in thirty minutes. I hope the flight has been enjoyable."

"Thirty minutes?" said Hoffman, surprised.

"Yes Sir!"

"These flights seem to be getting shorter. Or maybe it's just me that is getting drunker on them."

Hoffman's mind raced to the forthcoming meeting, fighting his way through the alcoholic fogginess, forcing concentration. He checked his watch, and moved it forward to Paris time. Then he thought about the meeting location, and how he would get to it. Taxi of course. As the Order's U.S. Master, his account was always bloated with cash. Their insistence to throw money at him had always paid off. He protected them with the full capacity of the most powerful intelligence gathering organization in the world.

***

Hoffman walked through Hotel George V to the corner of the lobby. A mixture of elegantly dressed women and men in their thirties and forties populated the bar. A group, thought Hoffman.

He spotted his contact. A middle aged man with a head of thick, shortly cropped grey hair, sat at a low table. Pierre Lacroix rose to meet him, a thin, forced smile on his face.

"Thank you, Zak!"

Hoffman was surprised by the comment. Such behaviour was not normal from France's Master of the Order. Something was wrong. "Have I ever reneged on your request for a meeting?"

"You have not, but I understand your work in the agency means that such requests might eventually constitute a conflict."

"Thank you for your understanding, Pierre."

"Please!" The French Grand Master gestured to a seat. "What would you like to drink?"

"A double whisky! It's been a long week."

"How do you take it?"

"Straight, on ice."

The Frenchman rose to attract the attention of one of the waiters who immediately approached. "Two double whiskies on ice!" He returned to his seat, his face stone cold. "Chernyaev is dead. I was contacted yesterday."

"I suspected as much," replied Hoffman, unmoved. "What happened?"

"He was assassinated."

"Do we know by whom?"

"That, we have yet to ascertain."

"How do we know he is dead?"

"As you know, our order has secret, diplomatic relations with four countries, Portugal, France, Scotland and Russia, apart that is from the Vatican and the Knights of Malta."

"Let me guess, Russia gave us the news!"

"Your intuition serves you well my friend," confirmed the French Master. "He was involved in a traffic accident last night in central Moscow, along with his driver and bodyguard."

"And I guess that in Moscow such accidents usually result in bullet wounds to the head?"

"Do you know for a fact that?"

"Pierre. I am deputy director of the CIA. Our man was gunned down just outside the Kremlin. There was nothing accidental about it."

"So what now?"

"We will have to call a meeting of the Council, to choose a new Grand Master."

"But such Councils have traditionally been held in Tomar Castle."

"We will accommodate our traditions."

"Where is our third member?" enquired the American, referring to the third of the three sénéchaux who had, by order of law, to be present at every meeting between sénéchaux members.

"Right there!"

Lacroix nodded towards a tall man striding towards them across the lobby dressed in heavy black coat, carrying a large leather briefcase. Antonio Bellisai was a quick tempered Italian and had spotted the two seated men and was making a beeline through one side of the group meeting.

"Sorry I'm late. The traffic!"

Hoffman said, "Glad you could make it, Tony!"

Antonio Bellisai, the Italian Master of the Order, sat down with the two other sénéchaux, and opened the leather briefcase. "I have something!"

"Tony" said the French Master. "Zak already knows about it. Chernyaev was shot in the head."

Bellisai looked up. "I wasn't referring to Chernyaev."

"What is it?" asked Hoffman, raising an eyebrow.

"It concerns the choosing of our next Grand Master. I have just got off the phone to Javier Siena in Barcelona."

"And?" probed Pierre Lacroix.

"Siena is inside Chernyaev's mansion in Barcelona and has just opened Chernyaev's safe, which is a matter of order protocol, you know."

"Go on," urged Hoffman.

"Chernyaev may have had a premonition of his death since inside the safe there was a single document. This document, as you know, was part of the same ancient document presented to you at Temple Church, London. Apparently, not only did the parchment taken by the Knights Templar to Ethiopia contain information concerning Anna Kuznetsova, it also described exactly certain events leading into the End Times."

"What?" exclaimed Hoffman and Lacroix in unison.

"Yes. Apparently, on the parchment now in Javier Siena's possession is written that during the start of the Great Tribulation, a Grand Master will be assassinated. A way into Solomon's Temple will allow members of the Order to penetrate. There their new leader will be revealed to them!"

"But that's impossible!" complained Hoffman. "All of us know that the Temple of Solomon was destroyed by the Babylonians."

"No," said Bellisai, simply. "The Temple of Solomon exists still, right under the Al Aqsa Mosque."

"Yes," chipped in Lacroix. "But it has been kept secret by the leaders of the city of Jerusalem all these years. They refused to let anyone into the area of the temple Mount, and rightly so . . . It would cause a riot, even a war. The second Intifada began in such a way."

Hoffman said, "So why will they let us in now? What has changed?"

"We do not know why, but we have faith. If God wants the secrets of the Temple to be defiled, he will show us the way."

Bellisai said, "All we know is that the Temple of Solomon exists still, and when the End Times begin, the next Grand Master of our great Order will be determined within its walls."

"How will we determine which of us three will become the Grand Master?" enquired Hoffman.

"The Gods have already decided it!" replied the Italian seneschal.

"How is that?"

"His name will be revealed to them, inscribed on a golden object on the stone altar in the Temple which used to hold the Ark!"

"Be revealed to them?" queried Hoffman. "It will be revealed to us you mean?"

"Zak," began the Italian seneschal. "Without seeing the document itself, I cannot tell you what it means."

"One thing however, is certain!" said the French seneschal. "It will be one of the three of us."

"You are right," said Hoffman. "It will be one of the three sénéchaux, that is, one of us. It is also imperative that the leadership of the order is determined as quickly as possible. Leaving our holy Order leaderless during what we all know is the beginning of the End Times is paramount to betraying every Templar who has ever walked the earth. The final battle between good and evil is about to begin."

"Or has already begun," said Pierre Lacroix. "First, we have to determine the originality of the document in Siena's possession. Then, we have to address the leadership issue."

"I concur," said the Italian seneschal. "Siena is at this very moment airborne, and will be arriving in Airport Charles De Gaulle within the hour. Gentlemen, time is limited. My car and driver are waiting outside."

Chapter 57

A vehicle was twisting its way up the mountain road towards the high pass where Anna had parked the Jeep. The vehicle was coming from the north.

Anna pronounced an obscenity in Russian. It was the second time she had been at the mountain in the Negev Desert. And the second time she had had to think about escaping from it. All she wanted to do was to stay there, be alone and not have anything more to do with the world of men. But the world of men would not let her go.

Time to take a decision. In a matter of seconds they would see her Wrangler Jeep.

She took off, revving the engine to its limits; first gear, second gear, third gear. Just like on the steep, stony track earlier. She only managed to go a few hundred meters before she lost it.

The Jeep flew off the road in one of the tight corners, landing on all four wheels on the steep rocks below the road. The ten meter drop gave the Jeep considerable momentum. Ten meters free-fall at 9.8 meters per second squared. It landed with its nose pointing straight into the gorge hundreds of meters below. In mid-flight Anna forced her foot onto the brake lever with everything she had. All four tires locked up on the firm, white limestone rock as the massive, dynamic weight of the vehicle came to bear. For an instant the Jeep slowed.

She saw her chance and took it, jumping, hitting the rocks hard, and whipping the breath straight out of her. She spun across a smooth boulder and careered headlong straight down a rocky incline coming to rest in the branches of an evergreen oak growing out from the side of a cave below. The Jeep disappeared over a rocky bluff, landing in the rocky gorge, exploding on impact.

The noise reverberated across the valley reaching the hillside opposite in seconds. Nine soldiers in three green Israeli Defense Force Toyota Land Cruisers rushed from their vehicles to the edge of the wide car park, clutching their rifles. Only they weren't Israeli soldiers. They were Iranian Special Forces, and they were on a mission.

"What happened?" said one officer to another. Another trained a pair of binoculars on the source of the thick black smoke which rose from the gorge 300 meters below.

"I missed it."

"A Jeep fell into the gorge," said one.

"I can see it, down there. Nothing left but twisted metal and burning tyre," said another.

"Was anyone inside?"

"If they were, they're history!"

Then the tenth soldier climbed out of the lead vehicle. He had been calling up a satellite link with the Iranian base at Fordow. Casually, he approached the edge of the car park where his team had congregated.

"What do you make of it?" asked President Khan of Iran, putting his own binoculars to his face covered in three day stubble.

"If there was anyone in the vehicle, they must be dead, Sir!"

"Good guess!"

Khan trained his binoculars on the slope between the burning wreck and the curve on the road 400 meters above. He searched for the point where its driver must have lost control.

A movement a third of the way down the rocky, boulder strewn slope caught his eye. Inside the mouth of a cave, on the flat limestone of its entrance there was a woman crouched next to the base of a group of evergreen trees. He increased the power of his lenses. Even from that distance Khan could see she was blonde, beautiful and injured, writhing in pain and clutching her stomach.

He took out a marble tablet from his pocket, the one given to him by Karim, at the airport, just before he left for Moscow. Karim had told him that he had received it at Alamut, at the place where the eagle had landed. During his 'Expedition of the Assassin', he had learned that at the site where the eagle had looked at him, there would be a message from Allah. So he had returned to the fortress of Alamut and he had found the tablet, lying there on the rock.

The inscriptions on the tablet provided for reconciliation between the faiths of Judaism, Christianity and Islam. At Tehran Airport, just before Karim boarded his Moscow bound flight, he had given it to him, saying, "Take this tablet to the Battle of Armageddon. You are the Mahdi, the twelfth Imam, and it is your destiny to save the second son of God when he arrives on Earth. The location for the Second Coming is Mount Megiddo, a cave below a road on its Eastern slope. On the day and time given on the reverse side of this tablet you will meet and protect the child and his mother, Anna Kuznetsova."

Khan flipped the tablet and read the time coordinates. He checked his watch, and marvelled at the power of the Ancients, of Allah, or of God, or whichever higher power had brought him to that site. With every passing second, his position in space and time brought him closer to that of the Second Coming written on the tablet of rock in his hands.

There was a movement on the other side of the valley, so he plastered his binoculars back to his rugged, weather beaten face. Black Hummer vehicles were coming into view on the road leading from the other side of the mountain, twisting up towards the high pass. He counted four as they climbed towards the curve directly above the cave where the injured woman lay. When they reached the curve, they stopped, doors flying open, well-armed troops with Kalashnikovs, and heavy machine guns swarming out like angry bees. "Russians!"

"Sir?" said the first officer.

"Men, we have a situation! Group One take your weapons from the vehicles. Group Two, listen up. I want you to identify the four Hummers on the road above the gorge."

"Yes Sir!"

"Anna Kuznetsova, our target, is one hundred meters below them. Drive around this road as close as you can to their position and then engage them with everything you've got."

"Yes Sir!"

"We will approach Anna's cave from here. God willing, we will rescue her and her child."

"Yes Sir."

"Group One, listen up: They have not seen us, so we have the advantage of surprise. Neither do they know the exact location of Anna. But I am guessing they know her approximate location. They, like us, also have her as their objective. The Russians, like us, know of the importance of Kuznetsova, and of her location. That is why they are here. We have to advance as near as we can to her before engaging them. They have the advantage of height. From here, we have to descend to the gorge, and then climb to the girl's position. Are we clear?"

"Yes Sir!"

"Good. Follow me!"

President Khan led his men swiftly down the barren hillside into the depths of the gorge.

The thick pungent smell of burning filled the air when they reached the bottom. The wreckage of the Jeep was not visible, obscured below a rocky bluff, but the powerful mountain up draughts carried its fumes to the men now contemplating the climb to the cave.

Khan was a seasoned rock climber who had climbed high altitude rock routes in the Alps. He led the way effortlessly up the sheer cliff which the river had cut a gorge of smooth limestone 30 meters high. When he reached the top, he secured the two ropes he had been trailing behind him.

As his men hauled themselves up to his position, the Iranian President looked up to the cave. Thirty minutes had passed since he had last seen the girl. He had hated having to leave her alone. It was a calculated risk. He hypothesised that the Russians Special Forces were unsure about who had been driving the Jeep. *If they knew that Anna had been the driver, they would have been all over the slope by now.*

Khan trained his binoculars on the hillside between him and the Russians. The cave was not in view, and neither was the road. Then he looked down the sheer cliff as his men climbed the ropes, and then he looked back at the cave. It was time to act. He threw his rifle over his shoulder, and started his run towards the cave.

The rest of the hillside soon came into view. He crouched behind an evergreen bush for breath, and to take stock. The cave was 100 meters above.

Near the cave, on the hillside above and to its right, two of the Russians were running down the stony hillside. They were close. Not 50 meters from the cave's entrance. Two more were further right, towards a sheer limestone cliff. *They still do not know where she is.*

Crouching, still hidden, the Iranian President trained his binoculars back on the cave. He could not see Anna.

Then he cast the binoculars back up the slope. The first Russian was closing fast.

President Khan flicked his Kalashnikov to single shots, off safety, and took careful aim. The Russian appeared in the telescopic crosshairs. The Iranian waited for the right moment, and squeezed.

The high velocity bullet pounded his head backwards, into the scree-slope, killing him instantly.

The gunshot echoed around the cliffs, followed quickly by Russian shouts. Khan flicked his rifle to automatic, opening fire on the hillside above and to the right of the cave. The Russians had the advantage. But he was closer to Anna.

The Sergeant of Group Two arrived breathless below him, at less than 50 meters, along with two riflemen.

"Give me cover!" shouted Khan.

Two Kalashnikovs and a single heavy machine gun opened fire below him as he sprang to his feet, sprinting to the cave.

***

"Anna!"

A head appeared from inside the cave. "How do you know my name?" shouted the blonde woman across the mountainside. "Who are you?"

"My name is Khan! You can trust me!"

Anna emerged from the cave, cradling a silent new-born child in her arms. She had not even known she was pregnant. Not until the Jeep crash when she had landed in the tree, thrown clear of the stricken vehicle. Only then had she gone into labour. She didn't understand, but neither did she care. She was simply happy.

"We have to get you out of here!" said Khan.

"Why?" responded Anna, smiling. "I feel so safe here! I don't want to go anywhere. Look!" She held up her child in her hand, the sound of gunfire drawing closer. "He is so brave!"

"That's because he doesn't know fear! Give him a while!"

A dark figure dressed in military fatigues appeared above the cave and reached for his pistol. Too late. Khan beat him to it. The Russian Special Forces officer fell heavily to the limestone pavement in front of the cave.

Khan turned back to Anna and her child just as the voice of one of his men came crackling through on the radio on his belt.

"Sir! You must fall back. I repeat. Fall back to our position."

He could guess why. The Russians had considerably more numbers and fire-power. The cave was fast becoming a death-trap.

The Sergeant from Two group appeared at the cave. "Sir, they are setting up a heavy machine gun above. We have to leave right now."

"How many are they?"

"More than three times our number."

They both turned to Anna, who understood that she was about to be captured yet again.

"Anna!" shouted President Khan. "You and your child are at risk. Please come with us!"

"No. I will not leave this cave!"

"Then let your son live!"

The Russian girl looked lovingly at the son she had always dreamed of. "Can you protect him?"

Khan answered, "I can and I will!"

"Then take him and leave me here!"

"I will leave my Sergeant to protect you as much as he can."

Anna kissed her son. "Go now!"

Chapter 58

The orders of Flight Lieutenant Paul Bremmer had been unequivocal; get his two passengers to Mount Megiddo by 13.20 that day. That meant he would have to take the modified F-16B three seater Fighting Falcon right to the edge of its operational envelope.

They flew at Mach 2 and 80,000ft for over an hour before Bremmer throttled back the engines from maximum power to fifty percent. The instruments indicated a return to safe operation levels, as if the aircraft was breathing a sigh of relief. Not many planes in the world could take such punishment. Brenner thought, *the engineers State-side sure did a good job modifying it.* Its engine and airframe had taken the sustained abuse without as much as a splutter.

Bremmer took his piercing grey eyes off the dark blue horizon for a second, glancing at his Breitling Aviator. 12.20am. If he wanted his passengers to have any chance of meeting their deadline, and stemming the planet's descent into anarchy, he had three minutes to get the plane on the deck.

He considered letting his two passengers know about the landing, about how the manoeuvre coming up differed from normal landings, but in the end decided against it. Valuable seconds would be lost. Seconds they didn't have. He now only hoped that the Stateside engineers had done an equally good job of hardening the plane's landing gear.

He put the aircraft into a dive without reducing power driving the speed straight back above Mach 2, cutting its altitude dramatically. Then he pulled back on the thrust control, applying pressure to the aircraft's ailerons. The 3G force of the dive kicked in, and so did the constriction of the flight suits, preventing him and his two passengers blacking out. The characteristic outline of Mount Megiddo registered in the dizzy minds of Ross and Maria as their heartbeat and adrenaline levels came down from the heights.

The F-16 banked sharply onto short final approach to the tiny airstrip. Bremmer dropped the landing gear and hit full flaps at the last moment, reducing the engine's power output and speed to absolute minimum. With the stall warning indicator screaming in his ears, he fought his instincts to increase thrust relying on the increased strength of the landing gear to counteract the force of impact.

The instant the fighter's rear wheels slammed onto the runway, Bremmer hit the entire breaking system with all he had. It appeared that they were not going to make it, the cliff which fell from at the end of the runway streaking closer and closer. At the last moment, on the last meter of the runway, the aircraft shuddered to a complete stop, its nose cone literally hanging over the cliff.

"Welcome to Mount Megiddo where the local time is 12.25!"

"We need a moment," said Ross.

"You don't have a moment! Not if you want all this to have been worth it!"

Ross and Maria extricated themselves from the straps and buckles of their seats, grabbing their rifles from their feet before jumping the two meters which separated them from the deck.

"It's 12.26," said Maria.

"That gives us forty minutes to get across to the mountain itself," said Ross looking around. "According to the map, its base is 4km to the east. That means if we run, we will make it."

"Here," shouted Bremmer from the cockpit above, throwing down a radio transmitter receiver. "If you need air support, call me."

Ross raised an eyebrow, "This thing is armed?"

"It has an M61 Vulcan cannon, plus a few little extras!"

"Will do!" said Maria. "Shall we Lee?"

Ross nodded, "Let's do it!" He pointed into the haze. "Mount Megiddo is that thing over there."

They set off at a fast jog, along the road from the deserted airfield directly to the base of the mountain.

***

Sergeant Mohamed Abdul kept the entire team of Russian Special Forces at bay for thirty minutes. The problem, he knew, was not a lack of courage, neither his, nor that of the Russian girl. The problem was lack of ammunition. His had tried to conserve it, allowing his attackers to come close to the cave before picking them off, one round at a time. In the last five minutes however his position had become untenable.

The outcome was inevitable. The Russians knew now what the cave held. That was obvious. Why else would Iranian Special Forces have chosen that particular side of Mount Megiddo for a fire fight? They knew the cave contained Anna Kuznetsova, the girl President Khodorov had ordered them to secure.

Sergeant Abdul checked the contents of the Kalashnikov's magazine for the last time. Then he turned to the place where he had instructed Anna to hide. The low boulder at the cave's entrance at least provided her cover. She looked back at him with a mixture of apprehension and admiration. The last time their eyes would meet.

Turning back to the point on the nearby hillside where he had last seen movement, he began his run. If there was a chance that he would be able to successfully liquidate the entire team, he would take it. Or he would die in the process. Either way, he knew what five dead colleagues meant in the world of combat. If they took him alive, the revenge on both him and the girl would be terrible. If he died, their demand for reprisal would be lessened.

Chapter 59

The U.S. military flight was passing over the island of Cyprus when the satellite transmission from Washington came through. The flight's dark, slim flight attendant strutted quickly down the narrow aisle to Hoffman's seat. "Sir. I have a communication link to the White House."

If there had ever been a time when Zak Hoffman had been truly happy to have had a decision over-ruled it was now. If he had had his own way, a business class Air France flight would have been more than sufficient for his flight from Paris to Tel Aviv. But Business class Air France flights are not equipped with the communications technology now at his disposal. Director Shepperton had insisted he continue to Israel aboard a military jet. "Zak Hoffman," he said, unsure of who exactly at the White House he would be speaking to.

"Deputy Director Hoffman?" It was a woman's voice.

"Yes, Ma'am," he replied. "Zak Hoffman."

"Please wait while I connect you to the President."

"Okay."

The unmistakably low voice of George Robertson, President of the United States came through as clear as a bell. "Zak Hoffman!"

"Mr President, it's a pleasure."

"Hoffman, as CIA Deputy Director of Operations I am calling you first, to give you the news. Approximately thirty minutes ago Director Tom Shepperton was assassinated outside his home."

The President's words echoed vaguely in the empty silence of the line, and Hoffman knew he should react. The President of the United States was not a man to be kept waiting on the end of a line. Despite the fleeting moment of clarity, to Hoffman's fertile mind came only confusion. While his mind was racing, the President was still talking.

"The reason I am calling, Hoffman, is more about understanding the agency's reaction to the on-going situation. I'm putting you in charge, at least for the moment, until a replacement is found. And as acting CIA head, you have great responsibilities. Even in peace-time those responsibilities are immense; responsibilities most men are unable to assume. In the current crisis, the pressures are greater still. I want to impress upon you the necessity to work together. The survival of our nation is at stake."

"You can count on me Mr President," responded Hoffman, without the slightest hesitation.

"I know I can," said the President. "Your file says it all. You mix ambition with power. Knowledge and ability seldom go hand in hand, especially in the military."

"Yes, Mr. President."

"On hearing the news of Shepperton's assassination, I exercised emergency powers and confirmed you as temporary head of the agency."

"I understand Mr President," replied Hoffman, solemnly. "Thank you."

"We need to work together, as a team, and teams are based on trust."

"Yes, Mr President."

"Please tell me, what exactly are the current agency objectives?"

Hoffman said, "We believe Iran is a clear and current threat to global security."

"Tehran has just been nuked! How can they still be a threat?"

"Very simply, Sir, because we believe they possess a nuclear capability and have clear intent to use it, even more so now that Tehran is destroyed. What is more, the President Khan of Iran, believes himself to be the Mahdi."

"The what?" uttered Robertson.

"The Mahdi, Sir. The redeemer of Islam prophesied to return to the world, during a period of time known as the Great Tribulations."

"Go on!" urged Robertson.

"Because he believes he will redeem Islam during the catastrophic events of the Great Tribulations, he will not be party to the usual restraints on the use of nuclear weapons."

"Meaning?"

"Meaning, he will purposefully seek to perpetuate the chaos by actively destabilising the Middle East in an attempt to bring about the End Times."

"End Times?" queried the President.

"Yes Sir. The End Times is the period of Christ's return to the realm of men, believed by the Abrahamic religions to be ushered in by the Great Tribulations."

"I see," replied Robertson, calmly. "And what exactly is the Agency's reaction?"

"Mr President. It is essential that we prevent Iran from striking at Israel using the nuclear weapons we believe them to possess, and to have at present operational. We have our best agents actively engaged in the field in an attempt to prevent such a scenario."

"You mean people like Lee Ross?"

"Yes, Mr President."

"Very well, Hoffman. I am putting my faith in your knowledge, ability and judgement. America depends on the success of your mission. If you need any extra executive power to pursue what you believe to be sources of danger, do not hesitate to contact me via this channel."

"Yes, Sir," said Hoffman.

"I will be on standby until the present crisis dissipates. Good luck. Out."

"Hoffman out."

Chapter 60

The mental map that had existed in Ross's mind ever since he had pored over his laptop computer at the space time coordinates of the final two skirmishes in the Battle of Armageddon told him that he and Maria still had some way to go. They had been running for twenty minutes along the hot asphalt of the road leading to Mount Megiddo and now the mountain itself reared up above them, capped by its ancient ruins. They stopped beside a low stone wall which crossed the dry landscape, intersecting perpendicularly with the road. Ross glanced at his watch. "We still have twenty minutes."

"Twenty minutes," repeated Maria. "But twenty minutes to get where?"

"To half way up the mountain!" responded Ross.

"I thought the location written in the fourth tablet was the summit of the mountain itself!"

"No," said Ross. "It's a cave on the eastern side. There opposite the deep valley towards the left. You see?"

"You mean that cave in the trees below what looks like a road which circles up towards the ruins on the summit?"

"Yes!" said Ross. "That's where the space time coordinates are located."

Suddenly, the noise of heavy cracks shattered the calm.

"Small arms fire!" exclaimed Ross, grabbing his binoculars. "It's coming from the mountain."

He focused the powerful lenses on the cave, seeing a fire-fight engulfing the entire hillside. "What the hell is the Russian military doing here?"

"Russians?" enquired Maria.

"Yep," said Ross, his gaze fixed on the backs of a group of Special Forces near the mouth of the cave.

Maria said, "Yuval must have had the same coordinates as us, and given them to Khodorov! Who are they firing at?"

"I can't see."

"What's our plan? If we approach the cave directly from here, they will not see us."

"No!" said Ross. "They will see us. Russian Special Forces would have someone protecting their rear and flanks from surprise attack. We have to use our brains, not only our balls."

Ross checked the rest of the hillside. The road beside which they crouched snaked up the mountain in a series of bends way to the right of the cave. On reaching the furthest point, roughly on a level with the cave and a kilometre to the right, it doubled back to pass above it. It was on the point of the turn that Ross now focussed his binoculars. The Russians had set up a roadblock. Three black Hummers. Two were blocking the mountain road as it began its long left leading stretch. The third was set back to the right on the axis hairpin bend.

"Bremmer, do you copy? Over."

"Loud and clear."

Ross pulled out the crude Israeli military map of Mount Megiddo, locating on it the hairpin on the mountain road. "The Russian's have a roadblock on the road, on the mountain itself. Do you copy? Over."

"Copy," said Bremmer, initiating the F-16's engine start sequence. "Give me the grid reference and targeting details, over."

"Target is at 40 minutes 9.5 seconds North, and 38 minutes 0.28 seconds East, just west of a hairpin bend in the mountain road. Target is two black Hummers blocking the road. Try not to hit a third Hummer on the apex of the bend. Do you copy? Over."

"Target at 40 minutes 9.5 seconds North, and 38 minutes 0.28 seconds East, two black Hummers. I should avoid a third Hummer on the apex of the curve. Check. Over."

"Affirmative. Ross out."

"Bremmer, out."

Flight Lieutenant Paul Bremmer increased the power output of the F-16 to fifty percent full and then released the aircraft's brakes. Seconds later the grey 'Falcon' rose into the clear blue sky, banking sharply right, the target coordinates locked into the on-board computer, his electronic targeting system identifying the target.

As the F-16 screeched above Ross and Maria, two Hummers appeared to Bremmer as 'locked on' by the targeting illumination of his visor. He fired a single ASM and pulled up, narrowly missing hitting the summit. The missile slammed into the Hummers destroying them in a blast which rocked the mountain. The F-16 went vertical before coming back to the deck ten kilometres to the south, approaching for a second run.

"Ross to Bremmer. Abort second run, repeat, abort second run. Over."

Bremmer took the F-16 vertical again, afterburners engaged, counter measures released, feeling the 4G hit deep. "Abort second run. Affirm."

"Second target, is the lone black Hummer further along the road, above a large black cave on the hillside. Do you copy over?"

"Second target is a black Hummer further along road, above a large cave on the hillside. Check. Over."

"Affirmative. Ross out!"

Approaching the mountain from the South at 500 knots, Bremmer acquired the target and locked onto it, firing a single ASM. Again he took the aircraft vertical. And again he fired counter-measures to protect himself.

And then a warning tone filled his helmet.

Two stinger missiles were in the air, gaining fast, tracking for the massive heat source generated by his after-burners. Bremmer extended the Falcon's vertical trajectory, pulling it into a powered dive. He couldn't yet see the lone Hummer he had noticed above the cave, but knew it was his only chance. With no time to spare on using the computer, Bremmer targeted the missile manually, releasing it as soon as the Hummer appeared in the targeting imagery of his visor. As the explosion of the missile and Hummer rocked the hill-side above the cave, he guided the F-16 into a manoeuvre he knew would test both him and his plane. He executed a maximum thrust, minimum radius loop, drawing the missiles behind him, bringing the heat source of the explosion of the Hummer in direct view of the stinger's guidance system. One stinger tracked into it, and exploded, but the second Stinger remained on his tail, closing fast.

Ross and Maria looked on in horror from their run toward the hairpin, as Bremmer took his aircraft vertical one last time on maximum power, maximum speed, maximum thrust. But he was powerless to shake the heat seeker. Catching up with its target, the sky broke into a huge explosion, ripping apart Bremmer and the F-16.

***

Ross and Maria ran on, soon reaching the hairpin bend. The lifeless, burnt remains of four Russians lay on the edge of the road, testimony to the violence of Bremmer's attack. Heaps of twisted, mangled metal, plastic and rubber lay across the road, still burning, filling the air with choking, acrid fumes.

"No survivors!" affirmed Ross, checking his watch while making for the third Hummer.

"How long do we have?" asked Maria.

"Ten minutes!"

"Ten minutes to get a kilometre up the mountain, and then to the cave, and to whatever is waiting for us there!"

"I'm pretty sure it's Anna who is at the cave," said Ross.

The two of them climbed into the one remaining Hummer. The one Ross had told Bremmer to spare in his attack. As Ross had envisioned, the lack of survivors meant that all of the roadblock's personnel had been adjacent to the explosion. Luckily for them, no one had remained in the third Hummer. And as he had hoped, a set of shiny keys had been left, hanging from its ignition.

"Check the back," shouted Ross, firing up the 3 litre engine. "Maybe they left some goodies for us!"

Maria climbed over the seats into the rear as Ross hit the gas, skirting the remains of the roadblock at full throttle.

"What's back there?"

"One big gun, which I'm guessing is an anti-aircraft machine gun, and Kalashnikovs."

"Throw over the anti-aircraft and two Kalashnikovs and get back here! Things are about to get hot!"

The hillside with the cave came into view as the Hummer swerved around the last corner, its high revving engine labouring to keep up the speed. Despite the Hummer's screeching tires, the staccato sounds of gunfire reached the ears of Ross and Maria loud and clear.

"Three minutes!" informed Maria. Ross pulled the vehicle to a halt directly above the cave, next to the remains of the last Hummer targeted by Bremmer.

"If it's the Russians that have Anna at the cave, we might be able to get close enough to help her," said Ross.

"But how?" countered Maria. "They're in a fire-fight with forces on the on the opposite hillside. They are in a well-armed defensive position."

"We will approach as close as possible, from the rear, engaging them with everything we've got," said Ross, man-handling the Dshk anti-aircraft gun. "Go!"

They bounded down the scree and boulders making it almost halfway to the cave before they came under fire. One of the Russians had spotted them, a big, muscular man in his twenties. He spun round, dragging a heavy Russian Dshk machine gun around with him as if it was a plastic toy. Ross dived for cover behind a large boulder, bullets ricocheting around him, pulverised rock chips spurting into the air. Maria had dived for the deck too, coming to rest in a natural hollow in the scree slope, cowering behind a large boulder which protected her from the onslaught of high calibre rounds.

When the burst of bullets from below the cave ceased, she lifted her head, already in a position to see into the cave. Less than a minute remained before the space-time coordinates written by the Ancients on the fourth stone tablet coincided with hers. Whatever battle she had been destined to be part of was to be fought then and there, between her and the cave fifty meters in front of her. *Within the next minute! It was now or never!*

She took the Kalashnikov in her hands, and sprang to her feet, sprinting headlong towards the cave. Watching her move filled Ross at the same time with admiration and horror. The Russian position was strong, extremely strong. The number of combatants deployed to protect Anna at the cave was at least five, probably more.

Ross deployed the Russian made Dshk machine gun against the Russians, bringing down an intense rain of armour piercing rounds which pulverised the rocks behind which they lay. Under the protection afforded by the onslaught, Maria managed, in the last seconds before the deadline, to get right up in front of the entrance of the cave.

There was Anna, alone, safe, sound, and standing just inside the lip of the cave. Maria had succeeded in reaching her! She had succeeded in defying the dark forces which intended to hijack Anna for their own selfish ends.

But before she could pronounce a single word to Anna, or run and embrace her, something made Maria spin around, or try to.

Two things had happened which made spinning round impossible. A bright flash filled the sky, dazzling her, and rooting her to the spot, and a sharp pain spread throughout her torso. She found herself on her knees, in shock from the bullet fired at close range by a Russian Special Forces officer, and in shock from seeing the amazing light.

A fireball was shooting through the atmosphere above the Western horizon in the direction of Tel Aviv. Two Russian Special Forces officers appeared at the mouth of the cave, silhouetted against the light of the explosion, their weapons trained on her as her life became a silent, frame by frame slow motion enactment during which her consciousness slowly faded. With her eyes fixed on the mushrooming nuclear explosion, her body fell lifeless onto the smooth limestone floor of the cave.

Chapter 61

The pilots of the United States Special Operations Gulfstream V, 29,000 feet above the Eastern Mediterranean and a hundred kilometres short of the Israeli coast, had a bird's eye view of the 20 kiloton air-blast detonation 500 meters above Tel Aviv. They took the aircraft left, towards Haifa.

"I advise you to abort this mission, Sir," said Flight Commander Roberts to Hoffman as he arrived in the cockpit. "If this is the Iranians, there is a high chance they will nuke Jerusalem and Haifa as well."

"Negative, Commander," countered Hoffman. "Continue to Jerusalem as per your flight plan."

"Yes Sir!"

Hoffman went back through the cabin, the flight engineer following him closely, a telephone in his hand.

"Call for you from the White House, Sir."

"Thank you," said Hoffman, taking the phone.

"Hoffman here!"

President Robertson's voice crackled through the line. "Hoffman. You are approaching Israeli airspace right? Thank God you're all okay."

"Thank you Sir. It seems the Gods are on our side!"

"For the moment, at least!" said President Robertson. "It looks like your hunch was right, Hoffman."

"Unfortunately, yes, Mr President."

"What's the CIA's reaction to the crisis?"

"Sir, our priority is preventing Israel from resorting to a nuclear response. Such preoccupations will be spelt out when I meet with the Israeli defense minister on my arrival."

"I have just got off the phone to the Israeli Prime Minister who has personally assured me they will not respond to the attack."

"That's good Sir," said Hoffman. "But it won't last. They will respond, and soon. No country can take such punishment without responding, least of all Israel. I will report back to you this evening, Israel time."

"Very well, Robertson out."

Hoffman heard the line go dead, his mind already racing to the future. How the hell was he going to arrange the meeting in the Al Aqsa Mosque now that Tel Aviv had been nuked? The two other sénéchaux, both present on the flight, would not be allowed to be present at his meeting with Israel's political leaders. However, the Mayor of Jerusalem, the Israeli Master of the Order, would also be present at the forthcoming meeting of political leaders. He would be able to accommodate them in the evening. The other two sénéchaux had already informed him of their assent to the meeting. The Mayor, they had told him, knew of the Templar legend, that of the last Templar Grand Master being inaugurated in the actual Solomon's Temple.

"Gentlemen," began Hoffman, as he moved to the rear of the Gulfstream to brief the other two sénéchaux. "We will be landing in around thirty minutes in Jerusalem."

"No!" exclaimed Pierre Lacroix, horrified. "You've got to be kidding! What about the radiation?"

"And the pandemonium that must be awaiting us in Jerusalem?" added Bellisai.

"You need not worry about that!" said Hoffman. "Jerusalem will indeed be in tumult, but we will be provided with a security detail. They will be greeting us when we touch down. You will wait under their protection while I meet with Israel's political leaders. God willing, we will find a way to access the Al Aqsa Mosque, and the secrets that lie beneath."

"Take your seats and strap in," came the voice of the captain over the aircraft's communication systems. "We will touch down in ten minutes."

***

Lieutenant Colonel Lee Ross approached the last functional Hummer on the road above the cave as the last of the five Russian Army MI-25 helicopter gunships disappeared behind the mountain, flying north, towards Tiberius. They had laid down concentrated fire on both him and the Iranians before evacuating the Russian Special Forces in the vicinity of the cave.

Ross and the Iranians had been out-gunned by the Russians, and powerless to prevent Anna Kuznetsova being taken back by Khodorov.

Ross expected the three litre diesel hunk under the Hummer's bonnet to burst into life as soon as he twisted the silver set of keys that dangled from the ignition. It didn't.

"It's dead!" shouted the Iranian soldier who had struggled to keep up with him up the scree slope, and now stood sweating, and panting, and suffering. The Iranian pointed to bullet holes in the bonnet. "It took fire!"

Ross needed an alternative, and quick if he was going to be present at the fifth and final skirmish of the Battle of Armageddon, that inscribed on the fifth marble tablet tucked into the pocket of his USAF flight suit.

"Do you have a vehicle?" shouted Ross.

The Iranian smiled. "We have a helicopter!"

Chapter 62

Al Aqsa. In Arabic, the name means The Furthest, and it refers to the destination of Mohammed's Night Flight from Mecca in 620AD. It is the second most sacred place for Muslims after Mecca.

Though still technically off limits due to its religious status, the strike against Tel Aviv had created an atmosphere of impunity in post-nuclear Jerusalem, and the last thing Israel's political leaders cared about was upsetting the religious sensitivities of its immediate Arab neighbours.

Four hours had passed since Israel's Ground Zero. Four hours since an 'atomic' anarchy had gripped the country. The wind had taken most of the radiation cloud out to sea, but that was not going to last. Night was falling and the wind was forecasted to swing back onshore.

A military convoy, a mix of armoured personnel carriers and Mercedes limousines, snaked up Temple Mount. At the heart of the convoy, rode Hoffman, deep in thought.

"We are arriving at the Al Aqsa Mosque," notified the chauffeur of the armoured limousine.

Scores of IDF soldiers made light work of securing the area. They cajoled the crowds to one side by brute force. In a matter of minutes, the entire square was secure.

Running across to the two lead Mercedes, two IDF Army officers gave the thumbs up.

"Okay Gentlemen," said Hoffman, in the front of the second Mercedes. He twisted round in his seat. "Let's do it!"

No air of urgency from the two other sénéchaux, sat in the back seat.

"What's the matter Guys?"

"Under the present circumstances," began Bellisai. "We feel uncertain about entering such a location as Al Aqsa."

Lacroix added, "We just witnessed the fervour with which Arabs are reacting to the attack."

"Yes," concurred Bellisai. "Being caught in the confined space of whatever underground crypt or chamber lies beneath Al Aqsa does not grab us."

"Gentlemen," said Hoffman. "Nothing is sure in this brave New World that is fast becoming reality. We owe a duty to every Templar Master, indeed every Templar Knight who has ever walked this earth, for giving us the opportunity to be right here right now. We must grasp this opportunity to make the future of our planet better than the present. We face God's calling Gentleman. Our ancient Order needs a leader. We need to fight the Antichrist, whoever and wherever he is, and if the Israeli Master Templar considers it safe, I think we can trust him."

The Israeli Master Templar got out of the car ahead, making his way towards them. "Time, Gentlemen!"

Yitsak Mayer, the Order's Israeli Master was a man of considerable stature, despite his age, whose punishing daily fitness schedule endowed upon his large frame a toned musculature.

As the group of Templar Masters approached the doors of Al Aqsa, he called a halt. "Sénéchaux! This is an historic moment not only for our Order, but for the entire human race. The annex of Al Aqsa given to our Order by King Baldwin in 1119 has never been fully explored. In the last decade documents shedding light on this the Templars first headquarters have come into our possession. Their provenance has been rigorously tested, as has their date. They include copper scrolls from Quran and Ethiopia."

The three Templar sénéchaux walked through the opened doors of the great mosque catching the first glimpse of its opulence.

Mayer led the group to the southern wing of the building, thrusting a stapled set of photocopied documents into each of their hands. "The originals of these documents are in the depths of my personal safe. They talk not only of the location of the First Temple, the one we know as Temple of Solomon, but also of the identity of the last Grand Master, the one who will be revealed during the End Times."

They followed the Israeli Master through an annex of vaulted arches to a more massive, inner building. The three sénéchaux studied the stapled sheath of documents that the old man had given them. One was a plan, recently drawn and superimposed on that of the present Al Aqsa Mosque. It showed the location of the First Temple.

Mayer said, "We are now standing in the center of what used to be the Knights Templar's most sacred building, the North Eastern Annex."

The three sénéchaux looked around in silence. The building was a simple rectangle whose imposing stone walls were split by stone pillars and a low, vaulted ceiling. Yitsak Mayer broke their concentration, his words echoing off the walls and filling the space and the occasion with a grim solemnity. "According to the plans in your hands, the southern wall is not original."

Hushed whispers of exclamation passed the lips of the group.

"But the vaulted ceilings!" murmured Lacroix looking up. "They have perfect symmetry. How could they possibly . . . "

"Look again, Pierre. You are mistaken! The ceilings too are not original. Ask yourselves the following question: If you had decades of time to conceal a passageway in such an exquisite and ornate location, how would it best be achieved?"

"By creating a fake of equally exquisiteness!" said the Italian master.

"By creating a fake of even greater exquisiteness! The pillars of the southern wall are exact replicas of those on the northern one."

"And what we are looking at above?" asked Pierre Lacroix.

"The ceiling you see has been built underneath the original."

The men looked with renewed interest at the walls and ceiling, as if its secrets were assailable by sight alone.

"Unbelievable!" gasped Bellisai. "If a secret passageway to the First Temple did exist inside the southern wall, what better way to conceal it than by building a second wall against the first?"

"Quite," continued Mayer. "The Templars had until 1187 to protect their biggest secret, a period of sixty eight years. Notice the construction of the walls, built of colossal, highly chiselled sandstone blocks weighing many tonnes each, intricately interlocking. What we see here is reminiscent of the engineering of the ancient Etruscans of Italy. It's a parallel, my friends, which did not come about by happy chance. Many of the Knights Templar of the times, our ancient brethren, came from the Apennines of Italy, an area populated in antiquity by the Greek-like Etruscans. They chiselled the gigantic blocks before us, copying the Etruscans, so that they would fit intricately together countering a threat to their secret: earthquakes."

The Israeli had a point. The Al Aqsa Mosque had been destroyed on numerous occasions, both before and since the capture of Jerusalem by the Crusaders in 1099. No better method of protecting the secret of the North Eastern Annex could be imagined than building it using tight-fitting, interlocking and earthquake resistant Etruscan-like blocks.

Hoffman broke the silence. "Okay. For the moment you've convinced us of the plausibility of both the false wall and earthquake resistant 'Etruscan-block' thesis. But if the remains of the First Temple lie directly beneath us, led to by a tunnel inside these massive walls, how do you propose we proceed? After all, the southern wall, the original one, would be, if you were right, concealed behind a wall made of ten tonne, intricately assembled blocks. Ten tonne blocks which fit so tightly together that one could not insert a needle between them."

"Nothing, my friend, is as it appears," replied Mayer studying the documents. "Look, if you will, at the sheet numbered three, and then look at the wall. The Etruscans certainly knew how to create strength. The wall appears as an interlocking jigsaw puzzle. And just like every jigsaw puzzle there is a solution. The solution to this particular puzzle is now within our grasp. Sheet number three is a part of the ancient Hebrew scripts found in the Church of Saint George, hewn out of Ethiopia's rocky, monolithic landscape of Lalibela."

"This is meaningless!" exclaimed Hoffman.

"To those unschooled in ancient Hebrew," replied Mayer. "To me they say one thing."

"Which is?"

"That one of the blocks in that wall is different from the others."

"Different?" mocked Hoffman, scoffing at the Israeli's naivety. "Different how? Do you really think that if one had been different nine hundred years of scholars passing between these walls wouldn't have been sufficient to get to the bottom of it?"

"One characteristic of the human state is to turn to complicated answers before the simple ones are exhausted," retorted Mayer. "Wouldn't you agree?"

"We seldom notice things right under our noses," shrugged Lacroix, his face twisted.

"Precisely," continued Mayer. "Gentlemen, identify if you would, the most massive block in the wall."

The three sénéchaux looked up and down the surface of the wall, shaped and chiselled, impregnable.

"That one!" yelled Bellisai, pointing to a particularly huge block a third of the way up the wall, slightly to the right of its center. "That block is the biggest."

It was an immense sandstone block, six feet up at its base was at least a third bigger than most of the others. Apart from its size, four meters long and a meter high, there was nothing to single it out.

"So what now?" asked Hoffman, vexed.

"Simple!" said Mayer. "Through the application of...," he took another brief look at the Hebrew inscriptions in his hands, "a horse weight of lateral force."

"A horse weight of lateral force?" said Hoffman, contemptuously. "And then what?"

"It doesn't say!" replied Mayer.

Hoffman said, "How in hell's name are we going to get a horse weight of lateral force on that block?"

Mayer was not a man to waste time when he was close to achieving something he had set his heart on. For the exact same reason that he had managed to reach the dizzy heights of a leader of the Likud Party he now managed to cut through the red tape of getting a horse weight of lateral force on a block in Al Aqsa Mosque. He approached one of the two IDF officers present and explained the problem. In a matter of minutes a force of twenty soldiers were assembled. They constructed a wooden contraption capable of converting the weight of ten men sat on a wooden beam, laterally against the huge block.

When the wooden machine was finished and ready, the officer in charge of the platoon sized group conducted a test to assure that the construction was up to withstanding and converting the weight of ten men into the wall. "Take your positions, men. Ten of you sit on the beam, and ten support the sides of the contraption," he shouted, his cries echoing off the walls.

As they sat on the beam, their weight transferred to two diagonal legs abutting the massive block. Nothing happened. The block did not move a single millimetre.

"This is an absolute waste of time!" derided Hoffman. "Anyone have any more bright ideas?"

"Wait!" shouted Mayer. "Soldiers, you, you, and you, get on the beam!"

A general commotion hit the group of IDF personnel as the soldiers on the beam made way for the addition of three more to their number. As their additional weight applied through the contraption, quivering and shaking, a subterranean rumble became audible. All watched in amazement as the massive block began to move into the wall.

A low pitched but powerful report punctuated the distant echoes which rang and rumbled throughout the chamber. The massive fifteen tonne block of finely chiselled sandstone came to a halt, two meters back from the front of the wall. Where there had been a smooth, vertical expanse of stone, now opened a gaping, rectangular slot just right of center.

It was a passageway to a secret world, a world not seen for over nine hundred years. A secret the ancient Knights of their Order, the brethren of the four who stood there, had deemed worthy of building the wall that appeared before them.

Two ladders were found and propped against the bottom of the rectangular space left by the block.

"Who will go first?" said Bellisai, echoed by Lacroix.

"We are in Jerusalem," pronounced Hoffman, "Therefore I propose to let the Israeli Master of our Order to be the first."

Murmurs of agreement passed the lips of the little group hunched around the base of the ladder.

Mayer, torch in hand, ascended the ladder and shone a bright pencil beam of light into the narrow, half meter slot of darkness, illuminating its long hidden secret passageway.

"How far does it go back?" shouted Hoffman.

Mayer's muffled reply drifted down to the group. "Come and see for yourselves!"

Hoffman was second up the ladder, quicker and considerably more able. He shot into the horizontal slot like a letter into a post box, contorting himself, cupping his hands around his mouth to project his words backwards. "Come on guys! The identity of our Order's next Grand Master and its future direction awaits us?"

A flight of stairs cut through the inner fabric of the wall, a spiral, its massive blocks twisting and turning. Hoffman marvelled at the ability of the Templar masons, and at Mayer's speed of descent. *The fire of ambition burns brightly in the old man.*

He reached the bottom. A low, horizontal passageway, barely wider than a man, cut through the solid bedrock of the Temple Mount. It led in a compass bearing which he could only guess at. He stood still and switched off his light for a moment. He had been completely disoriented by the countless spirals which had led him to that place, at a loss to know in which direction he was facing. *Which way was north? Which way was south?*

There was no light, not even a faint, diffuse illumination. No sign of Mayer. *The man had not been hindered by any inward circumspection.* He hadn't lingered either, well-motivated for such an outwardly religious person.

The sounds of the descending feet reached Hoffman's ears from above, softened into murmurs by the walls.

Why hadn't Mayer waited for him and the others before continuing? He switched on his flash light and shone it along the length of the passageway, taking off in pursuit of Mayer. It went straight for fifty meters and then curved to the right. He heard voices. Up ahead, about two hundred meters, a dim, diffuse light reaching his eyes.

Who else had gained access to the Templar's secret? Who was Mayer speaking to? A vast subterranean chamber was opening up ahead, illuminated by a flickering light. He took out his Glock and entered.

"You don't need that!" said Mayer, smiling. "Put it down!"

Hoffman swung around, looking straight down the barrel of a Makarov pistol.

Despite his age and outward frailty, Mayer's aim was steady, professional looking. CIA Director Hoffman felt in no position to dictate terms.

"Put-the-Glock-down, if you ever want to walk again!" Mayer ordered, stressing every word as if each one carried similar weight of purpose, switching his aim to Hoffman's legs.

For Hoffman the voice and attitude of the man in front of him indicated he was absolutely capable of firing. "Okay!" He capitulated, his arms already held high. He stooped, laying his pistol carefully on the ground. "What the hell are you doing?"

"Shut up and move to the left."

The sounds of the other two sénéchaux were getting louder all the time. Hoffman turned his head slightly left, distracted, noticing how the darkness swallowed the light from the torches. The light reappeared on distant walls and on the very center of the chamber, where on a huge stone table a golden chalice appeared.

"Stop right there!" shrieked Mayer, as Lacroix emerged, followed by Bellisai.

Mayer moved further to his left, deeper into the space, towards the stone table at the center of the chamber.

"What's going on?" blurted Pierre Lacroix.

"Shut up, old man. and move to Hoffman."

"Old man?"

Mayer held up three plastic hand retainers, throwing them down on the floor of the chamber in front of the three sénéchaux.

"Put those on!"

"No!" announced Lacroix. "I will not do anything you ask. Shoot me if you want, but you can go to hell!"

Without warning Mayer switched the aim of his Makarov from Hoffman to the right foot of the French Master and fired. Screams of agony reverberated around the chamber, drowning out the echoes of the shot.

"Put them on! Do it now! Or do I need to make another example of my resolve?"

Hoffman and Bellisai moved forward, picking up the plastic handcuffs. Lacroix squirmed and writhed in a corner of the chamber next to the entrance to the passageway.

"We should treat him!" suggested Hoffman. "He will die of loss of blood for God's sake!"

"He's not going to die," said Mayer, coldly. "The blood will coagulate inside his shoe before he does that."

"You are crazy!" shouted Bellisai.

"You're right, I am. But I'm also capable of repeating what I just did, so just do as I say and no one else needs to get hurt."

"What do you want?" wailed Lacroix in spasms of agony.

"What do you want for yourself, Old Man?" replied Mayer. "To be the Last Templar Grand Master?"

Despite the pain which stabbed like a knife, Lacroix managed to cast a glance around the chamber.

"If it is written . . . "

"God has already decided it," said Hoffman, procuring a modicum of calm in an otherwise desperate situation. "Somewhere in the darkness of this subterranean place, is the name of one of us, waiting for over nine hundred years for this very day."

"But where?" said Bellisai. "And when we find the name, we find also salvation. With the Last Templar Grand Master identified, the Order's strength will return. He must be respected by each and every one of us present, including you, Yitsak Mayer!"

"Unfortunately for you three," said Mayer, with calm. "This will not be how we will proceed."

"What?" said Lacroix, attentive to Bellisai's plan. "How then will we proceed? If we do not attempt to find the identity of the Last Grand Master, why did we come to this God-forsaken place?"

"Oh, you are mistaken, Pierre," said Mayer. "We will indeed be finding the identity of the Last Grand Master. The myths of our

Order hold that it will be inscribed on a golden object located in this very chamber."

The eyes of those present fell on the low stone table at the center of the chamber and focused on the golden chalice.

"You mean that what we see there before us is the Holy Grail?"

Mayer walked slowly towards the center of the chamber. "Why else would our ancient Templar brethren go to the effort to build the wall we witnessed above, to construct a fortress capable of defending the secret through the ages? They wanted the Grail and its secret to remain hidden until the day of the explosion, the day which heralds the End Times, this very day."

For the first time in centuries human fingers wrapped around the most sacred object in Christianity.

The chalice weighed much more than Mayer thought possible. It was made of pure gold. He turned it seeing the Hebrew inscriptions. "With the nuclear explosion in the sky above Tel Aviv, such a day has finally arrived."

In silence, Mayer lifted the golden chalice, taking care to keep his gun pointing at the three sénéchaux cowering at the entrance to the passageway.

He read the first of many Hebrew inscriptions on its surface, the one at the chalice's very top.

***

He who will lead the order through the End Times is the Wolf-Man

***

"A Wolf Man?" cried Lacroix, incredulous. "Hoffman!"

"Wait a minute," shouted the Italian Master. "The Ancients were never vague! Wolf Man could not be the only indication of the next Grand Master. Hoffman might seriously look like a wolf, but he's a man like the rest of us."

"Unfortunately, for you, Tony," said Mayer, turning the golden vessel in the light, "I did not finish the inscription. The initials ZH also appear."

He turned to Hoffman. "Congratulations Zak! You are the last Grand Master of the Templar Knights."

"Excellent!" shouted Pierre Lacroix jubilantly. "His first act will be to order your arrest and execution!"

"Not so fast!" said Mayer. "The Knights Templar, the foot soldiers of Christ, have always been the sworn enemy of Satan. Without a Grand Master to lead them, they will be unable to continue to oppose him, to bring to Earth their so called Kingdom of Heaven."

"What are you saying?" shouted Bellisai. "That you are working now for the forces of darkness?"

"What I am saying," said Mayer, aiming his Glock at Hoffman's temple, "if I am saying anything, is that the last Grand Master is about to die."

The terror of death froze Hoffman, transfixing him to the spot as surely as if he had been turned to stone. And just as the certainty of what was about to befall him spread through him, he noticed a movement in the shadows.

There was a second passageway hidden in the cave's dingy recesses, and his eyes fell on the dimly illuminated figure of Lee Ross, who said simply, "Pull that trigger, Mayer, and you die."

Chapter 63

The straps of the heavy backpack cut into Karim Hosseini's shoulder blades as he walked along Indian Head Highway 210, Washington D.C. Two hours had passed since the female agent had dropped him off at Potomac Heights, four hours since he had landed on the coast of the United States.

"We can't get you closer than twenty kilometres," had announced the controller a stocky, muscular Arab man when they had shaken hands on the rocky shore.

"You mean I will have to carry it all the way from there? It weighs thirty kilograms!"

"That's exactly what you have to do. Unless you want all of your sacrifices to have been in vain."

The Arab indicated which path they were going to follow with an outstretched arm. "Your contact and transportation is waiting on the road to take you to the device. She will then drive you and the device as close as she can to Washington D.C. The rest is up to you."

"And what of my request to have a dagger placed under the President's pillow?"

"Oh yes," said the Arab, breathing heavily behind him as they climbed towards the road. "As far as I know, she managed to place it, but you will have to ask her to be sure about it."

"You mean the girl who will drive me to Washington is also our sleeper in the White House?"

"She sure is!"

***

Parked at the top of the rocky shore and illuminated by the moonlight was a black Japanese import, a tall female figure standing alongside.

"It's a pleasure to have met you Karim," said the Arab, outstretching his bare arm. "Good luck!"

When Karim had descended from the rocks above the road, the tall female drew close.

"My name is Susan," she pronounced, outstretching a hand in welcome.

"And the dagger?" asked Karim, accepting the handshake. "Is it in place?"

"Just as you requested," said the tall woman. "And I know that the President already found it. Let's hope he is as aware as me of its meaning."

"America's time has come," said Karim. "Take me to its heart!"

***

Mayer delayed a critical instant in reacting to Ross's ultimatum, so Ross responded instead. The 9mm bullet shattered the outstretched arm of the Templar's Israeli Master, ricocheting off the rough wall behind. Mayer came to rest in a heap on the floor of the chamber, screaming in agony, his body seized by wild tremors.

Despite the pain and convulsions Mayer managed to press a red button on the warning device thrust into his hand at the last moment by the head of the IDF security brief.

Ross jumped to the Israeli Master applying his foot to wounded arm, "How long do we have?"

"Three minutes," uttered Mayer, between spasms.

"Over here Buddy!" shouted Hoffman. "Cut these God damned bracelets."

"We have two minutes!"

"Where do you expect us to go?" screeched Hoffman, eyeing the golden chalice lying on the rocky floor next to where Mayer had fallen.

"Follow me!" shouted Ross headed for the hidden tunnel.

"But what about the other two?"

"Leave them!"

"Wait!"

Hoffman reached for the golden chalice.

"What are you doing?" shouted Ross at the entrance to the second tunnel. "We've got no time for sight- seeing!"

"Just a little unfinished business!"

As the sounds of soldiers running along the first tunnel became perceptible, the two agents slipped quietly into the darkness of the hidden tunnel.

***

They emerged on the slopes of the Mount of Olives. Half an hour earlier the tiny entrance to the passageway had been as concealed from humanity as it had since the time of Christ himself. And it would have remained hidden had its location not been inscribed on the fifth and last tablet of the set given to Ross by Maria.

The two Americans squeezed and contorted until they were out of the tiny cave entrance and past the huge block that Ross had had to move to gain access to the tunnel.

"This way," shouted Ross. "My transport is down there."

***

"Some transport!" said Hoffman stooping below the accelerating rotors of the Sikorsky UH-60 Black Hawk. "Since when did you have friends in the Israeli Army?"

"Iranian Army!"

The rotors achieved take off revolutions within seconds, the young pilot taking her airborne and swinging her around, unopposed, towards the west.

***

"Tell the pilot to fly to Kalandia," shouted Hoffman above the din of the engines.

"Right!" shouted back Ross. "It's to the north, right?"

"He'll know."

Ross shimmied into the cockpit as Hoffman extracted the golden chalice from his military fatigues.

"Is that really the Holy Grail?" shouted Ross, on his return from the cockpit.

"Why else would our ancient brethren have gone to such lengths to protect it?"

"Why else indeed?" said Ross. "The fifth tablet confirms it. I was brought here to protect it and you as soon as it was discovered."

"There are inscriptions," said Hoffman holding it up, before thrusting the golden chalice into Ross's hands indicating the second inscription from the top of the chalice. "What does this say?"

Ross traced the inscriptions onto his mobile phone and hit 'translate'.

***

Twenty hours later

The modified Gulfstream V was nearing the western coast of the Atlantic, its wings oscillating wildly as it hit strong turbulence. The buffeting had no effect on Ross who was curled up in a cosy corner of the executive jet's rear cabin. On the contrary, turbulence soothed him like a tonic, similar to the constant vibrations and chatter of a night train or the blowing of a gale. Welcome lullabies. Through them he felt a connection to the terrain, a connection to nature. And far below him the Atlantic had special meaning. When he was a teenager he lived on its coasts. He climbed its cliffs in the baking hot summer sun. And on stormy nights, he would climb to the top of the coast's windblown pine trees just to feel nature's full fury.

Hoffman on the other hand was sat in the forward part of the cabin, deep in thought. He had the remnants of a double whisky on ice in his hand, the remnants of the previous two double whiskies on his mind, and the remains of a bottle of Johnny Walker Black Label on the table in front of him. He wondered how Ross could sleep, now that they both knew the prophecy. In particular they both now knew the meanings of the second and third inscriptions on the vessel. After reading, and translating them, sleep was impossible. He hadn't been able to sleep a wink the whole flight, feeling every shudder of the aircraft's tortured journey through and above the wide Atlantic maelstrom that was churning the ocean kilometres below.

The prophecy was now known to two men on the planet, him and Ross. Hoffman marvelled at the power of the ancient Israelis, the Israelites, who had inscribed the golden goblet which lay in his black leather briefcase.

He took it out and placed it on the tray table. *How had they been capable, hundreds of years before, to know more about the present than we, who live in the present, know ourselves?* The answer was obvious. *They knew it because the world was subject to Determinism, every event being caused by preceding events. Physics*, thought Hoffman. *The billiard ball model of the Universe where every event, even the thought processes of human beings, are predetermined by cause and effect.* The Ancients had been capable of tapping into the deterministic fabric of the Universe. They were able to calculate its status, its mass and the trajectory of that mass on the arrow of time, predicting its future with absolute certainty. They knew everything that would happen in the future, a future whose terrible events were written on the object before him, vibrating and resonating next to the bottle of whisky.

Hoffman refilled his glass and savoured its contents, wishing that the liquid would bring some relief. It didn't.

The inscriptions on the golden chalice told many things. The second inscription was simpler than the third:

***

Until the End Times, the world will be ruled by cause and effect

Thereafter, it will be ruled by Free Will

***

That meant that until the End Times the Universe would be subject to *Determinism*. Nothing knew or earth shattering about that, just pure physics. The billiard ball model. But then what?

Then came the problem. It was a problem that had to be acted upon in the next hour, a problem spelled out by the third inscription on the golden goblet.

What did the end of *Determinism* mean? Did it mean that what the third inscription described could be avoided? Could it be that the Third World War it prophesised was not predetermined? If so then he and Ross had the power to do something about it. Perhaps such a scenario, a no holds barred nuclear war with Russia could be avoided. But they would have to be quick. They would have to have a meeting with the American President within the next hour.

With its wings shuddering violently, the aircraft passed over the Atlantic's western seaboard, jets throttling back, the high pitched wine transformed into a lowering, rasping hum. The intercom crackled into life, robbing Hoffman of further insights. "We just began our descent into Andrew Air Force Base, Gentlemen."

A tall, skinny hostess with long black hair appeared from nowhere carrying a tray replete with culinary offerings from the galley.

"Isn't it a bit late for that?" asked Hoffman, looking up from his whisky. "The pilot just informed us that we will be landing in ten minutes!"

"Oh, that!" exclaimed the pretty brunette, laughing. "Don't worry. You still have time."

The breakfast was continental; two hot croissants, butter, jam and orange juice. She poured black, steaming coffee into a paper cup. "Shall I wake your friend?"

Chapter 64

They touched down at Joint Base Andrews and taxied straight up to one of the two Boeing 747s parked on the apron.

The Gulfstream V was surrounded by heavily armed troops who checked every inch of the plane's exterior before swarming aboard.

"Are you Hoffman?" barked the leader of the group as soon as he entered the cabin. "Where's the other guy?"

"Your social skills are quite astounding!" snarled back Hoffman.

The SEALS officer brought up his Glock straight and steady to Hoffman's face. "Are you Hoffman?"

"Yes!"

"Where is Ross?"

Hoffman nodded towards the aircraft's rear.

The SEALS officer said, "Show me your ID!"

Controlling his urge to protest, Hoffman showed him his ID. "Are we cool?"

Holstering his side arm, the SEALs officer motioned to his men to go to the rear. "Get Ross! The President is waiting!"

***

Air Force One surprised Ross. It was just different to his expectations. He had heard the rumours, of course: luxury beyond the realms of one's imagination, spaces like five star hotel penthouses. He shook away the last remnants of sleep as the SEALs officer strode ahead of him down the aircraft's central passageway. Hoffman was right behind him.

The SEALs officer stopped at the open door to the presidential cabin, and knocked loudly on its polished hardwood surface.

"Yes!" came a low voice from within, softened by the sheer size of the room and by the quality of its furnishings.

"CIA Director Hoffman and Lieutenant Colonel Ross, Sir."

With a wave of the hand, the SEALs officer motioned Ross and the CIA Director to enter. They were met by the President of the United States. He was statuesque, a tall man with fair hair and a white complexion. He had an angular, square cut face and a strong jaw which looked like it had been shaped out of a block of stone. His blue eyes wore the kind of distant, glazed look which bore witness to a sleepless night, though his smile, broad and white was distinctly genuine. He said "I trust your night flight across the Atlantic allowed you to sleep."

"The situation demands it!" replied Hoffman, moving around Ross to be the first to grasp the President's hand. "Two cities nuked in the last twenty four hours! Millions incinerated alive."

President Robertson gestured to the area opposite his chaotic desk. There was an expanse of black leather sofas set deep into a semi-circular recess behind an Indonesian hardwood coffee table. "Coffee?"

As President Robertson laid down the silver coffee set onto the table, Hoffman caught himself thinking: *on any other day in my life, being served coffee by the President of The United States on Air Force One would be cause for some kind of personal celebration.* On the day following the nuking of two cities it seemed completely normal. A sense of overwhelming tension pervaded everyone and everything, especially their thoughts. All that was certain was that each of the three members knew that the future of billions of people was in their hands.

President Robertson poured the thick black liquid from the silver pot into three large mugs emblazoned with the logo of the President of the United States. The smell of fresh coffee filled the air and brought a modicum of normality and a moment for reflection.

"The coffee is a nice touch, I'd say," said Hoffman. "The world can wait!"

"But not for long," said Robertson. "What's this all about?" Now at last he had sat down, on the coffee table, in front of the two men looking at each in turn as if he was a father wondering how to begin a difficult conversation with his sons.

"Well, Mr President," said Hoffman, reaching for his briefcase and extracting the golden chalice. "It's because of this!"

President Robertson took the ancient golden vessel in his hand, in awe, caressing its fine, smooth lines. "This can't be . . . ?"

"The Holy Grail? Yes, Mr President, we believe it is. Sir, the object in your hands proclaims many things. Take a look for yourself. Take a look at the three inscriptions, and the translation in English."

Hoffman passed President Robertson a sheet of paper, a printout of the translation of the long Hebrew inscription.

"So long?" said the President, looking up.

"Yes Sir. Ancient Hebrew is more concise than modern English. Please, Sir. Read it. And take your time!"

After reading it, the President flared up. "Why didn't you communicate this to me as soon as you got it?"

"Because they are already in control of Israel," butted in Ross. "They would have intercepted the communication from our Gulfstream V, precipitating the attack. I am in agreement with Hoffman on this. This had to remain secret."

"The Russians are going to attack!" Robertson reached behind Ross's head, to the communication link with Air Force One's flight deck, hastily pulling it from the wall.

"Yes, Mr President," came the voice of the aircraft's captain.

"Captain, get this aircraft airborne immediately."

"You got it, Mr President."

The sound of the aircraft's four huge Rolls Royce engines throttling up could be heard as much as felt through the fabric of the plane. The President turned to Hoffman. "But how can we be sure that this cup, this Holy Grail or whatever the hell it is, tells the truth?"

"Firstly, Sir, because it was written over two thousand years ago. We found it hours ago in a place where it had been hidden since antiquity. Look at what the Ancients knew millennia ago. They knew of the nuking of Tehran and Tel Aviv. Inscribed right here." Hoffman pointed to the translation of the inscriptions. "And they knew I would find it." He pointed to his initials written on its base. "If they knew such things, they must have had access to the very deterministic fabric of the Universe. At least until the End Times began."

President Robertson read the translation of the third inscription.

***

Russia will attack Washington DC at the start of the End Times

Less than one day after the destruction of Tehran and Israel

***

Hoffman nodded. "Yes, but they don't stop there. They proclaim that the deterministic nature of the universe terminates once the End Times begin. Look here."

Hoffman indicated the first inscription, saying, "It proclaims that God himself made the universe this way. God wanted men to fight for the Kingdom of Heaven at least once in the history of mankind. The object in your hand proclaims that once the End Times are in progress, the Universe will become ruled by Free Will. That moment is approaching, if not already begun. We have now to make the future good. We have to fight the forces of darkness right here, right now Mr President."

The aircraft was taxiing at frightening speed towards the holding point just before the runway, where its pilot did not intend to hold.

"Those damned Russians!" said the President. "I always knew there was something about that man., something evil, devilish. And now, it seems, he is the very Antichrist himself. Complete with the False Prophet as adviser."

An ageing, uniformed officer rushed into the office, oblivious to protocol. Hoffman and Ross recognised him as Chairman of the Joint Chiefs of Staff, General Bruce Peters. He blurted, "Why are we taxiing? And why was I not informed?"

"Take a seat General," said the President calmly.

"But I . . . "

"General, take a seat! I'll fill you in on take-off."

"Take off?"

"You got it!"

"Take off to where?"

His demands for knowledge were met only by a crackling of the intercom as the Captain calmly advised them to take their seats. The modified four jets were throttling up as the aircraft passed the holding point and swung onto the runway, accelerating towards maximum revolutions, pressing the passengers back into their seats.

Shortly after Air Force One became airborne, banking sharply towards the Atlantic coast, Karim Hosseini succeeded in martyrdom, the mission entrusted to him by the Eagle of Alamut carried out to perfection.

Chapter 65

A blinding flash of incredible intensity centred on the White House penetrated the gloom of the dimly lit presidential cabin, bathing it in its sinister light.

"Don't look at it!" bellowed Hoffman.

Speechless seconds passed in which each man dealt with the unthinkable. How to say anything in the seconds when hundreds of thousands of living souls were being incinerated?

The first officer steered Air Force One away from the fireball, reducing the steepness of the climb, accelerating, putting crucial distance between it and the expanding fireball which was engulfing Washington below. Even he was not sure the aircraft would make it. Air Force One was hardened to the electromagnetic pulse which accompanies a nuclear detonation, the pulse of energy which would have already downed it had it been an ordinary flight. The blast from the explosion, which was streaking towards them, however, was a different beast altogether.

Ross looked at his watch, notifying the men that twenty seconds had passed since the detonation. "It will be safe to look at it now."

But then the blast hit, a wave of energy which tore through the plane. A second passed and it continued to fly.

"Gentlemen, your Captain speaking. Please remain with your seatbelts firmly fastened."

"And I thought the Air Force didn't possess a sense of humour," quipped the President. He turned to the Chairman of the Joint Chiefs. "Didn't you once tell me that, General?" He reached once again for the intercom, saying, "Fine flying, Son!"

"Thank your First Officer!" said the Captain. "He flew it!"

"I will, Sir, later."

"Mr President?"

"Captain, make our destination Area 51."

"Yes, Mr President."

"Area 51?" said Hoffman, doing his best to stay in control of his emotions. "Might I ask why?"

"Director Hoffman. If you are correct about the inscription, then this country is under a pre-emptive attack. Who knows what will happen in the next hour. We will fight back against the aggressor from the most secure location we have. Area 51!"

The General regained some composure. "Mr President! Might I hazard a suggestion?"

"Go ahead, General."

"Cheyanne Mountain would be a better choice. It's located under a mountain!"

"Just tell me, General Peters, which of the two has the best missile defense against Russian ICBMs?"

"Area 51."

"There's my answer, thank you General."

The President turned to Ross. No words were necessary for them to understand that he was searching for help.

"That would seem like the best option!" advised Ross. "Even if the Russians are not behind the nuking of Washington, they will feel compelled to follow this with a pre-emptive strike, unsure of how we will react."

An Air Force officer appeared at the door, a grim look written on his grey, ashen face. "Mr President, we have just received warning that a number of incoming SLBMs, have been identified off the U.S. Eastern seaboard. We have yet to ascertain their targets, but it would appear that our Eastern seaboard cities are under attack!"

Hoffman had moved towards the window to see exactly what had become of Washington. As he looked down on the destruction of the city, further flashes, which came from nowhere and everywhere simultaneously, hit his eyes. He opened his mouth to speak, before his thoughts were fully formed. No words came out.

Ross said, "The Russians are launching a pre-emptive strike, Mr President. It's called a countervalue strike, Sir, against our population centres. The only option left open to us is a full scale retaliatory strike, to hit them with everything we have! Their control centers. Their major cities. The lot."

Hoffman had his own view of what he had just seen. "Did you see that?"

"See what?" said General Peters. "You mean the destruction of the city? I'll wait for the report!"

"No, no, no! I just witnessed further nuclear explosions, high above us! In space!"

"What?" exclaimed Peters, bewildered, clamouring to the nearest window.

"It could be EMP," suggested Ross.

"What?" said President Robertson.

"The Russians knew the decapitation strike against the Pentagon and the White House was going to take place. So they prepared for the simultaneous detonation of satellite based fusion bombs above the United States."

"Electro-Magnetic Pulse!" said Robertson. "They're disabling our capability to retaliate."

"Yes, Mr President," confirmed Ross dryly.

"Full scale nuclear war?"

"Yes, Mr President."

President Robertson turned to General Peters. "I want a full update of the situation, before I make a decision."

"You will have it," said the General, pulling a communication link from the wall.

"Command and Control Air Force One," came through a voice on voice active, so that everyone present could hear the conversation.

"This is General Peters. I need the latest assessment of the threat. Right now!"

There was a pause of twenty seconds before the voice returned. "NORAD reports multiple Russian SLBM launches targeted at our Minuteman ICBM silos in Wyoming, Montana and North Dakota, Sir, from Russian submarines off our Western and Eastern coasts."

"Damn it!" exclaimed the President. "X-ray pin-down!"

X-ray pin-down. The Russians had launched a barrage of submarine launched ballistic missiles on depressed trajectory flight paths that would not only be extremely difficult to intercept, their reduced payloads of fuel meant they would reach their targets in minutes.

"Yes, Mr President," continued the voice on voice active. "Expected time to impact four minutes. We have also detected multiple Russian ICBMs targeting the same Minuteman hardened ICBM launching sites. They were launched from Russia's Strategic Nuclear Forces inside Russia. That's to say a counterforce strike, one targeting our launch sites, coming in over the Arctic, Sir. Expected time to impact twenty minutes."

"So they are not launching against our cities?"

"No Sir. But the fallout from 15 megaton ground blasts in the Great Plains would be enormous."

"They are trying to decapitate our retaliatory capability with a SLBM onslaught backing it up with a major ICBM pre-emptive strike!" fumed the President.

"Well, technically speaking Sir, the decapitating strike has already taken place, committed by whoever was behind the ground blast in Washington."

"Is there any possibility that what we are seeing is a mistake?" said the President, turning to the Chairman of the Joint Chiefs. "An accident?"

"An accident?" General Peters laughed openly. "No Mr President."

"Launch a full retaliatory strike," screeched President Robertson into the communication link. "Get our ICBMs and SLBMs in the air immediately. OPLAN 8011!"

The Chairman of the Joint Chiefs looked white as a sheet. "A countervalue strike?" he said, horrified. OPLAN 8011 referred to a massive nuclear strike against Russia's main areas of population. And one the Russians would reciprocate with.

"Just do it!" shouted the President.

"You do understand that launching this kind of strike would have the effect of encouraging the Russians to launch a countervalue strike of their own, against our major cities?"

"Yes, General, I do!"

Air Force One climbed to its ceiling of 55,000 feet, considerably higher than the normal operational limits of the Boeing 747. The aircraft had many modifications, not least the hardening of its electronics against the huge electromagnetic energies produced during the initial stages of thermonuclear explosions. The consequences of the massive fusion explosions which shook outer space hundreds of kilometres above the Great Plains were now in the process of being visited, not only upon those operating vchicles on the ground, but also in the skies. The pilots of Air Force One could only watch and listen as they witnessed the fate of scores of pilots, whose aircraft were plummeting to their fates. X-ray pin-down! The Russians, by detonating a series of weapons in outer space, were preventing a U.S. response.

"Already their ICBMs are in the air. How do we know they are targeting our Minuteman ICBMs? Tell me that!"

"We do know it, Mr President. And they would know we know it. Theirs is a counterforce strike, Sir, preceded by X-Ray pin-down. They are giving us the chance to choose between losing and surviving, or losing and dying."

"You seem to be forgetting the fact that if we don't launch, America will cease to exist anyway. If we lose, then the Russians would invade and defeat us in a conventional war. On whose side are you on anyway, General?"

"On the side of rationality and logic informed by an instinct to survive. We face a choice, Mr President. A countervalue strike will encourage Khodorov to launch at our cities."

"So what do exactly do you recommend we do General?"

"Launch a counterforce second strike, keeping significant capability in reserve just in case they do indeed launch a countervalue strike."

"Do it!"

"Yes Sir!"

As General Peters hurriedly departed from the presidential cabin in the direction of the aircraft's control room, the two CIA agents and the President rushed to the cabin's windows to gain insight into exactly what X-ray pin-down really meant. Huge flashes from multiple hydrogen bombs were visible right across the sky. It was incredibly beautiful, and yet profoundly disturbing. It was a nuclear onslaught high above continental America. Its huge energy pulses were preventing the U.S. from making a retaliatory strike. The time to impact of the ICBM's, Russia's counterforce strike, targeting the US's Minuteman hardened missile silos with ground impacts of huge 1.2 mega-tonne devices was getting closer. America was being pinned down, held down for a real pummelling, helpless to launch a counter attack from continental U.S.A.

"They have the upper hand!" said Hoffman.

"They sure do," replied the President, his voice laced with melancholic regret. He thought: *That they should do it on my watch!* "They may have won the opening round, but we will win the war!"

"How can we be so sure?" asked Ross.

"Because we are American!"

Hoffman thought: *Your confidence is touching, Mr President.*

An Air Force officer appeared at the door. "Mr President, Gentlemen!"

The President walked towards him. "Make your report!"

"We have launched multiple submarine SLBMs against their intercontinental ICBM launch silos keeping a large capability in reserve, but . . . "

"For God's sake spit it out soldier!"

"It seems we are as yet unable to launch any of our land based ICBMs against Russia."

"X-Ray pin-down?"

"Yes Sir," replied the young officer.

"I knew it!" cursed the President. "How long will they be able to maintain their blanket?"

"We estimate that unless some of the incoming ICBMs are tasked with it, the X-Ray pin-down will be over in a matter of minutes."

"And what then?"

"After a few minutes we will be able to launch our LGM 30 Minuteman in a counterforce ICBM strike against their missile silos, Sir. But . . . "

"But what?" asked the President.

"The first of their ICBMs is due to impact the Great Plains in the next five minutes. Depending on the accuracy of their attack, the window for the launch of our ICBMs will be very narrow. It's going to be tight, Sir."

"And what will happen if we can't retaliate using our land based missiles?"

"Then our attack will be limited to our submarine launched ballistic missiles."

"What about our strategic bombers?"

"They're kept in reserve, Sir."

"And if we felt compelled to use them? Which bases can we rely on to deliver?"

"We could use Thule Air Force Base, Greenland, and Kunsan and Osan Air Force Bases, Korea, Sir. All are battle hardened and ready to go at short notice Mr President."

"Get me an update from NORAD! Now! I want to know what we are up against."

"I'm all over it."

The young officer saluted and hurried out of the presidential cabin in the direction of the aircraft's control center. President Robertson made his way back to the window just as another flash illuminated the distant, dark blue horizon. Neither he nor Ross nor Hoffman could see it. But without a doubt it came from the West, the same direction the huge aircraft was now flying in.

The President approached the place where Hoffman and Ross were crouching, their faces pinned to the windows in efforts to gain whatever information they could. "Are they still keeping us pinned down?"

"They are!" replied Hoffman. "We can't launch against them until a few minutes after the last pulse of EMP hits the Great Plains. What's the latest from NORAD?"

"Continuing detonations above our Minuteman silos. Russian ICBMs still incoming over the Pole. ETA is a matter of minutes. It doesn't look good."

"And what about our response?" asked Ross looking up at President Robertson.

"We're launching a counterforce second strike using our submarine SLBMs."

"Not Massive Retaliation?" asked Hoffman, a confused look written on his face.

"If we do that we will be committing suicide," informed the President. "They're launching against our ICBMs, not against our cities."

"Rationality dictates we would launch a massive retaliatory attack," said Hoffman. "Why would the Russians expect otherwise?"

"Why is neither here nor there, Mr Hoffman," said the President. "Rationality dictates that they should have launched a massive countervalue attack along with the counterforce strike, taking out our major cities as well as our ICBM launch silos. They did not. And we have not launched against their cities. That too is rational, Mr Hoffman!"

The young Air force officer returned to the door, breathless.

"Make your report!" said the President.

"NORAD reports massive Russian ICBMs launches. They are launching continuously. First ICBMs one minute from impact."

"Countervalue or counterforce strikes?" asked the President.

"Counterforce, Sir! They're launching against our Minuteman silos only."

"Well, I suppose we should be thankful for that at least. What is the status of our own SLBMs launched in retaliation?"

"Sir, 12 out of the 14 of our Ohio Class submarines have just launched their strategic missiles targeting Russian ICBM silos. Time to impact 12 to 14 minutes, Sir."

President Robertson turned to Hoffman and Ross, but it was Hoffman who spoke, saying, "Mr President, their ICBMs could take out most of our missile silos."

"And so what, Mr Hoffman?"

"That would mean the elimination of the ICBM leg of our nuclear triad. From that point on, any retaliation against Russia would take the form of submarine launched missiles only, along with our strategic bombers, the B1, B2 and B52."

"And what is the chance of our Submarine Launched Ballistic Missiles to get through to their ICBM launch silos."

"Very good Sir."

"Very well. It looks like we will prevail after all."

Ross gave the President a look as cold as he had ever experienced, and said, "You consider having all our ICBMs taken out by megaton range Russian nuclear weapons in the heart of continental USA as prevailing, Mr President?"

"Do we have any choice, Ross?" answered President Robertson, severely. "They have the upper hand."

"Yes, Sir, we do. Launch all our B2s right now on stealth missions and take this war to the Russians!"

"Do you really think that is necessary, Mr Ross? Half of America's strategic missile fire power lies on our Ohio Class submarines. Even the 4 cruise missile submarines would dwarf any attempt to manually deliver a reprisal attack."

The young Air Force officer returned, the latest NORAD report, hot off the printer, in his hands.

"What is it, Son?" asked the President, aware of the worried look on the officer's face.

"Sir, NORAD reports their ICBMs are targeting our population centers, Sir. A massive countervalue strike!"

"God damn it!" exclaimed President Robertson. "They are annihilating us!"

"That's not all, Sir," said the Air Force officer.

"Could there be anything else?"

"It seems the Russian Navy is making preparations. An invasion force is under-way, Sir."

"Get General Peters out here right now!" yelled the President.

The young officer saluted hurriedly and left.

Flashes of a different nature now commenced to fill the windows more yellow in colour than those which had just occurred.

"The first of their ICBMs are hitting our ICBM sites," exclaimed Ross. "Why did our Ballistic Missile Defense system 'Safeguard' not take them out before they could hit us?"

"That's not our concern. The fact is, they did get through. We'll just have to ride it out," answered the President. "We can do it!"

Ross gave him another look, cold as ice. "And their countervalue strikes against our population centres, Sir? Can we ride them out too?"

Chapter 66

Deep beneath the Kremlin in a vast presidential suite hardened against direct 1.2 megaton attacks at ground level, the President of the Russian Federation Ivan Khodorov slouched into a black leather sofa, a wicked smile braking across his face. On the wall opposite where he lounged, three screens linked to Solnechnogorsk, Russia's equivalent of NORAD, showed him the latest updates about the conflict, his war, his latest 'reality' video game.

A blonde woman wearing a white, translucent one-piece dress which accentuated her black underwear and huge breasts appeared from nowhere. She covered the vast suite quickly, her long legs striding confidently, her arms bearing a silver tray replete with soft drinks, ice, bottles of imported liquor and three glasses. "Where would you like it Mr President?"

"Right there, Marina," squawked Khodorov indicating the solid oak table on which his feet were rested.

"Your guests will arrive in ten minutes, Mr President. Shall I show them straight in?"

"Yes, yes, Marina. Show them straight in. Thank you."

The tall blonde walked to another door, the curves of her body followed for a long moment by the hawkish eyes of the Russian

President before he managed to get his mind back on the conflict. With a feat of will power he succeeded in putting thoughts of undressing her out of his mind, replacing them with war against America and missiles, 22 meters long and 2 meters wide.

The plans hatched by him and Yuval on many an evening spent in that very suite were working to perfection. The Americans were well and truly pinned down. Karim's decapitation strike had gone according to plan, wrecking their control and command center, destroying the Pentagon and White House. They had taken out a good part of the American capital too, taking a psychological toll on the American people. X-Ray pin-down had prevented them launching their ICBMs. Then Russian ICBMs had taken them out. Just as Yuval had predicted, when President Robertson had had to make a choice on whether or not to launch Massive Retaliation, he had erred on the side of caution. He had ordered a counterforce attack only, against Russian ICBM launching sites. Yuval's psychological profiling of the American President had been spot on. When faced with a decision to retaliate, rationality prevented him from launching against Russia's major cities. It was a last bid to show restraint, to beg for the sparing of his people and the American nation.

The Russian President watched the massive screens on the opposite wall of his lounge, his piercing grey eyes now gleaming. The left hand screen was linked to the Russian Space Forces, at Solnechnogorsk, 40 km north of Moscow. It displayed two sets of figures. The left hand figure, slowly clicking away into the hundreds, was the verified number of direct hits on Americas ICBMs. The right hand list showed the corresponding number of Russian ICBMs taken out. It flickered slightly, but continued to indicate zero.

The middle screen displayed a carbon copy of the display screen of Russian Space Forces. It showed the progress of both American and Russian ICBMs, SLBMs and Strategic bombers. It had been now ten minutes since he had switched from a counterforce strike to a countervalue one, against America's population centres. The tracks of 15

SS-19 ICBMs he had launched from that very seat, using a console set into the thick oak of the coffee table, were visible on the screen as red traces, accelerating now through Mach 15 over the Arctic. The 35 Topol-M SS-29s launched seven minutes ago appeared as orange traces, flying on low trajectories, Mach 10 and accelerating, reaching over 7km per second on their way to deliver ten 250kt warheads a piece at 500 meters altitude above all major American cities. As for the submarine and strategic bomber legs of Russia's nuclear triad, he kept them in reserve, for now at least. They would be kept to neutralise unwanted surprises. After all, the land invasion of the USA and Canada would necessitate tactical nuclear weapons.

President Khodorov looked at his watch. He had five minutes remaining before the arrival of his two guests. Enough time to launch one more missile. The right hand screen showed the progress of the American Submarine Launched Ballistic Missiles. It indicated many blue traces converging on the Russian ICBM fields in Teykovo, Kozelsk and Novosibirsk. He flicked the cap off one of the nuclear triggers of his console. It protected the launch of a single R-36M SS-18 "Satan." It was the last remaining original type SS-18 fitted with a high yielding 20 Mega Tonne warhead which the Strategic Rocket Forces had kept from decommissioning expressly for the purpose of targeting Cheyenne Mountain nuclear bunker, Americas NORAD control center.

He plugged in the coordinates of Area 51 and with scarcely a second thought, flicked the switch to 'launch,' just as the door swung open revealing once more Marina in all her stunning glory. "Mr President, your guests."

"Very well, Marina. Show them in!"

Yuval appeared, pulling behind him a chained creature, tall and with golden hair.

"Yuval! And you've brought me the girl! But why is she chained?"

Anna Kuznetsova held her head high in obvious show of defiance, her blue eyes cold as ice as she looked past the Russian President, focussing on infinity.

"Get those chains off her right now! She's not an animal."

"President," replied Yuval. "She can't be trusted. That's all I know."

"I don't want to hear it!"

"Okay, but don't say I didn't warn you," said Yuval, unlocking her chains. "She has escaped us once before and I will not be held responsible!"

The tall blonde Russian stood, rubbing her wrists which were red, cut, and swollen.

President Khodorov motioned to her to sit down on the second sofa situated beneath the central screen, opposite the one he had used to direct the Russian nuclear forces. "Anna Kuznetsova. How have you been treated?"

Like a bull with a raging fire in her eyes, Anna turned to look. "Go to hell!"

President Khodorov laughed aloud and gestured towards the sofa before installing himself back in front of his console. "Please sit, Anna. We can at least be cordial, can we not? I respect you, you know. More than you know for sure. You have remarkable qualities."

He took a swig of French Cognac as he looked at her. "If only my highest ranking officers had your ways of seeing and doing... We can at least be amicable about this now, can we not?"

Anna stared back at him, fixing a point between his eyes, hate written on hers. "What do you want from me?"

"You still don't understand do you?"

"I understand you want me!" said Anna. "You want everything that is beautiful. But then you destroy it, just like you are destroying the world."

"That's right. I want you more than anything in the world. In fact, for me, you are the world."

"Well, you've got a pretty fucked up way of showing it!"

"Would you like a drink?" said the Russian President watching Yuval as he came back into the room.

"Double whisky and coke on ice," replied Anna.

President Khodorov prepared three glasses and passed them to his two guests. Then he got back to following the conflict.

The left hand screen displayed 429 of America's 450 ICBM launching sites had received direct hits in contrast to ten of Russia's. In total, only 20 American SLBMs, the Trident II missiles launched from the 14 ballistic missile submarines had made it through the ballistic missile defense system which ringed Russia's ballistic missile fields. The system had been deployed only a month previously, a secret defiance against the Americans who believed Russia's promises not to develop ballistic missile defense.

Khodorov knew it would only be a matter of time now till his Strategic Rocket Forces detected a U.S. counter-value attack against Russian population centres. Now that the U.S. ICBMs had been neutralized, their retaliation would take the form of their remaining submarine-launched ballistic and cruise missiles. Moscow had the A-135 ballistic missile defense system. Other cities did not. To Khodorov, that was not a problem. For each Russian city the Americans, British and French took out, he would destroy one large European city. Let the Westerners destroy themselves.

A movement on the right hand screen caught his probing eyes. The Americans and British had commenced their counter-value attack. A series of red traces indicated that St Petersburg, Novosibirisk, Nizhny Novgorod and Kazan had been selected. Again Khodorov laughed out loud.

"Sorry! It's just that . . . " There was a pause. "While we are wiping USA off the face of the planet, they launch against Kazan. Take Kazan, my friends! See if I care!"

"Boss?"

"For God's sake Yuval, just spit it out!"

"Shouldn't we get to a safe location?"

"Yuval, we are in a bunker twenty meters under the heart of a city under a ballistic missile defense shield."

"Of course, Mr President."

"My dear Anna?" said Khodorov, sitting close to her on the black sofa.

"Yes?" replied Anna.

"As we were saying, the reason I need you is not only because I love you. That goes without saying. Love has a purely physical basis. When I look at you I desire you. When I touch you I feel electric because I know you to be beautiful. You are, without a doubt, the most beautiful creature ever to walk the earth."

"Is this meant to impress me?"

"No!"

"Good, because you don't!" The tall blonde looked more aggressive than ever. "Did you ever consider the fact that love is deeper than beauty?"

"Never!"

"Well it is!"

"Thank you but I can do without the insight. I know that I love you!"

"The feeling is not mutual. You are not handsome!"

"My dear Anna!"

"And stop calling me 'My dear!' That's an order!"

"The world as we know it will cease to exist this very day. Actually, it has already ceased to exist in the form we know it, dictated by America and its western stooges."

"And as far as I know, you are the reason for its destruction! Congratulations!"

"Be that as it may, I am a simple man and I was not auto-created. I was brought into existence by a process which began with the Big Bang. Whatever I do was simply written in its configuration of mass and energy. I am simply fulfilling what was set in motion by my creator. I therefore am not responsible for my actions."

"Oh please, Mr Khodorov, spare me the *Freud*. You created this war for your own narrow- minded, pathetic interests!"

"What do you know about my interests? What could be more important than bringing about the Kingdom of Satan? Satan knows something about true happiness. Evil is the most extreme form of happiness. It is infinitely more powerful than other forms. Through evil the human race will be able to maximise happiness in its populations. Satan will show us how it can be done."

He motioned to the screen. "What you are witnessing is the final battle between good and evil. And evil, thanks to me, Yuval and you my Dear, has the upper hand. The human race is made for evil. Through evil we realise ourselves." He chuckled. "Tell her Yuval!"

Yuval looked up, looking bewildered. "Mr President? Tell her what?"

"Tell her what part she has to play in all this."

"Oh yes, the trip!"

The Russian President thought quickly. He reconsidered the wisdom of telling Anna about her own part in everything. Not yet. The time was not right, and so said, "Yes Yuval. Tell her about the trip."

Yuval turned on the sofa to face Anna, leaving President Khodorov to return to his console, to make what seemed like fine adjustments to strategy.

"Anna," began Yuval. "Russia is under a nuclear onslaught by the Americans. The traces you see on the screen above us are incoming missiles targeting our Intercontinental Ballistic Missiles. Soon we expect the British and French to join the American attack. The Chinese are expected to launch against Korea and Japan as soon as they realise that America has been destroyed."

Anna replied, "The USA has been destroyed?" Somehow, she had always believed she would witness the Third World War. What she hadn't believed was that she was going to see it from the room where it was put into action.

"Let's just say, it's a work in process." His look had turned more serious. "In the next six days, most of the world will become uninhabitable. Sustained, total nuclear war between us and the Western world will take out all of the European population centres. Asia will not fare much better. India and Pakistan will launch against each other, as will Israel against her enemies. We could send you to Africa or South America, but we fear the chaos which the Third World War will bring will be translated to massive civil unrest. You will not be safe there either."

"Send me? To Africa?"

"Don't worry, we won't! It's too dangerous."

Anna looked both horrified and distraught. Not only was she being held captive, her captors were deciding on where to send her. "Why are you telling me this? You are holding me against my will, so if you want to send me somewhere why don't you just do it."

"We are, but it is not a state of affairs which pleases us. We would prefer you to stay with us of your own free will. We like you. Hell, we love you."

"I got it. You like me so much you keep me prisoner!"

"We would like to think of it as saving you. In a matter of hours, Jerusalem will be destroyed. If we had not taken you, there is no guarantee that you would not have been vaporized along with it."

"Your consideration is most touching. What is your point? What do you want from me?"

"Cooperation in exchange for moving you to the safest, most secure location in Eurasia, if not the World. President Khodorov has spent the last three years constructing a complex there capable of riding out the nuclear winter that the Third World War will most definitely cause. Even without the complex and nuclear bunker, the location is deemed safe. It is a cape at the northernmost point of mainland Europe. North Cape, Norway."

"Okay," said Anna, coming up to speed. "And if I don't agree?"

Before Yuval could craft a response, the door swung open and a green eyed, voluptuous beauty appeared in the doorway. After hesitating a brief instant, Kira strode right up to Anna without even looking at or seeking the consent of the Russian President.

Chapter 67

Air Force One flew for three hours and 3000 kilometres from America's East coast to just south of Salt Lake City. For some of that time and distance, its modified Pratt & Whitney engines were straining at the edge of their operational envelope, the pilots attempting to gain even more height and speed above the nuclear holocaust unfolding 15 kilometres below.

Its passengers had viewed with horror what Russia's counterforce and counter-value strikes had done to continental America. They had watched as the aircraft flew close to what remained of Illinois, St Louis and Kansas. When it passed 100km north of Denver they witnessed a nuclear air burst 500 meters directly above the city. They had watched in awe as the shock wave from the blast deflected the fireball skywards, leaving, under its epicentre, nothing but a darkened area of debris. Buildings, cars, highways and people all destroyed in the blink of an eye.

Air Force One's pilots had deviated only slightly from their course, taking the modified Boeing 747 just a bit further north in order to avoid at least some of the radiation that would be emanating from such a blast. Any large deviation would only lengthen the flight. It would add time and distance, and risk.

The command and control center was still in direct contact with Area 51, but that did not mean it was not a target. The longer Air Force One remained airborne, the greater the chance that it too would become engulfed in one of the nuclear blasts that was raining down on the continental U.S.

President Robertson took a last look at Salt Lake City as Air Force One banked slightly left, towards the mountains of the Nevada Desert, a manoeuvre replicated by the two F 22 Raptors which had in the last hour taken up station on either wing. He recited a silent prayer that at least one state capital would be spared the nuclear fury, as suddenly yet another flash propagated out across the Earth from below.

"They just hit Salt Lake City!" shouted Hoffman. "When will this be over?"

"When we win!" said the President, seated opposite.

"Well, we're a long way from winning just now."

President Robertson pulled the nearest phone off the wall, eyeing his CIA acting director. "Command? Where is the latest NORAD report? . . . Get it to me! . . . Fast."

The young Air Force officer appeared breathlessly at the door moments later. He was done with saluting. His job was to give relevant information as fast as possible.

"What is it?" said the President, detecting a hesitation in the young officer's attitude. "Make your report!"

"Sir! Russia's Strategic Rocket Forces have taken out all of our major cities. The total number of destroyed cities is 125. Even Hawaii has received a direct hit, Sir. All except fifteen of our ICBM launchers have been destroyed, Sir. That means approximately 435. We are still detecting launches against the remaining ICBM launchers, although it seems they are no longer launching against our cities."

"What about our own attack? How many of their cities and ICBM launchers have we destroyed?"

"Well, Mr President . . . Unfortunately.."

"It's okay, Son," soothed the President, composing himself. "Take your time!"

"Latest Intel suggests we have taken out 25 of their ICBMs and 10 of their major cities."

"Why so few?"

"Sir, as you know, we were unable to launch our ICBMs due to the high levels of radiation associated with the Electro Magnetic Pulses. Our ICBM force has been destroyed by high yielding direct attacks on our launch silos. Most of the SLBMs that made up our second, retaliatory strike never reached their targets due to what appears to be a Russian Ballistic Missile Defense system."

Hoffman jumped up, unable to contain his anger a second longer. "Son-of-a-bitch! I knew it! I had been saying it for the last year!"

"What exactly were you saying?" asked the President. "That the Russians were reneging on their commitments to the provisions of the Anti-Missile Defense System?"

"Yes. Exactly that!"

Clearing his throat, Ross rose to his feet. "Well, it does not matter how they managed to do it, they have managed to get ahead in this war, and so we had better get down to figuring out how we are going to take back control. Arguing is not going to help!"

"Ross is right," asserted Hoffman. "We need reports and decisions. Right now!"

"Expecting the worse," Ross continued, "Russia will continue on its present course, reducing our capacity to wage war. Then they will prepare a ground offensive."

"In your view, Ross, what is our best response?" queried the President.

"First, and this should be within the next day, we need to hit their command and control centres with tactical nuclear weapons."

"Decapitation strike?" asked the President.

"Absolutely. We need to bring to bear surgical nuclear strikes and take out their political leader President Khodorov. Latest Intel places him under the Kremlin. We should move on this within the next six hours."

"How do you propose to do this?" asked Robertson. "Moscow is protected by a fully functional defense system against ballistic missile attack, the A-135."

"Well," said Hoffman "Apart from a lightning ground invasion, the only options are a raid, or a surgical strike."

"A stealth raid! B-2 Spirit aircraft!" suggested the President.

For hours Ross had been secretly hatching a plan to carry the fight directly to Khodorov. More than anyone else, he knew exactly where he would be. The Russian President would choose to ride out the nuclear war consuming his country in one of his presidential suites, deep below the Kremlin. He said, "Interesting idea."

"What?" remarked Hoffman. "The stealth raid or the B-2 Spirit?"

"The stealth raid, naturally!"

"And why not the B-2?"

"Because such a raid, to have any chance of remaining undetected, needs to be carried out by a lone aircraft capable of looking after itself. It would need an aircraft capable of flying 3500 kilometres on internal fuel under combat conditions."

"What are you thinking?" asked the President. "What kind of mission?"

"What's more, the strike needs to be surgical. For stealth mode to be maintained, the strike weapon would have to be carried internally. Sorry to cut you off, Mr President. I meant no offence."

"None taken. I still think a multiple force of B-2s would be the best way to take out the Kremlin."

"If the aim was to take out the Kremlin, I would be inclined to agree."

"But?"

"But our aim is to kill Khodorov, not just take out the Kremlin."

The three men seated in the presidential cabin felt the aircraft decelerating, its engines throttling back. President Robertson looked confused, and in need of explanations but just sat and listened.

Ross said, "If we just wanted to take out the Kremlin, a force of B-2s would do the job. But we don't."

"What?" asked Robertson. "I thought we were sure the Russian President was in the Kremlin."

"No Sir," said Ross. "He is not *in* the Kremlin, he is *under* it. Approximately twenty meters to be precise."

"How can you be so sure?"

"Because I've been there! What is more, I am absolutely certain he is there right now. He'll be one of the presidential suites down there, directing the attack, and will remain there as long as we keep up the nuclear onslaught using our submarine based nuclear missiles."

"He is there? You know this for sure?"

"Yes, Mr President. He is there and he will stay there until he feels our attack has terminated. And for probably many days after, just to avoid the radiation."

"And if we keep him there, do you have a plan to get at him?"

"Yes, Sir, I do."

"Explain!"

"Sir, I can identify the exact location of President Khodorov's underground complex better than anyone in the United States Air Force. I know the Kremlin like I know my own home! I can get that bomb in to within 20 meters. I can kill Khodorov."

"And how do you propose to attack it?"

"By using the only weapon that can successfully attack a complex that deep, a modified B61 nuclear bomb in lay-down mode."

"Go on," urged the President.

"The bomb would be released from a fast moving bomber at very low altitude, say 200 meters. Its depleted uranium casing would allow it to penetrate deep enough before impact for its blast to rip apart the substrata to a depth of over 50 meters, well below the 20 meters necessary, killing anyone unfortunate to be within its vicinity. That, Gentlemen, is my plan to decapitate the Russian threat."

The President looked at Ross carefully. "Are you able to carry out the mission, Ross?"

"Yes Sir. Before joining the CIA, I was a United States Air Force test pilot. In fact, I am an F-35 test pilot. It's a stealth capable bomber, fifth generation. It can deal with anything the Russians can throw against it. Most certainly, it is capable of such an attack on the Kremlin. We could reconfigure its internal ordnance points to carry the B61 Mod 11 bunker buster nuclear weapon internally. It could be made to carry an extra 8700kg of fuel externally. That would give it a combat range of approximately 3000 kilometres."

Hoffman looked at him sternly. "Where would you begin the bomb run Ross?"

"Off the east coast of Sweden, Sir, over that big island in the Baltic. From there it would be only 1200km to Moscow, or about two hours flying at just under Mach 1."

"You are presuming of course that the Swedes will allow use of their airspace," said the President.

"Oh I think they will," said Ross. "I think by tomorrow they would be open to a request to do just about anything to Khodorov. Already Russia has attacked targets right across Western Europe. Look at the board. London, Paris, Rome, Berlin. Do you think they feel secure? Even if they do not launch against Stockholm, the Swedes, trust me, can be relied on to authorize an over-flight. All I need is one KC-135 Stratotanker loitering somewhere over Greenland to refuel me, and two F-22s to accompany me from here to the start of my bomb run."

Robertson nodded slowly. "You are absolutely sure Khodorov will be where you say he is? In his bunker?"

"Absolutely certain!"

"How can you be so sure?"

"Two things, Mr President. Because I know him, and because I once heard him mention something to his right hand man, Yuval. You can be sure. He will be there until we terminate our attack."

"And how about the mission itself? You are capable of delivering the B61 directly above the bunker?"

"Absolutely!"

"That's quite a feat, Soldier. After piloting a transcontinental flight you will attack the most heavily fortified location on the planet at Mach 1, and drop a bomb on a 20m target? How?"

"Mr President! Air Force pilots are trained to do such things. Just leave it to us."

"Where will you fly to after you complete the attack?" asked the President.

"Sir, in view of the situation, that's not important. All that matters is that I get through. Let's just say I have some ideas."

The aircraft intercom sprang to life, informing them that in several minutes, Air Force One would be on the ground. President Robertson took the nearest phone off the wall. "Make an urgent radio call to Area 51 control. Tell them to prepare F-22s and F-35s for immediate extended combat mission, a handful of each. And Officer, make sure the F-35s are all nuclear equipped with B61s, adapted for lay-down detonation, one a piece."

Chapter 68

Kira Kamenskaya had just spoken alone with Anna in a room adjacent to Khodorov's presidential suite, advising her to agree to go wherever they wanted to take her. She told her that there was no other way to survive the war, that she would be safe there, that she would personally make sure of it.

"But what of my son?" Anna had asked. "He was taken from me just before I was captured, at Mount Megiddo."

"I have no information about him," had replied Kira. "But as soon as I do, I will find him, and arrange for him to join you."

***

Anna arrived at Vnukovo Airport thirty minutes after leaving Khodorov's presidential bunker aboard the Maglev train. Yuval tried to lead her by the hand as the doors of the train opened.

"Take your hands off me!" she growled.

"Steady Girl!" said Yuval. "Khodorov may have given you back limited freedom. But I'm in charge from here on in. Just follow me, do what I say, when I say it and you will be okay."

"Bullshit Yuval!" replied Anna, following him along the well-lit marble passageway. "Don't twist what he said around. I am free!"

"You are free as long as you remain with us! That's what he said. Don't try to push your luck!"

Anna Kuznetsova walked briskly behind him. "Just so you know, I've seen what's going on and once I get to North Cape I can assure you I won't be going anywhere."

Casting a wary glance over his shoulder, Yuval stopped, saying, "I know! I will be there to make sure of it."

"It's not necessary, really. Doesn't your 'Boss' need you?"

"He does need me. He needs me to secure you, to keep you out of harm's way."

"That's very touching of him. Have you ever asked yourself why he needs me?"

"No," replied Yuval. They had come to the end of the passageway. A huge lift occupied the space where they now stood, a wide expanse of blue grey marble where the passageway ended. Selecting VIP from the choice of buttons, Yuval turned to face her. "I never question orders."

"I'm not asking you to. I'm just asking if you ever thought about it."

The lift doors slid open with a hiss of escaping air.

"After you," invited Yuval.

Following Anna inside, the doors closed and the lift accelerated upwards for five seconds. Then it decelerated for ten, almost reaching the VIP lounge at the surface. Anna pressed the stop button.

Yuval said, "What?" He looked at her with eyes as cold and blank as the Moscow sky, powerless to react.

Ann said, "Why is he helping me?"

"It's maybe because . . . "

"Yes?"

"He loves you!"

"No, Yuval. We both know that Khodorov only loves himself."

"And yet . . . "

"What?"

"He spends millions on protecting you. Why?"

Anna said, "Somewhere inside him he believes in the power of good over evil. He is not as bad as you think."

"You are forgetting that I think he is pretty bad! Better put this on. It's minus 20 outside."

Yuval wrapped her in the full length fur coat he had been carrying. Anna released her pressure on the red button and the lift finished its journey and the doors opened. A cold blast of snow filled air hit them as they exited onto the tarmac. A sign appeared just to their right, along with an arrow. It said Military Departures, and led out across the airport's apron, just about obscured by the blizzard.

"We will continue this discussion on the three hour flight," shouted Yuval, gritting his teeth as the sudden freezing gusts hit him.

"Three hour flight?"

She glanced at him warily, as she followed his lead towards 'Military Departures'. "Two questions, Yuval. Where are we going; and on what type of aircraft?"

"North Cape, Norway and Gulfstream V. Our flight is ready and waiting."

"Is it really necessary to go so far north?" asked Anna, trying to keep up and not slip on the ice at the same time.

Yuval stopped dead, drawing her close to him, until his face was next to hers. "Strange as this may sound, North Cape is the safest place to hide right now. It's the safest place to ride out a nuclear winter. To the west, north and east, there is only sea, and to the south a range of mountains."

"It sounds so remote, won't I be lonely? What will I do those long winter nights?"

For the first time Anna sensed the sweetness of his aftershave. And for the first time she felt... Well, even she did not know what exactly she felt. Her nerves were at a dead end.

Yuval led her to the shelter afforded by three conifers, on the edge of the apron. On their windward side, the wind had driven the snow into a deep drift. There, protected from the wind's cruellest savagery, they became stationary. His hand moved up over the soft surface of her fur coat until it reached her cheek. He caressed her ear for several instants, before applying pressure to twist her face towards his.

"Stop right there!" said Anna.

"Why?"

"Are you trying to seduce me?"

"No. We are friends. Besides, my boss would kill me if he found out."

"How would he do that?"

Yuval pulled his face away from hers, searching their dark surroundings as if the answer to her question lay somewhere out there. "He has eyes everywhere, you know! Let's go."

Chapter 69

Ross climbed at a rate of 200 meters per second, well below maximum for the F-35 Lightning II, reaching cruising altitude in a matter of minutes. At last he was back in control of a Lightning II, otherwise known as the Joint Strike Fighter. Like old times. Well . . . almost.

Pushing the aircraft to its limits now was going to be different from putting it through its paces two years ago. This was real.

He levelled out at 45,000 feet. Post climb and pre-cruise automatic system checks filled his carbon fibre helmet. He tried to relax. Never had flying been this easy. It would have to be. The aircraft would fly many hours by itself, allowing him to sleep some of the way. Otherwise he wouldn't have a hope in hell of completing the mission. Once the checks were complete, he applied pressure to the throttle, accelerating the aircraft through the sound barrier.

Seconds into the cruise, the flight computer voice came alive, speaking to him for the first time. "All systems checked. Normal. Altitude 46,000 feet. Speed Mach 1.2. Destination, Moscow Kremlin, Initial bearing 14.6521. Latitude: 55°45′00″N. Longitude: 37°36′50″E. Final bearing: 159°03′28″. Distance to destination 9397 km. ETA 9 hours 44 minutes at current speed."

"Way point destination: Rendezvous with KC-135 Stratotanker at Northwest Passages just off Mathe Point, Baffin Island, Latitude: 70°23′59″N Longitude: 89°38′11″W Final bearing: 36°48′59″. Distance to way point 4022km. ETA 4 hours 8 minutes at current speed."

Ross cast his eyes to the right and left, and gave the thumbs up to the two F-22 Raptors which lay off each wing. They wouldn't be able to accompany him in the most crucial part of the mission, but he was glad they were there all the same. As long as they were there during the two in-flight refuellings, the rest, he could handle.

The glass touch-pad control in front of him glistened sleek, spotless and silky in the evening sun which was just dipping low towards the curved horizon. The yellow disc would soon turn red, and crimson. And then it would disappear, leaving him alone with his F-22 escorts to face the night. Moscow was twelve time zones to the east, but after a flight time of, eleven hours, he would arrive an hour before sunset.

Ross applied slight throttle pressure, decreasing the power output of the modified Pratt & Whitney F135 after-burning turbofan to slightly over 50 percent. He felt the removal of 20kN thrust vectoring through the airframe, decelerating the aircraft to Mach 0.95. If the engineers back in Connecticut were right, keeping the speed just below supersonic at 49,000 feet was the optimum for sustained, fuel efficient transcontinental flight. Several seconds passed and then the on-board computer came alive again, with updated flight parameters.

"Way point destination: Rendezvous with KC-135 Stratotanker at Northwest Passages just off Mathe Point, Baffin Island, Latitude: 70°23′59″N Longitude: 89°38′11″W Final bearing: 36°48′59″. Distance to way point 3604km. ETA 3 hours 4 minutes at current speed."

Ross took his left hand off the throttle, lightly touching the left hand of two eight by ten-inch glass screens. Two map displays flashed onto the right hand screen, one for each refuelling way point. The upper flight profile indicated that he would arrive at the refuelling way point just short of Baffin Island's Mathe Point with 10 percent fuel remaining at the aircraft's current speed and altitude. Touching the glass screen again induced an immediate reaction from the on board computer.

"Maximum loitering time at Mathe Point forty minutes at twenty percent engine power not including emergency reserve of 100 litres."

Forty minutes! Ross smiled, remembering the pre-flight conversation he had had with Hoffman. Not exactly cutting it fine!

Piece of cake! His eyes wandered for an instant to the second of the two screens. Things would be drastically less easy if he had visitors to deal with!

The last flickering rays of the dying day hit his black, combat visor as he looked dead ahead, out over the planet. Never had he seen its beauty so clearly. The purples and reds, and blues of the curved earth below him were mesmerizing. Would it have been so had hundreds of nuclear explosions not just occurred?

The flight computer informed him he was leaving U.S. airspace. He gave a thumbs up to the two F-22 Raptors, watching them peel off, and dropping down and dropping back. From then on, he flew alone. His next human contact would be just short of Baffin Island with the tanker, in just under three hours. From then on, the only thing to keep him company on the subsonic dash across the Canadian wilderness would be the continual raw, rasping of the turbofan. He could feel it, immediate below him, the most powerful engine ever installed in an aircraft. Then a familiar voice came through on the still active fighter escort frequency. It was the lead Raptor pilot.

"Shark to Ross, are you still there, buddy?"

"Thought you guys were long gone! What's up?"

"Bad news I'm afraid."

"What happened?"

"Area 51 just received a direct hit from a Russian ICBM. Yield was in the 20 megaton range. Thought you should know."

Silence filled the airwaves as Ross digested the information. Zak Hoffman. The President of the United States. Not really friends, but more than acquaintances. Certainly no-one at or near ground zero could have survived, unless they were in a nuclear bunker protected by blast doors. Which was possible, but unlikely.

"Thanks, Shark. Where are you headed?"

"Don't worry about us. Just get that B61 through and nail that Khodorov son-of-a-bitch."

"I'll do my best! Good luck, you guys! Ross out."

For the fifth time on the flight, a myriad of sensors attached to Ross's body tripped a warning threshold. An enslaved program built into the F-35s on board computer was activated. Deep inside the dark green flight suit, a mechanized contraption clamped around his left arm came alive, and inserted an amphetamine laden needle into a vein of his forearm. And yet again the time when sleep could envelope the CIA's most valuable asset was put back indefinitely. The F-35, for all its autonomy, was not a drone. It needed Ross as much as he needed it.

Chapter 70

President Khodorov settled back into the black leather upholstered luxury of his cosy little nook beneath the walls of the Kremlin Armoury, admiring his handiwork. A broad smile broke across his ageing, squirrel-like face. Directly opposite him, three screens bore witness to the nuclear holocaust he had recently visited on planet Earth. On the right hand screen, the demise of the U.S. second strike was all too obvious. All but 20 of the SLBMs making up the attack had been neutralised high in the Russian atmosphere, taken out by Russia's ballistic missile defense.

The American SLBMs that had penetrated had mainly targeted small cities and were of little consequence. Luckily for Khodorov, Russia's 140 million people were spread across a vast territory. If the American strike had taken out one tenth of them, that still left over a 120 million willing recruits to avenge the American aggression. How would they know what had really happened that day if the only news they received originated in the offices of Alexei Nesterov, the newly appointed Chairman of Rostelekom?

Reaching for the remote control which lay before him on the oak table, the Russian President cast his eyes to the central screen, and flicked through several displays. A world map appeared, showing how the world's other nuclear powers were responding to the situation. China had launched pre-emptive strikes against Japan, Korea, and India encouraging the Americans to retaliate, launching a massive countervalue attack against China's population centres. As he watched, China was cowering under a rain of U.S. SLBMs and Indian Intermediate Range Ballistic Missiles, attacks which would reduce the threat China placed to his own project.

Pakistan and India had just launched against each other.

He had lit the fuse of the world's nuclear tinder box and was now watching it go up in flames.

On the coffee table in front of him his iPhone vibrated in spasms, and lit up and rang. Calmly, he reached for it.

"Mr President, General Valery Karimov."

Khodorov's heard the familiar voice of his Chief of the General Staff, who he had been in close contact with since the operation's planning stage. "General Karimov. How are things beneath Kosvinsky Mountain?"

"We believe there was a more or less direct hit above us. Caused an earthquake which we measured as 6.8 on the Richter scale, but we'll ride it out. What can I do for you Mr President?"

"Our Strategic Rocket Forces are holding up pretty well."

"Ninety percent intact, Sir. We retain hundreds of ICBMs, IRBMs and SLBMs ready to go at a minute's notice."

"And nuclear armed cruise missiles?"

"About five hundred."

"Good, General. The U.S. invasion plans: cancel them."

"Sir?"

"Call them off. We don't need to invade the U.S."

"But Sir, may I enquire as to why?"

"It's no longer necessary. Our first strike went better than expected."

Khodorov flicked through his remote controls until the correct display popped onto the left hand screen. "The U.S. has been militarily and politically destroyed. All of their ICBMs received direct hits, as did every state capital city, and many smaller cities besides. We will retain both our conventional and nuclear forces intact for our assault on the rest of the world."

"Yes, Mr President."

Khodorov flicked the screens to display the world. "For the moment, the world's nuclear powers are consuming themselves. All we have to do is wait."

"And then what, Mr President?" enquired Karimov.

"And then? Then, General Karimov, we monitor the world. We destroy hope, wherever it appears. Where there is nostalgia for the past. We destroy where there is freedom. The world will become ours. Its remaining populations will be ravaged by violence, by the rule of abuse, which will serve to reward the few.

"Rape of both sexes will be systematic, because sexual pleasure is sacred and Satan given. Torture too is a route to the Lord of Darkness. Torture of those who would fight to return the world to the rule of non- violence, to the rule of law. There are two ways to live General. To suffer, as in the world we just left, or to use suffering for higher pleasure. True happiness lies in the latter, the way indicated by Satan. Maximising one's own pleasure.

"We will champion the rights of everyone to pleasure. The stronger the pleasure, the stronger collective happiness. In my world, everyone who chooses Satan can be a winner. All it takes is know yourself, know that pleasure comes to those who act to satisfy themselves. So, in answer to your question, General, we will retain our nuclear forces in readiness to destroy any location fighting against us.

"Anyone, any actor, individual or state, who seeks to oppose us will be destroyed by me. By us. By Satan's dark fist. Our army will be instructed to act in accordance with Satan, to spread his teachings. Soon enough, the world will be ours. The first World Empire of Satan is Russia. It is us. And it will spread to the world."

Karimov shrugged, "All good and well, but how will it all pan out, Mr President? What are our operational priorities?"

Khodorov got up from the couch, pacing up and down the suite, suddenly anxious. Then he stopped, as if an idea had just materialized. "The creation of a revolutionary force of our best, most aggressive men and women soldiers will be created."

"And then?"

Khodorov scratched his head. "In a matter of days they will have swelled their own ranks to millions. They will be given training, ideology, funds. They will go forth from Russia to the four corners of the globe, spreading the Russian Empire of Satan. Anywhere where they will be resisted will come under attack. Attack from our conventional and nuclear forces. In less than two weeks, the world will be ours."

"Very good, Mr President, I will get onto it."

"General Karimov, before you go. Speed is of the essence. In a week I want this revolutionary force to number two million."

"You will have your Revolutionary Army, Mr President. You can rely on me."

Khodorov hung up the call, installing himself back on the leather couch behind his console. Flicking through the remote, he found the mission that had been occupying his tortured sub-conscious for the last few hours. He looked for the position of Anna Kuznetsova. Without Anna, all that he had done meant nothing. Because without Anna, the power to perpetuate his grip on the world would be lost. Anna was still the key.

***

"Tell me we're not travelling to North Cape on that!"

Anna had just emerged from the heat of the VIP lounge into the cold of a Moscow winter night. Ahead of her were the glaring lights of a huge hangar, ahead of Yuval who was striding along confidently and swiftly towards the towering hulks of two huge, twin tailed fighter aircraft.

"We are. One of us on each of them."

"You lied!"

Yuval ignored the remark. He carried on striding, like a man on a mission. He expected Anna's surprise of having to get into a Su-35, but not outright reluctance. If she needed reassurance of the necessity for getting out of Moscow, she need only look out of the hanger. She only had to look behind the twin tail fins of the two jets, to the continual flashes of nuclear detonations in the upper atmosphere. Moscow was under a prolonged attack, a missile shield bombarded by constant incoming American, British and French SLBMs. The missile shield was holding up pretty well, but... It would only take one missile to get through. Yuval thought, *Surely she could see that.* The last thing he needed right now was to have to sedate her for the flight.

Anna stopped dead as they approached the two Sukhoi Su-35s, so Yuval swung round. He was just short of the leading edge of one of the two aircraft's wing, half a meter above his head, Anna facing him, barring him. "You have got to be kidding!"

"Fortunately for us, I am not."

Yuval took a deep breath, grasping her firmly by the shoulder. "Look Anna. The missile shield is working, but that does not mean it will continue to work. My orders are to get you out of Moscow to a safe location. Without delay. And that's exactly what I am going to do."

"But I hate flying!"

Ominous shouts pierced the loud whine of the two aircraft, interspersed with the sound of heavy feet reaching them from the other side of the aircraft. A group of men dressed in green flight suits were coming straight for them.

"Put these on, right now!" shouted one of the pilots, throwing flight suits to both Anna and Yuval.

Two flight engineers hurried through final checks before descending the ladders from the cockpits.

"Sir! Both aircraft fully fuelled and ready," said one, saluting.

"Very good."

"What happened?" asked Yuval, squinting through the icy blasts of the wind.

"Just get them on!" answered one of two pilots. "Now! There's an imminent threat. No time to explain. I'll do that once we get airborne."

Anna and Yuval busied themselves with the flight suits. The pilot was still speaking, but they couldn't hear his words, because they were too absorbed. One thing alone on their minds: Survival. The attitude of the pilots told them that the nuclear explosions in the sky outside were about to come closer.

"I am Lieutenant Colonel Ivanov, and this is Major Kuznetsov."

They handed Anna and Yuval pills, two apiece.

Anna said, "What are these?"

"To help you," answered Lieutenant Colonel Ivanov. "First timers usually have difficulty adapting to life at Mach 2. Good luck!"

Anna quipped, "That's great, just great!" and strapped herself in as tight as she could behind the pilot of the lead aircraft. She felt a strange mixture of fear and excitement. A strange, alien cocktail of hormones and drugs were being pumped around her by her thumping heart. A high pitched roar reached her ears, only partially muffled by her helmet. The fighter jet was already in motion, accelerating briskly through the wide hangar doors into the hostile, nuclear night.

They reached the end of the taxiway less than forty five seconds later, side by side, accelerating right onto the runway.

Chapter 71

"The Kremlin is under attack. Get Khodorov out of there immediately!"

To Kira, Yuval's voice blaring out of her smartphone bordered on the hysterical. She was approaching Red Square from Kitay Gorad in a black armoured Hummer of the Russian Interior Ministry, the MVD. "Obviously!" she replied, looking up into the night.

"Not the strategic bombing, Kira, it's a specific threat. A lone stealth fighter-bomber broke through our defenses, undetected until a few minutes ago. You've got to get Khodorov out of there!"

"A single stealth bomber?"

"You got it. It's probably an American B2. It's headed straight for the Kremlin."

"How long have we got?"

"About five minutes. Maybe more, maybe less. Get him out!"

"It's too late for that. Best place for him is where he is. He's in the bunker, twenty meters below the Armoury!"

Kira thought: *No time to alert Khodorov. His time might have come quicker than I had anticipated.* "Driver, the Saviour Gate, and step on it!"

"Yes Ma'am."

The Hummer's studded wheels clawed to a halt on the icy cobblestones of Red Square, just shy of the Saviour Gate to the Kremlin.

"Defense Minister Kira Kamenskaya!" shouted the driver to the nearest guard.

The presidential guard frowned and squinted through the blinding snow at the visitor. "What the hell is this? A mistake?"

Kira threw open the passenger door, jumped out and rounded the vehicle. "There is no mistake, Officer. I am Defense Minister Kira Kamenskaya." She flashed her ID. "Let us through immediately!"

"Yes Ma'am! My apologies!"

"Officer!" answered Kira. "Your name please!"

"Major Popov at your service, Ma'am."

"There is a nuclear-proof guard station under this gate, if I am not mistaken."

"That's correct, Ma'am!" he said, making no attempt to conceal his surprise. "The entrance is right over there, on the other side of the guard's office."

"Is it locked?"

"No, Ma'am. It is always open. That's a kind of tradition."

"Show me!"

"But Ma'am, we're not authorized to . . . "

"Take me down to the guard room right now! And bring the other guard and my driver with you. That's an order!"

***

Despite everything that Ross was going through on his bomb run, he felt relaxed. He was confident and in control. The modified F-35 Lightning II was still flying an automatic, its altitude constant at 40 meters above the frozen surface of Park Parbedy, on the outskirts of Moscow. He was under no illusion that his mission was still a secret. He may have been skimming the treetops ever since he had crossed the Finland-Russia border, but there was no escaping it. Russian A-50

Mainstay early warning aircraft would have picked him up. That was okay. Picking him up was one thing, shooting him down was another.

Ross's squinting eyes focussed on his fuel. He would have liked to have pushed the Lightning-II already on the outskirts of Moscow to above Mach 1, but that would have reduced his ability to wage any kind of combat mission on his way out. Mach 0.9 was the best compromise between speed and security.

The flight computer was talking to him again, its electronic tones informing him that the target was two minutes ahead at current speed. He took back manual control, finally permitting himself to increase the aircraft's speed through the sound barrier as he armed the single B61-11 for lay-down mode detonation. Released at Mach 1.2 the depleted uranium bomb casing would resist impact with the ground, and penetrate several tens of meters. Then it would detonate, all 340 kilotons worth in a place adjoining the presidential suite.

Dead in front of him, coming rapidly into view, was central Moscow, grey and solemn. He identified the key way mark on his approach to the target, the soaring towers of Moscow City business district. They appeared well to the right of his trajectory. He banked sharply to the right, listening to the on-board computer recalculating the heading required to bring him to the target. He and only he knew the position of the Russian President's underground bunker, simply because he had been the only one from the West to have been there. He had calculated the bunker to be directly between the Kremlin Grand Palace and the Aleksandrovsky Sad Garden Wall. His original incoming trajectory would have approached the wall obliquely, presenting a difficult target. So he banked again, correcting.

Chapter 72

The two Su-35s climbed steeply, in formation, towards the north east, a direction which would lead straight to the Kremlin. Lieutenant Colonel Ivanov accelerated to take the lead position, ramming the aircraft's two Saturn turbofan engines into afterburner. If the threat was real, and the communication link had told him that it was very real, they had less than five minutes. Five minutes to get into position to intercept an F-35 advancing towards the Kremlin at above Mach 1! Ivanov had no illusion of the threat to himself and the young woman behind him. But an order was an order. An order trumped everything. It trumped even what Defense Minister Kira Kamenskaya had told him earlier that day. "Your mission is to fly Anna Kuznetsova to safety at the northernmost point of Europe. Nothing else matters."

Despite nothing else mattering, an order was an order, and an order from the Chief of the General Staff to eliminate the threat posed by the American intruder trumped absolutely everything. No problem. If any aircraft could successfully identify, track and engage such a target, it was the Sukhoi Su-35.

He levelled out at 500 meters, Mach 0.8. He tasked the aircraft's passive phased array radar to search for the American. With the Kremlin just coming into view, the radar connected.

***

Just like he had done countless times before during the long hours en route using the aircraft's built-in flight simulator, Ross lined up the three way marks ahead and below his F-35 as it roared supersonically towards the Kremlin's red-bricked ramparts. This time it was for real.

The first way mark, the Russian government White House Tower was dead ahead, and then passed directly beneath him. He pulled slightly to the left onto final approach, engaging the auto. From that point on until the bomb was away the aircraft would fly itself. It was going to hit with total accuracy, a pin point bombing run which would deliver the half tonne device slam bang into the bank of the Aleksandrovsky Sad beneath the Kremlin wall. Speed on impact: Mach 1.2.

He roared low over the high rise apartment blocks of New Arbat. Seconds later he was over the Russian Ministry of Defense building on Arbat Square, a high-pitched tone filling his helmet. The bomb was away.

A green light flashed onto the bomb run display in front of him, confirming release. Ross took back control, slamming the ramjet for the first time on the mission. The aircraft was a prototype, its hybrid turbojet-ramjet engine never before used operationally. He needed every little bit of thrust to get him away from the blast which would be mere seconds in coming.

Ross fought the controls as the ramjet cut in, its massive thrust catapulting the aircraft forwards, pushing him deep into the back of his seat. Then a warning tone he knew all too well filled his helmet.

I've been painted by a weapons system's radar. But by whom?

Unchained by the ramjet, the F-35 had become a flying tiger with Ross hanging on to its tail. Already it was over the period palaces of Kitay Gorad. Speed Mach 1.5 and increasing. He pulled north. The enemy was a plane, a Sukhoi-30, no, Su-35. *Shit!* He fired.

Chapter 73

Lieutenant Colonel Ivanov had engaged the American as soon as he had identified him. *Fox Three!* An air-to-air missile on active radar homing was away. The F-35 deviated towards Ivanov's Sukhoi 35 with 1000 knots closure. The American had banked sharply to the right, presenting the Sukhoi-35 with a brief firing opportunity. He took it.

Then a new Sun, an apocalyptic vision, a fireball of incredible brilliance filled his entire left hand view. Half instinctively, half consciously he yanked the Sukhoi's joystick to the right, literally hitting the throttle with the palm of his hand to engage the after-burners at maximum. He knew what had happened. He knew that very, very well. The priority now was not the American; it was survival as the shock wave of the nuclear detonation approached his aircraft.

The blast hammered through the Russian fighter like a battering ram, wrapping it in its sinister, deadly grasp. Lieutenant Colonel Ivanov fought to maintain control, knowing it was useless. Wind velocities that close to a nuclear explosion were of the order of hundreds of meters per second, approaching the speed of sound in air. No aircraft could stand up to them. But his instinct and training told him otherwise. *Get out of the spin. Throttle back, nose down and ride out.*

Amazingly, he remained alive. His eyes re-focussed, this time on his instruments. Instinct and training. The Sukhoi was stuck in a steep dive. Though he couldn't see it, he could sense the fireball from the detonation deflecting high above and to his left, lighting the sky and the ground. It was casting its light onto the rapidly approaching blackened area of ground now spreading out at the speed of sound over what had been Moscow. He had a split second opportunity to react, and he took it, pulling the aircraft out of its dive in the nick of time.

Re-established on level flight he was appalled at what he saw. The center of the city had been reduced to rubble and ash. Ground blast! That was why he had survived! The bomb had detonated on the surface, possibly underground, limiting considerably its blast effects. He said, "Lay-down mode!"

Which brought him back to reality. *Anna! Yuval! The President!* "Anna! Are you okay?"

"I am fine! Thank you very much!"

"Sure you are!"

Ivanov had heard various noises from his passenger coming through his helmet. Major Kuznetsov! Yuval!

"How do you know? Didn't we just fly through a nuclear explosion?"

"Because you're with me!"

He switched the radio frequency. "Kuzy? Are you there?"

No contact from the other Su-35. The screen in front of him was blank. Though there was nothing flying within 10 kilometres, the aircraft systems were working perfectly. *The Sukhoi! Even a nuclear explosion could not affect it!*

"Are we on our own?"

It was Anna, and Ivanov was happy to have her aboard. "Looks like it," he replied, absolutely composed. During the confusion, the F-35 had vanished from the radar screen.

Ivanov switched his attention from the instrument checks and accelerated to Mach 0.95. He made his altitude 20,000 feet as the mushroom cloud of the explosion was left well behind them. But other mushroom clouds had come into view due to their height. There were dozens of them, especially towards the west. It looked to him as if most of the cities of European had been taken out.

"So shouldn't we be heading towards the north, towards North Cape?"

"We are!"

On the screen in front of him appeared the route to Mehamn Airport, the nearest airport to North Cape. It was a great circle route, and 1840km long. It would take them into Norwegian territory just west of the barren Kola Peninsula. No need to worry about NATO aircraft taking them out. Russian forces would already have moved in to occupy the entire region.

Anna and Lieutenant Colonel Ivanov cast their eyes to the west, dazzled by the beauty of the sky. The sun was dipping low towards the horizon, throwing its dying rays onto the clouds, and painting them purple. Perhaps the air had become filled with particulates from the explosions. Perhaps that was why the sunset had assumed such splendour.

The radio burst into life on one of its prefixed frequencies.

"Sukhoi-35, Beriev A-50 your heading north on bearing 348, acknowledge ident, over."

The presence of the Soviet-built airborne warning and control system (AWACS) did not surprise Lieutenant Colonel Ivanov. Even though a nuclear war was being fought, they were still up there, patrolling the Russian skies, doing what they could. That was their job.

"Beriev A -50, this is Lieutenant Colonel Ivanov, Sukhoi-35 ident. What can I do for you guys?"

"American F-35 intruder heading north on bearing 348. He's 12 kilometres in front of you at Mach 0.5. Engage this fighter, over."

"Engage American F-35, bearing 348, 12 kilometres ahead of me. Sukhoi- 35."

Ivanov jammed the turbofan engines into afterburner, taking the Sukhoi supersonic in seconds.

The phased array Irbis radar spotted the American, a fast moving blip at low altitude, trying to avoid radar. But why was the American flying the F-35 on a heading of 348 degrees, the same as his own? *Why would the American choose to head towards the Russian-Norway border instead of towards closer and safer escape destinations? Why had he chosen North Cape as his intermediate way-point?*

Ivanov closed the range to 5km, and then he fired two R-27 air-to-air missiles on active radar homing, one straight after the other. "Fox three!" he said, indicating he had launched air-to-air missiles. He watched the missiles streaking ahead of him.

"What?" Anna had seen the missile launches, wondering what was going on. "Fox three?"

"It's just a code!"

"Who are you firing at?"

Ivanov did some quick mental arithmetic. The computer was telling him that his destination airport, Mehamn, was now 1708 kilometres distant. His current range was 2500km, but that was at altitude. His range would drastically reduce if he flew sustained combat operations, something he wasn't planning on.

Chapter 74

Fox three! Air-to-air missiles on active radar homing! Ross took the F-35 supersonic, punching the throttle lever to maximum to engage the ramjets, accelerating the aircraft through the sound barrier. *Dammit! Who the hell is engaging me?* The ramjet kicked in, its thrust staggering, in seconds the F-35 travelling above Mach 2 and still accelerating. But he was still being painted by two missiles on active homing, and they were closing fast. There was only one way to escape. *Outrun them.*

The electronic voice was talking to him again. "Time to impact 45 seconds at present speed. Deploy counter-measures and pull up."

Ross smiled wryly, and followed the computer's instructions. "Come on! Fox three? No way!"

The manoeuvre would be a first. No one had ever taken the F-35 Lightning II above Mach 2.65. Not even at altitude. That would have damaged the F-35's single F135 turbofan. His particular F-35 was different, however. It was a prototype, modified, and fitted with the USAF's first operational jet-ramjet hybrid. The ramjet side of the half-breed would start producing thrust at just below Mach 1, and could theoretically keep on producing it. Right up to Mach 6!

He glanced down at the cockpit's touch pad screen. Mach 3.2 and increasing. Then the on-board computer gave an update.

"Identity confirmed. R-77 Adder missile with active radar homing. Maximum Velocity Mach 4.5. Time to impact 40 seconds at present speed. Deploy counter-measures and pull up."

Not necessary, thought Ross. His aircraft had already matched the speed of the missile. Pulling up at Mach 3.2 would do nothing except needlessly subject the airframe to forces above 10G. And anyway, what difference would it make? R-77 missiles were tested to turn at a rate of 150 degrees per second. Which would be a 15G turn. *No way! No way to break missile lock.*

"Time to impact, 55 seconds. Deploy counter-measures and pull up. Change your vector to break missile lock."

Another smile broke across Ross's face. *From where had the computer found the extra advice*? Change your vector to break missile lock? No need! The missile had reached its maximum velocity and would not be able to catch him. The F-35 was already pulling away. He reached forward, and selected missile speed and distance from the menu. Just to be sure.

The electronic voice gave him good news. "Incoming R-77 Adder missile velocity: Mach 3. Time to impact: 60 seconds."

Lay off the gas! If he was ever going to reach North Cape he had to conserve fuel. The route appeared in red on the left hand screen. A great circle route, first to the Russian-Norwegian border and then on to the coordinates he had plugged into the computer all those hours ago, on the runway at Area 51. They were the same coordinates inscribed by the Israelites on the golden chalice which hung before him. The golden chalice found under Al Aqsa Mosque, and handed to him by Hoffman just before he had climbed aboard.

"The fourth inscriptions are space-time coordinates for a place near North Cape," Hoffman had said. "They're for tomorrow. And only you can get there on time!"

The Adder missile fell further back, finally disappearing from his radar. Ross smiled, this time less wryly. The on-board computer had already given up talking about it.

The ancient chalice rattled in front of him against the digital dashboard as he decelerated the F-35 back to super cruise at Mach 1.2. Leaning slightly forward, he adjusted the position of the golden goblet, pinning it tighter to the instrument panel by a woven band which had been given to him by Kira Kamenskaya, days before, in Moscow. The golden chalice! The Holy Grail. The inscriptions! Further commandments from the Ancients about the present crisis! Written there was so much. So much more information than just America's annihilation. He hesitated a moment, deep in thought. He caressed its deep inscriptions. There was his name, as there was Kira's. Ancient inscriptions linking him to the one he had tried to seduce all those months before in a Moscow club. Then a long set of numbers pinpointing a place, a time. The sixth space-time coordinates! *They were for a place near North Cape, ten hours from now.* But a place and a time of what? For what? Could he really have been so important to the Israelites? His mind filled with a heady mixture of awe and confusion and a million things between. How could the Israelites have known all this about the future? How had they been able to determine, with certainty, that he was capable of reaching those coordinates at all?

He glanced at his watch feeling the effect of the amphetamines which the on-board computer pumped at regular intervals into his veins. Ten hours still remained. The space-coordinates on the golden chalice were not for an airport, however, not even a town. He had looked them up on the flight, checked them, and double checked them, and then checked them again. They had formed part of his on-board entertainment on the transcontinental flight. They were the coordinates of an ancient hut, Smorbringen, situated above a rocky headland, several kilometres from the most remote point in Europe, North Cape. What could possibly be his connection to such a place? And why had the Israelites been interested in him getting there at a time which was approaching at a rate of knots?

He throttled back the F-35 to Mach 0.5 to conserve fuel. The on-board computer had happily informed him yet again of the situation. He looked at the twin control panels, just to be sure. He had a range of 1750 km left at that speed, and it was 1528 kilometres to Mehamn airport, on a heading of 348.2 degrees. No problem.

Twilight had descended on European Russia, the view from 45,000 feet captivating him. He noticed the lights of the city of Bezhetsk immediately below the aircraft, visible through the digital eye on the aircraft's belly. A huge expanse of water appeared below and to the right of his flight path, towards the west, its surface a silver sheet reflecting the moon. Rybinsk Reservoir.

Ross made his altitude 55,000 feet or 16,700 meters. He continued on the heading of 348.2 degrees at Mach 0.5. His helmet visor displayed the aircraft parameters. Everything was functioning to perfection.

Taking a last look towards the huge reservoir, he felt suddenly overcome, pervaded by a strange yet familiar sensation. In a split second it was gone. His tell-tale signs of drowsiness had activated the on-board computer which had in turn injected its latest cocktail of drugs, amphetamines for the most part, into his arteries. They were a necessary ill. An integral part of long duration missions. One got used to them. A tell-tale blip which served to highlight that his body was being pushed to its limits, a blip brought to his attention by the serenity of the scene, the reflection of the metallic moon, starkly penetrating his consciousness, inciting drowsiness.

Or maybe it was quite simply severe fatigue. His mind forced by the drugs to focus, and focus hard. Eventually, he would have to sleep, and he knew it. But right now, the drugs were doing their job.

He was as awake as ever. Despite having been awake for 38 of the preceding 48 hours. In the last week, he had only slept 60 hours.

***

Innumerable mushroom clouds and nuclear fireballs of the conflict fell behind him as his jet streaked for North Cape. He had witnessed scores of them since he had left Moscow, to the left and the right of his route northwards. Mainly to the left however, towards which he again cast his gaze, towards Western Europe, obliterated. Russia was winning World War III.

The last bomb had exploded clearly in view, dead west of him, St Petersburg flattened under its heavy 140 kiloton blast. Ross guessed it was a submarine launched missile strike, from the U.K., U.S. or France.

Russia's aggressive use of their first strike, and their indiscriminate bombing had taken out every major European city. Paris, Berlin, and London would take decades to rebuild, if ever. What was there left to destroy? America was history.

Ross climbed higher still, to extreme altitude, even for the USAF. Not its operational ceiling however. Much higher, towards an altitude never before attained by a fighter jet. Not even on test flights. The stars in front and above him shone intensely, their white brilliance reflecting off his visor, studding the deep black of endless space. Up there was space, pure and infinite without history, nor humanity. There was just vacuum, or near to it, until other stars, planets and civilizations light years distant. Space was neither good nor bad. Those characteristics belonged only to humans who claimed on them a monopoly, and who, far, far below were killing each other as fast as they could.

Ross climbed higher still, and the setting sun reappeared to the west, its crimson disc again above the Earth's blue-white curvature, throwing its multi-coloured light onto the flattened, anvil shaped tops of nuclear clouds, blown north on the jet stream.

Then the silvery disc of the full moon appeared low to the east, directly opposite the setting Sun, reflected in a winding ribbon of water which led to a city whose lights were now clearly in view. *Murmansk had survived!* Ross feared the worst for all those living in cities which had, until now been spared. How long would it be before they too were targeted, by the residual stocks of submarine SLBMs?

Suddenly a red warning light flashed onto the screen in front of him, a fast moving radar contact, directly behind him.

Another aircraft was closing fast at Mach 2, 20 nautical miles behind him but gaining. At that speed the intruder would be in a firing position in seconds. His on board computer sprang back to life. "Two Su-35s, range closing at 15 nautical miles. Increase speed."

Ross rammed the throttle forward, engaging the ramjet as the fighter became supersonic. Possibly, one of the Su-35s was the same one that had engaged him over Moscow. Ross thought: *He knows my capability, my speed, destination. That means he also knows about my fuel situation.*

"Two Su-35s, range closing at 12 nautical miles. Increase speed."

The two Su-35s had increased their speed to Mach 2.2, a speed which would wreck their engines. Ross thought: *They don't care. They know I will run.*

"Range closing at 10 nautical miles. Increase speed."

Another warning, more sinister, flashed across the twin touch pad screens. There was no need for the on board computer to inform him what he already knew.

They fired, a missile a piece.

"Two R-77 Adder inbound. Radar active. Range 9 nautical miles. Increase your speed. Dive!"

Ross ignored the advice, unwilling to commit the aircraft to the stress. He deployed anti-radar jamming countermeasures instead. The range of the R-77 Adder missile was low when fired at a stern target. 25 kilometres at most. With the ramjets engaged, he could outrun them. His velocity was Mach 2.5 and increasing. He reached forward, touching the screen, straining against the large acceleration forces raking through his body as the ramjet thrust ahead. With it running on maximum, at 20 kilometres altitude, the aircraft would literally keep on accelerating. Right up till Mach 6.

"Two inbound R-77 missiles on active radar homing, range 8 nautical miles, speed Mach 3. Time to impact 15 seconds. Time to missile range limit 20 seconds."

It was going to be closer than he thought. He needed to reach Mach 3 within the next twelve seconds to be in with a chance. He looked down at his speed. Mach 2.75. Another warning, now distressingly familiar, flashed across the hi-tech cockpit screens. "What? Another one!"

As if he did not have enough on his mind with the two Sukhoi Su-35s on his tail, his on board computer was again alive, this time indicating a bogey on head on approach.

"MiG-31, Foxhound, inbound, closing at high speed from bearing 010."

Severomorsk Naval Air Base! thought Ross. Why hadn't the airfields of the Kola Peninsula been destroyed by cruise missiles? Was the U.S. war machine already completely destroyed?

"Two R-77 missiles, inbound, speed Mach 3. Range closing, 1 nautical mile."

The F-35 accelerated through three times the speed of sound, reaching Mach 3.1 and still accelerating. The R-77s fell back, two seconds before impact.

Chapter 75

The threat now came from the north. Head on!

The on-board computer sensed Ross was tired, selecting a higher dose of amphetamines, and injected them straight into his artery, with instant effect. As wide awake as a tom cat on the rampage, he took control once again of the situation. Or at least he tried to.

"Intruder inbound, range 75 nautical miles, bearing 010 at Mach 2.85, altitude 18,000 meters. Change your vector and pull up."

The MiG-31 was coming straight for him, at Mach 6 closure. Ross smiled. Did the computer not realise that already the F-35 was operating at its ceiling? Had he pushed the computer, as well as the aircraft, past its limits?

A warning flashed throughout the cockpit, wiping the smile off his face like a slap.

"R-77 missile with active radar homing in bound. Calculating time to impact. Change your vector and pull up."

"Changing our vector's not an option, Babe," said Ross, out loud. "We have no fuel for that!"

He rammed the throttle to its forward limit once more. He thought: *I might not be able to reach Mehamn on present fuel, but at least I will survive the engagement with this MiG-31 son of-a-bitch!*

His cockpit displays indicated that the aircraft was accelerating through Mach 3.8.

"R-77 inbound, bearing 010, range 30 nautical miles at Mach 2.9. Time to impact 26 seconds. Change your vector and pull up."

Pulling sharply back on the control column, Ross converted the aircraft's incredible speed to height. Feeding G forces through his body faster than a space module on re-entry, he took the F-35 to its very limit. In the space of several seconds, he reached 30,000 meters, and continued to climb. The R-77 Adder missile's speed would be little affected by the scarcity of the atmosphere, because it was a rocket, not an air-breathing jet. Its ability to turn, however, to use its tail fin lattices to track towards a target would be curtailed by the lack of air. At least that was the theory.

He levelled out at 35,000 meters panting heavily from the G forces and from the mixture of adrenaline and amphetamines which had been forced into his veins. It was going to be close. The Adder missile was locked on, its radar active, calculating. It was updating the F-35's position, its bearing, altitude and trajectory.

"5 seconds to impact."

Ross pulled the control column sharply right. The missile reacted instantly, electronic impulses sent to the four tail-mounted control lattices. A manoeuvre which could out fly any known turning capability... at low altitude. At 30,000 meters the story was different. The airflow across the lattice surfaces was insufficient, its control sluggish. It missed.

The vortex created by the high speed pass sent the F-35 into a flat spin.

Instinctively Ross fought to control it, and succeeded.

Approaching fast, but well below his altitude, the MiG-31 had fired again. Ross was glad he had not reduced his speed, had not disengaged the ramjet during the spin. Speed was going to be a factor once again. The MiG-31 was at close range, not directly ahead, but not directly below either.

"R-77 with semi-active homing inbound at bearing 015, range 5 nautical miles. Calculating time to impact."

Ross banked slightly to the left. It would take precious seconds, for the missile to accelerate to Mach 3 and even more to reach his altitude. The missile would simply not be able to attain him if he continued on his bearing and speed of Mach 4.5.

Ross's breathing and heart rate came down, out of the extremes. Though the MiG-31 had turned to pursue him, he was falling back. It was the fastest Russian jet. But Mach 3.2 was just too fast, and would be causing irreparable engine damage. Its pilot didn't seem to care. Probably he was under strict orders to continue the chase to its deadly conclusion.

Ross looked directly below him. A high pressure weather system had moved in to cover Northern Scandinavia, enveloping it with cold, clear skies. It was midnight. Not a single light was visible below him. His GPS navigation told him that he was approaching the Russian — Norwegian border. Again he looked, more closely this time, squinting down into the darkness.

Minute, twinkling lights pricked the blackness. Kirkness. Right on the border.

***

Ross disengaged the F-35's ramjet. He had pulled a comfortable buffer between him and the MiG-31 Foxhound. Coming in from the east over the Varanger Peninsular, at high but decreasing altitude, his mind numbed from lack of sleep. Yet still functioning. It was numbed too from the amphetamines which had kept him alive.

Dead ahead was Tanafjord, a broad, hazy blue line. Above it he could make out the steep slopes leading to the tundra plateau of the North Cape Peninsular. Mehamn Airport, right ahead. Fuel was critical. But he was going to make it

He reduced the aircraft's speed further. Thundering in low above the first deep inlet of the Barents Sea, he made final landing checks, expecting the friendly computerized voice to confirm everything. He was home and dry.

Only he wasn't.

He had messed up, probably more due to the drugs and his tiredness than anything else. Then the on-board computer sprang again to life.

"MiG-31 inbound at Mach 3, range 5 nautical miles bearing 150 degrees. Increase your speed, change your vector."

Ross wondered how the computer had failed to inform him that the threat was so close behind. Had it informed him? *Was I too fazed by the drugs to hear the warnings?*

Five nautical miles? Things were much worse than he thought. They were pretty dire in fact. He was already running on vapour, so any kind of combat flying would put a crash landing categorically in his future. Five miles? So why had the MiG not fired?

The MiG-31 is out of missiles.

For the last time, Ross gunned the throttle, knowing full well the action would mean putting Mehamn out of range. The thrust pushed him into the seat as the ramjet pulled for a last time on maximum thrust.

"MiG-31 radar locked on. Execute immediate evasive action."

The F-35, at less than 300 meters over Tanafjord, pulled up, thrust vectoring. It reduced its speed to cause the following MiG to overshoot. Too late.

Before the MiG-31 overshot, its pilot let off a burst of fire from its rotary gun. 23mm calibre depleted Uranium cannon rounds. They slammed into his F-35 from close range.

Chaos erupted around Ross, as he fought with the controls. A vicious fire of shrapnel had smashed not only into the aircraft's vital avionics and the on-board computer, silencing definitively the electronic voice. They had smashed through his helmet too, though he had not felt them penetrate. Maybe he was numbed by battlefield adrenaline. Maybe it was the amphetamines, or a combination of the two. His mind was set on one thing and one thing alone: putting the aircraft on the ground.

Chapter 76

The cold bit savagely as a wolf, and wolves that night were in his dreams. And wolves fought close to the place where he lay, oblivious to his presence. Play fights, as wolves do to keep themselves alert and in tip-top-killing-machine condition. And to allay the effects of the cold, which at that very time was relentless, even to wolves. Its face was stark and hard, its teeth of steel. Deeper and deeper it penetrated into every layer of his garments, from the hard, ice encrusted shell of his flight suit, fused by the wind, through to the surface of his skin. The night was drawing towards its close, towards its coldest, most inhospitable hour. The dawn.

Lieutenant Colonel Lee Ross lay semi-conscious, half-camouflaged, half-hidden by a rocky recess of the slope. He was young, only 29, and he was resilient. His body was warm from the drugs. Most importantly, he was protected from the whistling wind by a huge boulder which towered above him on his northern side. There was a huge snowdrift too which formed around him, and insulated him.

The crash landing run had left the aircraft in a mangled mess against a low rock outcrop, and a last cocktail of drugs injected into his veins. The amphetamines had done their job one last time, focussing and clearing his mind on the crash landing roll. When it finally had come to a stop, he knew only one thing: *Get out before it blows!*

Once out of the wreck, he went out of his mind. Partly it was the drugs. Partly the shrapnel lodged deep in his skull. Already he remembered absolutely nothing of his mission. The name Mehamn meant nothing to him, Anna Kuznetsova even less. Only survival mattered. And survival meant getting out of the open, out of the snow filled wind which blew incessantly across the tundra.

The drugs burnt inside him; a raging fire, turning what little reserves he had to heat. There were other effects too though. Even without the shrapnel wound, he would not have remembered the hours leading to the crash. The drugs did not come without side effects. There were consequences, drawbacks, pay-offs. Nobody could expect to have their cake and eat it. Not even him. He had needed to remain awake for days, and fly as if he were fresh as a daisy. But he had survived. Thanks to the drugs he was there, alive and warm.

Hours passed, and the wolves moved on, up towards the plateau, towards Mehamn, but not that far. They kept away from the Russian patrols who were already numerous in the border regions between Russia and what used to be NATO controlled territory. Before the war.

The north-eastern horizon grew lighter, heralding the dawn. Then the sound filling the air changed.

To Ross's slumbering world, the noise was no longer the soft whispering of the snow filled wind. It grew to a chattering cacophony which extracted him from his dreams. He knew only too well the noise. It was that of helicopter rotors.

Part 3. After The War

Chapter 77

Seventeen Years Later, Finnmark, Norway

Sat on a huge boulder, overlooking Rafjord, Ross felt a wave of happiness envelope him like a breeze on a warm, autumn day. Of course there had been times when he had experienced feelings of wellbeing during his seventeen years of captivity. No matter how dreadful are the conditions of one's existence, happiness comes and goes. The human brain learns. The capacity of the human race for adaptation is equalled only by that of the brain for survival. Hope had kept him sane. Hope kindled by the knowledge that he was still close to North Cape. Why they had never moved him, to a location deep inside Russia, had remained to him a source of contemplation for years. It was a mystery.

Close to Anna Kuznetsova! Was she still there? Somewhere in the wilderness through which he now trekked, seventeen years after the crash? But even if she was still there, even if he succeeded in finding her, what then? Would he then remember something about her? Why, despite all the pain and hardship he had endured, did the memory of her keep him alive?

It was something about the mission. That much he knew. That much was obvious, ascertained from the flight suit he wore when he was captured.

Ross guessed that was also the reason why they had interrogated him so cruelly. They wanted information. His identity. Information about his mission. About his plane. But how could he have helped them when he only remembered two things; the name Anna Kuznetsova and the airstrip at Mehamn.

It was a late September evening on the tundra, and for only a week he had been free again.

Ross was sitting contemplating the setting sun, a warm wind on his face. He had made good progress and was now close at hand to the location of the crash landing. Each step he took in its direction brought more memories rushing back. He now remembered more clearly than ever the icy wind in the boulders, the snow, and the wolves.

He knew too that he had been but 29 when he had guided his stricken F-35 inland above the dark, frigid waters of Tanafjord. He knew now for the first time in all those years of captivity that he had done the impossible, putting the aircraft onto the steep rocky sides of the Rafjord valley, and surviving. Forcing his mind to think about it, to fill the gaps in his memory, had been one of the main ways he had kept sane during the seventeen years.

In captivity he had been unable to remember anything before waking from a dream of wolves in which the sound of the mountain wind filled his ears with its sweet music. The whistles of the snow filled wind in the snow drifts was transformed into that of thunderous down draughts of helicopter rotors, as real as the boulders amongst which he lay. Beyond that, he had had no memories at all.

The valley which stretched now before him was long and deep. Its sides led steeply to the plateau on which he sat. Ross scanned the rocky landscape with the powerful binoculars he had acquired during his escape. He thought: *seventeen years since I saw this place. I am now 45.*

For three and a half years now, the Russian Army was the only military power left on the planet. That much he knew. His captors had eventually given him access to a computer, and the internet, considering him no longer a risk. America, the UK, Israel, Japan, France, Turkey and Italy all had been destroyed within weeks of the strike seventeen years before, China and South Korea in a matter of months. The rest had been won over by treaties and threats. The world, despite the several thousand nuclear detonations, continued to revolve. Life went on, just differently.

They were out there, thought Ross, the Russian Army. Probably they were closer than he dared believe.

He had done well in laying a false trail towards the south for the first two days following his escape. Close to the former Russian-Norway border, he had turned westwards, doubling his previous speed at the start of the equinox nights to fool them even more. Sometimes he ran for hours thankful of the long hours spent training in his cell for each day of the seventeen years. The exertion relaxed him, toned his muscles, a tonic for his body and mind, burning much of what little body fat he had left, making him stronger.

He was thankful that his captors had not denied him a diet which had fuelled the athletic, muscular body that had carried him to freedom. His escape had depended on speed that first night. Following that night, the helicopters no longer passed constantly overhead. But they still passed. Even now it was still necessary that he blend into the landscape at a moment's notice.

On the second night after turning west, he had begun the long trek north. Then as now, he did not know what was guiding him. Just that somewhere in his mind he had a picture, an image, a mental map of where the answers to his questions lay. But the answers to what, and to why, he did not know. Anna Kuznetsova? Mehamn? What did those names mean, and why had he remembered them alone?

Instinct led him on. The 'Wolf Instinct' as he termed it often in his mind. The wolves he had met in the past two weeks were many, and he felt strange kindred towards them. They knew he was there, in their midst, and after days and nights, they drew close. There was mutual respect.

He hoped that the answers would become clearer as he got closer to where his instinct was taking him. The 'Wolf Instinct' had led him to the present spot, spread-eagled on the flat boulder, looking down the deep valley towards Rafjord, glittering in the distance, towards the wreck of the F-35.

For forty minutes now he had scrutinized every corner of the southern panorama, binoculars held steady to his piercing blue eyes as they caught the dying sun. Nothing. He swept them towards the east, down the axis of the valley of Rafjord. He knew the name because it had been engraved on his memory, wiped almost clean during the crash, but never completely. The amnesia, he now knew, was a combination of the cocktail of drugs and the piece of depleted uranium embedded into his skull. Or so the operating doctor had told him days after the surgery which saved his life. He never saw the doctor again, but remembered the boulders, the snow, the wolves, and the helicopters when he was captured. Rafjord.

Why had they kept him alive? He had posed the question many times, as he did right then. They could have got all the information they needed from the plane itself. Yet they wanted him. Why? Probably that meant that the plane was not only a wreck, it was a burnt wreck.

Looking carefully straight down the valley towards Tanafjord, the deep inlet of the Barents Sea, Ross thought: *So this is the valley of Rafjord, where I crashed.* He did not question how he knew it. He just did. His instinct had brought him back to the place where his previous life had ended; full circle.

He panned the binoculars from one steep side of the valley to the other. He sought to relive the last moments of the flight. Still nothing. His mind was blank.

Lounged stomach down on the flat boulder, his legs wide apart, he switched methods. He put himself in the shoes of the pilot of a stricken jet who had no choice but to put the aircraft down in the valley before him. Still nothing. The valley sides were steep and rocky in all directions.

The breeze tore at his camouflaged jacket, the one he had taken from one of the guards on the day of his escape. The day had given way to twilight's long hour and a radical shift in temperature. The season of change was already well advanced on the tundra. With no distances left to cover, and no chance to locate the crash in the hours of darkness, the need to find shelter pressed on him.

He fell asleep under the same flat boulder in a bed of dry heather, his body overcome. Fatigue worked in strange ways, as did the radiation of the depleted uranium still lodged in his brain. The one the surgeon had been unable to remove. It had happened before of course, many times. Usually at the end of the day, when he was lying down, his body still. Drowsiness hit him like a shot, his muscles twitching on the border between wakefulness and sleep. Then he slept.

He woke with a start, aware of something strange, something alien. Though he had not seen anything, he knew he was no longer alone in that wild and lonely place. *How had I become so lax?*

"Don't worry. I'm not going to turn you in!" said a girl's voice carried to him on the breeze. He hated being prone, but he dealt with it. If she had wanted to kill him, he would already have been dead.

She was behind him. Even if he had turned 180 degrees, he would not have been able to see her. The night was cloudy. The darkness was thick.

"Who are you?" he said, without moving an inch.

"A friend!"

"How do you know that if we haven't even met!"

"We haven't met, but I know who you are. I know many things about you. You're the pilot!"

Through Ross's confusion, he heard the girl was speaking again, her voice louder, closer. He spun onto his back.

"Don't be afraid," she whispered. "I am your friend. Get up if you want. I am not armed."

He moved to a sitting position.

"It's funny," she said as she looked at him, really close now. Her eyes were as acute as an eagle's and accustomed to the dark. Ross too was able to pick out the features of her face. She had a wide mouth, full lips and large intense eyes. Her dimples disappeared when she smiled, as she was doing at that very instant.

"You're just as I imagined you would be," she said. "Just as they said you would be."

"They?" answered Ross. "They who?"

"Don't worry, we'll get to all that later. Quick, we don't have much time."

"Why? It seems to me we have all the time we need!"

"Seems?" she answered. "Lee. You weren't born here! Please, we need to leave."

Ross got up and grabbed her arm as she turned briskly to leave, pulling her close to him. "How do you know my name?"

Her jaw was wide, yet finely tapered. He noticed the fine lines of her face, the small nose, her deep-set eyes painted the colour of the sea.

"Listen . . . " began Ross before the girl cut him off.

"Lee. Don't argue. They patrol the peninsular at night, and believe me; you do not want to be caught by them. It happened to me once and I vowed I would never let it happen again. We have to go. Right now!"

Again Ross pulled her around. But now he saw fire, not water, in her eyes. She was no more that seventeen. He said, "Go? Go where?"

"To my place, just over the hill." She pointed towards the highest part of the plateau. "An hour away, at my pace that is." She turned to look in the direction that she indicated, as if looking there gave the gesture meaning. "Ross. Let's go!"

She led him straight up the mountain by way of a path.

They had gone no further than half a kilometre when they saw a line of torches, moving leftwards towards them on the far side of the valley yet on their level, just above the cliffs which fell to the waters of Tanafjord. Then the girl stopped dead, and spun around towards Ross. "Hurry! We don't have much time!"

She began running up the path.

"Russians?" said Ross, following at her pace.

"You got it. And they are heading this way."

"How fast?"

"Faster than us, that's for sure. We could be cut off at the top. They are running along on the high path. Maybe they already know you are here in the valley, though I doubt it."

"Why would you doubt it?" asked Ross, doing his best to keep up. He was a strong runner, the strongest in his school and later, in the Air Force. But a week on the run had taken its toll.

"I would have heard it on the radio."

She stopped for a brief moment and tore open her jacket, revealing a radio. "A year ago, one of them slipped on the cliffs of Tanafjord and fell to his death. By luck, he was small, not much bigger than me." She smiled. "I guess his uniform was also a little too small, because it fits me perfectly."

The lights were already closing. The girl had been right not to underestimate them. They were obviously not going to make the top of the slope before being cut off. There was only one thing for it. Hide. "Quick! Run for the boulders. Over there."

They camouflaged themselves in seconds, pressed together under Ross's jacket, hardly daring to breathe. The heavy footsteps were closing, passing close by. They were right on top of them, and then they receded, swallowed by the night.

Chapter 78

The next morning, the sun's first rays hit the high, cirrus clouds above the eastern horizon, turning them deep crimson. It was the following day, and Ross and the girl were already back on the top path after a night spent at her hut on the plateau. Below them stretched Rafjord valley.

His young escort was making her way down the other side of the ridge, following a steep path. Without a word, Ross followed, his mind, still mulling the events of the previous night.

***

"What's your name?" had been one of Ross's first questions, once they got to her hut, a small, wooden construction with a black chimney sticking out of its top.

"Lena Berntzen."

Later he had sat cross legged on the warm floor as she busied herself around her simple home. He was dead tired and could think of nothing else but sleep. And yet, his desire to find out about the girl who knew so much about him was overwhelming. Since the talk on the boulder where they had met she had hardly said a word. "Where are you from?"

"Here," she answered. She felt comfortable with him, as if they had known each other for years, not feeling the need to make constant small talk.

"You were born here? In this hut?"

"I don't know exactly, I don't remember being born."

She was tall and slim with an athletic body honed by years of running on the tundra. He put her at no more than eighteen, which meant she would have been born about a year after the war. Or maybe she was seventeen, which mean she would have been conceived when the war started, around the time he had crash landed into her neighbourhood.

"Tell me about your first memory," suggested Ross, eager to know more. She was busy preparing the fire which he supposed was going to be used to cook the meal. Above the amassed tinder and wood, a solid stove shone bright.

Lena knelt down, a mass of tinder in her hands, and a contraption which looked like a bow. She looked into the tinder as if the answer lay there, concealed, waiting to be found.

"It was late autumn because the days were becoming really short. We had gone out just before dark, with rifles and paraffin fuelled Tilly Lamps, hunting hares on the tundra."

"Why do you remember it?"

"Because of what we saw," said the girl, working the bow back and forth with a vertical rod of hardwood turning at high speed inside an indentation in a hardwood, wooden base. "It was either an asteroid or a rocket re-entering the atmosphere, its red and yellow shining brilliantly in the dim light of the night. I remember my father saying it was a rocket re-entering."

"What happened to your parents?" asked Ross.

"I was raised by the Sami, the local tribe, and the man I called my father, wasn't really my father. He was the owner of this hut, that's all, and I grew up with him. He protected me since as long as I can remember."

Ross noticed tears had formed in her eyes as she began to work the bow faster than ever. She stopped momentarily, to wipe them away. Smoke had started to rise from the base of the vertical rod, so she dropped dry tinder powder into the indentation on the wooden base, blowing softly the fire into existence.

She straightened up as the flames took hold, adding dry sticks to the fire. "He died last summer and I buried him at the top of the plateau, as that's where he loved to watch the sunset, above the boulder where I met you."

"I'm sorry for your loss."

"Thank you," said the girl, smiling.

"Do you do that every day?" said Ross, crouching beside her as she finished building the fire.

"How can you tell?"

***

Lena Berntzen cooked a meal of stew on the fire using a large, cast iron cauldron. She told him she had a secret store of reindeer meat in a nearby farm, while the potatoes she had grown on the wild, empty tundra surrounding her home. During the time she had taken to cook for him, Ross had lain on a bed of reindeer and polar bear fur which she had made for him next to the fire, listening to the sounds of nature which penetrated easily from outside. There was a strong, gale-force wind blowing and the rain which had just started pelted against the hut's two windows. A feeling of happiness ran through him. He was free, in the company of an amazing young woman and the night was filled with the sounds of nature that he loved. He fell into a state of deep sleep, not even feeling the characteristic twitches as his body and mind passed out of wakefulness.

"Hey! Wake up!"

Ross awoke with a start, scooping up Lena's rifle which he had cleaned just before he had laid down.

"It's okay," said Lena soothingly. "Supper is ready!"

"How long was I asleep?"

"An hour I suppose. Come on."

She led him to the tiny, low table which she had laid in front of the flames of the pine fire which crackled and sparked in the fireplace.

"It's funny. It seems like I had been asleep for hours. I feel completely rested."

"It's the effect of the storm. My father always said the storm invigorates, better than a sauna."

Sitting, cross legged in front of the fire once they had finished their supper, drinking tea, Lena looked at him as he sat beside her, outlined against the flickering light. "Now it's your turn to tell a story. Tell me about your first memory."

Lena detected a change in him as her question sank in. Then she thought that the feeble light which illuminated his face must have misled her. Then she was sure. The question had unsettled him.

"My earliest memory is being woken by the sound of wolves in the morning following the crash."

"You don't even remember the crash?"

"No, I don't."

"Kira?"

Ross felt a bolt of energy, a shock, though he could not understand its provenance. "What did you say?"

"Kira!"

"How do you know that name?" Ross felt as if he had just found something he did not know he had lost. Though it was just a word, and a name, when he heard it he knew it was more. It was a key, a way to unlock his past. Already it was opening doors.

Something inside him had changed, but only partially. His mind still contained secrets, even to him. "Kira." He said, out loud, doorways to the past opening further, the name burning a hole back in time from the memory of the wolves and the sound of helicopter rotors which woke him among the frozen boulders. Like a computer system, the name was a point of reference, a 'system restore' to a point in his past.

"Say it again?" said Ross.

"What?"

"The name you just said, say it again!"

"Kira."

"How do you know anything about her?"

"It was in your phone, the one I found at the crash site. The Russians didn't do a search of the area. They didn't even search the burnt out plane. I guess that due to the events of the war that was the last thing on their minds."

"You found my smartphone?" demanded Ross, incredulous. "Where is it? For God's sake, show it to me!"

He got up agitated, walking, pacing up and down the wooden floor of the single room of the hut.

"Hey!" replied the girl, getting up. "Take it easy. I'll get it, but don't get your hopes up. The battery died seventeen years ago!"

She moved across the single room hut to a rustic chest of draws which stood against the wall adjacent to the fire and took it from the second draw from the top. "Here you are."

He took it, grasping it firmly, turning it this way and that, feeling its contours, remembering. Having it again in his hands was unlocking some of the secrets of his mind, blazing a trail into his past.

There was no need to talk to Kira to unlock at least some of his past. He felt hope, and excitement, and doubt. He remembered her curves, her green eyes, even her touch. She was in his past and that was enough.

"I remember!" he said finally, half to himself and half to Lena.

"What do you remember?"

"I'm not completely sure, not yet. There's something inside the F-35, something I need to find. There are numbers and inscriptions that were important for the mission I was on."

He scratched his head, pacing up and down.

"You need to rest," said Lena. "Tomorrow, early, before the sun rises, we'll go to the wreck, if you like."

But Ross was in no mood to sleep. "There is gold there too," he said. "Inside the plane there is gold! I don't know whether it is important, just that the memory of gold is linked to my memories of the F-35, of the numbers and inscriptions."

"What does it mean?" asked the girl. "Numbers, gold, inscriptions? You're being too vague. We need to know specifics."

"I don't know. All I know is that there are two distinct entities in my memory of the plane, things important for me, for us."

"For us? What do you mean Lee? You aren't making sense!"

Ross sat back down next to her, in front of the fire. "Listen, Lena. For years in captivity, I searched my memory for clues of my past, of the mission I was on that night of the crash. During the long months of solitude inside my cell, I willed my mind to clarity. It was as if I knew what the plane wreckage contained, but was unable to see it."

"And now?" asked Lena, returning to the fire and stoking it with peat fuel for the night. Outside the gale was reaching its climax with the sound of driving rain on the hut's windows and roof adding to the charged atmosphere.

Ross had to speak up as the girl came and sat next to him. "After I escaped, the closer I got to the wreckage, the greater the illusion that clarity would return. Yet . . . "

He left the word hanging, seized by a sudden doubt.

"Yet?" pronounced Lena, sitting cross legged in front of the fire looking up at him.

"Yet even when I reached the head of the valley of Rafjord, from where I could have seen the wreckage . . . Even from there my amnesia, the God-damned shrapnel uranium shit lodged in my head, prevented me from reaching it and opening the secrets of my head."

"And now?" said Lena.

The American put his arm around her shoulder. "Now, thanks to you, Lena, the clouds are clearing. If you are sure that no one has searched the plane wreckage, then what I know was there, the gold object, the inscriptions, the key to my past and to the mission, are all still there."

"It's still there," said Lena. "I am sure. I think my father too knew of the importance of the aircraft. You see, that plane was something of an obsession to him. Never a day passed that he did not visit it. Even in his final year he studied it, with binoculars from the rocks at the head of the valley, sat on the flat boulder where I met you. It was as if he was waiting for its pilot to return, as if he knew that to return he must. He was somehow sure that if only he kept looking, kept going back to it, the plane would reveal the secrets he longed to solve. Alas, he died too early."

They sat cross legged on the reindeer rugs staring into the fire, warm now, listening to the storm outside. Although neither spoke more, each was attuned to the other, and to the place where they found themselves.

Lena inserted her hand inside her clothing, producing the most precious object she had ever possessed, given to her by her father just before he died. "Here, take this," she said, pushing it into Ross's hand. "You know how to use it, I don't."

Ross took the Beretta M9 pistol and removed its magazine, checking its contents.

"It's full, 9 rounds."

She sprang up and walked over to the chest of draws, extracting three boxes from the bottom drawer. "There! Three boxes more of 9mm rounds; for tomorrow!"

Ross followed the young Sami girl down the well-worn trail. The rocky path led steeply down from the valley head towards the switch-backs, leading into the valley bottom.

Lena jumped onto the huge, flat granite boulder where they had met the previous day. "We can see the wreckage from here, with binoculars. See? Down there, at the foot of the cliffs."

Lena indicated the left hand side of the deep valley ahead of them, an outcrop of rock, at the foot of cliffs which slanted up and leftwards, to the plateau. On one side of the outcrop, a long grassy area led straight to the sea, to Rafjord, and in the distance, Tanafjord.

"That's it!" exclaimed Ross. "I tried to put the F-35 down on the long grassy strip which I saw coming in over Tanafjord!"

***

Unknown to Ross and the Sami girl, the hut belonging to her had been under observation since the previous evening at the time when the storm reached its zenith. The observer was also of the Sami tribe, a boy of fifteen and a native of Kirkines the town where Ross had been imprisoned.

He had heard the rumours of a hefty bounty on the American. In the New Era, the Russian's paid well for information. Everyone had become police, and information had become a kind of second currency. Information leading to the American would eclipse everything else which the Russians had ever paid.

When he had finally caught up with the American night had already fallen across the plateau. The storm allowed the boy to move close to the hut, right up to the window where he remained hidden, invisible to anyone on the inside. He had peered in, through the stinging rain which pelted his face, soaking every stitch of his clothing.

The American was not going anywhere that night. Since the boy had no way to communicate his find to the Russians, nor could he be sure of navigating through the night to the nearest Russian camp on the road to Mehamn, he decided to stay put, until the morning.

Due to the storm the night before the Russian patrol was late in setting out from Mehamn. When they finally came along the plateau, the watery sun had just risen above the waters of Tanafjord.

The Sami boy had followed the American and the Sami teenager since they left the hut, and now took one last look last look at them as they jumped onto a huge flat boulder which commanded a fine view of the steep valley below. He noted their position before sprinting up the slope towards the Russian patrol which he knew must be close on the plateau behind him. He did not know if he felt scared, elated or just plain stupid. He was sure about one thing however, that he was about to become very rich.

Chapter 79

Standing on the flat topped boulder next to Ross, a thought suddenly flashed through Lena's mind. *Shit! How could I have forgotten?*

"Jump!" she said, giving Ross a firm enough shove to overbalance him, leaving no alternative but to leap.

If Ross had not been trained or not kept his body in tip top condition during his long imprisonment, the two meter drop and heavy landing onto the heather below the boulder could have easily sprung an ankle, or worse. With the agility of a cat, he forward rolled as he hit the deck, the Beretta already drawn.

Lena landed right behind him, and Ross threw an arm to grab her waist to stop her from careering further down the steep slope.

"What is it?" said Ross, surveying the slopes below. "Did you see something?"

"Not down there," she answered. "On the plateau behind us. Today the Russians restart their early patrols after a week. I forgot."

"And where will they come from?"

"Right now they should be close to the top of the plateau."

The Russian patrol planned their operations to be on top of Koifjordfjell at dawn. That was just midway between their present position, and Lena's hut on Koifjordvatnet. From the top of the

Koifjordfjell, they would have been in a position to see them, clearly silhouetted on the flat boulder against the backdrop of Tanafjord.

Ross said, "Maybe the storm and the wind delayed them."

"Maybe. But I don't like it!"

"What is it?" asked Ross. "We are so close to the wreckage. Show me again where it is."

Lena pointed. "In the direction of the point, can you see where the steep cliffs of Koifjordfjellet meet the base of the valley? Do you see the rock outcrop at the end of the grassy slope where you crash landed, before the waters of Tanafjord?"

Ross lowered the binoculars for a second, trying to locate the plane wreck. Suddenly, he saw it. Just as she had said, the wreck was at a rocky outcrop on the edge of steep cliffs leading above the grassy valley floor. "Got it. Let's go!"

"Wait!" commanded Lena. "We have to move slow, and keep down. The Russians could be watching the valley from the top of Koifjordfjellet. Keep close to the deck."

After weeks of tracking him, the Sami boy knew exactly the shade of colour of Ross's camouflage fatigues. "There they are!" he said, handing the binoculars to the commander of the Russian squad, who had come to join him, laying down next to him on the heather at the top of the valley. "They're two kilometres, directly ahead of us, halfway between here and the valley bottom."

"I see them," replied the commander. His options were few. He knew Ross would be watching periodically the plateau, watching his rear. Once they moved towards them, they would be seen. "Damn it!" *Too far for a quick kill,* thought the commander. *We don't have anyone who could carry out that kind of shot.*

He noticed that the two were heading for the position of something he knew only too well, the F-35 wreckage. But the F-35 had been classified as completely destroyed. *Why in hell's name would the pilot want to get back to the site of his own crash?*

***

Ross saw the wreckage of the F-35, buckled and broken against the low, rocky slabs of red granite which had ended his crash landing run. He felt a surge of memories, a rush of insight into his past, the first time in seventeen years. He got to his feet. He wasn't going to crawl the last hundred meters. Not when he was so close. Not when the power of curiosity was that strong. Not now that the secrets of his past and of the F-35 were so close at hand. Taking Lena's hand, he motioned to the wreckage. "Go!"

High velocity rounds ricocheted all around, shattering the calm. Despite the rain of lead they managed to reach the granite slabs, the momentum of their bodies carrying them over the first boulders, and into the dead space behind, hidden from line of sight and line of fire from anybody located at the head of the valley.

Ross said, "Are you all right?"

"I'm fine, thank you very much."

Breathing deeply Ross began to figure out a plan. And there had to be a plan. There was always a plan. Even in the middle of the wilderness, with a single Beretta, three spare magazines, and a young girl in tow, there was a plan.

Another wave of bullets pounded into the rock, pinning them down in their rock lair.

"Who the hell is firing at us?"

"The Russian patrol!" shouted back Lena. "I told you they would be up there, but you didn't listen. You made a mistake!"

"Maybe not. We're here aren't we, and alive!"

"Maybe not for much longer!"

For a brief moment there was a pause in the onslaught, and Ross was out in a flash, taking four quick shots with the Beretta. He took in the scene, before ducking back behind the boulder and reloading. The Russian patrol was closer than he had expected, 700 meters and running at full tilt towards them. He repeated the action, firing twice and counting four Russians before a new wave of bullets exploded around him, sending him back into cover, back to the dead space behind the boulder.

"How many Russians did you say make up the patrol?" said Ross, reloading the Beretta.

"Five!" she answered. "We don't stand a chance do we?"

"Not in the open, but if they keep coming, I'd give us fifty-fifty."

The heavy machine gun had stopped firing, which didn't bode well for him and the girl. It meant the patrol was upon them, their heavy machine gunner silenced out of necessity to prevent friendly fire casualties. It was now or never.

Ross somersaulted into a firing position, shooting twice and seeing the Russian patrol at less than a hundred meters, zigzagging, impossible for a single man with a Beretta to take down, even him. He could get one, possible two, but the chances of him getting them all were non existential.

He fired twice again in less than a second and took out the closest Russian.

He held his ground and fired twice more, taking out another Russian, before ducking back into cover and reloading.

Their position was hopeless, but he would take down as many as he could. At close range, he was at his most lethal.

When the Russian patrol was on him, three against one, another noise met his ears, that of the heavy machine gun. Only it wasn't. It couldn't be, because it was louder, closer. A second gunner had entered the fire fight. *It was coming from the wreck of the F-35!*

Ross dived back out and saw the three remaining Russians being raked by high calibre bullets.

Their comrade had taken them out!

Chapter 80

Only their comrade had not taken them out at all. Someone else had joined the fight, on their side!

As the echoes of the shots died away, Ross sprinted to the three dying Russian soldiers firing two safety shots straight into their chests. Lena appeared at his side, safe and sound, saying simply, "Who shot them?"

Ross didn't reply but instead scanned the hillside above the plane wreckage.

Lena said, "Lee!"

"What?"

"What are you looking for?"

***

Ross recognised the woman long before she came into earshot walking down the hillside. In the last few tens of meters, he noticed that her beauty had not changed, despite the passing of seventeen years. At ten meters, he said, "How did you know?"

Instead of answering the woman wrapped her arms around his waist, holding him tightly, releasing him only after seconds which seemed to last an eternity. She pushed him away in order to focus on him, hit by how much she had missed him. "That's not important, Lee. All that matters is that you are alive, and that we are here."

After the initial embrace, she pointed to the F-35 wreckage crumpled against the low granite outcrop by the force of the final impact. "Did you really survive that crash? Do you even remember?"

"No. I don't remember the crash, or the flight for that matter."

"Do you remember me?"

"Yes, I do. I remember you Kira. It seems you were an obsession for me. I remember Hoffman, the CIA."

"What about Anna?"

"The name yes, but that's about it. Anna Kuznetsova. Who is she?"

"She was your last mission. I guess the details were wiped by your concussion during the crash and by the radioactive shrapnel still embedded in your brain."

"You even know that? The shrapnel." asked Ross.

Lena said, "Guys!"

"Sorry, Lena," said Ross. "Lena this is Kira, Kira, Lena. I owe Lena my life."

Lena smiled, saying, "We had better go. It's inconceivable that the Russian patrol would not have radioed it in. Either their machine gunner would have gone for help, or he is up there, waiting, watching our position. Their best reaction time out here is thirty minutes."

Lena was already up the path which rose diagonally from the granite crag.

"Wait, Lena," shouted Ross after her. "Aren't you forgetting that we have unfinished business with the plane wreck?"

"No. I'm not. You don't know the Russian patrols like I do. Like what they will do to us if they catch up with us. If we want to live to see another dawn, we have to leave now."

"Impossible," said Ross. "I have a mission to complete and I don't even know the first God damn thing about it. It's taken me seventeen years to get back here, to this point, and I'm not going to give up now. Lena, get down here and help Kira get the weapons off these guys. If you are right about the Russians, and I God damn hope you're not, then there's going to be one hell of a fire-fight when they catch up with us, and we need all the weapons we can get our hands on. I'll be at the plane wreckage."

For someone with only a vague idea of what he was looking for, Ross found it pretty fast.

That he knew absolutely nothing about it was not however, entirely true. Already he knew the object was golden, that it had inscriptions. And since he had met Kira, he knew it was in the cockpit of the aircraft.

The wreckage was in better shape than he had expected. There was no evidence of the fire he had presumed must have engulfed it on impact, the fire that had meant that he had been found huddled in boulders a full two hundred meters from the crash site. He climbed atop the wreck and into the pilot seat where he sat still a moment and closed his eyes. The key had indeed remained there all the years and his memory too had been frozen in that place.

Now he remembered everything. Anna was in danger! But that was seventeen years ago!

In front of him, the golden chalice was where he had left it, fixed with the woven band which had been given to him by Kira. He prised it out of its place and ran his fingers over the inscriptions. He remembered now that the fourth inscription were the space-time coordinates of North Cape. The place would be the same, presumably, but time had moved on.

As he studied the inscribed coordinates, a name flashed in his mind, Mehamn Airport. But Mehamn Airport was not where the coordinates lay. During the flight from Moscow he had estimated a three hour trek at a fast pace from Mehamn Airport to the Cape. He had thought that it was possible, but on the limit. September 21st. The weather seventeen years ago had also been stormy. He remembered the wind, cold and strong, as he huddled in the rocks.

"Ross," shouted Lena from across the tundra. "We should go!"

He needed time to think. He caressed the ancient goblet, turning it in the light. Was not time running out for humanity? That he knew now more than ever. He remembered Yuval, the False Prophet, and Khodorov; the Antichrist himself! The Kremlin! The decapitation attack!

Kira appeared in front of the shattered aircraft, her dark hair blowing wildly in the new gale force winds which were suddenly tearing up the valley. "Time to go Ross!" she shouted up to him, her words all but carried away.

They caught up with Lena at the top of the steep path that led diagonally up the steep side of the rocky fjord. Sat beside the path, she looked relaxed, the weapons she had hauled dumped on the heather.

"Been here long?"

"I've got a bad feeling about this."

"Where are we headed?" asked Kira.

"Away from the crash site at least. Lena is right about that."

"And then?"

"And then . . . " He took the golden chalice out of his camouflaged fatigues. "And then we need to find the location of these coordinates."

"What's that?" said Lena, approaching.

Ross handed her the relic.

"What is it? Where did you get it?"

"This, Lena, is what I have been looking for the past seventeen years, first inside my mind."

She was holding it now, running her fingers over the inscriptions. "So this is it. This was the golden numbers from the cockpit. It's beautiful."

She looked at the numbers of the space-time coordinates that were written there, feeling an unexpected chill run down her spine. The time coordinates were the year of her birth, but . . . earlier . . . Nine months earlier!

"What's wrong?" asked Kira, discerning apprehension in her attitude. "You look like you've seen a ghost."

Lena looked up at Ross and said, "This is important, right?"

Ross asked, "What do you mean?"

"You said this object was a key to the future of humanity."

"It is. It was inscribed over 2000 years ago. I was supposed to have been there, at those space-time coordinates, to do battle with God knows who for the future of humanity. Then my plane was shot down, I lost my memory and missed the rendezvous. Why?"

"This date is nine months before the day of my birth."

"Yes. And three hours after my F-35 was shot down. So what?"

She said, "Where is this location?" She was indicating the space coordinates.

"I don't know. I guess I had searched and located it on a map during the flight. I can't remember specifics. I guess I was planning to use my phone's GPS tracking device once I landed."

Suddenly, a new sound could be heard, above the sound of the gale. It was the drone of helicopters. The Russians were back!

"Quick," said Lena, running. "This way!"

They reached the cave after a ten minute sprint, just in the nick of time.

Two MI-25 helicopter gunships had just rounded Tyfjordneset point and by some miracle they hadn't been spotted.

Ross checked his watch as the sound of the two helicopters was tempered by distance and the sounds of the wind howling across the tundra. In less than an hour it would be dark. They were dry but cold, and in need a good night's sleep, and sleep, in those latitudes and in that season, meant fire. "It'll be dark in an hour. We'll stay here the night."

"What about my hut?" answered Lena, unable to hide her disappointment.

"Of course not," said Ross. "That's the first place they will look. You can be sure it's well staked out tonight. The same goes for your tent Kira. Besides, this cave is not so bad. There's soft heather and the sound of the sea will be our lullaby."

"But we'll freeze. Another storm is already upon us."

"We'll have a fire!"

Within the hour three fires were burning in the level area between the mouth of the cave and the steep cliff which fell to the sea. They formed a triangle. At the center was the place where Ross intended they sleep, a huge bed of heather and a rough wall of rocks. Ross had sent Kira to her base camp, to get the tent where she had spent the last week.

When they settled down for the night, the wind had increased further, to storm force. Lena had said it would, the sea whipped up into a huge swell which crashed against the rocky shore below them. Rain was mixed with the wind, though it didn't affect the fires.

Ross plied them with dry wood from the huge pile which Lena had brought from the beach below the cave. He then went to check that the tent was well secured against the makeshift wall he had constructed from the large, flat granite stones which littered the plateau above the cave. The wall protected them from the wind and the rain which was now driving horizontally from the south, while the fires provided warmth. He climbed back into the tent's dry, warm interior to find Kira and Lena not sleeping. They wanted answers.

"Before the helicopters came," began Lena, "you asked me why I was interested in the golden chalice."

"I remember. You said you were born nine months after the time coordinates inscribed on the chalice."

"That's right. I want to know where the space coordinates are. To which place and time exactly."

Ross reached inside his camouflaged jacket, extracting the golden vessel. "These coordinates are for a place on North Cape Peninsular. That much I remember. I remember calculating it was an hour's march from the place I planned to land the F-35, Mehamn Airport."

"Is there no way we can find out where the coordinates lie?" asked Lena, sitting cross legged on the heather at the entrance to the tent. She looked first at Ross and then at Kira. "Neither of you have a map?"

"I have a phone," said Kira.

It was the latest model smartphone, produced in Jerusalem. She took it out, switched it on, and waited for it to become active. Then she plugged in the coordinates, as Ross read them off the chalice.

"71.0716139 latitude. 27.80115137 longitude."

A location flashed onto the screen along with a name, Smorbringen. They saw that it was a place on an arm of land which struck out into the Barents Sea 2.55 kilometres northwest of Mehamn, just east of North Cape itself.

"Smorbringen!" exclaimed Lena, clambering for a view of the screen.

"Yes," answered Kira. "That's where these coordinates refer to."

Ross said, "It means something to you, right?"

"That's where I was born."

"You were born there?" exclaimed Kira. "Unbelievable! That's got to be more than sheer coincidence."

"Not really," said the young girl. "My foster father owned Smorbringen. It is an ancient habitation, a fortress dating back to the Iron Age."

"But you just said it was not a coincidence that you were born there," said Ross. "What do you mean?"

"Don't you see Ross? My life has always been connected to you, the aircraft, and that golden chalice. You see, it was no coincidence that we met. My father arranged it. He bought the hut where we spent last night because it was the nearest habitation to the F-35. I don't know how or why he knew you would come back to it at some point. But he knew it. And he was right. After all, here we all are."

"But why," asked Kira, lost. "Why did he want you to meet the pilot of the plane?"

"You see, my father was also born in Smorbringen, and inherited abilities for clairvoyance, for seeing into the future. Some say he was a wizard, a modern day Merlin. That's why he knew that my destiny was to meet that F-35 pilot. Why, we can only guess at, but I too believed in it."

"That's an awful lot of faith for something so invisible, so lacking in substance," said Ross.

"You are mistaken!" said Lena, whose eyes were suddenly lit up by the flickering fire.

"What?"

"You see, he was not really my father, as I told you."

"No?"

"No! Although he never told me directly, I came to know it. Everybody in Mehamn knew it."

"Knew what?" asked Kira.

"The arrival of my real parents at North Cape was the biggest event which ever befell Finnmark. Their arrival from Moscow occurred on the very same day that the nuclear war began."

"Anna and Yuval!" exclaimed Kira. "Are you saying that Anna and Yuval are your real mother and father?"

Lena looked at her, startled. "How do you know their names?"

"Lena! Don't you see? They are the reason we all are here. We are all connected to their arrival at North Cape!"

"Not them!" said Ross. "They are only pawns in a bigger game. The reason we are all here is because the Israelites who inscribed this chalice, this Holy Grail, knew something about the world we would be living in in the 21st century. They knew that the battle during the End Times, the battle between good and evil, the conflict that has endured through the ages, would lead mankind to North Cape, to you and to us."

"How could they know it?" blurted Lena, confused.

"We will never know how, but they did know it. They knew that your parents were the key to the battlefields of Armageddon. They knew that I would have to intervene in order to ensure the victory of the power of good over evil. That's why I needed to be present at your birth, not to kill you, but to protect you and your mother, Anna. I had to protect you both from Yuval, your father. Yuval was and is the False Prophet. Unfortunately, the world is no longer pre-determined, as it was before the war, so I was unable to reach the rendezvous."

"So why did you come back? What is your present mission?"

"Your foster father, the wizard, knew there was still hope to save the world from the evil which Yuval and his overlord, Ivan Khodorov, would have us endure. He knew too that I would need help when I came back to the plane wreckage. He knew I would need guidance to complete my mission. That's why he bought the hut nearest to the crash-landing site and taught you in the ways of the world. He did it so that you would be able to help me."

"And your mission, now that I have helped you, now that you are in a position to complete it?"

"My mission now is the same as it was seventeen years ago, to keep Anna from Yuval and Khodorov, to prevent them controlling her and using her power to ensure the survival of their Kingdom of Satan. My mission is still to save the world from the dystopian future that awaits all of us if we do not act."

"Dystopian world?" asked Lena. "How do you know what world is out there? All you have known for seventeen years is the walls of a prison in Kirkenes."

"I know. The question is do you know? Prison was a school, a place of learning about the unjust, corrupt world government in Jerusalem. Without democracy, without justice and with absolute power over the world government which he heads, the world we live in is indeed a living hell. It is indeed the Kingdom of Satan." He looked at Kira, who had been listening quietly. "Isn't that right Kira?"

"What you say is true. The world *has* become dystopian. We live in a world of maximum order and minimum justice where the powerful have complete freedom, and the weak are enslaved into lives of servitude. It's a world where the powerful maximise their happiness at the expense of the weak."

"Khodorov rules from Jerusalem, right?" said Ross, looking towards Kira.

Kira said, "Yes. He rules from the Temple that has once again risen from the ashes, the one he calls the Third Temple."

Ross said, "The future, our future and your future Lena, is not written. We have a choice and the world can be changed. We just have to want it enough. Khodorov is a powerful man, but a man nevertheless. His star will wane, and when it does, another will come to rule. We have a chance to make that future bright, to start again the fight, and from what better place than right here, right now?"

***

The gale continued through the night and yet, despite the wind's wailing and the waves roaring as they crashed ceaselessly onto the rocky shore below, it was the soundest night sleep of their lives. They had talked late into the night, until tiredness had finally closed their eyes. It was going to be tough, not one of them harboured doubts about that little detail. The next day, however, would be easy, a day for rest and relaxation.

Chapter 81

They arrived at Smorbringen in the early hours, two days later, an hour before sunrise, and found it deserted. They conducted a search for signs which might lead them to Yuval and Anna. Nothing. Then Lena came clean.

"They are not here!"

"Right!" said Ross. "We noticed. Do you have any idea where they might be?"

"North Cape!"

"North Cape?" said Ross. "But the Cape is just a desolate black cliff jutting out into the sea. There's no house there, no place to live."

"You're mistaken. There is a villa, a short distance from the Cape, built by the Russians before the war. Everybody in Finnmark knows about it."

"Why didn't you tell us?" asked Kira.

"I didn't know for sure, but I guess I wanted them to be living here, in Smorbringen, the place that my father owned. And anyway, it doesn't matter. North Cape is just over there."

She pointed in the direction of the north-western horizon, across the fjord, the inlet of the Barents Sea which intervened between Smorbringen Point and North Cape. Actually, the stretch of water which separated Smorbringen from the villa at North Cape was the shallowest of all the fjords in Finnmark.

The sky in the west was just beginning to change colour, heralding the dawn, so it was just possible to make out the outline of the cliffs. Lena said, "There's a villa on the nearest side of the point and a road linking it to the airport. I know it from my father. He drew me maps, recounting many times over and over again, just so that I would have it all in my mind, for this very moment."

Tears appeared in her eyes. "Anna and Yuval, my real parents will be there, where they've always been."

Kira and Ross put their arms around her, one on each side of her. Kira said, "They will not be alone."

"What do you mean?" asked Lena.

Kira said, "The place will be heavily guarded. It won't be a question of just wandering up, knocking on the front door and asking for Anna."

The three of them went outside to watch the dawn, sitting down on the fortress's ancient veranda.

"How do you know that?" asked Ross, rubbing his eyes.

"Following the war I was kept in Moscow by Khodorov for whom I continued to be an obsession. He told me everything, or close to it. Anna's location, however, was one thing he did not confide in me. All I knew was that she was in a secure location, somewhere safe.

After a year, because he was more and more involved, Khodorov made me one of the highest ranking Generals of the Russian Army. Then he moved the seat of his power from Moscow to Jerusalem, but still needed to keep control of what was left of Moscow and Europe. I was someone he could trust. But he never let me, or anyone else for that matter, know the location of Anna Kuznetsova."

"And what about the plane, the F-35?" asked Ross.

"That was different. It was a matter of security. You see, the pilot of that plane was a threat to Khodorov. Actually, you were the only threat once America was taken down. I always knew where you were, that you were safe. I kept tabs on you, using my position in the Army, and was informed immediately of your escape. That's when I knew I had to act, to help you. To do something to arrest the terrible course history had taken since the nuclear war. I knew your psychological state from the prison reports and knew you would head back to the wreckage for answers. You needed to know what the details of your mission in order to move on with your life. The details were only to be found at the crash site, so I disguised myself, bought equipment, and went straight to the plane wreckage to wait for you."

"And Khodorov?" asked Ross. "He escaped my bombing raid without injury?"

"Yes, he did. His bunker was simply too deep for your bomb to get at him."

"And he doesn't know you are here?"

Kira said, "He doesn't know I am here. He's in Jerusalem, busy spreading the Kingdom of Satan over the whole planet." Then she added. "But he will know by now that I am missing, that I am not in Moscow."

"We have to stop him," said Ross.

"Yes," said Kira, "But how?"

"Through the power of Anna, and of this, the object in our possession." Ross took out the golden chalice. "With Anna and the Holy Grail, I think we can do it."

***

President Khodorov sat on his gold engraved throne overlooking Jerusalem, bathed in the rays of the warm afternoon sun which were hitting hit him face on. The view he commanded was breath-taking, which was why he had chosen that place. The presidential palace had been constructed to his exact specifications and the place where he now sat overlooked the Dome of the Rock and Mount Zion, a location which gave legitimacy to his rule. He had constructed both the Third Temple and the New World in the battlefields of Armageddon, the Third World War. And now he ruled the New World from the Third Temple.

Khodorov looked out across the city, but was unable to see it. His mind was far away, in Moscow, in the place where he really longed to be; in the arms of Kira. Her disappearance from the Kremlin had shaken him more than he liked to admit. It had been four days now since he had heard the news, and he doubted she would ever be his again.

He noticed one of his Korean bodyguards, a Special Corps Officer, striding fast below on the paved rocks of the wide open space which had been laid in front of the Third Temple.

"Mr President," called out the bodyguard as he climbed the smooth marble steps which led from the paved rock expanse to Khodorov's throne. "The time is approaching."

"The time?" answered the President, confused.

"Yes, Sir, the mass execution. Had you forgotten?"

"How many?"

"Two hundred."

Khodorov sighed deeply. "Two hundred thousand rebels? Are there any left?"

"Unfortunately, Sir, there are likely to be a similar number every day this week."

Khodorov flicked a switch on the control panel of his throne and a screen above the altar to the left of his field of view flickered to life. He scrolled through the details of the execution, randomly checking the numbers of those to be executed, their names, and their crimes. There remained a minute to go.

He selected <All> from the menu on the touch-pad screen on the control panel in front of him and at exactly 3pm, tapped <Execute>.

He looked up at the video camera recording him. It was tough to kill 200,000 people in a single second, but absolutely necessary. Without fear in the general population, he would be no longer able to rule.

He got up and left the temple, followed by four advisers who he in turn left in the antechamber, without reason. He didn't need to give them one since he ruled with an iron fist, which they should know better than anyone.

***

Striding across the palace, there was someone who he needed to meet. Sirirrat Kakandee had not objected to moving with him to Jerusalem, and took up residence at the palace. Things were coming to a head.

"How many today?" she asked, as he walked into her apartment.

"Too many," replied Khodorov, weakly. "Two hundred thousand. I feel it's finally getting to me."

"It will keep getting to you, Darling, until you do something to change it!"

"But what can I do? A world empire is impossible to maintain without fear. And fear comes at a price."

"There is another way," said Kakandee.

"You're talking about the infant Christ," said Khodorov. "Any news from your side? Any visions?"

"He is not an *infant* any more. In fact, he will be seventeen already. And no, no news."

"So what can we do?"

"You know it already!"

Khodorov said, "You're talking about bringing Anna to Jerusalem."

"She knows where her son is. It's hard-wired inside her."

"How can you be so sure?"

Kakandee said, "It's written. She will always lead to him. Like computer software, programmed. All you have to do is arrange for her to become lost in the desert, on her own, and she will lead you straight to him."

"As you know, I can't do that. I can't bring her here."

"You can but you won't," retorted Kakandee. Frankness was her strength, and she knew it.

"You're right. I can but I won't. I need her where she is, in North Cape. Can I see you on Sunday night?"

"You can, of course. Have a good flight to North Cape!"

Sirirrat Kakandee watched him as he left her presence, and felt sorry for him. Despite his wealth, and his power, his status as humanity's first global ruler, he was intensely unhappy. She saw it growing through the years, clinical depression of the worst kind. He had lost touch with reality, with himself. No longer did he know how to be happy. He didn't know how to learn life's most important lesson. All that made him happy was Anna and Yuval, in North Cape, sexual energy of the most brutal type. He craved it now more than ever, addicted.

North Cape had become his real power base, the reason he had been able to survive all these years. In North Cape he could indulge in his obsession, indulge in the mixture of good and evil, Anna and Yuval, the archetypical Beauty and the Beast, a drug. They so intoxicated him with their life-giving energy that every weekend, without fail, he flew to see them in that cold, desolate place which to him was paradise, just to get his fix.

Kakandee knew that as long as Khodorov kept Anna at North Cape, their searches for the location of the youth would be futile. So long as he kept her in his little 'love nest' the boy was safe.

Khodorov was in need of his pleasure fix more than ever. He had dispatched a death squad to find and execute Kira, the other sexual mainstay of his life. Before her disappearance he had flown every Wednesday to the Kremlin, to find comfort in her curves, to find solace in her deep green eyes. Now even that had ended. He needed Anna and Yuval's sexual energy now more than ever.

Chapter 82

Kira lay listening to the waves inside her sleeping bag, warm despite the cold outside. The fire had burned late in the open hearth, and now a pile of red embers was giving out heat.

She got to her feet, letting the soft nylon of her duck-down sleeping bag slip down her bare white thighs to the floor. Taking care not to wake the others she picked up a pair of binoculars and walked to the window. The view was outstanding. She put the binoculars to her eyes and looked out across the arm of the windswept Barents Sea. There in the distance were the black cliffs of North Cape, falling vertically for a hundred meters into the boiling waves of the tempest. The northernmost point of mainland Europe was starkly beautiful, yet also dark and menacing.

Lena had said there would be a Russian military base at the Cape, and she was right. Kira saw the guards that Lena had told them about, armed and camouflaged. Finally, she focussed the powerful lenses on the imposing building which stretched out behind the rocks of the shore which could only be North Cape Villa. *So this is the place where Anna and Yuval had spent the last seventeen years. Anna is there, somewhere, in front of me!*

Kira listened to the sound of the wind as it whistled through the ancient stones, feeling the jets of freezing air entering through cracks in the window; the Barents Sea in a storm was really something. It came straight from the Arctic, straight into the granite cliffs. The location was without a doubt potently exciting, but worth giving up a life for? Did Anna really love Yuval enough to give up her freedom? Or was she really kept there as a prisoner?

Suddenly she discerned another noise, different from those of the sea and the wind, growing louder. It was mechanical and high pitched but at the same time humming and rasping. It was a noise unlike anything she had ever heard before.

Ross was by her side in a flash, so fast that Kira wondered what could have energized him to such a degree, motivating him to jump out of bed. Both watched as an aircraft neither had seen before flew across that desolate arm of the Barents Sea.

Kira turned to look at him as the light disappeared from view, towards Mehamn Airport. "What was it?"

"Must be a new type of aircraft," replied Ross, turning to return to his sleeping bag. "One developed in the last decade, probably in Jerusalem. Or maybe it's just an out dated, pre-war type."

"Impossible, Lee. Don't lie. You know what it was, don't you?"

Slipping back into the warmth of his sleeping bag, Ross said, "When was the last time you were in Jerusalem Kira?"

"I was kept in Moscow, as you know. Despite being a General, I was unable to leave. I know all about our technical expertise. Believe me, I would have known about such an aircraft."

"What we just saw was the X10-Mercury, otherwise known as Spacejet. I came across it last summer. It fell into my lap."

Ross got back out of the sleeping bag, realising he ought to rekindle the fire.

Kira watched him stoke wood onto the red hot embers. "Meaning?" she asked.

"Last summer, my captors felt sufficiently confident I would never again be in a position to threaten them. They allowed me access to a computer, which, thank God, was connected to the main servers in Jerusalem."

"So?"

"So, I am a pilot, and the only thing that really fuels my interest, on a virtual level, is flying. I managed to set up simulator programs for all their latest projects. The X10-Mercury, Spacejet, was just one of many. When I woke up just now, I thought I was dreaming, or at the very least, reliving some X10-Mercury mission played out through the computer interface. The noise of its four engines are unmistakable."

"So just how sure are you that it was a Mercury?"

"Sure?" asked Ross. "Absolutely certain. The question is not there, but what they are doing with it here in the most northerly point of Europe. What's for sure is that it has something to do with that villa." He nodded in the direction of North Cape. "That is why we have to get into it."

"Get into it?" answered Kira, startled. "You're not seriously considering trying to get in are you? Have you seen the installations, the guards?"

"Not in daylight, of course. We will be moving in the dead of night, between three and five in the morning to be exact."

The fire had returned, its flames licking high up between the wood Ross was busy stacking up on it. He said, "Today, we just have to get close to the North Cape Road, to gain as much information as we can about what is going on at Mehamn Airport and at North Cape. That's all."

"Shouldn't we just lie low, and risk everything tomorrow night?"

"No," said Ross, getting back into his sleeping bag. "We need to know their numbers. And we need to be well rested. Get some sleep Kira!"

***

"What is it?" said Lena, seeing Ross at the window, when she woke.

Ross spun around. "Armed men coming this way, ten or more, and they'll be here in minutes."

Kira woke in a flash, having heard what Ross had said.

Lena said, "They knew we would be here. They always knew!"

"What do you mean?" asked Ross, eyeing her briefly before checking one of the automatic rifles and throwing it to Kira.

Lena said, "Nothing is the way we think it is. Nothing happens by chance. Neither does it matter how they knew. They knew. They always knew we would be here. Right here, right now, in Smorbringen."

Ross noticed a change in Lena. She had suddenly become confident. He thought it was because their lives were now in real danger. He checked another automatic before tossing it into the hands of Lena. "Let's go down fighting!"

"We don't have to!" said Lena.

"Meaning?" said Ross.

"Do you really think I would have led us to this place, encouraging you to light a fire, telling tales of how safe it is, if I did not have a back-up plan?"

"I guess not," replied Ross, raising his eyebrows.

"Quick, this way!"

***

The Ancients had cut the tunnel that Lena led them into millennia before. They had cut it out of the tough granite rock below Smorbringen Castle, towards the northwest, deep under the arm of the Barents Sea which separated the ancient fortress from North Cape.

Lena was in the lead, knowing the tunnel like the back of her hand. Many times had she been along it, sometimes in the company of her mother, sometimes alone. Ross and Kira followed close behind.

Lena knew too that soon they would be at the halfway point of the tunnel, at its deepest point under the Barents Sea. Soon they would be at the 'fort' as she used to call it, the chamber cut into the tunnels left hand wall, the furthest she had ever been to North Cape. From that point on, even for her, every step would be a step into the unknown, and every step a little closer to her real mother, Anna Kuznetsova. It seemed like as good a time as any to take stock of the situation. "Guys, are you okay?"

"Perfect get away," announced Kira through deep breaths.

"Yeah! You really saved us back there," said Ross.

"As long as they don't find the secret entrance," said Kira. "I think we're safe."

Lena said, "Don't worry. They will not be able to do that."

Kira asked, "How can you be so sure?"

"This tunnel was constructed at the time of the Pyramids, by people who knew how to make it secure. You see, as soon as we pushed the stone doors back, it locked."

Ross marvelled at the Ancients. The tunnel reminded him of Israel, of the chamber below the Al-Aqsa mosque, chiselled into the rock. *Could it really have been constructed by the same people?* "Why had it been constructed?" he asked, as they neared the lowest point of the tunnel, now walking, not running. He reckoned their position to be half way under the arm of the Barents Sea.

"It leads straight under the Barents Sea, to North Cape. To the Villa . . . " said Lena, who had read Ross's thoughts. She paused, for effect, before adding, "To Anna. Come on!"

They reached the deepest part of the tunnel, the lowest point of its journey where it began to climb again, to North Cape.

Just as Lena had remembered, a large, chambered room had been carved into the left hand wall of the tunnel, its dark, chisel etched walls steeped in mystery. "This is the 'Fort'."

There were benches carved into the walls of the chamber, and iron torch holders, complete with torches, ready to be lit.

Ross lit them one by one, having to stretch his arm high above him in order to bring the flame of his lighter into contact with the combustible material at the center of the torch holders. They burst immediately into flames. The flickering light revealed the chamber. Stone benches encircled the square perimeter, but apart from them and the iron torches which now shone, the chamber was empty.

"What's that?" shouted Kira, pointing to a hole in the back wall of the chamber.

Lena remembered it. "It's the keystone. My mother never stopped talking of it."

At the very middle of the chamber's back wall, a curved recess had been carved, and at its center, a large hole.

"What did she say about it?" asked Kira.

"She said he who had the key would have to reclaim the world from the butchers and thieves that had stolen it. She said another tunnel, lies on the other side of this key. She said it led somewhere special."

Ross approached the curiously shaped hole in the wall of the chamber and felt a cold current of air on the smooth, white skin of his face. It was proof that what Lena was telling was true; there was another tunnel on the other side of the wall!

"It must lead somewhere," he said, lowering his head. "And I wouldn't mind betting it leads to the airport."

It was Kira's turn to be surprised. Somehow, the pieces of a gigantic jigsaw puzzle were fitting into place. The trouble was, she did not know what picture the finished puzzle would depict. "What?" she exclaimed. "Why would it lead to the airport?"

"The airport!" shouted Lena.

Ross and Kira looked at the young girl.

"What, Lena?"

"It rings a bell, you see."

"What does? The airport, or the key hole in the wall?"

"I always thought it was a late night story told sometimes by my mother, when the wolves were howling a bit louder than usual, or when the winter gales had become intolerable. You see, she was telling me a story about this, about what is happening right now."

"Déjà vu!" said Ross, studying her face in the flickering light.

"And how did the story go? How did it end?" asked Kira.

Lena looked at Ross, as if seeking guidance, tears welling in her eyes, the previous confidence gone.

"I never found out," she sobbed. "I always fell asleep before my mother had finished telling the story."

Chapter 83

Kira said, "The key hole is the shape of a chalice, meaning a chalice would be the key."

Ross said, "And because the only mechanism of the lock was the weight of its key, it would seem obvious that the material chosen by the Ancients to make the key would be gold, the heaviest known naturally occurring metal. Let's see if it works."

Ross introduced the chalice into the recess. "Look at how well it fits!"

"To perfection!"

Ross carefully placed the golden chalice on the base of the recess on the key hole's other side, taking great care to let its considerable weight act fully, applying only its true force. He guessed that if the Ancients had been capable of designing and building such a locking mechanism, they would also have been able to calibrate it exactly, possibly even building into it fail safe aspects which would lock the system down if anyone tried to open it by a process of trial and error with differing weights.

As he drew back his hand through the keyhole a subterranean rumbling became audible, as if an earth tremor was hitting the tunnel with its epicentre in the granite slabs under their feet. The rock door began to move, slowly at first, then faster until stopping with a jolt. It stood open, for the first time in millennia.

The three adventurers waved their torches into the darkness, holding their breaths, then gasping, as their eyes focused.

In the center of the chamber, chiselled out of the granite rock, stood a stone platform composed of a different rock, dark and finely crystalline. But what captivated them most, however, was what stood on the platform.

Nothing could have prepared the three of them for the sight. Ross had seen pictures of it. Who hadn't? It was beautiful. A golden chalice, like the one he had just used as a key, but bigger, more ornate.

"It's beautiful!" said Kira.

"The real Holy Grail," declared Ross.

The two girls looked at him with sudden suspicion.

"How do you know?" asked Kira. "Why was the golden chalice we found on the F-35 wreckage not the Holy Grail?"

"No. This is the real Holy Grail," replied Ross matter-of-factly, approaching it, lifting it. "The proof is our present position, that the Ancients buried it deep under the Barents Sea. Why else would they have constructed these tunnels, if not to hide one of humanity's most treasured prizes?"

From the chamber led a new tunnel, just like Ross had expected, in the direction of Mehamn Airport. Holding the heavy chalice, Ross looked along it. "The Holy Grail gives us the power to confront the guards, save Anna, and get her to the airport along this the second tunnel."

He looked down at the huge vessel in his hands, and ran his fingers along its golden surface, searching something he suspected would be there. Finally he looked on its base. "And look here!" He held the chalice in the torch light so that the two girls could see the inscription. "This is a coordinates of a specific place in space and time, a location which can mean only one thing: the final battle of Armageddon."

Lena and Kira again looked at him with suspicion.

Then Lena said, "Whatever it is, we have to use it. It has the power to change the world, just like the Ark of the Covenant." The other two looked at her, surprised by her tone, which they had grown accustomed to hearing at times. Her confidence had returned with a vengeance. "Whoever possesses the Holy Grail controls its power. The Ancients knew we would be right here, right now. They gave us the power to change everything too."

Kira said, "Whatever. Ross, give me the coordinates."

Kira plugged them into her smartphone, a map of the space-time coordinates flashing onto the screen. She said, "Looks like somewhere in the middle of the Negev desert, tomorrow at 14.00."

Ross reached for the smartphone, hoping to gain a better understanding by seeing the location. He said, "But why? What could it possibly be the location of?"

"I don't know, but I have a feeling we are going to find out! Can you give me the chalice?"

"Why?" answered Ross.

"I want to touch it. Hold it. It's not every day that one gets the chance to hold the most celebrated artefact in human history."

It was not like Ross to refuse her. But that's what he did, right then and there, when it counted most. Kira found him cold, unfriendly. Instead of answering, he put the chalice inside his jacket, in an inner pocket. Their connection was gone, and strangest of all, Ross didn't seem to care.

"Guys. We have little time, if we want to save Anna," said Lena.

Ross said, "Getting her out will not be easy, but we have two important things on our side."

"Two?" asked Kira. "I count one, the Holy Grail."

"The power of surprise should never be underestimated. Yuval doesn't know that we are coming, and neither that we are so close."

"What about the guards at the ancient fortress?" said Lena. "They know we are close! They will have radioed it in."

"Guards can be neutralised."

"And the second thing?" asked Kira, turning to face Ross.

"The Ancients think we have a chance. I think that speaks for itself. After all, we have all got this far, and they knew that we would. Our mission was not only written in the stars, it was chiselled by Ancients into this rock. They knew that at this very place at this very moment, we would be coming along this tunnel."

Lena had sat down on the platform, tired.

Kira tried to say something, but Ross cut her off, his eyes lit by an inner fire. He took a deep breath, and looked at Kira. "I can't give you the chalice, the Holy Grail, or whatever it is, because its power will be directed against Khodorov in Jerusalem, and the Israelites wanted me to get it. They wanted me to get on time to the location of the space-time coordinates, and I alone will use it to end the Kingdom of Satan."

Kira said, "Why you? Maybe the Ancients wanted all of us to work together on this."

"They knew I would have already found the golden keystone in the Al-Aqsa mosque. They knew that I would have flown the F-35 all the way from the U.S. to the Kremlin. They would have known that I would have bombed the Kremlin, and flown on, all the way to North Cape. They knew too that I would be here with Lena and you. They gave us a mission, to end Khodorov's Kingdom of Satan, and they made me leader of that mission."

"Then why are you so sure that this golden chalice is the Holy Grail, and the coordinates are for a final battle?" queried Kira, accepting his authority.

Ross looked at her, aware that he still needed her. Without Kira, someone who knew Khodorov and had access to him, there was no way in hell they were going to get all the way to Israel, to the middle of the Negev. "Think about it Kira. Look around you! Do you think they would have gone to so much trouble as burying it under some obscure corner of the Barents Sea without a pretty good reason?"

To Kira Ross's attitude continued to cause concern. Where did his anger come from all of a sudden? His tone again, was harsh. But he was right. Their mission needed a leader, and despite her rank, he had obvious authority and legitimacy.

Ross said, "The only way any of this makes sense is if all this really was built by the Ancients, and that this really is the Holy Grail."

"And that we must use it to do the right thing!" said Lena. "Don't forget that!"

"Of course, Lena. Why bring that up?"

"Just so we are all clear about just what it is we are doing here!"

"Which is?" asked Ross.

"To get Anna back, of course. Why else? The primary reason we are all here is to rescue her."

Kira said, "Of course. Without Anna, neither does our mission have much point. She is the key to everything."

"But?" said Ross.

"But she is not the only reason we are here. She may be the key, but we are also here because we have become aware that we now live in a world governed by Free Will. And we believe it has become a world in which Satan has the upper hand. We are here to change it, to bring about the Kingdom of Heaven."

"Nice speech Kira," declared Ross. "So let's do it!"

***

The mountainous rock doors at the North Cape end of the tunnel opened like clockwork when the weight of the second golden chalice acted on the keystone. It rumbled and grated, and finally stood wide open, allowing the arctic twilight to penetrate the tunnel entrance for the first time in over a thousand years.

They emerged from the tunnel's granite doors in the middle of a rock formation, concealed from all directions. The Ancients had obviously spared no trouble in taking special care to leave them in no danger as they emerged from the tunnel.

To Ross that made perfect sense. *If they had been visible on exiting the tunnel, all the work done in building the tunnel to rescue Anna would have been in vain.* He said, "You two stay here while I take a peek from up there," indicating the 50m high rocks that towered above the tunnel entrance.

"Be careful!" warned Lena.

"Don't worry Lena. If the Ancients predicted we would be here, they probably could predict that we would all be okay."

"But don't forget that we now live in a world of Free Will," reminded Lena, as he began climbing the smooth rock face.

From ten metres up Ross looked down, motioning her and Anna to come close, saying as softly as possible, "Or maybe the deterministic world continues for the time being, until the final Battle of Armageddon. The one indicated on the Holy Grail."

Ross froze on the top of the outcrop, above a dark figure which walked across the tundra between the outcrop and the road. The North Cape Villa was clearly visible, outlined by the purples and browns of the setting sun, no more than half a kilometre to the north, along the road, towards North Cape itself.

The figure had stopped. For brief seconds Ross feared something was wrong, that he had been given away, so he ducked his head low, plastering it against the flat top of the rock outcrop.

He saw a spark pierce the gloom, followed by a flame. The guard had lit a cigarette.

Carefully Ross brought his binoculars to his eyes.

The sound of distant vehicles drowned out that of the wind through the rocks as the sight of flashing lights up ahead on the road met his eyes. A motorcade had just left the villa and was now approaching head on. That meant it was heading to the airport.

The guard below him moved briskly toward the road, due Ross guessed, to boredom. For the guard, the long hours of waiting, checking and killing time were going to be cut short for a few moments. Unfortunately for him, he chose to pass right under the rock where Ross waited.

Ross launched himself like a missile, with gravity for acceleration. Five meters at 9.8 meters per second squared. The guard heard the flapping sound of Ross's jacket, like wings, through the air, but heard it too late. The power of the blow knocked the Russian to the ground. Permanently.

Ross changed his jacket for the Russian's, grabbed the guard's rifle and radio, and ran to the road.

He saluted as the motorcade approached. It was a hundred meters in length. There were cars, armoured vehicles, motorcycles. At its very center was a black armoured limousine, placed carefully, the most protected, the least at risk. There had to be a reason, thought Ross, and then he saw it. He had recognized the figure seated inside by its silhouette, lit from the car behind by its powerful headlights, a figure he knew personally, and had already been tasked with executing; Ivan Khodorov.

Chapter 84

The rest of the guards Ross encountered on the way to the villa were easy to deal with. They were a walk in the park, picked off one by one, some with one of the silenced Berettas picked up from the Russian soldiers near the plane wreck. Others he terminated with a knife. Then he closed on the villa, sprinting, directly to the main entrance.

At the wooden door surrounded by massive stones and two granite pillars, one on each side, he froze. The building was massive too, grandiose even. There were two burning torches situated high on the pillars.

Ross signalled a pre-agreed code to the rock outcrop; five flashes meant the coast was clear.

"How many are left?" asked Kira, in hushed, out of breath gasps as she and Lena attained him.

"I can't be sure. But there will be more."

"Shall I make the call now?"

Ross said, "Yes! Make the call." He moved into position, ready to silently slip into the villa, but before entering whispered something to Kira. "Just make sure Anna is kept alive, whatever her psychological status. No matter what she says or does, we need her on board to complete the mission, either with or without her consent. See you at the airport."

Then he was gone.

Seconds later a shot, cracked the air, followed by two more shots. Ross had twenty minutes remaining to do what he did best; cleaning.

***

"Mehamn Airport, this is General Kira Kamenskaya. Come in, over!"

Heavy interference came through the receiver, then a reply. "General Kamenskaya, this is Mehamn Airport. Code in."

Kira punched a ten digit military identifier, and waited, trying to imagine what was going through the mind of the person on the other end of the line. General Kira Kamenskaya was a legend in military circles. No matter what had happened in the preceding two weeks, she was still the head of the Army. But she was also listed as missing.

The small military garrison of Mehamn Airport was about to become legendary too, but for considerably less commanding reasons. She said, "I am at North Cape Villa where a rebel attack is under way. I request immediate reinforcements, over."

They responded immediately, because they had to. Their military careers depended on it. Their lives depended on it too. Everybody knew of the connection between Kira Kamenskaya and Khodorov. Which meant any delay at all in sending a force to retake North Cape, would have savage repercussions.

In less than twenty minutes the best part of a company of men and women arrived at North Cape Villa bristling with automatic weapons. There were tracked and armoured vehicles too, mounted with heavy machine guns. They surrounded the villa and threw open the main door.

Kira stood in the center of the cavernous entrance hall, with bodies still oozing blood and guts littered around her on the stone floor. Ross's handiwork.

Lena was at her side, safe and sound. Both held Kalashnikovs. The air was heavy with the smell of blood, and cordite too.

As the main force entered the villa, a tall blonde woman appeared from nowhere, looking directly at Kira.

"Anna!"

"What?" said the tall blonde woman. "What did you call me?"

"Anna," repeated Kira. "Anna Kuznetsova. That's your name."

The tall blonde woman seemed confused. It was just as Kira had expected. *She was hypnotized, or worse.* Probably she had been kept at North Cape, but not against her will; she had been kept at North Cape because she did not even know her will.

"Anna Kuznetsova!" Kira pronounced the words a second time, slower, but still without effect. The thick lips of the tall woman continued to tremble, but whether with fear or emotion, the Russian General could only guess.

The tall blonde woman knelt down beside one of the bodies. He had been a dark man, obviously good looking, with Middle Eastern features. She searched for a pulse, first on his wrist and then his throat which she pinched in a way she had learned in Russia in a previous life. Then she looked up. "He's dead, and you killed him!"

Kira stood her ground. She was under orders from Ross not to allow her to escape, nor take her own life. "Wait, Anna . . . "

"That is not my name!"

"Anna *is* your name, and whatever just happened was not your fault!"

"You're damn right it wasn't. You killed him!" Emotion had taken hold of her, sadness more powerful than anger.

"Who is he? Do you even know his name?"

Between sobs, Anna said, "Of course I do. He is Yuval, my husband."

***

Ross ran as fast as he could sure that all he ever wanted would be his. Now it seemed almost certain, deterministic world or free will world.

Maybe the deterministic world had not ended yet. Maybe the Ancients knew he would get as far as he had. Maybe they knew he would get to Jerusalem too, to the Negev Desert and the final battle of Armageddon. The battle whose coordinates in space-time was inscribed on the Holy Grail which banged around inside his military fatigues as he sprinted. All he needed to do was to get to the other end of the tunnel before Kira and the others got to Mehamn Airport. Anna would be there. She would be safe and sound, with Kira and Lena. Of that he was sure. The Ancients had known that they would!

Ross guessed that only if he got to the airport before Kira and the others, could they leave on time and have any chance at all of reaching the final battle. He planned to fly Spacejet-2, the second X10-Mercury to Lod Airport, Tel Aviv, where he would leave them before continuing alone to the final battle, the final coordinates in the Negev.

Thanking the Ancients, Ross's boots batted along the tunnel. Though the illumination was dim, his eyes had become accustomed to the night, as the Ancients had known he would. He could see just fine. All the way down, to the tunnel's deepest point, to a place where torches were still burning, to the chamber where they had found the Holy Grail, hours before. From there, it would be easy. He would just have to take the second tunnel, to the airport.

When Ross arrived at the chamber of the Holy Grail, he stopped. He looked at his watch. Fifty minutes had passed since he had entered the villa. Thirty minutes had passed since he had shot dead the last men holding Anna. Twenty minutes had passed since Kira, Lena and Anna had left with the Russian Army for Mehamn Airport. Ross thought: *I am going to be late!* But they would have to wait. *I have the Holy Grail.*

***

General Kira Kamenskaya looked disapprovingly at the commanding officer of the garrison controlling Mehamn Airport. She walked directly up to him, stood in front of him, looking even closer at him now, into his cold grey eyes. He was a Colonel, but she was a General, and even if Khodorov had put her on a wanted list, she still had authority. And if looks could kill, the Colonel would already have been dead.

"Fuel the second Spacejet immediately, Colonel."

"Just give me the destination and it will be done, General Kamenskaya," he replied, without hesitation.

"Jerusalem," said Kira.

***

Spacejet-2 stood on the dark apron of Mehamn airport. It was one of only five prototypes. Following the war, the best Russian and Israeli engineers had been installed in a secret, exotic location, where they had been supplied with huge resources. They had been given a year to come up with a space-aircraft capable of covering the distance between North Cape and Jerusalem in one direct, 45 minute flight. The space-aircraft Spacejet, otherwise known as the Mercury-X10, was the result. It was a hybrid, one which took off and landed as a conventional jet, but travelled into low orbit on twin rockets.

"And the girl?" began the Colonel.

Kira transfixed him with her dark green eyes. "Lena comes with us."

"Not Lena," said the Colonel smiling. "Anna Kuznetsova!"

"Colonel. Do I need to remind you of something?"

"So Anna goes with you?"

"Of course," replied Kira, dryly.

"Then I'll make sure everything is ready and waiting in Jerusalem, for her arrival."

Kira had expected he would. It was too much to hope for that a Russian Colonel would be negligent of his duties. He was therefore going to send a message to Khodorov, which meant that Khodorov would send his most trusted agents to meet the flight, wherever it landed. Probably Khodorov's orders would include sending agents to every known landing strip in the Middle East. He was going to take back Anna Kuznetsova into his safe keeping and Khodorov, not her and Ross would be back in control of her.

Chapter 85

The news was given to President Khodorov of the New World Authority while he was still aboard Spacejet-1. The huge hybrid aircraft was twenty minutes into the flight, in low Earth orbit, and half way back to Jerusalem when the flight hostess handed him the message. He digested the news with a mixture of fear, pleasure and sadness.

He experienced pleasure on hearing the details of a massacre at North Cape, even though they were his own men. Then he felt sadness at the news of the passing of Yuval. Finally he felt fear for the possibility of losing Anna.

As to the reason why Kira had shown up in North Cape at the precise moment of the rebel attack, to that he could only guess. He knew Kira had a special connection to Anna, but for her to escape from Moscow, and travel to North Cape just when it came under attack? That was worrying. Either she too was involved in the rebel attack, or her presence at the event was a product of pure woman intuition.

Either way, Khodorov was happy to hear that she was on her way to Jerusalem. If she was guilty of association with the rebels, his Thai spiritualist would find it out soon enough. And she would be executed along with the rest of them. But if she was innocent, he would be free to pursue more sexual encounters with her. It was a win-win situation.

Then he settled back into his flight seat, took a swig of Cognac, and thought about Anna. She was safe had said the message from the Colonel in charge at Mehamn Airport. The message said she had arrived at the airport under the protection of Kira and a company of presidential guards. She had then ordered Spacejet-2 to be fuelled for Jerusalem.

But without Yuval, the False Prophet, he feared the sexual essence which welded him and Anna together would be gone. How could he do what he liked to do to her without him?

With Kira? The thought had already crossed his mind. He would have loved nothing more than for the Russian beauty to perform the role played by Yuval. There was, he admitted, the possibility.

Now that he thought again about it, the idea became more and more attractive, and he wondered about why he had not pursued involving Kira before. Yes, Kira was the answer. And, as if destiny had connived with science and fate, she was at that precise moment about to take off for Israel, with Anna.

***

Colonel Lippman was a tall, six foot five inch block of muscle who had headed the elite of the elite Special Forces, Russia's Presidential Guard for the last two years. His thick black hair cropped short and square complemented his robust physique. In fact, everything about the man seemed to be cut and angular, including his jaw which was straight and strong and not without profound severity.

Colonel Lippman received the presidential call as he was on his way to personally lead the Lod operation. The call was a surprise. He was not party to the wisdom of telling those under his command the stakes of failure. If he had any doubt at all about the capability of the team waiting down at the airport, hearing the threat coming straight from Khodorov's mouth might have unsettled him. The rumours of what forces failure would automatically set in motion had been enough to keep all members of the presidential guard on their toes for years, so having it spelt out exactly did not affect him.

"How long Colonel?" snapped President Khodorov curtly into the receiver.

"Spacejet-2 just left Mehamn, Sir. In thirty minutes, they will be on the ground at Tel Aviv, Lod."

"Thirty minutes. Copy. I know I do not need to impress upon you the importance of the cargo aboard the flight, do I Colonel?"

"No Sir, you don't. My men won't let you down Mr President. Colonel Lippman, out."

Lippman's team was the world's best-trained and equipped reaction force. Nothing had been left to chance. He had even arranged a force on all of the airports surrounding Lod, lest something dramatic would require the incoming Spacejet to divert, itself a very unlikely event. He had been in direct contact with its pilots ever since they had taken off from Mehamn. They had informed him of their passengers, of an unconscious agent who General Kamenskaya had said had been working with her, and the two young women. The operation was going to be a walk in the park.

A scene of military preparation met Colonel Lippman's eyes as he approached Lod airport along the Cyprus tree clad road which led down towards the airport's perimeter from the hills towards the east. The sight pleased him. Similar scenes were on his orders being repeated across the whole of the Middle East too. But Lod, was the stated destination of the inbound space-aircraft, a destination he had personally checked and re-checked. Nothing had been left to chance.

Lippman pulled his green coloured convertible Wrangler Jeep off the winding road into a dry and dirty lay-by directly overlooking the airport, skidding to a halt in a cloud of dust. He swung open the door and grabbed a pair of binoculars from the dash, making his way around the vehicle to the precipitous edge which descended steeply to the airport's perimeter fence. He brought the binoculars up to his dark, sunken eyes, trying consciously to put thoughts of failure out of his mind.

Chapter 86

Unable to comprehend how he was going to be able to keep on subduing a whole division of trained soldiers with a single Kalashnikov rifle and two clips of ammunition, Ross decided to let the matter slide. He just had to get to the plane. That was all that mattered, and he felt assured it would be waiting there, just over the granite outcrop next to the tunnel exit. A granite outcrop similar to the one at the tunnel's other exit, near North Cape Villa.

The reason as to why the division was there at all did not bother him. It was natural. To get anywhere in life, you had to fight. Getting to the revolutionary aircraft, Spacejet-2, was no different. A mother of battles it may have been, but just a fight none the less. It was his fight, a fight that he alone could win. He was the hero of the world, and only he could save it.

Instinctively, he pushed aside the person who had got too close, obscuring his view from the tunnel exit.

"Get off," he shouted, as the figure became real.

Shock turned to relief as he realised he had been dreaming and that he was now looking straight into the deep green eyes that he loved so much.

Then a high pitched humming met his ears. The humming was real, as was Kira's presence. He muttered, "Where are we?"

"Aboard Spacejet-2. And you were out of it."

"Why can't I remember anything?"

"It's the effect of the drugs," replied Kira. "They usually cause such things. But you're going to be okay."

"What drugs?" Ross sat up on the bed which was soft, bedecked in white cotton sheets with an equally soft duvet covering his legs. He was in a cabin, the surface of which was curved white above him, and to the side of him punctuated by three oval Perspex windows. The smell of Kerosene, the distinctive odour of every air-plane hit him like a hammer, "We're on Spacejet!"

"Yes," replied Kira. "I told you."

"How long have we been in the air?"

"Fifteen minutes."

"Then why can't I remember getting on?"

"Because you were already unconscious. You were shot at Mehamn Airport." Kira leant forward, towards him, and took his hand, which she guided to a place on his head. He felt pain, and a bandage. "The bullet just grazed your skull. A fraction of a centimetre to the right, and you would have been dead, but serious enough to cause some memory loss."

"Retrograde amnesia? Again?"

"Probably. But you will be fine. The drugs brought you round faster than perhaps they should have, but . . . "

The fading of her words told him something. She was scared.

"What is it?"

"We have a problem, which is why we had to bring you round early."

"The wonders of modern medicine," said Ross. From the look of worry on her face he thought she could use some humour. She did not smile. "Okay, I'm ready. What is our situation? Where are we headed?"

"In less than thirty minutes we will be landing in Lod airport, Israel," informed Kira hurriedly. "At least that is where the pilots have been instructed to fly us."

"And Anna? Is she safe?"

Kira cast a knowing glance in his direction. So he did remember, at least the name, the mission. His interest in Anna was natural, she thought. After all, the mission had been centred on getting her out of Yuval's control, and then flying her to Israel where she would lead them to whichever place she had hard wired into her pretty head. Quite simply, he could have been just concerned for a friend. But whichever, the circumstances, the flight to Israel and the fact that those on the ground knew of her arrival, were at risk of putting her straight back under the control of Ivan Khodorov, the President of the World Government in Jerusalem.

"So you do remember. Yes. She is safe. You can see her if you like. But, be warned Ross. She does not want to have anything to do with you."

"What did I do?" said Ross. "I saved her, didn't I?"

"Unfortunately, she has been totally brainwashed. She sees you only as the killer of her husband Yuval. She says she loved him."

Ross looked at her, unable to mask his surprise, or maybe just unwilling to make the effort to try. After a moment's thought, he managed to say carefully, "Is that a problem for us. Does just controlling her bring us divine power? Or does she need to be on-board, conscious of who she is and her role?"

"That is left to be seen, but I believe the less she knows the better. She is, as yet, unaware of our mission, unaware even of what she had gone through to get here. She is unaware that we intend to use her to find whatever place and thing controls the distribution of power in the world. We must get her back to where she was kidnapped, to Mount Megiddo, and then with the help of the object, the golden cup we found under the Barents Sea, we will be able to uncover the last hiding place. From then on the world will be in her hands, not in Khodorov's."

"Look Kira," said Ross, his voice suddenly hushed. "Do you remember the chalice?"

Ross had already located it, just where he had left it, in his jacket, surprised that it had not been removed whilst he had been unconscious. "This is the key!" he said, holding it towards her. "These inscriptions are for space-time coordinates. They are the coordinates of the hiding place of Anna's son, in the Negev Desert."

Kira looked at him coldly. "I thought you said they were for the Final Battle of Armageddon? So what now, you changed your mind? What are you saying?"

"They are for that too. There will be a final battle at those coordinates, the coordinates of her son. Of that I am sure. But what I am also saying is that we don't need her." He held up the chalice. "Look! They are written right here!"

"No way, Lee!" said Kira, with fire in her eyes. "We all came this far for one reason, to find the power to stop Khodorov from going on to destroy the whole world. Now is our chance to push back the Kingdom of Satan. Anna is a part of that mission, and always has been. So are you. And so am I. There is no way we can go it alone without her."

"So what was it that I can help you with," said Ross disappointed. If she did not want to be part of his own vision of peace, power and happiness for the populations of the planet, then he would have to do it without her. Eventually, he would win her to his side, on the other side of the battle at the space-time coordinates which were almost upon them.

"Can you fly this plane?"

"You bet I can!"

"Then come with me. We have about fifteen minutes to put this thing right."

Kira led Ross, stumbling and staggering and faltering, though the aircraft's main cabin towards the cockpit. His body was raked by the effects of both concussion and the brutal cocktail of drugs. But somehow, somewhere, his body had become used to dealing with it, continuing to function, something at that very moment registering in his peripheral vision. He turned to look at it and through the oval windows of the surface of the white cabin saw the unmistakable outline of a MiG-35 flying in formation just off Spacejet's wing. He stopped dead, wobbling back and forth as if teetering on the edge of a cliff.

Kira said, "Yes, we have attracted a fighter escort, one on each wing."

"That's just great!" replied Ross. "If you have any more great surprises, now would be a good time to tell me, don't you think?"

"There's really no need for explications," retorted Kira, bluntly. "You'll understand for yourself the extent of our problems if you just keep following me."

On entering the cockpit, Ross could not prevent vocalizing profound surprise. "My God! What in hell's name is going on?"

"It was absolutely necessary, Ross, believe me!"

On either side of Lena, who stood there in the middle, both pilots were tied up, their hands immobilized by immense knots, their arms covered in tight coils of rope which attached them snugly to their seats. The same thick ropes passed loosely through their mouths, pulling their heads slightly rearwards, impeding any speech.

"Who the hell is flying the plane?"

"It's on automatic," said Lena, waving an arm and wagging a finger in the direction of the flight instrumentation as if to add meaning and legitimacy to the answer. Apparently, she had been in the cockpit for some time, maintaining the plane in flight.

"Are you CRAZY?" shouted Ross, unable to restrain himself, lunging forward to release the Captain.

"Stop right there," ordered Kira from behind him. "I am in control of this flight, and I say when to release the pilots."

Ross spun round to see the sharp end of a Beretta pointed directly at his chest, gripped firmly in both her hands. All traces of the concussion or drugs had vanished in a flash from his mind, as Ross's surprise morphed into a broad smile. "I thought we were on the same side!"

"We are, Lee. We are. I just didn't want to put any of us at risk. You needed to be brought up to speed."

"Who's putting who at risk right now?" said Ross frankly, casting an eye to the aircraft's instrument panel. The pilots remained firm and bound, their faces red, beads of sweat adhering to their eyebrows, tell-tale signs of recent, pointless, struggle. "One wrong command could put this aircraft into an uncontrollable dive. So what don't I know?"

"Let me fill you in," said Kira. "While you take over from Lena in overseeing the controls." She motioned to him with the same Beretta to check the instruments.

In fact, Kira now trusted Ross more than anyone alive, and secretly abhorred threatening him. She loved his straight talking down to earth nature, probably much more than she cared to admit. The situation was, however, too delicate to give any leeway to misunderstandings which could cloud reality: in the event of mistakes, there would be no second chances. "The pilots have been instructed to fly to Lod airport where this plane, and everything and everyone on it will be impounded. I can't let that happen, and neither can you."

"Because Khodorov will be waiting for us!" he exclaimed, suddenly remembering. He thought: *How could I have missed the connection.* "Of course! Anna Kuznetsova is on this flight!"

Kira nodded slowly and emphatically, visibly relieved that he now understood the sheer necessity of avoiding touching down in Lod. "That's absolutely right. Which means . . . "

Ross cut her off, brusquely, "We have to divert!"

"Agreed."

"But what about the MiG-35s? They will turn, burn and fry us long before we reach our destination, wherever that might be!"

Kira thought carefully, her green eyes, brighter than usual in the high altitude light, fixed on the distant horizon. "What is our fuel status?"

"What are you thinking?" Ross replied. "You want to run? Kira we are flying with two MiG-35s, like a fat lamb lumbering along with a hungry wolf on each flank."

"They would at least have to get clearance before opening fire. Don't you think? That would give us time." She looked at the altimeter. 20,000 feet and descending rapidly. "If we could trick them, increase our altitude slightly, slowly, and then make a break for it."

"No way," replied Ross. "They would realize what we were up before we even did it. Taking us up to above their service ceiling would take too much time, minutes at least. They would have time to receive orders from the top."

"Those orders wouldn't include shooting us down!"

"How can you be so sure?" said Ross.

"You don't know Khodorov like I do. He's crazy about Anna. A man like him is incapable of killing the one thing he loves. He would let her go, hoping that they would meet again, in better circumstances. He's a survivor. Look at him, an old man, but a man in control of the world. He didn't get there just because he is smart."

Ross's mind was working overtime. Amnesia or not, he felt the golden chalice in his flight suit pocket, digging into his side. He looked at his watch. Just over an hour remained to the last space-time coordinates indicated on the Holy Grail. He was so close, so sure. He thought: *No! I can't just let this situation slide out of my control. Not now that I am so close.* "No!"

"No, what?" said Kira. Her eyes moved from the horizontal line in the distance separating Earth and space, to focus instead on the deep grey-blue of his irises.

"You're forgetting one thing," said Ross. Now it was his turn to talk without emotion. It gave what he said added weight, the weight of someone who has considered carefully, the weight of someone who looks before he leaps. "Khodorov will track us to wherever we go. Satellites are watching our every move. Probably they are even eavesdropping on this very conversation."

"Running is not an option?"

"No!" said Ross, with a firmness which bore all the stamps of finality. "Khodorov will have military forces near every airport on the face of the planet. Believe me, they will be waiting at every little airstrip to receive us, especially the ones in Israel. We can run but we can't hide."

"So what do you recommend we do, Lieutenant Colonel Lee Ross? The moon is a bit inhospitable, is it not?"

Ross thought deeply for a moment. Airports. Problem. Solution. A fundamental rule. To every problem, a solution. Was this dead end, this flight to disaster really an exception? No way! His mind crunched the inputs. "Armageddon!"

Chapter 87

"Control. Did you hear that? Over," said Major Ilya Timofeev, call sign "Akula," into the mouthpiece of his helmet.

Timofeev was thirty six years old and a veteran of the nuclear holocaust, the three and a half year war which had engulfed the planet seventeen years previously. He maintained his MiG-35 in tight formation off Spacejet-2's right wing. Every now and again he turned his dark visor combat helmet towards his left, to check for movements. He had been surprised how easy it was to keep tab on the movements of Spacejet-2's passengers. He was engaged in a direct satellite link enslaved to the Spacejet's own electronics, allowing a precise, real-time picture of the entire aircraft, images displayed directly in front of him on the MiG's fourteen inch monitor. He knew the whereabouts, identity and life history of the each of the passengers. Without a doubt, the most interesting was Anna Kuznetsova, followed by Kira Kamenskaya. For the last ten minutes he had been listening to the digital, biographical readout. *If you want to win the battle, know your enemy,* he thought. As for Ross, he perceived a simple soul not dissimilar to himself, which accounted for his lack of interest. A seasoned fighter and brilliant test pilot, Ross was too predictable. He was egoistic too, and self-assured to the point of arrogance, which meant he could be counted on to follow narrow, masculine interests. At that moment, he was in the cockpit, probably checking the instruments which continued to show the tell-tale signs of hostile takeover. No radio call had been received from the pilots for the last fifteen minutes. Fighter control considered the pilots to have been incapacitated, and Timofeev knew no reason to disagree.

"Roger that. He said *Armageddon*," answered fighter control. "God knows what he meant!"

Major Timofeev thought carefully for a minute. A code? He cursed aloud for not having the context of the word. What had Kira, said to him in order to solicit such a response?

He reached hurriedly for the settings menu of the application that had enabled the snoop, cursing continuously. Selecting 'two minutes' from the drop down menu for playback and tapping 'enter' he waited anxiously for the program to engage. Valuable seconds were wasting, seconds that in combat meant the difference between success and failure, life and death. As the recording of the voice of Kira began to come through, a warning light flashed orange on his console, and the on-board computer voice came alive, over riding the voice recording. What it said gave him the immediate impression that the initiative had just been lost.

"Automatic pilot disengaged. Spacejet propulsion engaged. Revolutions indicate maximum power. Altitude set to Space."

His communication link to fighter control confirmed it. "Akula. Control. Target is running. Repeat. He has intention to evade and escape."

"Roger that Control. I heard it. Do I engage? Over."

Fighter control ordered, "Negative. Follow but do not engage. Await further instructions. Over."

"Roger that. Follow, but do not engage."

Breathing deeply but slowly, allowing the thick oxygen to saturate his blood and with several Gs of acceleration ripping through him, Timofeev gunned the MiG's afterburners onto maximum. The

Spacejet wanted to escape, and with its performance, he only had a minute to keep up with it, before it was out of range. He needed to fire right now. *Jesus! What are they waiting for?*

***

"Damn it!" cursed Lippman. Still in position overlooking Lod Airport, and with his radio set to listen to the fighter channels, he had heard everything. "They're running!"

He sprinted back to the Jeep's driving seat from the edge of the precipice overlooking the airport, to the satellite link to Jerusalem, doing his utmost to fight the feeling that he too had just lost the initiative. The satellite link became active. "Khodorov here. What is it Colonel?"

"Sir! We may have a problem."

"They're running!" said Khodorov matter-of-factly.

"How did you know?"

"Colonel. There is an American pilot on that flight, Lieutenant Colonel Lee Ross. I wouldn't mind betting he's now in control."

"Sure looks like it. They just disengaged autopilot and the controls are set to space. Sir, suggest we disable it now and bring it down."

"No, Colonel. Without my specific authorisation, there will be no shooting at that aircraft. Is that understood? Fighter Control is in the loop. You will liaise with them from now on. Find out where their new destination. Track them closely, but no shooting. We'll get them when they land. Khodorov, out."

Chapter 88

Beads of sweat clung to Major Timofeev's brow as he fought to remain within shooting distance of Spacejet 2, a difficult task in itself. The acceleration of Spacejet 2 was outstanding, coupled with a phenomenal rate of climb, its twin rockets pulling it through the sound barrier despite the slowing effect of gravity. His window of opportunity was closing rapidly, and he knew it, so he made an urgent radio call to fighter control. "They just went supersonic, heading through the roof. We're about to lose them. Suggest we bring them down."

Moments later, the response came through, crisp, clear and direct. "Negative Akula. You will not shoot. Maintain pursuit and standby!"

***

The chase away from the MiG-35 gave Ross crucial insight into his adversary. Its pilot had had plenty of chance to fire. He had even time to get authorization from the very top. Ross engaged its two rockets on fifty percent power, punching the air-space craft towards space. If Kira was right, the move would prove it beyond reasonable doubt, and at reasonable risk. Knowing the Spacejet's capability to evade and escape through speed and height, the MiG pilot would feel obliged to shoot. If he did, Ross had half rocket power in reserve, to outrun the missile. If he did not, it would prove the MiG pilot was unwilling to shoot. Or unable. Or both unwilling and unable.

A minute had passed since the start of Ross's run, and still no missile had been fired by the MiG-35. From that moment on, Ross's confidence was total. Kira was right; its pilot was unwilling to engage. He leaned slightly forward with brimming confidence, disengaged the rocket, checked the radio frequency and depressed the transmit button on his joystick. "Akula, this is Spacejet Two. Do you read me, over?"

Silence reigned across the fighter control radio frequency for long seconds before the radio crackled into life with the sound of a breathless voice. "Spacejet Two. This is MiG-35. Call sign Akula. I read you loud and clear. What do you want?"

Spacejet Two was flying at the edge of the MiG-35's performance envelope. Mach 2.25 at a tad over 18,000 meters altitude. If he fired, the MiG's AA-12 Adder missiles, capable of rapidly reaching Mach 4.5 could easily attain Spacejet Two. Within seconds. Still, the MiG pilot did not fire.

"An ultimatum!" pronounced Ross calmly and clearly. There could be no room for misinterpretation. "Both you and the other MiG will disengage, slow down and permit a twenty minutes of separation between us. Over."

After a momentary delay, came the answer from a now less breathless Russian pilot. "And what if we refuse your ultimatum?"

"Then I will destroy you!"

***

Ross throttled back the engines, holding Spacejet 2 steady at speed and altitude, to allow the two Russian fighter jets to close in on him, one on each wing, wolves back at the sides of the staggering sheep. Thirty crucial seconds had passed since he had given the ultimatum. And still the Russians had not agreed to his demands. Time for a reality check.

Major Timofeev saw Spacejet 2 shine its targeting Radar at his MiG-35. The targeting radar locked on. He had underestimated the American's resolve, and his haste. Too late! The American had already fired.

The R-77 missile, NATO reporting name AA-12 Adder, took a circular trajectory away from the left wing pod of Spacejet Two. Not such a lumbering lamb any more, but more of a venomous snake, about to bite. The lattice controlling fins of the Adder corrected its trajectory, second by second, while its computer processed the data received from active radar. Quickly it resolved which of the two MiG-35s to home in on. Both were deploying serious amounts of countermeasures. They were spewing them like saliva, splitting one towards the left and one towards the right. The missile homed on one the closer of the two, slamming into it head on with Mach 5 closure.

***

Kira strapped herself into the right hand pilot seat. "Cabin secure Captain," she said, smiling. "Everything is set for our landing!"

Ross glanced at her, his attention all but consumed by the landing check-list. "And what about the girls?"

"Anna, awake, and filled in on the situation. She seems genuinely happy, thank God," she said with a sigh. "The drugs sure worked a treat, the ones we gave her, and the ones she had survived on all those years. She does not remember a thing." She glanced at Ross. "I just want this to be over. You can't imagine."

"I know," said Ross, preparing for the landing. "Do me a favour please," he said, handing her the check-list. "Read them out, one at a time."

As she read them out, he felt more relaxed. *I can do it! I can pull it off!*

On final approach, Ross's workload shot up dramatically, and he thanked himself for all the hours of practice on short landings he had undertaken during his seventeen years in captivity. He marvelled at what higher powers had predetermined he would be right there, right then. *How and why had he known, deep inside him, that he would one day need such practice to end the reign of Khodorov?*

Ross thought: *how much of what I have become, of what I have learnt, is due to destiny? How much to my free will?* The question assumed singular importance as he contemplated the shortest landing he had ever undertaken. Many were the occasions when he had succeeded at such landings on the simulator. But on many he had failed. This was for real.

The landing strip came into view, looking even tinier than he had anticipated. The aircraft had descended below the mid-level lenticular clouds which appeared above Mount Megiddo and was already on short final for touch down. Taking a deep breath, he did one last, mental run through. He thought: *destiny is taunting me. For the second time I am attempting a landing in a jet aircraft at Megiddo airstrip. What were the chances of succeeding both times on such a short runway?*

Lower and lower, towards the strip, flaps set to maximum, speed to minimum and undercarriage down and checked. Through the cockpit window, he saw movements on the ground, and felt a quick panic strike deep in his heart. Had Khodorov left nothing to chance? Had he arranged for all airstrips regardless of size surrounding Jerusalem to be surrounded and secured?

Whatever. He was committed to putting the aircraft on the deck.

Seconds before touchdown, he thought about executing a necessary manoeuvre which would surely slam the aircraft forcefully onto the end of the airstrip. Such a manoeuvre risked breaking the aircraft's undercarriage, but without it, the aircraft's speed at the start of the landing run would be too excessive for the aircraft to stop before it reached the other end. So he banged his hand down onto an operating lever and two massive air-brake surfaces shot out of the rear of the fuselage.

The space-aircraft hit the rough tarmac surface of the airstrip with all its weight at less than ten meters from its northern limit and

Ross gritted his teeth, oblivious to the screams coming from Kira. *Ten meters wasted!* Then he deployed the parachute, and engaged full reverse thrust standing with all his weight on the massive brakes, straining every muscle in his body in a desperate effort to get every last Newton of breaking force through the breaking system and onto the surface of the tires. The anti-brake mechanism kicked in. Yet despite everything, Spacejet-2 was half way to the southern, rocky extremity of the rough landing strip. Half way to the cliff, which he remembered fell away vertically from that end.

The aircraft shuddered to a complete stop, a meter from the cliff.

***

A cloud of brown dust had been kicked up by the landing at the rough airstrip. Slowly it dissipated, blown into eddies by the wind.

Ross checked his watch. 14.30 local time. Forty five minutes before the time indicated on the chalice in his flight suit. Conscious yet oblivious to Kira's presence, he plugged in the coordinates into the on-board computer, selecting the fastest route to them, and pressed *enter*. Only then did he look at Kira, who sat watching him. He said, "Are you okay?"

"Ross, what are you doing? Why did you plug in another destination to the flight computer?"

Ross ignored the question having noticed movements through the swirling dust. Opening the cockpit window for a better look, he was hit by *déjà vu*.

The movements he had seen on the approach had been people, crowds. Already they were close at hand. He noticed their attire, thinking, *they are Bedouin. But what were they doing here, so close to Mount Megiddo?* They surrounded the aircraft, men, women and children.

It was the pretext he had been looking for. Ever the opportunist, he started the jets, leaning out of the window. "Back off from the engines," he screamed in Arabic out of the cockpit window.

Kira repeated, "You didn't answer me! What are you doing?"

"Not now, Kira!"

"No, I demand to know! You're planning to fly out aren't you? You're planning on flying to the final coordinates?"

"Of course not. We have less than thirty minutes before regime forces arrive. The second MiG-35 will not be able to land with us sitting here, but it can sure as hell use its missiles. I am just keeping the locals at a safe distance by spinning us around. Then we can all get out."

He swung the aircraft around, the deafening noise of the four jets combined with their blasts spreading the crowds with ease. He wondered about the strange destiny which had brought the crowds to that place, which to him was a welcome development. In a very short time the place would be streaming with the military. Yet with the crowds, Anna, Lena and Kira would be able to slip away. Possibly they would even be able to evade capture.

"Let's go!" said Ross, urging Kira to get a move on ahead of him, out of the cockpit and leaving the jets engaged at 5 percent power and the craft straining at its wheels, the noise serving to keep the Bedouin at bay while the girls got clear.

He followed closely behind Kira out of the cockpit, where they came face to face with Anna, who asked, "Where are we?"

"Megiddo, Israel," replied Kira. "We're close to the heart of the Negev Desert."

The sound of that name struck something deep. They all knew it. They had seen it in her face. It was obvious that she knew it. It was as if she was awakening from a dream, in which she knew what happened, but not when, why or how.

"I know the name," she said, looking past Kira, out of the aircraft door, to the desert and the Bedouin below the aircraft's steps. Then she moved to embrace her. They held each other for long moments before pulling apart, emotion swelling inside them, filling their eyes with tears which rolled down their perfect white cheeks. "Why do I know it?"

"Because you have been here before," said Kira with compassion.

"I don't remember."

"Don't worry. You will. You just need time. You're safe now."

Ross had been patiently waiting. He now moved uncomfortably, driven by a desire to be free of them. "Time ladies. Shall we get down these stairs and away from the aircraft?"

Ross thought he felt the presence of the real Ark in his bones, having the distinct and decidedly uncanny feeling that the Ark that Yuval and Maria had found, the one which had led them on a wild goose chase in search of the 'Battles of Armageddon' was false. It had been a paper chase and a side show. A required diversion which the Israelites had used to hide the tablets that would lead both sides, those on the side of good and those on the side of evil, to the locations of battle, to Moscow, and to Mount Megiddo, and to the Al-Aqsa Mosque and to North Cape. They were real locations, and real battles which went to determine which side won. They were battles which through treachery, had been won by the Antichrist.

But it was not the real Ark. Of that he was sure. The inscriptions on the chalice, the fourth set of descriptions, deciphered secretly by him whilst on the Spacejet, had confirmed it. They had told him and him alone of the real Ark, which to him seemed perfectly natural, as it had been him all along who had succeeded in unlocking its secrets. The inscriptions on the large chalice told another Ark, the true Ark, the Ark which Anna had been searching for when she had been picked up in the Negev desert, the one with the real power. And beneath the inscriptions there were coordinates. And there was a name inscribed there too, in ancient Hebrew, a mountain in the Negev Desert. Mount Hashem el-Tarif.

It was near, and it was his destiny alone to receive its power. He would do what no leader had ever done. He would lead the world according to morals and his vision, not according to power. The Ark was what locked access to a better world; and he was its key. How could it be different, when everything that had happened in his life since he had met Anna Kuznetsova led him to that dusty, sun drenched and infinitely remote airstrip? The Israelites had known him to be the one which would lead the world out of its modern crisis. They had led him every step of the way, to the Al-Aqsa Mosque, to the Kremlin, and finally to North Cape and the Holy Grail. By giving him the large chalice, the fabled Holy Grail, they had given him the legitimacy and the motive to carry out something he had been dreading. Now that time had come. He took a deep breath, and led the girls down the steps of Spacejet 2.

Seeing them descending from the aircraft, the Bedouin crowds rushed from their distance to meet them, no longer afraid.

"I need to return to the plane," shouted Ross as he turned to the three girls following slowly behind, their clothes buffeted by the stiff breeze. "Now that we are clear, and sure that the Bedouin are friendly, I'd better turn off the engines."

Although Anna and Lena's watched him indifferently, a look of disappointment animated Kira's beauty.

"You lied!"

The words shouted at his back were swallowed by the desert wind long before they reached his ears. Ross, sprinting now, was already half way back to the steps of the huge aircraft. By the time the first Bedouin reached the girls, enveloping them in hugs and gifts of fine clothing, Ross was strapping himself back into the cockpit. He was upping the take-off jet engines to full power, releasing the breaks.

***

Spacejet-2 roared off the northern extremity of the strip, banking sharply left into the sun, going supersonic soon after. If Ross wanted to have any chance of getting to the place on time, he knew he was going to have to use every ounce of raw power the aircraft's engines possessed. Full four jets till supersonic, followed by twin rockets at full power forced him deep into the back of his seat. He had about ten minutes to be at Mount Sinai.

Four minutes later, he throttled back, already on final approach to Mount Sinai. He put the aircraft on autopilot, the on-board computer better able to calculate than him, using the coordinates.

He took the chalice in his hands. He fondled it this way and that, feeling its every scratch as if it were his flesh and blood. He felt he had done it. Felt he had won. With the Ark in his possession, the world would be his, ruled according to his vision. Obsession had been a blessing. Without it, he would never have got to this point. But what point exactly was he at?

He took stock of the situation as the aircraft descended. 14.57 local time, September 23rd. The chalice indicated 15.00 on that very same day. The location: a rapidly approaching point on the planet's surface. He pinned the chalice into a recess on the side of his seat, before glancing at the glass cockpit console in front, for a reading of his position, as the huge aircraft came in low over the desert. He switched off the autopilot, squinting through the cockpit windows in a search for the landing strip, the one that he knew must be there. The Israelites had never lied. His needs when close to the space-time coordinates had always been met. There was no reason to think that the final Battle of Armageddon would be any different.

Suddenly, an alarm sounded, followed by a computerized rendition of the threat. "MiG-35 bearing 320.1 and 320.2. Three miles. Suggest you change your vector to 180 to evade. Climb! Climb!"

Ross shook his head almost imperceptibly to the left and to the right. He thought: *If I climb and evade, I will not reach the space-time coordinates. Whatever the Ancients predicted, whatever they knew about me, would be lost. Quite possibly, humanity would never receive the sacred Ark, condemned to eternal evil and rule by descendants of Ivan Khodorov. No way! They trusted salvation to me thousands of years ago, and I will not shy away from them when I and others have come this far.*

With that he lowered the aircraft's nose, bringing it in hot and fast on the space-time coordinates.

To Major Timofeev it seemed that the aircraft he was tracking could have divine protection. There was something, however strange, about the way its pilot flew, from the soul.

What he was looking at in front of him backed up what he had been angrily informed of by Colonel Lippman, who was making his way by helicopter gunship to the tiny airstrip where Khodorov had allowed Spacejet 2 to land. *No passengers on that flight. There was only its chevalier pilot.*

Switching to combat mode, Timofeev hesitated. He too, like the chevaliers of old, was against killing in cold blood. He could invent a thousand reasons for not firing, as he had done on countless occasions before. Maybe quite simply he did not want the fun of the chase to end.

Ross glanced momentarily at his watch, unable not to feel relieved, yet undecided if he would have to continue with plan B. Plan B was to take care of the MiG first, but miss the rendezvous. The MiG had switched off his targeting radar. But he could still fire. He was not about to commit suicide for humanity, but neither was he going to give up the chance of making good on plan B. Arriving minutes late at the rendezvous was still better than not arriving at all. He could not understand the MiG's action, but was thankful for it. He was sure that such an action was also built-in to the plan of the Israelites, pre-ordained. Plan A was still on. A minute remained. He engaged the landing gear, running through the checklist. It was going to be close. Very close. *But the Ancients knew I would be here! And I trust them!*

But he had failed.

Ross had been so sure that the coordinates had been for Mount Hashem el-Tarif, the name written below them on the chalice, that he had not checked them against a map. Nor had he checked visually, now that he was coming in, fast and low to put the aircraft down on the very spot. Now that he could see where the coordinates lay, he realised that there was not a mountain in sight. Below him, the dunes of the Negev desert stretched into the redness of the setting sun. There was only emptiness, from horizon to horizon, and beyond. He had been tricked.

A shrill alarm on his watch rang out indicating 15.00. It broke the silence of the cockpit. His aircraft flew low and slow over the correct coordinates, with the desert stretching to the horizon. He had made it. But he had lost. The coordinates were a nondescript point, a sand dune quite similar to the millions of others which crowded the desert.

Epilogue

Three months later, Sinai, Egypt

The beauty of the site chosen by the Bedouin shepherds for the night's rest had not escaped the attention of the three young women.

A vast, valley, wide, flat and fertile, nestled beneath a circular ridge of yellow, sand-coloured rock. Although a road passed close by, and decades ago, before the war, the Egyptians had built an army base on its summit, the view of Hashem el-Tarif had not changed since the time of Moses himself.

Since arriving in the vicinity of the mountain, two weeks earlier, life for the three women had become idyllic. A paradise. As on every night, camp fires burnt hot and bright, their main central flames thrusting incandescent sparks high into the starry sky. They were sitting at the chief's fire, which had become more and more routine in the months following their escape. Mohammed, the chief's younger brother got up from the rocky place he had chosen to sit. The yellows and reds of the fire reflected in his eyes, adding mysteriousness to his dark looks. He was tall and clean-shaven, strong as a horse and now, as always, wore his long black hair in a ponytail tied with a traditional white and black cotton scarf. The girls could not help admiring him as he began, bare chested despite the evening chill, with a deep, almost guttural delivery, to recount the evening story.

"Legends passed from father to son in our clans tell us of Moses."

His pleasure at telling the story was written in his pronunciation of every word and in his movements too. It was obvious too from the way he looked into the eyes of those lucky enough to be there.

"He led our brothers, the Israelites, through the desert and across the sea, to a wide and green valley beneath a rocky peak. There, they rested. They were warmed by big fires which burned under a starlit sky."

For effect, Mohammed made a wide, sweeping movement with his right arm, indicating the fires which were burning on a similar night, thousands of years hence. "And yet . . . " he continued, "Moses that night did not rest. He climbed alone, along a steep and rocky path to the jagged summit of a mountain."

"Where he rested forty days and forty nights!" shouted Lena.

Mohammed turned to look at her, smiling broadly. "That's exactly right, little sister. He stayed there, alone, for many days and nights." He turned and motioned to the peak behind him, still clearly silhouetted by the twilight left in the sky by the sun which had set twenty minutes earlier.

On the far side of the fire, half hidden in the shadows, a smile crossed the chief's face. His brother had a gift for the melodramatic which he admired. Mohammed was social, romantic, knowledgeable of history and of the ways of women. In fact, he was everything the chief was not, which was why they were a formidable team, capable of escaping the wrath of the Russian army and living off the desert.

"Finally," continued Mohammed, "God deemed him worthy of carrying a priceless gift to humankind. He trusted him with being his messenger. On the fortieth night, which started starry as this one, a great storm descended from the heavens. The Israelites sheltered in their tents which crowded the amphitheatre, scared to death for their leader exposed on the ridge above."

At this point, those present around the chief's fire could not help casting anxious glances upwards. They stared in awe and beheld a sky of stars. The attention of Kira, Lena and the rest of the listeners, the Bedouin, returned to Mohammed, enthralled by the story, and the truth of Moses.

The attention of Anna, however, did not return to Mohammed. She continued to look towards the heavens, conscious of a change. The brightest stars continued to shine, points of lights infinitely concentrated which twinkled at the casual observer. Their lesser companions of the night had, however, already been obscured by cloud. High altitude cloud had spread from the west, and she became restless. The night seemed welcoming and full of interest.

"Lightning struck ten times on that sacred summit, inscribing ten stones with the laws of man. The commandments are humanity's blueprint for containing the temptations of Satan. But one was missing."

"Which one, Mohammed?" burst out Lena. "The commandment to love?"

"No, Lena. The eleventh commandment is self-control of obsession."

"Why do we need it?"

"Obsession is a natural tendency among humans, one which can work for the Devil or for God. Mankind needs training in its ways. Who knows what the world would have become if it had it been received by Moses with the others? Self-interest competes with consideration in our everyday actions, leading us towards Satan, or towards God. Obsession is the joker in the pack, driving us with ambition's fire to fulfil our capacities. But it can become a law unto itself, assuming a momentum which we will blindly pursue."

"Like the obsession of Colonel Lippman?" asked Kira, darkly.

"That's exactly the kind of obsession I'm talking about," said Mohammed. "He knew an obsession which drove him to commit terrible things in the name of what he believed to be his calling, his mission."

Mohammed's words were followed by a silence which reigned for a long minute. The only sounds were the crackling of the flames fanned by a sudden wind which tugged at the white tents below the fires.

Only Anna found the courage to talk about the events which they all had witnessed and animated their nightmares ever since. She alone succeeded in bringing smiles back to dark faces, ridiculing the man they all knew was Colonel Lippman and the way his obsession with finding her had driven him to commit a massacre of innocent women in the two weeks following their escape. She knew the power of good and right would always win over those whose ways lead to the Devil, choosing to bring happiness to minds that had been turned to dark thoughts. "Why do they need me? They have all the women they want. When they want one, they just take."

"Anna. You are different," said Mohammed. "They cannot take you. They have heard what you do to men."

The comment had a strange effect on her, as if awakening a part of her that had died long, long before, before Barcelona. She got up, unnoticed, and looked towards the mountain, partly so that the group would not see that tears had welled in her eyes. Partly because she had become aware that instead of the clear night sky, the summit was almost obscured by dark clouds which must have descended rapidly during the second half of Mohammed's story.

A sudden impulse to discover the secrets of the mountain suddenly gripped her, and refused to let go. Over the months since they had escaped from Colonel Lippman and his army, she had developed the habit of walking far away from the camp site, usually alone and at night. To them, this night was no exception. Despite the storm which was brewing around them, they let her go.

***

Anna was far along the ridge above the amphitheatre valley before the first spots of rain splattered its dry rocks, still visible in the eerie yellow twilight. Above her dark grey clouds billowed towards her, their down drafts chilling her. Soon, huge, thundery spots of rain were soaking her long blonde hair, complementing her traditional attire.

The rocks would have necessitated a local shepherd constant care if he was not to slip. And yet, only occasionally did she look down. Her regard was focused on the ridge ahead.

A bolt of lightning struck, followed immediately by the crash of thunder. Then another, even stronger, which made the ground shudder. Anna peered through the stinging rain, making a mental note of the position of the place where the bolt had hit, though not knowing why. Then another flash hit, its blinding light illuminating the surroundings. Then came the thunder, loud and powerful, shaking the rocky ridge. Déjà vu transfixed her to the spot. The lightning had struck just below the summit, in a circular recess rimmed by rocks. One last flash touched down in front of her, on a flat slab of fine grained rock.

Though Anna saw it strangely out of place amongst the jagged rocks which surrounded it, her eyes were focused on what was 100 meters behind it. She saw a cave where the lightning had struck. It was a new cave, and at its entrance there was a pile of broken slabs of the same fine-grained rock. She walked towards it, overcome by a strange feeling, like she was coming home.

Then a face appeared, out of the misty gloom, as another flash of lightning hit nearby. In the mouth of the cave, there appeared the figure of a youth, and he was coming towards her, shouting.

***

Finally succeeding in finding her tongue and the energy to use it, Anna shouted over the thunder and through the emotion which pervaded every fibre of her soaked body. Following an embrace which seemed to last for eternity, she pushed him to arm's length.

"You look just as I knew you would, as I always imagined."

She stroked the thick black hair which fell around his shoulders

Anna wiped her tears of happiness. "Thank God you're safe, dear Son. How do you know I am your mother?"

"Come out of the rain and I will show you."

The tall youth led her through the lashing rain to the entrance of the cave along a path that seemed to have been paved by ancient hands. They entered awkwardly through the narrow opening in the rocks of the summit, past the slabs of fine white rock that had been broken by the lightning strike, to the cave. Anna saw that it was dimly lit by lamps, a line of them which led into the interior."

"A tunnel? To where?"

Her shouted questions went unanswered. The youth led her to the first torch burning on the right wall of the tunnel entrance. Behind it, the wall, flat, smooth and dead straight disappeared into the darkness. Anna held her breath, feeling like an explorer, an archaeologist just about to make the discovery of her life. Then she saw that the smooth wall was covered with inscriptions.

"What the hell is this?"

"Don't be afraid, Anna."

She advanced, surprised that she could read the script which covered the wall of the cave.

"It's Ancient Hebrew, the continuation of the New Testament," declared the youth.

Anna lifted her right hand, caressing the first words of the script, which commenced from the right.

"Have you . . . "

"Read it all?" The youth laughed out loud. "Only about a hundred times!"

Gripped by a strange realization, Anna turned to look at him. His face was illuminated by the soft reddish light of the torch which burned at his side on the wall. "What's your name, my Son?"

"My guardian calls me Dan," answered the youth. "It's short for Daniel."

"Your guardian?"

"I know he is not my real father, but I call him Dad anyway."

"And where is he?"

"Up ahead." The youth motioned towards the darkness.

Anna's thirst for knowledge was only partially quenched by her son's answers, each opening new vistas of incomprehension. She continued to fix him. "How long have you been here, Daniel?"

"I have always been here, at least ever since I can remember."

"And how do you know I am your mother?"

"Because it's written on these walls." The dark youth motioned again into the darkness. "It's all written here. My birth, the war, your coming. Everything. I read these walls again and again, year after year by torchlight until I knew every word. You see, though now we are near the entrance, this was a sealed cave until today's storm. The storm I knew would bring you, its hour written at the end of the script, the hour of your arrival. Come I will show you."

The tall youth picked up the torch, leading along the smooth, flat wall. Anna followed closely behind, her feet feeling the smooth cut block pavement as she kept one hand on the wall, constantly feeling its inscriptions. *A modern testament*, she thought, *conscious of the power of the ancient minds*. The Ancients had unlocked the secrets of the universe long before the age of science. She marvelled at their power. They knew she would be there, that she was the chosen one, but for what purpose? She could only guess that the secret was about to be spilled by the tall youth, her son, who now led her.

"Read it with me, aloud!" he said to Anna.

***

Seventeen years after the Battle of Armageddon, the one chosen to rid the world of evil and tyranny will appear outside this tunnel.

Taking control of the Object of Power, she will confer it to her son who will go forth to complete the purification of the world started on Judgement Day.

***

The words 'Judgement Day' were the last ones on the long wall, carved high and deep into the rock wall just before the edge.

"Where is the object of power?" asked Anna

"Follow me! It's here, in this chamber."

The tall youth led her around the corner.

After ten minutes, the tunnel came to an abrupt end. Beyond, a gaping chamber opened, swallowing the light from their torch.

***

Overcome by a feeling of *déjà vu*, Anna rounded the corner of the chamber.

And there it stood, the Ark of the Covenant, the real one, bigger and more ornate than the one found by Yuval and Maria in the sinkhole of the same mountain. The Ark whose location had been inscribed on the Holy Grail, the one whose exact coordinates had been known only to Anna, hard-wired into her head.

Anna saw it, and knew what it was. Even though she had never heard of it, nor seen it, nor studied it, nor even had known of its existence, she knew it was the force that had attracted her for most of the last decade. Only Anna and her son could feel it. Only they were attuned to it. Only they were connected through it, to God who dwelled within it.

In silence, they approached it.

"Let me show you the Commandments," said her son, "and one in particular, the eleventh."

Reaching inside the Ark, he extracted a white slab of marble, the one placed equidistant between two stacks of five tablets each. "These tablets explain everything which has happened to you," he said. "They explain the people who enabled you to realise your destiny. The eleventh explains obsession. It explains the impulses and motivations of Lee Ross."

Anna took it from him. She felt a desire to hold it, to feel the words which explained her life, explained those who had helped her.

Turning to his mother from the Ark, Daniel read the tablet, the eleventh.

Ross's heart is true. He is on the side of Good.

He worked hard to save you, to bring you to Jerusalem, to bring you home, to the Negev. Only, right in the end was he corrupted.

He felt the desire of power and greed, and became obsessed. But he learned his lesson. He is alive and will return to you. You must embrace him, for he too is your saviour.

Anna said, "It's written millennia ago, and yet speaks of things in the present in the past tense."

"It's because the Ancients knew we would be here."

"So the world is still deterministic!" said Anna.

"Apparently it is, though we will never be completely sure. Maybe the period of determinism ends right now. Maybe from now on I will have to fight the Antichrist without the luxury of knowing that the future being written. It is something I have accepted."

Anna felt a wave of tiredness overtake her, as if her entire life since falling in the Negev Desert had been one of tension driving her to that very place. Finally, she could relax. "Finally, I have come home! And you are my son!"

"Yes!"

"Then you know what you have to do!"

"I do!"

After meeting the guardian, who her son introduced as the Mahdi, the Iranian who had protected him on the Battlefield of Megiddo, his teacher, mentor and friend, Anna was shown to her room. The huge four poster bed, she sensed, had been prepared for years. If smelt fresh as did the whole vast chamber, and reminded her of an Arabian Palace of the desert. Although deep underground, it appeared to be a tent with fine tapestries hanging on the walls and real palm trees in the center. Oil lamps hung in the alcoves, and burned, filling the room with sweet perfume. Soft Arabic music played.

Anna woke naturally next morning, and stretched. Her son was there, having slept on a similar bed in the same chamber, waking in turn.

They had a simple breakfast of fruit, unleavened bread and yoghurt, a meal which they ate with black sugared tea. Then Anna led Daniel back along the tunnel, the way they had taken the night before. "Come, Son," she said. "Time is short."

Although she wanted him close to her, and wished for nothing more than to spend a thousand nights like the one which had just passed, she knew she couldn't keep him. His place was not there. Not now. Not until the thing which had been set in motion had been stopped, and the world returned to its peoples.

At the end of the flat tunnel walls, where the modern testament started, she stopped him, pulling him towards her. "Do your duty naturally, Son, without emotion. Even though the future is maybe no longer written on cave walls, you are guided by your heart. It is pure. It is true. Only you and I wield the power of the Ark, so go forth and rid the world of the tyrant who has seized it.

Anna snuffed out the torch with her bare hands, turning towards the first rays of the rising sun as it entered through the cave.

They walked towards the sunlight entering from the mouth of the cave still far ahead, and felt time cut short, the universe thinning, suffocating. Soon they would be alone. Only there was one last thing. Her son turned to her, an object in his hand. It was a VHS video cassette. It had a white label on its cover with black, hand written numbers scrawled there. And her son was saying "Mum, this is for you. It's something you have been searching for all your life, and there's one more thing you need to do. Spread what humanity has learned these last years — that total, 21st Century war is the true enemy. That message, that *information*, is your Holy Grail, and the true, modern Holy Grail of our times, for every person to guard and cherish. For our children are too innocent, our world too precious, and its animals and landscapes too beautiful for humankind to destroy them in a split second."

He turned, and without a further word or look, left her presence.

With the video tape clutched tightly she followed him along the smooth pavement of cut granite blocks. His stride and pace had opened a gap between them, and when she reached the sunlight, he was gone.

"Good luck!" she said, her voice softened into silence by the mountain breeze.

Printed in Great Britain
by Amazon